THE TEDDY
BEAR
CONSPIRACIES

WATCH OUT FOR ALIENS THAT LOOK LIKE TEDDY BEARS!

MYKE REINHOLM

YAY!

♡ Schawmy

The Paw soars above the city on patrol to protect the inhabitants.
(Photo by Andy Adorable for The Daily Times of Pawtropolis)

THE TEDDY BEAR CONSPIRACIES

MYKE FEINMAN

PHOTOS BY
ANTHONY FEINMAN

CREATIVE CONSULTING BY
CATHY FEINMAN

A portion of the proceeds from this book will go toward an art scholarship at
Herscher High School and a journalism scholarship at Streator High School.

To order additional copies of this book, contact:
Xlibris Corporation
1-888-795-4274
www.Xlibris.com
Orders@Xlibris.com
20368

CONTENTS

Part 3
The Secret War

List of photos:

DEDICATION:

I would like to dedicate this book to Good Bears of the World, an organization that gives gifts of teddy bears to traumatized children, or lonely, forgotten adults in the world. James T. Ownby founded GBW in 1969 after reading Peter Bull's book, "Bear With Me." The book tells of a man who dedicated himself to giving bears to hospitalized children. For more information about Good Bears of the World, write to: GBW, P. O. Box 13097, Toledo, OH 43613.

Other publications
by the author:

1. *The Mask Conspiracy*, 1991, with calligraphy by Cathy Feinman, published by Ink and Feathers Comics (novel-length comic book).
2. *The Ink and Feathers Comic Publisher's Guide*, 1993, published by Ink and Feathers Comics with Jim Ridings (one-shot magazine).
3. *The Crystal Skull Files*, 1998, with calligraphy by Cathy Feinman, published by Ink and Feathers Comics (novel-length comic book).
4. *In Search of the First Teddy Bear* with photos by Anthony Feinman, 2002, published by Ink and Feathers Comics (one-shot magazine). Second printing 2003.

Other publications
by the photographer:

1. *Escape in a Dirigible*, a prequel to *The Mask Conspiracy*, written and drawn by Anthony Feinman, Plotted by Myke and Anthony Feinman, 2003, published by Ink and Feathers Comics (one-shot comic book).

OUR EXPLORATIONS OF TIMES PAST HAVE SHOWN US SO MUCH THAT POSSESSES MEANING AND BEAUTY TODAY. IT IS SOBERING TO REALIZE THAT ONLY A TINY FRACTION OF THE SONGS, STORIES, AND ARTIFACTS OF ANCIENT TIMES HAVE MADE THE LONG JOURNEY TO US. THAT THOUGHT SHOULD SPUR US TO PRESERVE WHAT WE HAVE TODAY, ESPECIALLY THOSE MOST FRAGILE TREASURES OF ALL—THE LIVING ONES. DEPENDENT ON OUR DESIRES AND DECISIONS, BEARS AND ALL LIVING THINGS NEED OUR UNDERSTANDING, APPRECIATION, AND CONSIDERATION. WITH OUR HELP, THE TREASURES OF YESTERDAY AND TODAY CAN INSPIRE GENERATIONS TO COME. MY WISH IS THAT PEOPLE MAY HAVE THE CHANCE TO EXPERIENCE THE POWER AND BEAUTY OF EARTHLY BEARS FOR AS LONG AS THE GREAT BEAR CONTINUES HER HEAVENLY PROWL.

—REBECCA L. GRAMBO, IN "BEAR, A CELEBRATION OF POWER AND BEAUTY," A SIERRA CLUB BOOK

PREFACE

People pay me to write stories. I have been a professional journalist since the summer of 1972. So when someone drops a mysterious thick envelope filled with a manuscript on your desk, it begs a lot of questions. When you read the manuscript, and find it concerns someone claiming to be an alien from a planet in the Ursa Major constellation, it begs even more questions. When that "alien" claims his species has been visiting the Earth for many centuries, it gets downright fascinating—especially when the manuscript offers photographic proof of the claims.

The author of the manuscript wrote it as weekly episodes. He intended to electronically publish online. The author claims to be named Captain Schaumburg Harmony, a.k.a. the Paw. Schaumburg left no forwarding address or phone number. He offers no other evidence than his story. The manuscript includes a few photographs, including one he claims was taken at Roswell, New Mexico, July 1947. He says that his species is called the Orisha. He claims they look very much like toy teddy bears. He further states that the Orishans are here to protect Mankind from hostile aliens known as the Arjogun.

These claims are obviously fantastic. However, anyone who goes to a bookstore these days can find dozens of books claiming aliens visit this planet—many of them focusing on the now-famous Roswell incident in 1947.

I present the manuscript exactly as he dumped it on my desk at *The Paper*, a weekly free-circulation newspaper published in Dwight, Illinois. I have changed nothing. I prefer to let the reader decide if this is true or not.

I, for one, believe there may be intelligent life on other planets. It is only logical. Why would God create so much space and planets and only place intelligent life on one out of billions? If you accept the existence of alien life, is it so hard to make the leap that aliens really did land in Roswell, New Mexico in 1947?

And were those aliens little green men or—as this Schaumburg claims—were they really one small group of Orishans on the Earth posing as teddy bears?

Are there really teddy bear conspiracies—evil alien plots to destroy the Earth—going on right under our very human noses?

Don't ask me. Ask your teddy bear . . .

Myke Feinman
Streator, Illinois
Spring, 2003

INTRODUCTION BY CAPTAIN SCHAUMBURG HARMONY

The aliens landed at Roswell, New Mexico in 1947 . . . only they are not who you think.

The story I have written in the Earth language of English chronicles how beings from the planet Orisha, with a little help from some human friends, struggled against an evil plot by the Arjogun, creatures known on Earth as the alien grays. The Arjogun are beings from another world who abduct humans for nefarious experiments.

To piece together this bizarre tale, I have employed numerous primary source documents such as newspaper accounts of the crash at Roswell in 1947 in publications like the *Los Angeles Herald Express,* *Chicago Daily News* and *Spokane Daily Chronicle.*

I have also used the original press release issued by Roswell Army Air Base Public Information Officer Lieutenant Walter G. Haut on July 8, 1947.

Another main source for this incident is my own captain's log of the crash, which had been written in English in anticipation of our mission here on Earth.

The story begins with the crash at Roswell in July of 1947, but most of this story takes place from November 23, 1999 to May 6, 2003.

Once the story reaches 1999, I started using more current primary source material such as newspaper accounts, including some written by Samuel Arctophile, Versailles Bureau Chief for *The Daily Press* of Montreal, Illinois; Sam's private journals; the private journals of Cheryl Cruz, curator of the George Washington Museum in Versailles, Illinois; and newspaper stories by Fred Steinfeld in *The National Investigator,* a weekly national supermarket tabloid newspaper published in Kankakee that caters to stories about alien abductions of human beings and UFO sightings.

There are also newspaper stories written by yours truly, going by the pseudonym of Scoop Schaumburg while writing for *The Daily Times* of Pawtropolis.

To write this chronicle, I also employed my own notes of interviews with the primary sources in this story including but not limited to: Amy Sampson, Fred Steinfeld, Samuel Arctophile, Commander Black, Frank Largetooth, Armando Cruz and Cheryl Cruz.

Besides my own first-hand experiences and notes, I have also included the experiences of my Hug (a squad of Orishan operatives). My Hug on this mission included my wife, Millennium (Leni) Harmony, Wizard of the Mystical Order of the Golden Paw; my second-in-command, Captain Louis LaHug; and my baby sister, Chocolate Harmony, ship's guidance counselor and medical officer. Also, the Orishans Andy Adorable and Lavender Grace helped contribute primary source material to this chronicle.

Other primary source material included the *Journal of Bartholomew*, a secret book hidden from both humans and Orishans for two centuries; the secret writing hidden in the letters of George Washington; the archives of the secret Orishan society on Earth known as the Knights in Blue Satin, and their human counterparts, the Protectors.

I was also able to obtain some data disks detailing Arjogun activities here on Earth from some captured Arjogun soldiers, primarily one soldier known as Gobador.

Finally, for the benefit of readers of this chronicle, both human and Orishan, I must outline for you the structure of this report so you will understand the complex story. Since there is some time travel involved, the events of 1947 are linked to events from 1999 through 2003.

But the story is not told in chronological order. Instead, I have chosen to break the story into three main parts.

In the first part, the timeframe is the spring of 2003, just before May. The first part is called "The Adventures of the Paw," and introduces readers to many of the main players in this drama.

In the second part, known as "The Conspiracy Begins," we take readers through a flashback to 1947 and the subsequent journey through time to 1999 where my Hug first encountered Samuel Arctophile. In this second part of the story, which is also the longest, the events are basically in chronological order.

I have chosen to leave unimportant events out, thus there are some gaps in time from 1999 to 2003. I attempted to move the reader along by using only the most relevant events, sometimes skipping over days, weeks or even months in time.

Part two concludes right before part one, ending in April 2003.

In Part three, "The Secret War," we skip ahead to the end of April 2003 until the conclusion of the events that make up this strange, yet true story.

In truth, we have been fighting a secret war, right under the humans' noses. "We" being the Orisha and the Arjogun.

Humans will soon learn when they read it that we Orishans have been involved with human history for a beary long time.

It is the hope of all Orishans that humans and Orishans can go forward as staunch allies in our struggles against the Arjogun.

This is too important to keep a secret.

I believe that only through disseminating the truth about Orisha, and the Arjogun, will mankind understand what is at stake in the universe in the struggle of good versus evil. I also hope humans realize that it is we Orisha who are your friends, not the Arjogun, a.k.a. the alien grays.

As an act of friendship, I am reaching out to humans with the truth.

Don't just take my word for this. Investigate things for yourself. Do research on George Washington, and the origins of America. Prove to yourselves that these teddy bear conspiracies are truth, not fiction.

Sincerely,
Captain Schaumburg Harmony
Pawtropolis, Illinois
Spring, 2003

PROLOGUE

Roswell, New Mexico, July 3, 1947

Dr. Manuel Feinberg, United States Army Air Force Medical Corps, opened the front door to his Army base home to greet his wife, Madge, and son, Izzie.

"Manuel, you are home," Madge said, giving him a warm embrace. But Manuel pushed her away, not in the mood for a hug.

"What's wrong, darling?" she asked, pulling away and looking into his weary eyes.

"I was involved with some patients at the base hospital," Manuel said. "They were prisoners and they escaped somehow."

Four-year-old Izzie, short for Israel, sat in his bedroom playing with his teddy bear named Joey. He loved that bear. He'd had it since birth.

Just now, Izzie pretended to be reading a book to the bear, even though Izzie could not yet read.

Manuel saw Izzie seated on his bed, addressing the bear.

"Is that really a teddy bear?" Manuel wondered to himself.

He walked into his son's room.

"Can I see Joey?" Manuel asked his son, kindly.

"Sure, dad," Izzie said. "Joey likes hugs."

Manuel sat on his son's bed and took Joey from him, giving the bear a hug.

"Hmmm," Manuel said.

"What's wrong?" Izzie wanted to know.

Manuel put the teddy bear's mouth to his ear.

"Oh, really?" Manuel said, pretending the bear spoke to him.

"Your teddy bear said he's not feeling too good," Manuel said. "Perhaps I should take him to my office and give him an examination."

"Okay, Dad," Izzie said. "You fix him up and bring him back, good as new!"

"Right you are, son," Manuel said.

The father took the bear and stuffed it into the medical bag he had absent-mindedly brought into the boy's room with him.

"I'll buy you a bat and baseball glove tomorrow, Izzie," Manuel said. "I think you're old enough to start playing."

"Yay!" Izzie yelled, now excited.

Manuel gave his son a big hug then took his bag back into the living room to meet his wife.

"Madge, I'm going back to the office for a few minutes to examine Joey," he said, winking to his wife to play along with the ruse.

Madge and Manuel hugged and kissed, and Manuel left the living quarters to trek back to the base medical facility.

Back at the office, Dr. Feinberg pulled out the bear and gently placed it onto the examination table.

He took a surgical knife and carefully started to cut into the bear. But before making an incision, he stopped.

"No, this is just a teddy bear," he said to himself.

He once again started to cut the bear. At first he jumped, expecting to see internal organs as he pierced the tummy of the bear. Stuffing spit out instead.

"I guess this is nothing more than a toy after all," Manuel said to himself, out loud.

Nurse Jenna Armstrong came in.

"Doctor, can I help you?" she asked, seeing the toy on the examination table, stomach cut open to reveal the stuffing inside. "Are you okay?"

"They vanished I tell you!" Manuel said. "They just vanished right before my eyes! The Base Commander will not believe my story. I will probably be tried as a criminal. I have done nothing wrong!"

"What are you doing with that toy?"

Manuel took Joey off the table and handed it to the nurse.

"Throw this away, nurse," he said softly. "My son is getting too old for teddy bears, anyway."

*   *   *

A few days later, Izzie happened to ask Manuel about Joey.

"Did you fix him up, Daddy?" Izzie asked hopefully.

"Son, why don't you sit down," Manuel said to his boy, kindly.
"Daddy tried to save Joey, but he could not. Joey won't be coming
back."

Tears began to well up in Izzie's blue eyes.

After a long pause, he asked, "Joey's not coming back?" Izzie's
lower jaw trembled in sadness. "But you promised! You said you would
fix him!"

"I'm sorry son," Manuel said.

"You promised!" Izzie screamed. "You said he would be good as
new! You promised! Now Joey is gone! I'll never let you have my toys
again! My only true friend is gone! I won't trust anyone ever again!"

Then Izzie ran away from his father's arms, raced to his room and
slammed the bedroom door to sob away his unhappiness.

Later that day, at work, Nurse Armstrong watched the doctor,
wondering why he acted so oddly. He sat alone in an examination
room, muttering something to himself over and over. She crept up
more closely to hear Manuel.

"It's a teddy bear, not an alien," the doctor said. "It's a teddy bear,
not an alien. It's a teddy bear, not an alien. It's a teddy bear, not an
alien. It's a teddy bear, not an alien. It's a teddy bear, not an alien . . ."

Then Dr. Feinberg noticed Nurse Armstrong watching him.

"Doctor, what is it?"

"Those prisoners we had here yesterday?"

"Yes, doctor."

"They vanished into thin air."

"They will be located doctor, don't worry."

"No, nurse you don't understand. These creatures looked just like
teddy bears when they are sleeping. I believe they are evil aliens invading
from another planet. They have to be stopped. They will destroy us all
through our children, posing as teddy bears."

PART 1

THE ADVENTURES
OF THE PAW

CHAPTER 1

ONLY SUBSTANCE KNOWN TO HARM THE PAW

Captain Schaumburg's Personal Log, Earth Date April 23, 2003

My original assignment given to me by Orishan command: Discover what the alien grays are doing on Earth. The Better Bear Bureau has canceled that. My new assignment is to infiltrate the human cultures. When I am not in the human world, I live in Pawtropolis. I work as a newspaper reporter. I also save Orishans that need help while I use my secret identity, the Paw.

We are all from the planet Orisha, a planet far from Earth inhabited by beings that resemble Earth toys known as teddy bears. We come to Earth to protect and nurture mankind, especially small humans. But we like the big ones, too.

All the "teddy bear" inhabitants fly in spaceships to Earth, knowing it would be a good place to live. But there is one catch.

My enemies have found radioactive rock, known as Orishanite, here on Earth. Orishanite does not harm humans, but super-powered Orishans (like me and my sidekick Mardi Gras) are susceptible to the radiation when we are super-powered.

The good news is I am only super-powered when I eat a chocolate bar. But my super powers last just 20 minutes. While super-powered, Orishanite could actually cause me and Mardi Gras to be weak, and could kill us if exposed long enough. Orishanite is brown, glows, and looks a lot like dirt.

When I am not a reporter for The Daily Times *in Pawtropolis, and not fighting crime as the Paw, I work with a human known as Samuel Arctophile, Versailles Bureau Chief for* The Daily Press, *published in Montreal, Illinois.*

Sam is not a tall man—by human standards—though he towers over me. He is five feet, seven inches tall, in his mid-30s, wears glasses and is an award-winning, hard-hitting investigative reporter. He is fair-haired and fair-skinned, with bright blue eyes, similar to my wife, Leni.

When he is not reading science fiction novels, he watches science fiction videos like "Star Wars," "Star Trek" in all of its incarnations, and many others. He also likes fantasy like J.R.R. Tolkein ("Lord of the Rings") and Robert E. Howard ("Conan the Barbarian").

This makes him what some humans call a "nerd," meaning he is not a prime candidate for mating with human females, I am told. He has been single all his life, although I think he likes the young widow who runs the George Washington Museum in Versailles. There is also a female reporter he works with, named Amy, with whom he has a romantic history.

One time at a "Star Wars" movie, he told me if I found any single woman there, to "let me know," because he should marry her. Any woman who liked science fiction was his "cup of tea," he said.

I find it hard to understand why he does not have a mate. I find him very cuddly, myself. And he likes to laugh, a prerequisite for being a good mate, in my opinion. Just ask my wife.

The Paw Discovers The Frown's Diabolical Plot

Late April, 2003, Pawtropolis, Illinois

The Paw and his teen sidekick, Mardi Gras, found themselves trapped in a room with spiked walls as two sides slowly scraped toward the center of the room. This will eventually skewer our heroes.

"Quick, Mardi Gras," the Paw barked. "Pull out your secret laughing powder."

Mardi Gras pulled out his laughing powder from his utility belt and handed it to the Paw. The Paw quickly threw the powder at one of the spiked walls, causing a tremendous convulsion in the wall. Suddenly, the walls stopped converging on the center. Instead, the walls began to laugh. The more the walls laughed, the more the walls trembled until the sharp gleaming metal spikes fell harmlessly to the floor. The walls started to crack and break apart.

Finally, in a tremendous explosion of cement and wood splinters, the walls crumbled—allowing our heroes to escape.

"On to the secret headquarters of the Frown, Mardi," the Paw said to his pal.

"Right, Paw," Mardi replied.

"What about my right paw?" the Paw asked. Mardi said nothing, confused, and followed his older, more experienced superhero friend.

The Paw and Mardi Gras arrived at the heart of the Frown's castle, a monstrous structure with an evil frowning face and glowing eyes menacing those who passed by. The Paw and Mardi Gras moved silently through the castle built by the megalomaniac, the Frown. The Frown kept his computer complex at the castle's center.

"We must reach the computer room, Mardi," the Paw exclaimed as the two moved furtively from room to room.

"What's in the computer room, Paw?" Mardi Gras asked.

"The secret plans for the Frown's evil plot," the Paw said. At that moment, a voice boomed over a loudspeaker saying, "Take the second door to the right, and go through the hall."

"Who was that?" Mardi asked.

"That's the Frown taunting us," the Paw replied. "He thinks that even if we learn his plot, we won't be able to stop him. But I have a few tricks up my super sleeves."

In a few minutes, the heroes arrived at a door marked, "*Secret computer room. Do not enter.*"

"Stand back, Mardi," the Paw said. "It's a trap."

"How do you know, Paw?" Mardi asked.

"Because I can see a trip wire which undoubtedly extends to a bomb rigged to explode the moment we open the door."

The Paw ran across the hall and pulled down a nearby metal table to protect him and his sidekick.

Then the Paw removed a special vial from his utility belt.

"No hero is without his special all-purpose dissolving Paw Juice," the Paw said as he sprinkled some on the wire. "Take cover behind the table," the Paw ordered Mardi as both of them sought the protection of the metal table. Instantly, the entire wire dissolved, tripping the bomb device and causing a deafening explosion. Protected by the table from the shower of door debris, smoke and dust, the Paw and Mardi Gras safely entered the computer room.

Once inside, they spied the Frown busy at his computer console. The Frown, an Orishan who never smiles, whipped around, his evil blue cape (even the cape is evil) twirling around with him, facing the Paw and Mardi Gras.

"So, you think you can stop me, eh?" the Frown asked. The Paw pulled out another vial, throwing it onto the floor. The Paw and Mardi Gras instinctively held their breaths. The vial burst into smoke and flame, causing the Frown to start coughing and wheezing. The Frown slumped to the floor, unconscious.

"Quick, Mardi, see if you can figure out his computer system. We must learn his plot."

Mardi, a skilled computer operator, began to play the keyboard like a piano.

"Here, Paw!" Mardi said.

"Holy teddy bear!" the Paw exclaimed. "The Frown is trying to replace all teddy bears in the world with automatic ear lobe stretchers! How diabolical!"

"No children will be able to cuddle with those ooky ear lobe stretchers!" Mardi Gras said.

"Precisely, my young friend," the Paw replied. "We have to stop the Frown's evil plot before all teddy bears on this planet are transformed into those awful devices for earlobes."

Suddenly, the Frown stood pointing a ray gun at Mardi Gras.

"Thought you could give me the slip with that old gas pellet trick, eh?" the Frown sneered at the heroes. "I'm too smart for you fools! Now prepare for your doom!"

"Holy evil dude!" Mardi Gras said. "I'm not ready to die yet!"

With that, the Frown pointed the ray gun at Mardi Gras' furry head, while the Paw stood helplessly by, fearing the Frown would pull the trigger on his sidekick.

The Frown stands by his menacing castle located on the outskirts
of Pawtropolis.
(Photo courtesy of The Daily Times of Pawtropolis)

CHAPTER 2

EVIL UNLEASHED

Leni the female Wizard, watched over her husband (the Paw) and his sidekick by using a crystal ball.

"Say your prayers, little sidekick," the Frown sneered, about to shoot the helpless Orishan.

Thinking quickly, the Paw knew that he could gulp down some chocolate, giving him super powers for 20 minutes, which would save his pal. But just as the Paw began swallowing the chocolate and streaked to protect Mari Gras by allowing the Frown's bullet to bounce off his powerful chest, the Paw heard a loud "Noooooooooo!" in his head, a warning too late from Leni. You see, Leni had noticed in the corner of the room, the Chest of Sorrows. The Chest of Sorrows is a legendary casket used to house an unspeakable horror.

Leni recognized, too late, the trap the Frown had set for the Paw and Mardi Gras.

The Frown cackled a maniacal laugh as the Paw's chest deflected the Frown's bullet, saving Mardi Gras.

"Now watch the ricochet," the Frown said. To the horror of the Paw and Mardi Gras, the bullet bounced off the Paw only to head straight for a great casket in the corner of the room marked "Automatic Ear Lobe Stretcher Teddy Bear Converter Machine inside—DO NOT OPEN!"

The bullet blasted open the chest lock, and out slithered a frothy, monstrous blob of horribleness!

"That's the Splotch!" the Frown cried. "He will consume all Orishans posing as teddy bears in the world!"

Now the Paw, Leni and Mardi Gras knew what evil the Frown had unleashed upon the world, and it is far more dangerous than just eating aliens that look like teddy bears. The Splotch would consume all living creatures on Earth.

Leni knew from reading "The Encyclopedia of Magical Critters" that the Frown needed a super-powered ricochet from a bullet to open the Chest of Sorrows that held the Splotch captive by magic. As the Splotch headed toward Mardi Gras, the Frown scampered out of the room and locked the two heroes in with the monster. The Paw could save Mardi Gras for now, but only as long as his super powers held up. But soon the Paw would be defenseless against the Splotch as well. The Paw had eaten his last chocolate bar. Mardi Gras was also fresh out of chocolate, so he had no super powers at the moment.

"Leni, we could use a little help here," Schaumy said, knowing his Wizard wife was watching over them.

"Just hang on," Leni said, busily ripping through her magical tome to find a solution to her husband's situation.

Have You Seen H.A.R.V.E.Y.?

"Uh, Leni . . . ," the Paw said as he stepped in front of Mardi Gras to protect him from the oncoming Splotch.

"Use H.A.R.V.E.Y.!" Leni said in a flash of inspiration. "Grab his paw! Both of you!"

"Of Course!" the Paw said in delight. He and Mardi Gras touched the paws of what appeared to be a tiny rabbit and faded out of sight. Though cloaked, they could still see each other. H.A.R.V.E.Y is a sophisticated computer resembling a two-inch rabbit worn on the Paw's utility belt.

The Orishan High Command issues these units to all Orishan groups known as Hugs. H.A.R.V.E.Y. stands for Hand Activated Radix (computer center), with Variable Electronic Yashmac (veil). H.A.R.V.E.Y. can turn invisible and can render those touching it invisible.

The Splotch stopped its advance on them, beary confused.

"Now, H.A.R.V.E.Y., project our images into that casket," the Paw ordered. Instantly, H.A.R.V.E.Y.'s eyes projected an image of the Paw and Mardi Gras inside the casket.

In reality, the Paw and Mardi Gras moved away from the Splotch.

The Splotch turned around, slobbering acidic goo on the floor, and moved slowly toward the Casket of Sorrows.

"Good!" Leni said, speaking to the Paw telepathically. "Once the Splotch is back inside the casket, you can close it and seal him inside once again."

The Paw and Mardi Gras quickly trapped the monstrous Splotch in the magic casket, and then moved out of the Frown's computer control room, still invisible.

They heard the Frown speaking to someone in another room.

"Yes, master," the Frown was saying. "I have eliminated that pesky Paw and his sidekick Mardi Gras! The Splotch has likely devoured them by now!"

"Very good. Now, I, the Lemming, am free to implement my ultimate plan for controlling the planet! Ha,ha,ha,ha,ha!"

"Yes, master. I will continue the second phase of our mission, finishing the weather-control device."

The Paw and Mardi Gras already knew that the Frown was just a henchman for another menace who called himself the Lemming.

"He's talking to that Lemming guy!" Mardi Gras said aloud, revealing his presence.

"Quiet!" the Paw said.

The Frown turned around, but could not see the Paw or Mardi Gras.

"They're ghosts!" the Frown screamed in terror. "They are here to haunt me!"

The Frown stumbled away in fright, scampering down a corridor. The still-invisible Paw and Mardi Gras chased after him.

The Paw (foreground) and Mardi Gras fight crime in Pawtropolis with the Pawmobile.

The Evil Plot Thickens

The Paw stopped and restrained Mardi Gras from chasing after the Frown any more.

"But he'll get away," Mardi Gras complained.

"It's okay," the Paw said, removing his paw from H.A.R.V.E.Y.'s paw and turning visible again.

"I planted a homing beacon on the Frown," the Paw continued. "We can track him back at the Paw Cave."

The Paw pressed a button on his belt buckle, and the Pawmobile zoomed automatically to the front of the Frown's secret lair. The Pawmobile was a miniature vehicle, sized for the two Orishan agents for ground-travel on Earth. The designer made it for speed. The colors blue, red and yellow covered the vehicle, just like the Paw's costume. Mardi Gras (now visible, too) and the Paw hopped inside the Pawmobile.

"Don't forget to buckle your seat belt, young Orishan," the Paw reminded Mardi Gras.

"Right, Paw," Mardi Gras said.

"You can use any paw," the Paw said, confused.

The jet-powered Pawmobile zoomed away like a bullet toward Toleni and the Paw's secret hideout.

Moments later, inside the Paw Cave, Leni greeted our heroes.

"Come quick, Schaumy, I mean Paw," Leni said. "I have the Frown on the computer—tracking his movements."

The Paw and Mardi Gras raced inside to view the giant computer screen, which showed the Frown moving quickly across a map of the United States.

"He must have boarded a plane," Leni said. Then she took out her crystal ball from her Wizard's robes, and started gazing. "I can see him on board. He has hijacked a flight, and forced it to fly to Washington D.C.," Leni said, incredulous. "Here, let me project this image on your computer so you can see and hear him," she continued.

"It's a good thing you put that homing device on the Frown, Paw," Leni said.

"Why?" the Paw wanted to know.

"Because as I've told you two," Leni explained. "The crystal ball does not always give us real time images of those we seek. Sometimes it shows them in the past or the future."

On the view screen, the three Orishans watched the Frown.

"I want the Washington Monument cleared of all tourists," the Frown was saying on a cell phone. "No, I don't want to blow it up," the Frown said, disturbed. "For now, I just want to dig it up."

Leni, the Paw, and Mardi Gras all looked at each other puzzled.

"We've got to act fast!" the Paw exclaimed.

The Land of Toleni
(on the edge of a dream)
The Wizard Millennium (Leni) Harmony

Nimbus (Broomstick)   Hoot & Nanny (Owls)   Iggy (The Seal)   Scorch (The Dragon)

Millennium "Leni" Harmony, a Wizard of the Mystical Order of the Golden Paw, has many animals and instruments to practice her magic arts.

CHAPTER 3

TEDDY BEAR ZONE, PAWTROPOLIS DISCOVERED BY HUMANS

BY SCOOP SCHAUMBURG
THE DAILY TIMES OF PAWTROPOLIS

PAWTROPOLIS—The secret is out! Humans know about the existence of the Teddy Bear Zone, the secret portals under humans' beds that transport all Orishans posing as toys called teddy bears from their human homes to the gleaming spires of steel and glass in Pawtropolis.

As you all know, our city of Pawtropolis has been kept secret for 100 years, existing first as a tiny burg in Illinois, founded by Orishans who traveled to Earth for regular infiltration assignments by Orishan Command in Earth Year 1902.

The city now contains hundreds of millions of Orishan inhabitants, who live and work there while their humans are asleep, at work or otherwise occupied and don't know where we all are. We realized that our secret was out when we started seeing publications revealing our city's existence, the Teddy Bear Zone, and other secrets in books published about the teddy bear centennial in Earth Year 2002. We had no proof yet, but Better Bear Bureau officials have speculated that the Frown, the only Orishan in existence ever to tear up his License To Hug, has leaked the information. Then we learned of a plot by the Frown's human, the Lemming, to control the Earth's weather.

Further details will be published in The Daily Times *as soon as they are available.*

In the meantime, Orishans the world over are asked to report any suspicious activities to the BBB immediately. To date, no humans have been spotted in Pawtropolis, but officials believe it is just a matter of time now.

Secrets of the License To Hug Revealed

After the Paw and Mardi Gras learned that the Frown was digging up the Washington Monument, they changed to their secret identities and transported to Pawtropolis.

In Pawtropolis, Scoop Schaumburg works as a mild-mannered reporter for *The Daily Times*, an Orishan daily newspaper. Andy works as a cub reporter, and also shoots pictures freelance for *The Daily Times*.

As soon as the Paw and Mardi Gras waltzed onto the 32nd floor office of the newspaper (now dressed in their secret identities of Scoop Schaumburg and Andy Adorable), City Editor Perry Purple summoned them into his office.

"Did you see this dispatch from our D.C. correspondent?" Perry asked. Scoop Schaumburg rapidly scanned the printout.

It read in part:

The Frown, who just dug up the sword of George Washington here, publicly tore up his License To Hug before humans, and then gave a speech to the horrified crowd.

"This is issued to every Orishan who earns one. Orishans are aliens that look like toy teddy bears," the Frown said, almost spitting out the words with disgust as he tore the precious license to pieces.

"It gives them the right to hug other beings, to give them love," the Frown sneered as he shouted the word "love."

The humans looking at the strange "teddy bear" who called himself the Frown, did not comprehend what he was saying.

This irritated the Frown.

"Don't you see?" the Frown asked the crowd. "You have all been duped by a conspiracy of evil alien teddy bears to love each other! They secretly

transport to a city called Pawtropolis by using portals under your beds! They plan to take over your pathetic planet!"

Scoop Schaumburg threw down the printout of the Washington, D.C. article. He ran out of Perry Purple's office, tears streaming from his face. Andy was bewildered. He picked up the article and read it.

"I don't understand, boss," Andy said. "Why is Scoop so upset?"

"I think it's the Frown tearing up his License To Hug," Perry said.

"What's a License To Hug?" Andy asked.

At first Perry looked at Andy suspiciously, then realization came over his kindly old teddy face.

"Of course, Andy," Perry said. "You don't know, do you?"

"Know what?" Andy asked.

"That Schaumburg and his Hug of Orishans don't have their Licenses To Hug," Perry explained. "Something to do with a transportation accident when they first came to Earth in 1947."

"I don't understand," Andy said, still confused.

"You wouldn't know about that because it was more than 50 years ago," Perry said. "I was just a cub reporter back then, working in New Mexico. Someday I'll tell you the story."

"How come I don't have one of those licenses?" Andy asked.

"You were assigned to the Schaumburg Hug just two years ago," Perry continued. "You were an orphan Schaumburg took into his Hug. No Orishans in his Hug have their licenses. Just like Schaumburg and his Hug, you too will have to earn yours."

Andy still looked confused.

Just then, Schaumburg walked down the aisle between the computer terminals in the newsroom, filled with Orishans busy typing the day's news. Schaumburg heard a news bulletin on a television blaring away in one corner of the newsroom.

"This is Fatima Furbulous, reporting live for WPAW from Washington, D.C., with a news bulletin about the Frown," the female Orishan reporter said.

"The Frown was spotted tying a small human boy to the top of the Washington Monument," she said.

"We go live to hear him speaking to the crowd," she said.

"This human boy tried to stop me from digging up the sword of George Washington," the Frown announced as he pointed a huge cannon at the boy, from below. The boy squirmed to get free of his ropes.

"As I said before, all teddy bears are evil alien invaders from another planet," the Frown continued.

"I should know! I am one! Now this boy, Jose, will be sacrificed so I can prove to all humans the truth about the teddy bear conspiracies."

Back in Pawtropolis, Schaumburg received an urgent telepathic message from Leni. "Did you see the news on TV?" she asked him.

"I'm on it, Leni," Schaumburg said, racing back into Perry Purple's office.

"C'mon, Andy. We gotta run!" Schaumburg barked.

Schaumburg pulled Andy from the editor's office. "We have to get there fast, Leni."

"Both of you gulp down a chocolate bar and use the Teddy Bear Zone to travel to Washington, D.C.," Leni instructed Schaumburg.

The Paw and Mardi Gras had replenished their supplies such as chocolate bars at the Paw Cave a few minutes earlier.

"I hope we make it on time," Schaumburg said as they scrambled to find a portal.

The Frown Gets The Drop On The Paw

Leni perched on the side desk of journalist Samuel Arctophile in Versailles, Illinois.

Samuel's fingers flew across his keyboard as he banged out a story about what just transpired in Washington, D.C. to the Paw and Mardi Gras. Their story had a local angle. The boy tied to the Washington Monument resided in Versailles.

"You know they're never going to print that," Leni chided Sam.

"I know, Leni bear," Sam said affectionately. The bears and Sam had grown quite close over the last three years, Sam being enlisted by them to help them accomplish their secret mission on Earth.

"But I needed to document it. Perhaps I can write a book when this is all over. Or maybe Fred over at *The National Investigator* will print this. Nobody will believe it's real, but it won't be the first time fact is stranger than fiction."

Scoop Schaumburg works as a reporter for The Daily Times of Pawropolis. He often reports on the adventures of the Paw, but people don't know the Paw is his secret identity.

"You know we can't reveal our existence to humanity," Leni said.

Here's the story Sam punched out on his computer terminal:

Where Am I? Who Am I?

BY SAMUEL ARCTOPHILE
VERSAILLES BUREAU CHIEF
THE DAILY PRESS, MONTREAL, IL

WASHINGTON, D.C.—A pair of super-powered aliens who look like teddy bears saved the life of a Versailles boy this morning in our nation's capital.

Details are still sketchy at this time, but The Daily Press *learned an evil teddy bear known as the Frown tied Jose Cruz to the top of the Washington Monument.*

Jose is the eight-year-old son of Cheryl Cruz, curator of the Versailles George Washington Museum and George Washington expert doing research in Washington, D.C. this week.

Jose told The Daily Press *he spotted the Frown trying to dig under the Washington Monument and knew instantly the evil teddy bear was trying to find the fabled Sword of George Washington, a nine-inch long replica of the original sword worn by our nation's first President during his swearing-in ceremony more than 200 years ago.*

As the Frown attempted to blow up both Jose (tied to the top of the monument) and the monument to prove his wild tales about a conspiracy by aliens that look like teddy bears, the two super-powered bears intervened.

"It was really cool," Jose said in a phone conversation this morning. "I was tied to the top of the monument, squirming and trying to escape when Mardi Gras flew up to free me while the lead super bear, the Paw, flew to the Frown, tackling the Frown to the ground. But the Frown had already launched his shell toward me. Then the Paw flew up to block the shell from hitting me. It was fantastic!"

Jose said Mardi Gras flew him down to the ground safely. As the Paw proceeded to tie up the Frown, the Frown pulled out a glowing brown rock, which stunned the Paw.

The Paw writhed in pain on the ground, too weak to escape from the rock's strange brown glow.

"The Mardi Gras bear kept his distance so he was not affected by the rock's strange rays," Jose continued. "But he could not help his friend, the Paw, and had to let the Frown get away. I later heard the Frown boarded a train bound for Boston."

The Mardi Gras bear seemed to be talking to nobody, or perhaps somebody in his head, Jose said.

"He was given instructions to use his super strength to rip out some pipes underground that were made of lead, and fashion a box to contain the radioactive rock that was hurting the Paw."

Mardi Gras seemed to have X-ray vision that allowed him to see the pipes, Jose added.

Jose said Mardi Gras instructed him to help.

"'Hurry, Jose,' Mardi Gras told me," Jose said. 'Go to the Paw and shut the rock in this box so he won't get hurt by the rock's effects.' I ran to the Paw, placed the glowing rock in the lead box, slammed it shut and the Paw began to stop trembling in pain. But then, Mardi Gras was upset," Jose continued. "He said their super powers had just worn off and his friend Leni was scared because I was too late to prevent some damage to the Paw. When I gently woke up the Paw, he seemed confused. 'Who are you?' the Paw asked me. 'What am I doing here? Who am I?' Mardi Gras said the Paw seemed to have amnesia.

"So I picked up both Mardi Gras and the Paw and ran to the Library of Congress to see if my Mom could help us," Jose continued. "But when I entered the building, the bears suddenly became stiff like they were just stuffed animals. And their eyes grew vacant as if they were no longer alive."

Cheryl Cruz busied herself doing research on the very sword the Frown was digging up.

She had no idea her son had been in danger at all.

The Daily Press learned that Jose and Cheryl are headed back here to Versailles by car, and have both bears with them. We will keep readers posted of any further information regarding this strange conspiracy of aliens that look like teddy bears.

After Sam finished typing the story, he turned to Leni.

"Looks good," Leni said. "You know, we are going to have to

bring Jose into the loop. His mom knows about us. It's time for the boy to know the truth about us too. Meanwhile, we have to cure Schaumy's amnesia."

"I'll call Cheryl as soon as they get home," Sam said. "Jose should know what's going on with his mom. You know she is always looking for alien conspiracies and such."

"Maybe she's not too far off the mark," Leni replied.

Just then, a customer came into the Versailles Bureau, and Leni stiffened up, her blue eyes staring blankly up in the air. The customer ignored Leni, thinking the Orishan to be a teddy bear.

After finishing with the customer who wanted to pay for a subscription to *The Daily Press*, Sam received a phone call.

"Sam, this is Fred," the caller said. "I'm faxing over a copy of a story the Protectors are sending to newspapers to cover what just happened out in Washington D.C. You could rewrite it with a local angle about Mrs. Cruz if you like."

Moviemakers Stage Movie Stunt at Nation's Capital

BY SAMUEL ARCTOPHILE
VERSAILLES BUREAU
THE DAILY PRESS, MONTREAL, IL

WASHINGTON, D.C.—The Daily Press *has just learned of a movie involving aliens that look like teddy bears being filmed in Washington, D.C. A Versailles boy is involved with the film project.*

The movie company, New Teddy Bear Cinema, staged a promotional stunt at the Washington Monument yesterday, where a teddy bear, claiming to be an alien, makes demands of tourists.

The "alien," an animatronic actor, is part of a secret movie production that studio executives are planning to release later this year.

Repeated calls to New Teddy Bear Cinema resulted in executives declining to comment further on the production.

The stunt apparently involved a small boy from Versailles, Jose Cruz, whom some super bears "rescued" in the film.

Don't Forget Me, My Love

Cheryl and Jose Cruz arrived home in Versailles, unpacking their luggage and trudging their bags into their tiny apartment above the George Washington Museum. Sam greeted them as they were unpacking her 1974 Ford Pinto station wagon, full of rust and barely able to hit 55 miles per hour on the highway.

"Hi, Sam," Cheryl said.

"Good day, Cheryl," Sam said. "Do you mind if I take Jose back to the office to finish that story I was working on?"

Jose looked puzzled.

"I suppose," Cheryl said. "I have to unpack anyway. You don't mind watching an eight-year-old?"

"We'll be fine," Sam said.

"I thought you didn't like kids," Jose countered.

"Of course I do, Jose," Sam responded to Jose's challenge, messing affectionately with the boy's dark brown hair. "Don't I always treat you nicely when you come into the Bureau to talk about your paper route with the circulation manager?"

"Yeah, but you don't talk much," Jose said wrinkling his nose.

"Jose, could you bring those two teddy bear super heroes with you?" Sam asked. "I want to get a picture of you three."

Jose dived into the Pinto to retrieve the Paw and Mardi Gras, now stiff like toy teddy bears.

Back in the Bureau office, Sam asked Jose for Mardi Gras.

Jose handed Mardi Gras to Sam. Sam gently squeezed Mardi Gras' right paw. Instantly, the Orishan's eyes grew alive, as if a soul just entered him and he woke from his suspended hibernation sleep.

"I knew it was alive!" Jose said. "How did you know?"

"Jose, I have a story to tell you," Sam said. "But first, I want you to read the Paw's diary."

As Sam handed Schaumburg's diary to Jose, Leni, dressed as a Wizard bear, stepped out from behind a chair.

"Let me see the Paw," Leni said. "I think I can restore his memory."

"Wow, another live teddy bear!" Jose exclaimed when he saw Leni.

While Leni worked her magic, Jose began to read aloud a fascinating tale from the Paw's space diary:

Captain's Log, Captain Schaumburg Harmony serving aboard the Saturn IV on its way to Earth.
Star Date Juno 6, Orishan Calendar Year 21776. Earth Date: July 2, 1947.

To Orishan High Command:

As requested, I am writing this log in Earth English to demonstrate our Hug of Orishans has achieved versatility in Earth's languages and cultures.

This is my Hug's final mission that will enable us to earn our Licenses To Hug from Orishan Command.

Earlier today, after my briefing with Commander Filbert, my rival, Frank E. Vil, spouted off about his opposition to our missions to Earth.

"So, Schaumburg," Vil said. "You and your Hug may finally get your chance to earn your Licenses To Hug, eh?"

Vil slapped me on the back in a fake token of affection.

"Ow!" I responded.

"Look, Vil," I told him. "I know you think I failed in our last mission, but that's no reason to be sarcastic about my second chance to earn our Licenses To Hug."

"You four are a disgrace to the planet Orisha," Vil said, referring to me and the other three Orishans in the Hug. My Hug includes: 1) Captain Louis LaHug who will serve as executive officer, my good friend and second in command, 2) Ship's Wizard of the Mystical Order of The Golden Paw, Millennium Harmony, my wife of two years, 3) Chocolate Harmony, ship's counselor, medical officer and my little sister.

"You showed compassion to an Arjogun enemy officer," Vil barked at me. "Rather than accomplish your mission on the Planet Serena, you saved the life of an enemy soldier! You should have just shot that soldier in the back and put him out of his misery!"

"What?" I shouted back. "That would be against all Orisha stands for. You know the code of the Order of the Golden Paw forbids

fatal retaliation against an enemy, no matter what the circumstances. That's why we always operate in secret, to avoid that kind of contact."

"We should all teach love, goodwill and foster peace throughout the galaxy, right?" Vil said snidely, seeming to not believe in the code we all swear to uphold.

"You know that's right, and besides, Orishan Command gave us this second chance because they believe we were correct in sparing the Arjogun's life," I said.

"Schaumburg, you forgot the prime goal of any Orishan mission: Accomplish the objective, even if it means harming other beings," Vil said. "Sometimes, as an Orishan in command of a Hug, you may even have to order another Orishan to enter harm's way. You and I are both headed to Earth on separate missions. I, for one, have no intention of endangering the life of a member of my Hug just to save some miserable Earthling, or even worse, an enemy Arjogun agent!"

"You do what you have to do, Vil," I said. "Just leave me in peace."

"Listen to me, Schaumburg!" Vil continued, even though I wished to end the conversation.

"Earthlings are evil malcontents who slaughter every other species on their own planet for sport. They do not deserve to continue to exist. I am baffled when I hear the Elders of the Order of The Golden Paw spout off about how much potential Earthlings have. Bah! We should let the Arjogun just conquer their planet and be done with them!"

With that, Vil left for his space ship. I wondered to myself why he was coming out of the hangar where the Saturn IV was awaiting our departure. None of my crew was yet aboard her.

Jose stopped reading for a moment. At that time, Leni took out a specially carved bar of white chocolate and gave it to the Paw after reviving him by pressing his right paw. The chocolate bar was shaped like a bear with a super costume, looking just like the Paw in miniature.

"Here, this Remembear I fashioned with magic should restore your memories," Leni said to the Paw. "Eat up!"

Jose watched as the Paw slowly sat up. As he ate the Remembear bar, recognition seemed to come over the super bear's face.

"Leni," he said, hugging her very warmly. "Thank you."

"No sweat," Leni said. "You didn't think I would let you forget your own wife, did you?"

"How about another hug?" the Paw said.

"You're always trolling for hugs, husband," Leni said to the Paw.

"You know what I always say, 'Everyone can always use another hug.'"

They hugged again warmly for a long time.

"I love you, Schaumburg," she said, a tear streaming down her furry cheek.

PART 2

THE CONSPIRACY BEGINS

CHAPTER 4

THE SAUCER CRASHES IN NEW MEXICAN DESERT

In the office of Versailles Bureau Chief Samuel Arctophile, Jose continued to read the diary out loud:

Commanders, after reaching the space-time funnel, we were quickly on our way to Earth's solar system and will soon hit their atmosphere. The H.A.R.V.E.Y. unit is connected to the ship so we are cloaked to the humans.

Our mission: Find out why the Arjogun have secretly journeyed to Earth and what they are planning. In our previous encounters with the Arjogun, we know they plan to rule the known universe, favoring logic over emotions. Their colorless gray skin exemplifies their colorless souls, which know no art, no music, and no joy—only warfare. They wish to enslave all sentient beings so they can continue to add weapons factory planets to their vast confederation of slave worlds. Since we suspect the Arjogun have similar plans for Earth, we are to investigate and stop them, keeping our existence secret from the humans. Humans stand twice the height of an average Arjogun, and Orishans are half the size of an average Arjogun foot soldier. Earth has attracted the attention of the Arjogun because the Earthlings set off an atomic explosion two years ago and are now testing bigger and more destructive atomic devices.

Our intelligence sources say it is the atomic bombs that make Earth a target for Arjogunia.

Despite Vil's objections, I still believe the members of the Mystical Order of The Golden Paw are right to believe in the prime law: Treat all other beings as you would have them treat you. That universal law, which

*the Arjogun seem to violate every chance they get, is the reason the Orisha
have been able to evade the Arjogun and save countless planets from them
in the past. I hope we can save the Earth.*

Captain Schaumburg Harmony, reporting from deep space.

"Wow!" Jose said. "These teddy bears really are space aliens, aren't
they?"

"What's Jose doing reading my diary?" the Paw asked.

"He's seen too much, Schaumy," Leni said. "So we brought Jose
into the loop."

Electro Magnetic Pulse Stops
Schaumy's Mission Before It Starts

The Paw sat down cross-legged on the floor, as Leni and Mardi
Gras sat down beside him.

The stories the aliens were telling about how they crash-landed on
Earth more than 50 years ago transfixed Sam as well.

"We were on our way to Earth, and on the 23rd day of our journey
we pierced the planet's atmosphere with no great difficulties," the Paw
said.

*On this mission, Louis, as usual, acting as main pilot, with Leni
serving as navigator, steered the craft toward its destination: Pawtropolis,
Illinois.*

*The ship's H.A.R.V.E.Y. unit had been installed to provide a cloak to
the ship.*

As the Paw told his story, he lifted up his left paw, showing Jose a
two-inch white bunny rabbit. "This is H.A.R.V.E.Y.," the Paw said.
"He is a Hand Activated Radix (computer center) with Electronic
Yashmac (veil). He is very versatile. Although I think he was damaged
slightly in the crash."

*Before the trouble started, Schaumburg sat at the Captain's station,
monitoring Lou's maneuvering of the ship at supersonic speeds as the outside
of the hull turned a bright red-orange from the friction of entering Earth's
atmosphere. Schaumburg's little sister Chocolate was seated at the health
station, monitoring the health of the crew during the landing.*

Leni turned to Schaumburg.

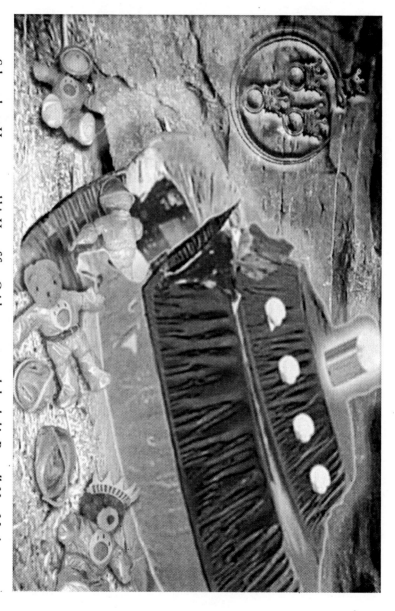

Schaumburg Harmony and his Hug of four Orishan agents crash-landed in Roswell, New Mexico, United States of America, planet Earth, Earth date, July 2, 1947.

"We will arrive in Pawtropolis at precisely 3:30 p.m., Earth, American central time, and be able to land at the Central Portal, where the Better Bear Bureau headquarters is located," Leni reported.

"Start the landing sequence Lou," Schaumburg ordered.

Suddenly, Louis lost control of the ship.

Red and white lights blinked on and off, and the control panels started sparking.

"What hit us?" Schaumburg asked.

"I don't know," Louis said. "I've lost control, Captain. I can't steer us at all."

The ship slammed sharply into a starboard angle, throwing all four of them out of their seats. No seat belts are used in Orishan vessels because of the special inertia absorbers built-in, invented by our very own Louis LaHug.

"We were hit with an electromagnetic pulse," the H.A.R.V.E.Y. unit said.

"From outside the ship? From Earth? How could they see us?" Schaumburg asked.

"The pulse generated from within the Saturn IV vessel," the H.A.R.V.E.Y. unit said, just as the ship lurched in the opposite direction, throwing the bears across the bridge, sliding on the smooth floor.

"None of our monitors are functioning," Chocolate said as she crawled back to the health station, a little bruised.

"I have no control here either, Schaumy," Leni said.

Schaumburg asked her to use some magic to try and stabilize the ship.

"Roger," she said and started to cast a spell.

"Captain, the computer is going haywire," Chocolate called out. "It is showing we are all dead. A message has already been transmitted to the B.B.B. indicating our deaths."

Lou looked at Chocolate, worried.

Chocolate threw back a look of reassurance, interesting since Chocolate was on her first flight while Louis experienced many missions in the past.

"We'll be ok," Chocolate told Louis. "My brother Schaumburg will get us out of this fix."

At that instant, the H.A.R.V.E.Y. unit began speaking nonsense about his functions.

"The H.A.R.V.E.Y. unit is a sophisticated hand-held device with a cloaking tool as well as other handy . . ." the unit said, sparking.

The ship lurched in the opposite direction again, violently throwing the occupants against the opposite bulkhead.

"Why is our H.A.R.V.E.Y. unit going crazy?" Leni asked.

"Lou, can you get control manually?" Schaumburg asked. Schaumburg crawled to his station to try and help Louis with the controls.

The ship lurched again. By then, the ship soared about 5,000 feet above the surface and was going down fast. Leni managed to take some control over the ship, and it started to descend over the New Mexico desert, near Roswell.

"Some of the tools a standard H.A.R.V.E.Y. unit is equipped with includes a special temporal displacement, which allows the wearer to pass through solid objects . . ." the H.A.R.V.E.Y. unit babbled on.

Before anyone could do anything else, the disk-shaped ship quickly plunged to the sand, bouncing along the desert floor as if it were a stone skipping on water.

The Orishans flew violently about the space ship.

"Go into suspended hibernation," Schaumburg ordered. "The stiff condition will protect us from the crash."

All complied.

Mardi Gras was also fascinated hearing the story from Schaumburg's diary.

"So how come you guys don't look 50 years older?" Mardi Gras asked.

The Paw pulled open a filing cabinet in Sam's office and pulled out a folder of yellowed clippings.

"Read this, my young friend," the Paw said to Mardi Gras.

He handed Mardi Gras the following story, which was first published in *The Daily Times*, Pawtropolis, on July 3, 1947:

It's Raining Teddy Bears in New Mexico

AN EXCLUSIVE, FIRST-HAND EYE WITNESS ACCOUNT BY PERRY PURPLE, CUB REPORTER THE DAILY TIMES OF PAWTROPOLIS

ROSWELL, NEW MEXICO—One of our Orishan ships crashed in the desert near Roswell, New Mexico last night, and four Orishan agents were seen strewn around the wreckage. I managed to arrive on the scene before the humans, took a photograph, and determined that all four Orishans were okay. They remained stiff in a state of suspended hibernation.

First priority: to secure the vessel so that the natives of Earth cannot study Orishan technology before they are mature enough as a species.

So I boarded the vessel. I found the H.A.R.V.E.Y. unit still intact and separated it from the ship. It was sparking a bit, but seemed functional. I hopped outside the crashed ship and strapped the H.A.R.V.E.Y. unit on the ship's commander's paw, knowing the commander can use its cloaking technology, if need be.

All the Orishans were dressed in their standard silver flight pressure suits, but some of them had lost their flight helmets.

The ship, Saturn IV, had smashed against a cliff face in the desert. There were no humans around at this point.

I jumped back onboard the wrecked ship. I planted a self-destruct instruction in the still working ship's radix computer center from one of the four keyboard panels still intact. For those readers in Pawtropolis who are not members of the Orishan High Command, Orishan spaceship keyboards contain paw impressions with buttons for each paw "finger." Each button can control different functions for the ship. All four crewmembers on an Orishan vessel fly the ship and all four can access the ship's radix computer. One panel is navigation, another monitors the crew's health and handles the ship's defensive systems, another is propulsion and engineering, and the final panel is the commander's that controls communications.

As I set the self-destruct, I heard a military Jeep approaching, an Earth land ship. I pulled the four "bodies" to safety just before the Orishan ship exploded, scattering flying debris across ¾'s of a mile on the desert floor.

Just as I was about to carry the four Orishans away to my waiting car, the Jeep drove up to the scene. Two army officers jumped from the vehicle, guns cocked on me!

"Back away from those bodies," one officer called to me.

At first I thought to freeze in suspended hibernation, but changed my mind.

I dropped the bodies I was dragging and ran for my car. Shots rang out. Even though several bullets whizzed by me, I escaped to my car unharmed and was able to drive away unmolested. They did not pursue me.

The officers picked up the four Orishans and placed them in their Jeep. Then the officers hoisted parts of the ship aboard the Jeep as well.

"These aliens look just like teddy bears," one officer said. "That other one looked like a teddy bear, too. And it drove off in a miniature car? Is this some kind of gag?"

"Orders are orders, Charlie," the other officer said as they grunted and groaned, lifting pieces of the wrecked ship to the back end of their Jeep.

I followed far behind the Army Jeep and learned that the ship and Orishans were taken to a U.S. Army Air Force base nearby.

I knew I had to get the Orishans out of there, fearing that the humans would try to do a medical autopsy on them if they did not think they were just toy bears.

I took out my B.B.B.-standard issue pocketknife, cut through a portion of the fence outside the base, and slithered to the medical building where the Orishans remained incarcerated.

All four Orishans lay stiff as boards on top of one bed designed for a human.

I cautiously woke each one, introduced myself as Perry Purple, correspondent for The Daily Times of Pawtropolis, and instructed them to use the Teddy Bear Zone under the bed to escape to Pawtropolis.

But before they could journey to Pawtropolis, things went wrong.

A doctor with a nametag that read "Dr. M. Feinberg, United States Army Air Force Medical Corps," came in and saw us conversing in our native tongue. He pulled out a pistol, pointing it at Chocolate, one of the females. I believe we frightened the human.

"My commander told me you aliens might wake up," Feinberg said. "That's why he left me his pistol. Now, hands . . . er . . . paws up!"

I instructed Leni, the other female in the Hug, to use her skills in the mystic arts to help her Hug escape. I recognized her magic spectacles, a sign of members of the Mystical Order of The Golden Paw.

"But what about you Mr. Purple?" she asked.

"Just go, before someone gets hurt," I said.

Feinberg, who could not understand our language, shouted in English for us to stand still, continuing to point his pistol at Chocolate's head.

"*Take our Hug far, far away in time and space,*" Leni chanted. "*Swish us away to a place that's safe so we can investigate our case.*" *After her incantation, the four Orishans evaporated from existence.*

The human doctor could not believe his eyes. That gave me an element of surprise to scamper under a bed and escape safely though a Teddy Bear Zone portal to the newspaper office in Pawtropolis.

I have no idea what that doctor told his superiors when he had to account for four missing alien bodies.

But we also have no idea where the Schaumburg Hug went.

The Daily Times *of Pawtropolis will report any further developments as we receive them.*

"Jeez, this would make a great science fiction movie," Jose said, still mesmerized by the stories he tried to absorb.

"Yeah, and our H.A.R.V.E.Y. unit has never been the same since that crash," Leni said. "Sometimes I wish Perry hadn't rescued it for us."

"The crash also caused the ship's computer to signal the Better Bear Bureau that we were all dead," Schaumburg said. "That's why they never issued us our License To Hug, Mardi Gras. Actually, after we contacted the BBB in 1999, they told us to remain 'dead' and gave us a new mission. At the time, we did not know that Vil was not who he said he was."

"You mean a spy bear among the alien teddy bears?" Jose asked.

The Paw stepped up to Jose who was seated at a nearby desk. The Paw placed his left paw gently on Jose's shoulder.

"That, my young friend, is another story, and in part why your life is still in danger," the Paw said, cryptically.

"What was it like to time travel?" Jose asked. ·

"Let me read this log entry," the Paw replied.

Captain's Log, supplemental:
To Orishan High Command,

Although I know some of you have time-traveled before, I must say the experience was beary unsettling.

My wife created a time storm with her magic. At first, a glowing mist appeared all around the four of us out of nowhere. The mists were colored greenish-yellow. We all heard humming and buzzing noises. I could feel a tingling paralysis, like we were all struck by lightning. Then we seemed to hear a rushing noise. Finally, we felt like we were floating out of space and time. It seemed like for us, all time had stopped. We awoke in a strange human apartment, slightly dazed. It is a good thing the human who inhabited the dwelling was asleep at the time.

"Okay, Paw. So how did you hook up with Sam, here?" Jose asked.

"For that story, I will take over," Sam said.

"I remember it very clearly as if it were yesterday. It was my 32nd birthday, Nov. 23, 1999," Sam said.

"I had just come back from dinner with my managing editor, Izzie Feinberg. Izzie was saying I should settle down and marry someone. I was resisting. Here's how it went:"

CHAPTER 5

CLOSE ENCOUNTERS OF A TEDDY BEAR KIND

November 23, 1999, Izzie Feinberg and Samuel Arctophile dine at Burger King, Montreal, Illinois.

"You're getting too old," Izzie said. "You should find a good woman and start your own family."

"I'm really not a kid-person," Sam told Izzie. "Besides, I'm too shy. I'm short for a man, 5 feet 7 inches. I am slight of build, no athlete. I wear glasses. What girl would want me anyway?"

"You'll never know until you start asking them out," Izzie replied. "Why did you break up with Amy, anyway? Say, how about that widow, Cheryl Cruz? You're doing that feature about her as curator at the George Washington Museum, right? She's pretty."

"She still thinks she's married," Sam said. "Besides, she already has a kid."

"All the better. Most of the hard part's already done in raising that one," Izzie said. Izzie has three children, all grown adults now.

After dinner, Sam arrived at his apartment in Streator, and settled down to read a good science fiction novel.

He fell asleep on the couch. He woke up an hour later and went to bed. About midnight, he awoke to some strange noises like scuffling and growling in his kitchen.

He sat up in the bed listening to detect where the sound came from.

Sam tiredly flipped on the light, and determined the noises seemed to be coming from the kitchen.

He went to the kitchen, turned on the light and the noises stopped.

Sam quickly opened up the kitchen cabinets, thinking some sort of animal might jump out. He found nothing out of the ordinary.

Sam returned to bed.

After a few minutes, the scuffling sounds started again.

This time he got up, a little bit more hurried, a little bit angrier.

"What the heck is going on?" he asked under his breath. "I'm trying to sleep here!"

He heard the noises again in the same place, the kitchen. He went in, opened up the kitchen cabinet under the sink. There were bags under there. He moved the bags around. Nothing happened. No noise.

Sam went back to his room and tried to sleep once again.

For the third time, a few minutes later, he heard noises again.

This time, Sam grabbed a baseball bat out of his closet and slowly moved toward the kitchen, trying not to alert the intruder to his presence.

He quickly flipped open the cabinet under the sink. At first he heard nothing.

Sam suddenly heard a growl, and then jumped back in surprise.

Sam quickly bent down to crawl into the cabinet, "Whoever you are, I'm not an easy target!"

He dragged his bat into the cabinet in a menacing way then heard a blood-curdling scream. Sam jumped, hitting his head on the top of the sink, then scrambled out of the cabinet.

He flipped on the kitchen light.

To Sam's surprise, an ethereal sight of four teddy bear-like creatures, dressed in silver pressure suits, greeted him. They rummaged through Sam's kitchen cabinets. The dark brown creature with a green crown grasped the arm of a honey-colored bear that wore a red belt with a golden ring looped around the belt.

All of them had paw insignias on their uniform chests. A third "bear," colored in golden brown fur, had a golden hook on his right paw, instead of the normal silver glove. Sam mused that this looked strangely out of place.

The final "bear," a white iridescent one with bright blue eyes, wore glasses.

In shock, Sam dropped the bat, which startled the "bears." Sam pointed at his chest.

"These cute little beings have to be just computerized toys," he said to himself. "Sam," he said, pointing at himself vigorously. "I wonder if they are interactive?"

Chocolate leaned over to Schaumburg and whispered in Orishan, "He's trying to communicate with us," she said in Orishan, then giggled.

Sam noted this, and cracked a smile himself. He picked up a Nestles' Crunch bar on his kitchen table, unwrapped it, took a bite, and then offered the bar to Schaumburg.

Schaumburg cautiously approached the candy bar, and then bit off a hunk.

"Mmmmmm," Schaumburg said, rubbing his tummy and smiling.

"Chocolate bar," Sam said.

Chocolate giggled again. "Should we tell him we speak English?" Chocolate asked Schaumburg in Orishan.

Schaumburg said nothing. Sam noted their voices were kind of growly, like a grizzly bear.

Sam held up his hands, palms facing the "bears"

"I am friend," he said.

All the Orishans could not contain themselves and burst out in loud laughter.

For some reason, Sam could not bring himself to believe these creatures were harmful.

"Speak to him in English," Leni instructed Schaumburg, knowing it was cruel to be fooling their host.

"We need your help," Schaumburg said to Sam. "We are travelers and are lost. Can you help?"

"This has to be some kind of joke, right?" Sam said. "Are you guys animatronic toys sent here by one of the boys in the newsroom to scare the wits out of me?"

Schaumburg, standing 18 inches high, slowly walked up to Sam. He stretched out his arms like a young child wanting a hug.

Still in a state of shock, Sam instinctively bent down to his knees, then awkwardly, but warmly, hugged Schaumburg.

Sam pulled Schaumburg away and held him by the waist about a foot away from Sam's face, staring into the alien's amber eyes.

For a brief moment, nobody said anything.

"I can see kindness in your eyes," Schaumburg said to Sam.

"You aren't toys, are you?" Sam said, not expecting an answer.

"My name is Schaumburg," the Orishan said.

"My name's Sam."

"Yeah, so you said," Schaumburg chided Sam.

Then all the aliens rushed up to Sam, giving him a group hug, knocking him down. They all laughed.

Sam sat up and the Orishans all sat down on the kitchen floor facing Sam. Schaumburg explained they were from another planet, crashed in the desert, and how the Army captured them. Then Leni used her magic powers to swish them away.

While the others listened to Schaumburg's tale of crashing at Roswell, New Mexico, Louis, the "pirate" and official procurement officer on the mission, started to fish around in the kitchen, searching for something to eat. He pulled down a canister of flour, spilling it all over himself. Then he took a can of soda, started shaking it, and used his hook to puncture it open. Frothy sweet foam sprayed him in the face, startling him. Lou licked his lips, liking the taste.

"Wait, little alien, you're making a mess," Sam said to Louis.

Then Lou opened the refrigerator door and started opening all the jars and sniffing them. While Sam was distracted with Louis, Leni walked into his bedroom rummaging through the dresser drawers. She started throwing Sam's socks and underwear all over the bedroom.

Chocolate now felt safe with Sam. She decided to walk over to a shelf of cassette tapes and CDs in the living room as Schaumburg continued to tell his story of the crash landing. Sam was watching Chocolate through the corner of his eye. He noticed that the aliens sort of wobbled on their stubby legs. She took out one cassette tape and began pulling the tape out, ruining Sam's favorite recording of Carly Simon's greatest hits.

Meanwhile, Schaumburg grabbed the Nestles' Crunch bar and began to eat the rest of it.

"Hey," Sam said to Schaumburg. "That's my last Crunch bar! And you, stop pulling out my tape," he said to Chocolate. "And what is that other creature doing in my bedroom?"

Sam felt out of control, like he was in a room full of mischievous children, and he was not accustomed to handling children.

Leni came out of the bedroom with a purple and red argyle sock around her neck.

"I like the colors," Leni said to Sam, smiling warmly. Sam tried to get angry, but Leni's smile melted Sam's heart.

However, Leni began to realize that their actions were disturbing their Earth host.

"Perhaps we should put him to sleep for now," Leni told Schaumburg in Orishan.

"Yeah, that way we can explore his dwelling undisturbed," Louis said enthusiastically. "He might even think it is all a dream."

"Go ahead and cast a spell on him, Leni," Schaumburg ordered. "But after we explore this dwelling, we must put it back in order without him knowing about it."

"Agreed," Leni said, zapping Sam to sleep with some sparkling pink powder from within a pocket in her pressure suit. She levitated him to the bedroom and floated him gently to his bed.

The Orishans continued to explore the "Earth dwelling," and turned on the television, watching the local television programs. A re-run episode of the original 1960s version of "Star Trek" was playing, which transfixed Chocolate and Louis as Captain Kirk and Mr. Spock helped the starship crew to escape from hostile aliens.

Leni and Schaumburg combed through books Sam had on a shelf, reading about everything from science fiction (namely the "Hitchhiker's Guide to the Galaxy") to the study of Earth life forms and cultures in *National Geographic* magazines. The aliens voraciously soaked up all they could about Earth culture.

"It's time to contact the Better Bear Bureau," Schaumburg said.

He pulled open his H.A.R.V.E.Y. unit and tried to call a special number by Orishan radio. The H.A.R.V.E.Y. unit responded with:
"The number you have reached has been disconnected."
"What?" Schaumburg asked.
"I have tapped into the Pawtropolis communications network," H.A.R.V.E.Y. replied. "The Better Bear Bureau is no longer in Pawtropolis. To reach the B.B.B., you will have to travel to the Arch in St. Louis, Missouri and follow these detailed instructions."
The H.A.R.V.E.Y. unit gave specific directions to the Hug so they could contact the B.B.B. in St. Louis. Schaumburg wrote them down.

*   *   *

The next day, Sam woke up feeling very rested, and thought the aliens could have been just a strange dream. He did not see any sign of them being there, except that his Crunch bar could not be found.

The bears hid in a closet that morning. Sam stopped by the store before work and picked up more Nestles' Crunch bars so he had a brand new stash waiting for him when he arrived home from work.

At the newspaper, for some reason Sam felt compelled to look up the famous Roswell crash on the Internet. Here's what he discovered:

Lt. Col. Walter Haut, press officer for the 509th Bombardment Group Intelligence Office at Roswell Army Air Field, New Mexico, released a statement July 8, 1947. It said in part that the Army came "into possession of pieces of a crashed flying disk." Very soon after making that statement, he retracted it. Major Jesse Marcel, U.S. Army Intelligence, Roswell, claimed the retraction of Haut's press release was a government cover-up. Marcel said the Army found debris strewn over an area three-quarters of a mile in diameter. Marcel had no idea where the wreckage came from. He also indicated there is no evidence remaining of any alien bodies, but some were found at the wreckage— four to be exact. All the stiff bodies wore silver pressure suits.

Sam found Haut's original press statement on the Internet:

"The many rumors regarding the flying disc (sic) became a reality yesterday when the intelligence office of the 509th Bomb Group of the Eighth Air Force, Roswell Army Air Field, was fortunate enough to

gain possession of a disc through the cooperation of one of the local
ranchers and the Sheriff's office of Chaves County.

"The flying object landed on a ranch near Roswell sometime last
week. Not having phone facilities, the rancher stored the disc until such
time as he was able to contact the Sheriff's office, who in turn notified
Major Jesse A. Marcel, of the 509th Bomb Group Intelligence Office.

"Action was immediately taken and the disc was picked up at the
rancher's home. It was inspected at the Roswell Army Air Field and
subsequently loaned by Major Marcel to higher headquarters."

At this point, Sam remembered his strange night with the four
"bear" aliens.

"Was it a dream, or real?" he wondered to himself, out loud. In
any case, he had an assignment that day, and had to get to it. He
planned to write a feature about Cheryl Cruz and her museum. Because
Washington camped for long periods near Versailles during the French
and Indian War, a lot of historical documentation and artifacts dating
back to the period remained in Versailles. So the city opened the
museum and hired Cheryl, a George Washington expert who had written
a book on the subject, to be the curator.

During that interview, Sam learned about Cheryl's obsession with
alien conspiracies. She started asking Sam if he had any way of checking
on the FBI's story about her dead husband. She thought it was a
government cover-up because Armando learned too much about aliens
trying to conquer the earth.

The Lady Is Either A Conspiracy Nut Or She's On To Something

Samuel Arctophile's private journal, Nov. 24, 1999

I woke up for work today, believing I remembered a weird dream
from the night before about aliens that look like teddy bears. I drove
my usual half-hour trek to Versailles from Streator, opened my office
and began typing the day's stories.

I like my job. I've been working as the Versailles Bureau Chief for about 10 years, uncovering corruption and crime in the shadows of local city government.

But despite my career achievement, I'm still a loner. At the age of 32, I not only remain single, I'm not even dating. I dumped the one girl I ever seriously dated, Amy, another reporter at the paper. So when my boss assigned me a story that required that I interview Cheryl Cruz, the beautiful, 28-year-old widow who runs the George Washington Museum in Versailles, the idea made me a little nervous.

Cheryl, however, believes she is still married, not accepting the official government explanation for her husband's death—an aircraft accident over the Nevada desert skies in 1997.

After filing my stories for the day, I walked to my scheduled interview with Cheryl Cruz. My office is across the street from the museum, and the fall weather remained warm enough to enjoy, about 60 degrees and sunny. The museum overlooks the Illinois River located along lovely natural rock bluffs and trees.

Cheryl's office is in the back of the museum, and she lives in an apartment upstairs with her little boy, Jose.

After an interview, I like to chitchat with my interview subjects— sometimes getting better, more in-depth quotes when the interview subject grows more relaxed and trusts me. So I proceeded to make small talk with Cheryl.

But Cheryl's conversation was anything but small talk. Here's how it went:

"I believe the government is keeping my husband captive in some secret prison," Cheryl said to me.

"Why would they do that?" I asked, a bit taken aback.

"Because he got too close to the truth about extraterrestrials and the government's weather control technology (which we are getting from the alien grays). The government agreed to this in exchange for allowing the grays to abduct humans for nefarious experiments."

My jaw dropped.

"What???" I exclaimed. I pushed my chair away from her kitchen table where we sat, dropping my pad and pen. "You're joking, right?" I asked, continuing to back away from her.

Cheryl's large brown eyes looked at me sadly as water welled up inside them. I felt guilty now, and pulled my chair back to the table.

"I'm sorry, Mrs. Cruz," I apologized. "I just think what you are saying sounds crazy."

"Look, Mr. Arctophile," Cheryl said to me, leaning closer, less than an inch from my face. This made me very uncomfortable.

"You are a reporter, and a very good one, I am told by the people of this town," Cheryl said. "They love reading your hard-hitting copy in the newspaper, especially when you root out government corruption."

"Thank you, but what's your point?"

"I want you to help me find my husband."

I drew a deep breath, still not believing what I was hearing.

"Okay," I finally said. "I won't promise anything. Why don't you tell me all you know and I'll pull a few strings with some people I know at various government agencies."

"I'll do better than that, my friend," Cheryl said. "I'll let you have my husband's letters. Everything is in there. He sent them to me at a post office box in San Francisco that nobody could trace. We lived in San Jose at the time. He knew that if the FBI believed he was revealing government secrets, he could be punished as could I."

"Your husband worked for the FBI?" I asked.

"Yes, he was a field agent working out of the San Jose, California, office."

With that she got up and went to a large bureau. I watched as the woman bent down on her knees to pull out a locked, metal cabinet. The short skirt she wore rode up, revealing more of her shapely upper legs.

When she got back up putting the small filing cabinet on the table, Cheryl realized I was watching her. I know I was blushing.

She giggled.

"I'm sorry if I embarrassed you, Mr. Arctophile," she said. "But remember, I am a married woman." Her voice was breathy. She was teasing me.

I cleared my throat, nervously. "Of course," I managed to stammer.

Cheryl unlocked the cabinet and removed a half-dozen envelopes with broken seals.

"These last letters tell all the details," she said. "Look them over. Tell me what you can do for me."

I nervously took the letters, picked up my notebook and pen, and stood up. I started to pull on my coat to depart. When she stood up, she saw eye to eye with me, tall for a woman. Her almost perfect hourglass figure showed favorably beneath her clothing.

"I'll do what I can, Mrs. Cruz," I said looking at her attractive body, instead of her eyes, showing I was visibly uncomfortable.

Then I started to leave, hurriedly.

Thinking I left my cap in her office, I started walking back. She had already closed the door.

I could hear her talking to herself.

"Finally, someone who will listen to me," she said out loud to herself. "He's cute, too."

Back at the Versailles Bureau, I learned that the information in those letters could be front-page news.

As I peered through them, I began to sweat. I was seated at the Versailles Bureau office, alone.

This story could be a science fiction novel.

Excerpts from Armando's letters:

Oct. 3, 1997:

Dearest Cheryl,

What I am about to tell you is unbelievable. I just interviewed an informant about a plot to reverse engineer alien space technology at Area 51 in Nevada. He said he has Unicorn 23 clearance, which is equal only to the President of the United States of America.

. . . He said he was shown several space vehicles hidden inside a range of mountains, which is painted with textured material to look like the sandy desert floor in Nevada.

. . . At one point he walked by a doorway with two scientists talking to what looked like an alien gray. He said the aliens are providing us with technology in exchange for allowing the grays to abduct humans for medical experiments.

. . . I was able to see inside the facility at last for myself. Cheryl, this place would blow your mind.

It's like a set from "Star Wars." There are at least seven spacecraft in here, of different designs. I crept up to one spacecraft in a hangar, touching the surface. It was smooth, with no visible seams. It was like the entire metal skin was poured into a huge mold.

I snuck onboard one of the craft. The seats were too small for human beings. The technology onboard looked alien too.

Oct. 5, 1997:

Cheryl, I have just learned that the technology our government is being given, besides the anti-gravity space propulsion for saucer-like crafts, is to control the weather on Earth. An Air Force General here in Nevada, Samuel Grant, is in charge of the program.

. . . The program, code named Project Unicorn, uses a group of soldiers assigned to construct a massive weather station somewhere off the coast of Africa. The station will be a base from which the United States can control all the weather on the planet. It's funded using secret CIA money. .

That station is not to help humanity. It is for a weapon, for God's sake! Cheryl, this stuff is dynamite. I have to blow the whistle on this, or too much power will be in the hands of some very unscrupulous people.

Oct. 6, 1997:

Cheryl, I am boarding a plane bound for Africa today. I'll get the evidence I need, then go public on this thing by contacting a newspaper or something. If you don't hear from me for a while, don't worry. I'll be going deep under cover.

I love you.

Armando

After finishing reading over the letters, I was not sure what to think. How would a low-level FBI agent get access to such high-level secrets? I am skeptical of what I have just read. Furthermore, aren't these people chosen so they do *not* reveal secrets to family members? Then, again, something strange *is* happening on this planet with regard to UFOs, that's for sure.

The Paw is Born

Sam composed his feature story about Cheryl Cruz.

Meanwhile, in his Streator apartment, the four aliens learned more about Earth culture.

"Schaumburg, watch this video story with us," Louis requested.

"What story is it?" Schaumburg asked, grabbing Sam's new stash of Nestles' Crunch bars.

"It's called Super Guy, about a humanoid who escapes a dying planet, journeys to Earth and gains super powers," Louis said. "Then he dresses up in a gymnast suit with a big giant snake design on his shirt and saves humans who need to be saved."

"That sounds silly," Schaumburg said, slurping a piece of chocolate that flecked onto his furry chin.

"No, brother," Chocolate said, snuggling up to Louis. "It's a really neat story." Chocolate and Louis sat transfixed before Sam's 27-inch color television, seated on the floor directly in front. They were holding paws.

Seeing Chocolate and Louis get cozy encouraged Leni to do the same with her husband.

She pulled Schaumburg down to sit with them and watch the movie.

About halfway through the show, Schaumburg was still eating his chocolate bar and became agitated when a bully was picking on young Bart Bent, the alien adopted by human parents. Bart, in high school now, fell in love with a cheerleader. But the bully, a football star, picked on poor Bart. His kindly father asked Bart not to show others his extraordinary strength by playing sports so Bart could keep his abilities a secret.

Schaumburg balled his right paw up into a fist, and pounded the floor of the apartment. To his astonishment, the fist went right through the second story apartment floor, to the ceiling in the floor below.

Wood and drywall showered down on the apartment below, abruptly waking Charles Letterman, an eighty-year-old who lived under Sam. Letterman snoozed on his living room sofa.

"What in tarnation was that?" the old man yelled, shocked and covered with pieces of his ceiling. He looked up to see what appeared to be teddy bears dressed in silver pressure suits peering down at him. Louis leaned on Schaumburg a little too hard, accidentally pushing Schaumburg down through the hole into the apartment below. But to everyone's astonishment, including Letterman, Schaumburg did not fall. He just floated. Schaumburg realized he could somehow fly now.

Schaumburg quickly flew down to the apartment below, at super speed, gathered up the chucks of ceiling/floor, and then repaired the damage at super speed so nobody would know the difference.

Downstairs, Letterman fell back into a deep sleep, thinking it was all a bad dream.

"What was that?" Schaumburg asked himself as well as his three friends.

"You just displayed the same super speed as Super Guy in the movie," Louis said.

"Don't be silly," Schaumburg said. "I can't bend steel in my bare paws." With that, Schaumburg picked up Sam's clothes iron and crushed it within his paw like tinfoil. Then he started to soar around the room like a bird.

"I'm Super Guy!" Schaumburg said. The other three bears tried repeating the super feats. Louis tried pounding in the floor, with no success. Leni and Chocolate tried to fly, again, both falling on their fannies.

Then, suddenly, Schaumburg fell to the apartment floor, no longer able to fly.

"Ouch!" Schaumburg said.

"Get off me," Schaumburg heard from under his right paw. It was the H.A.R.V.E.Y. unit, complaining about the abrupt fall.

"What happened to my powers of flight and super strength?" Schaumburg said, now unable to bend the iron as easily as he had a few minutes ago. "My strength seems to have worn off."

On the television set, Bart Bent's mother was fashioning Bart a super suit to wear when he was performing his super feats of strength.

"Wear this whenever you go out as Super Guy," Martha Bent said. "When you are just ordinary Bart, you can wear these glasses. Nobody will recognize you."

"You've got to be kidding," Louis said. "How can those stupid glasses prevent people from recognizing Bart as Super Guy?"

"Louis, will you forget about the dumb video story!" Schaumburg yelled. "I just experienced those same super powers, and you three did not. What gives? H.A.R.V.E.Y., can you give us some answers?"

"What is different about you vs. the other Orishans?" H.A.R.V.E.Y. inquired.

"I am the commander," Schaumburg said, not thinking straight.

"Eat some more of that brown confection," H.A.R.V.E.Y. said. "None of the other Orishans have consumed any."

Schaumburg ate another piece of chocolate and found his super powers had returned. The other three bears grabbed the candy bar out of Schaumburg's hand and started to eat it. But they did not experience the powers like Schaumburg.

"It must be the power ring on your commander's belt," H.A.R.V.E.Y. said. "It is reacting to your physiology and to the confection you consume."

So Schaumburg took off his belt with the power ring on, and allowed Louis to try it on. Louis took a bite of chocolate. Nothing. The other bears also could not obtain the super powers when eating chocolate and wearing the belt with the power ring.

After a few minutes, Schaumburg's super powers subsided again.

"It seems the powers don't last long," Schaumburg said.

"They last exactly 20 minutes," H.A.R.V.E.Y. said.

"This could be useful. Perhaps it will aid us in our mission here on Earth."

"Schaumy, I could fashion you a special gymnastic suit and cape like the one Super Guy wears, and you can use it when you are fighting the bad guys as a super bear," Leni said.

"What are you going to call yourself?" Chocolate wanted to know. "You can't call yourself Super Orishan. That's too corny."

Leni looked at the paw symbol emblazoned on all their chests as part of their flight suit insignia.

"He'll become the Paw," Leni said.

"Right," Schaumburg said. "Listen, Lou. I'm going to need a real computer. This H.A.R.V.E.Y. unit is unreliable since the crash."

"I resent that," H.A.R.V.E.Y. said.

"Never mind, H.A.R.V.E.Y. Lou, we'll also need to set up a secret HQ, away from prying eyes, like the human downstairs. Meanwhile, Chocolate, you rustle up as much of this chocolate as you can. I am going to need to be able to stash it in strategic places for future use."

"You could keep bars in pockets on your belt," Chocolate suggested.

"Good idea," Schaumburg said. "And I can keep some of our other Orishan technology on the belt in pouches as well."

*   *   *

Sam checked out Cheryl Cruz's story about her husband being held prisoner by the U.S. Government.

"What's that, Fred?" Sam said on the phone. "You have the final report written by Armando Cruz just prior to the supposed plane crash at which Armando was supposedly killed? That's great. Fax it to me, won't you?"

While speaking, Sam watched as documents began spitting out of his news bureau's fax machine.

"And while you're at it, Fred, send me those news stories of the 1947 crash at Roswell I asked you about."

Again, his fax machine began spitting out documents. Sam reviewed the Roswell crash stories first. He was not sure why he was so curious about Roswell, all of a sudden, but convinced himself that the research on Armando Cruz was directly related to Roswell.

"I sent you the front page newspaper stories from across the country in July of 1947," Fred told Sam on the phone.

Fred, a clerk at the Chicago FBI office, grew up with Sam in Kankakee. For a time, Fred worked as a reporter at the same newspaper, alongside Sam and Amy, Sam's former girlfriend. At the FBI, Fred often helped Sam obtain government documents.

"I sent you the *Chicago Daily News*, the *Los Angeles Herald Express*, the *Spokane Daily Chronicle*, and the *Sacramento Bee*," Fred said. "They are all from Tuesday, July 8, 1947, the day the nation's papers carried the Roswell crash story. I find it interesting that naysayers only quote the Roswell papers about this story."

Sam read the headlines, "Army finds flying saucer," "Army finds air saucer on ranch in New Mexico," and a sidebar head, "General orders flying disc (sic) to Wright Field for tests."

"Amazing that the next day they all claim this was a weather balloon," Sam told Fred.

"The Army Air Force lied that second day," Fred said. "The first articles contain the facts."

"Can you tell me of any connection this crash has with what Armando Cruz was investigating?" Sam said.

The line went dead.

Look Ma! I Got Super Powers!

Sam clicked the receiver to try and get his friend Fred back on the line. No good.

He quickly looked up the number to the Chicago FBI office in his Rolodex and dialed it again.

"Federal Bureau of Investigations, Chicago District, agent Malone speaking," came a voice on the other line.

"May I speak with Fred in research please?" Sam asked.

"Who?"

"Fred, Fred Steinfeld! He works in research! Is he there? Please, I need to speak with him now!"

Suddenly, Sam heard a dial tone.

Sam, frustrated, hung up the phone.

"My God, what is going on?"

The phone suddenly rang.

"Versailles Bureau, Sam speaking," he said.

"Sam, it's me, Fred," said the voice over the other line.

"What happened?" Sam asked, now calmer.

"Sorry, Sam. My boss is monitoring my phone calls. Everything's okay now."

Sam was a little bit suspicious now and he could sense nervousness in Fred's voice.

"I gotta go now, Sam. You got my faxes, right?"

"Got them."

"Read them, Sam. See ya."

It was nearing lunch, and Sam had to cover a meeting that night so he went home for lunch. He took the faxed news clippings and Armando's report along with him.

Sam walked into his apartment. The Orishans were caught by surprise, and quickly stiffened into suspended hibernation. But they had no time to turn off the television. The Super Guy video still played. At first he paid no attention to the "teddy bears" on the living room floor facing the television, wearing silver flight pressure suits. It was as if they were supposed to be there.

"Hmm," Sam said. "That's odd. I don't remember leaving the video player on."

Sam walked into his kitchen, noticing his bag of groceries from this morning. All but one of his Crunch bars were gone.

"I know I bought more candy bars than that," Sam said to himself.

Schaumburg woke himself from suspended hibernation. He walked into the kitchen.

"Are you all right Sam?" Schaumburg asked.

Sam started, noticing a teddy bear was talking to him.

"It's me," Schaumburg said. "Schaumburg. We met last night, remember? We told you how we crashed in Roswell, New Mexico yesterday and how my wife Leni whisked us here with her magic."

"That wasn't a dream?" Sam said to himself. "What's happening to me? I'm going crazy!"

At that moment, there was a knock at the door.

It startled Sam, who was already a little jumpy.

"Who is it?" he called, without opening the door.

"It's Mr. Letterman," said the man from the downstairs apartment. "I heard some noise up here. Just wanted to make sure you were okay."

"I'm fine Charles," Sam said. "I just came home early today. I've got to cover a meeting tonight so I took the afternoon off."

"Oh," Letterman said. "Okay . . . Oh, and the cable TV guy came and said your cable is okay. He just left a few minutes before you got here."

Sam flew to the door and flung it open, scaring Mr. Letterman.

"What cable TV guy?" Sam said. "I didn't order any cable TV guy to come here!"

"He was just here, said he was checking the system," Letterman said. "What's gotten into you, boy?"

"Oh, I'm sorry, Charles. I'm okay. Thanks for checking. Good day, Mr. Letterman," Sam said, slamming the door shut.

At that instant, upon turning around, all the other bears looked in wonder at Sam.

"That cable TV man put a box on your television," Schaumburg said, pointing to it.

Sam slowly looked at the box, which looked innocent enough.

Schaumburg took out a Crunch bar and gulped down a piece.

"Hey, that's my chocolate," Sam complained.

Then Sam watched Schaumburg peering strangely at the box installed on the television.

"There's a bomb in that innocent-looking box," Schaumburg said. "I can see it with my new X-ray vision."

"What???!!!" Sam screamed. "A bomb?"

At that moment, Sam saw the most shocking thing of the day. Schaumburg gingerly removed the box, then smothered the cable box with his body. A muffled explosion shook the apartment, blowing air but nothing else from underneath the "teddy bear."

"It's okay, Sam," Schaumburg said. "I used my super strength to muffle the blast, protecting you and the others."

"Super strength? X-ray vision? What are you talking about?"

Sam picked up the phone and dialed 9-1-1.

"There's been an explosion in my apartment. Send a fire truck right away please," Sam said to the dispatcher.

"I can't have these teddy bears underfoot when the fire department arrives," Sam said.

"We should not let them know Schaumburg muffled the blast with his new super powers either," Chocolate said.

"Right," Sam said. He looked around the room. Then he snapped his fingers.

"That's it!" Sam exclaimed.

He went to his house safe, opened it up and dumped out the contents. The bears thought Sam was going crazy.

"What are you doing?" Leni asked.

"It's okay," Schaumburg said. "I think I understand." Schaumburg picked up all the pieces of the now harmless bomb and helped Sam throw them into the safe.

"We'll say you put the bomb into the safe, closed it, and it safely exploded inside," Schaumburg said, understanding Sam's plan.

"But you'll have to punch out the inside walls to make it look good," Sam said.

Schaumburg complied, still having super-strength.

"Ouch!" Schaumburg suddenly said. His powers had worn off.

"This super stuff only lasts about 20 minutes," Schaumburg explained to Sam.

While Schaumburg and Sam made the safe look like the bomb had exploded in there, Louis noticed the faxed news clippings about the Roswell crash. He picked one up and started to read.

"Hey, listen to this guys! We made the newspaper!" Louis said.

He began to read an article out loud from the *Los Angeles Herald Express*:

BY ASSOCIATED PRESS

ROSWELL, N.M., July 8—The Army Air Forces here today announced a flying disc had been found near Roswell and is in Army possession.

Lieut. Warren Haut, public information officer of the Roswell Army Air Field, announced the find has been made "sometime last week," and had been turned over to the airfield through cooperation of the sheriff's office.

"It was inspected at the Roswell Army Air Field and subsequently flown" by Major Jesse A. Marcel, of the 509th Bomb Group Intelligence Office at Roswell, "to higher headquarters."

The Army gave no other details.

(Officers at the base say that the "disc" was flown in a Super Fortress to "higher headquarters" undisclosed. The air base refused to give details of construction of the disc or its appearance, but residents near the ranch on which the disc was found reported seeing a strange blue light several days ago at 3 a.m.)

Haut's statement:

"The many rumors regarding the flying disc became a reality yesterday when the intelligence office of the 509th (atomic) bomb group of the Eighth Air Force, Roswell Army Air Field, was fortunate enough to gain possession of a disc through the cooperation of one of the local ranchers and the sheriff's office of Chaves County.

"The flying object landed on a ranch near Roswell sometime last week. Not having phone facilities the rancher stored the disc until such time as he was able to contact the sheriff's office, which in turn notified Major Jesse A. Marcel, of the 509th Bomb Group Intelligence Office.

"Action was immediately taken and the disc was picked up at the rancher's home. It was inspected at the Roswell Army Air Field and subsequently loaned by Major Marcel to higher headquarters."

"Listen to this one, guys," Louis said, starting to read another article, which accompanied the first.

General Orders Flying Disc To Wright Field For Tests

FORT WORTH, Texas, July 8—Brig. Gen. Roger Ramey, commanding general of the Eighth Army air forces field, asserted tonight the purported "flying disc" found in eastern New Mexico is "evidently nothing other than a weather or radar instrument of some sort."

BY INTERNATIONAL NEWS SERVICE

DENVER, July 8—Senator Ed C. Johnson, of Colorado, told the Denver Post by long distance from Washington today that the object found in New Mexico might have been "either a radar target or a meteorological balloon."

BY ASSOCIATED PRESS

WASHINGTON, July 8—Brig. Gen. Roger Ramey said today that a battered object, which previously had been described as a flying disc., found near Roswell, N.M., is being shipped by air to the A.A.F. research center at Wright Field, Ohio.

Ramey, commander of the Eighth Air Force with headquarters at Fort Worth, received the object from the Roswell Army air base.

In talking by telephone to A.A.F. headquarters at Washington, Ramey described the object as of "flimsy construction, almost like a box kite." It was so badly battered that Ramey was unable to say whether it had a disc form. He did not indicate the size of the object.

There were "some fragments of junk" found near the object near the New Mexico ranch where a rancher sighted it last week.

Ramey reported that so far as the A.A.F. investigation could determine, no one had seen the object in the air. Asked what the material seemed to be, A.A.F. officials here said that Ramey described it as "apparently some sort of tin foil."

The object, after being found by the rancher, was turned over to the 509th Armored Group at Roswell airfield.

When asked if other agencies including the FBI would examine the exhibit, A.A.F. officials said they understood that if the airplane carrying the material had not left Fort Worth up to now the FBI representatives in that area might make an examination.

"And get a load of this final article below the one debunking the 'disc' as a balloon," Louis added, reading another smaller newspaper story:

Site Where Disc Found Near Atom Bomb Proving Ground

Announcement by the Army Air Force of the finding of a "flying saucer" on a ranch near Roswell, N.M., excited speculation here today about a possible connection with the famous proving ground at White Sands.

White Sands, where the first atomic bomb was tested in an explosion that marked a new era in world science, and where numerous captured German V-2 rockets have been fired, is only a short distance from Roswell.

The state of Washington, where the first saucers were reported, also is the site of one of the great atomic processing plants at Hanford.

"That's interesting, Louis," Schaumburg said. "The humans are already connecting the flying ship with the human atomic testing."

"Already??!!" Sam said. "Those clippings are from 52 years ago!"

"Excuse me, Mr. Arctophile," Leni said. "What did you say?"

"I said those news clippings from the Roswell crash are from 1947, more than 52 years ago."

"But we just crashed yesterday," Louis said, taking a paw to his furry head and scratching.

"Leni, you must have swished us into the future with your magic," Schaumburg said.

"What does that mean?" Chocolate asked.

All the Orishans looked at each other, a little worried. Sam seemed a little confused, too.

At that moment, off in the distance everyone could hear the sirens of the Streator fire truck approaching.

"Quick, you guys," Sam said. "Go back into your stiff conditions so the fire department will think you're just toys."

CHAPTER 6

MONSTERS EATING BARNS OR BARNS EATING MONSTERS? THAT IS THE QUESTION

After trying to explain to the authorities how a bomb ended up in his apartment—with no success—Sam reported to his Managing Editor, Izzie Feinberg, in Montreal.

"Sam, I have a feeling your checking into this woman's story about her husband and his alien conspiracy theories has led you too close to something," Feinberg said. "I want you to use the Investigative Reporter's Fund and take the rest of November and all of December off. Lay low. Leave the area until this all cools down. I have a feeling somebody tried to scare you with that bomb. They probably did not think you would be home during the day."

"I can't just take off," Sam complained. "What about my job? Who's going to cover the Bureau while I'm gone?"

"You let me worry about that," Izzie said. "Your priority is your own safety and well-being," Izzie said.

"Izzie," Sam pleaded. "Please don't pull me off this story now. I'm just starting to get into it."

"Sam, this is an order!" Izzie barked back, scaring Sam a little. "You are to take the rest of the year off! Period!"

Sam realized his boss was growing angry. He decided to drop the issue.

"All right," Sam said finally. "I'll take a little vacation. I'll see you January 2."

Back at Sam's apartment in Streator, Sam explained to the aliens he was taking a few weeks off.

"That's great!" Schaumburg said. "Then you can take us to the Better Bear Bureau where we can straighten out this time-travel mess."

"The Better Bear Bureau?" Sam said.

"Yes," the H.A.R.V.E.Y. unit answered. "It is located in the human city of St. Lou . . . Mo." With that the H.A.R.V.E.Y. unit sparked, burning Schaumburg's paw slightly.

"Ouch!" Schaumburg said.

"What is that?" Sam asked.

"This is my H.A.R.V.E.Y. unit," Schaumburg said, rubbing his singed paw. "It's like a computer, when it works right."

"Did it say the headquarters is in St. Loumo?" Sam asked. "Does it mean St. Louis, Missouri?"

The H.A.R.V.E.Y. unit sparked again, then said, "Yes, that's it. According to the Pawtropolis communications network, the headquarters is in the Gateway Arch at St. Louis. The HQ has been relocated by Orishan High Command from its previous location in Pawtropolis."

"That's a four-hour drive from here," Sam said. "I can take you. I'm off now for a few weeks anyway and should leave the area." Sam picked up the faxed newspaper clippings about the Roswell crash and Armando's report, stuffing them into his shirt pocket.

"Great!" Schaumburg said. "Leni, you're with me and Sam. Louis and Chocolate, procure us some clothing so we can blend in better with these humans. We need to look more like toy bears, not space faring aliens. And Louis, you take the H.A.R.V.E.Y. unit."

"Roger!" Louis said, saluting his commander. "C'mon, Chocolate. This should be fun."

*   *   *

On the road trip to St. Louis, Leni and Schaumburg peered out the window, asking Sam many questions about what they saw on this strange planet humans called "Earth."

As Sam drove south on Interstate 55, they passed through miles of agricultural areas where farmers harvest corn and soybean fields each year. Many of the fields contained corncribs, some very old and falling apart. Schaumburg grew animated when he noticed a lot of the cribs seemed to be rotting away.

"There are big chunks eaten out of those buildings," Schaumburg said, pointing.

"Those are barns," Sam said, indicating they were agricultural buildings. Sam grew amused at the alien's alarm.

"There's a barn-eating monster on the loose!" Schaumburg said. "Look at the evidence!"

Leni also grew visibly frightened as her blue eyes grew wider.

"A barn is eating a monster?" Sam asked.

"No, a barn-eating monster!" Schaumburg shouted. "Look at the big hunk taken out of those barns!"

"But barns cannot eat monsters," Sam said.

"No, the monster eats the barns!" Schaumburg said.

"But you said a barn eating a monster," Sam repeated.

"No, the monster eats the barns!" Schaumburg said, pointing to another barn rotting away as they passed by on Interstate 55. "I said a barn DASH eating monster," Schaumburg yelled at Sam.

"Yes, a barn that eats a monster," Sam said calmly, holding back a chuckle.

"No, there is a dash between the barn and the eating," Schaumburg complained, now frustrated.

"Humans use a dash of spice in foods that they eat," Sam said. "I think you are a confused little alien."

"AARRRGGHHHHHHH!" Schaumburg shouted. Leni realized Sam was joking.

Leni and Sam laughed. Schaumburg realized Sam had been teasing him too, and began to laugh. Sam began to think to himself that these aliens seemed like human children.

"Maybe kids aren't so bad after all," he thought to himself.

Meanwhile, the car whizzed by Towanda on its journey to the Better Bear Bureau.

*   *   *

Back in Streator, Louis and Chocolate waited until after dark, then began to skulk around, hiding in the shadows. They prepared to "procure" some clothing for themselves, Schaumburg and Leni.

They arrived in downtown Streator, slipping through an alley behind several storefronts on Main Street.

"They use paper currency to purchase things," Louis said. "Perhaps we can exchange our stash of gold for goods and services."

"I do not know if humans value gold like us, Louis," Chocolate said.

"We will see," Louis responded, then peered around at the signs in the alley.

"Look, Chocolate," Louis pointed out with his hook paw. "A gift shop. It says they carry doll clothes."

Chocolate pulled out her handy, dandy Orishan lock-picker. Louis stood under the lock and hoisted Chocolate onto his shoulders so she could reach the door lock. Chocolate began working the lock.

Suddenly walnuts and almonds rained on them.

"What gives?" Louis said. "Ouch! What is this?"

"Someone is throwing nuts at us," Chocolate replied. "Ouch!"

Chocolate jumped off Louis and turned around. To her surprise, she saw a huge squirrel, taller than her, throwing the nuts at them. She ducked as another nut almost beaned her in the head.

Louis turned around as well. Then, Lou's and Chocolate's mouths hung open as they watched the huge squirrel transform itself into a Bengal tiger standing about 18 inches tall. It stood on its hind legs and wore a Wizard's robes; similar to those Chocolate and Lou had seen Leni wear.

"What business do you two have here?" came a voice from the tiger. Louis and Chocolate looked at each other, now worried they were in deep trouble.

*   *   *

In the Chicago suburbs at the FBI office, a superior officer instructed Fred on the proper ways the FBI employees must deal with the media. He sat in front of his boss' desk.

"Mr. Steinfeld, you work with very sensitive government documents," said Agent Malone.

"Yes, sir," Fred said.

"You are not to just go giving away sensitive intelligence to the news media, especially to your friend at *The Daily Press*. Is that understood?"

"Yes, sir," Fred said.

"From now on, any information that is given to the press has to be approved by me first. I don't care if it is already declassified. I want to see what you are sending to the media. Understand?"

"Yes, sir."

"That will be all, Mr. Steinfeld."

As Fred got up from his chair to leave the office, Malone said one final ominous statement to Fred:

"And if I find out you've been digging into that dead agent's file—what's his name, Cruz? I will have you fired on the spot and sent to prison! Is that understood?"

Fred said nothing and quickly scampered out of the office. All the blood had rushed out of Fred's face.

Teddy Bears Have Been on Earth For More Than 100 Years

"Ah ha!" came the tiger's voice from the shadows. "Silver flight suits. Beings that look like Earth teddy bears. What are you two trying to do?"

Louis started to stammer.

"Please sir," Louis said. "It's not like it looks."

"Oh, no?" the tiger asked, coming out of the shadows. In one paw, the tiger held a leash on his dog and in the other paw, he held what looked like a walking staff made of silver.

"Then why was the female Orishan trying to pick the lock on Maxine's gift shop?" the tiger asked.

"Uh, er . . ." Louis said.

"Never mind," the tiger said. "You two are obviously from the

Planet Orisha. Gee, Orishans on Earth. What a surprise," the tiger added sarcastically.

"No need for sarcasm, Mr. Wizard," Chocolate said, still frightened.

"You are correct," the tiger responded. "I am being very rude. You may call me Nerwonduh. I am a Master Wizard of the Mystical Order of the Golden Paw from the planet Bengali. We are staunch allies to Orisha since your kind saved us from enslavement by the Arjogun many years ago."

"A friend!" Louis said, relaxing.

Nerwonduh's dog began to growl at Louis as the Orishan stepped forward to hug Nerwonduh.

"It's okay, Fritz," Nerwonduh said, giving Louis a big hug. The dog sat down calmly. "I think I know why you were trying to break into that store."

"Why?" Louis said, as if he did not know.

"To secure better clothing, no?"

The tiger spoke English very well, but with a strange growling accent.

"Of course," Nerwonduh said, slapping his forehead in realization. "You must be the source of the magic I sensed late last night."

"My sister-in-law, Millennium Harmony, also a Wizard of the Order of the Golden Paw, sent us here from the past," Chocolate said. "We are on undercover assignment for Orisha to investigate the Arjogun who are secretly invading this planet."

"No! Don't tell me you are what remains of that crew that crashed more than 50 years ago in New Mexico," Nerwonduh said, with a chuckle in his voice.

"It appears we are," Louis said. "But there are two others, Captain Schaumburg Harmony and his wife Millennium. They are on their way to the Better Bear Bureau as we speak."

"Come with me. I will obtain the clothing you need. And tell me how you wound up here, 52 years out of your time."

As Nerwonduh the Bengal tiger took care of Louis and Chocolate, Sam drove through Bloomington on his road trip to St. Louis.

"So tell me, little ones," Sam said. "Why do you guys look like teddy bears?"

"The better question would be 'Why do teddy bears look like us?'" Schaumburg replied.

"Okay, I'll bite," Sam responded. "Why do teddy bears look like aliens from another planet?"

"We have been visiting your planet for many centuries," Schaumburg said. "We have been watching secretly, occasionally befriending a human along the way."

"Yes, your first president, George Washington, was a friend of an Orishan more than two centuries ago," Leni said.

"Fascinating," Sam said. "Did you know there is a new George Washington museum in Versailles?"

"No, we did not."

"Yes, it seems Washington was in Versailles during one of his campaigns during the French and Indian War between England and France."

"The Orishan who lived with Washington is legendary on my home world," Schaumburg said with reverence.

"He made friends with Washington when your first President was still a very young boy and they stayed friends all of Washington's famous life. His name was Bartholomew, and he is said to have given Washington a magic sword which protected him in battles," Leni said.

"He also advised the Founding Fathers of your country, helping them to decide to form a new, independent state from England," Schaumburg said.

"I will have to discuss that one with Mrs. Cruz, the curator at the George Washington museum," Sam said. "Okay, so why did humans start making teddy bears?"

"It was only natural," Schaumburg said. "Orishans have been coming to human children for many centuries, knowing they would be more accepting of fuzzy, cuddly creatures than adults. So some toy manufacturer must have reasoned that his cuddly friend as a child would make a great toy for other children."

"Yes, there were actually two who created teddy bears at the same time," Leni added. "One was a man named Richard Steiff in Germany. He worked for his aunt Margaret who owned a plush toy company. The others were Rose and Morris Michtom of New York who founded an American toy company making teddy bears."

"Yes, I have heard that teddy bears are named for President Theodore Roosevelt," Sam said. "Roosevelt was hunting for bears in Mississippi. Hunters with the president tied a bear to a tree because no bears had been bagged that day. But when Roosevelt came upon the helpless animal tied to a tree, he refused to shoot it. Two days later, a Washington newspaper cartoonist drew a cartoon about Roosevelt refusing to shoot the bear. It was that cartoon that inspired the New York toy company to create 'Teddy's Bear' and the rest is teddy bear history."

"Yes, and many of the so-called Teddy Bears on your planet are actually Orishan operatives out to protect your planet from an invading force of evil aliens," Schaumburg said.

"You mean you are an invading force of evil aliens?" Sam asked, joking.

Leni and Schaumburg looked nervously at Sam.

"I'm kidding," Sam said. "I know you guys are not evil. How could you be?"

"How do you know?" Leni wondered out loud.

"My grandfather, Frederick Arctophile, was a Washington, D.C., correspondent for *The Daily Press* about 100 years ago," Sam said. "He did a series of stories about the birth of teddy bears. I have a picture of him with his teddy bear . . . Say, you don't suppose his teddy bear was from Orisha, do you?"

"The next time we are at your home, show me the picture," Leni said. "I will be able to tell if the teddy bear is a toy or an Orishan agent."

And while Sam, Leni and Schaumburg zoomed south on Interstate 55 on the way to St. Louis, Sam's friend at the FBI, Fred, sped south on Interstate 55 as well, only coming from the Chicago suburbs and heading to Streator. He sought his friend, Sam, trying to warn him of possible danger from the FBI for investigating the mysterious death of one of their agents, Armando Cruz.

He was trying to reach Sam at Sam's apartment number by cell phone, but kept getting Sam's answering machine.

"Sam," Fred said into his cell phone, frantically. "If you are there pick up . . . It's me Fred . . . Sam, when you get this message, meet me at your office. I have something I need to show you. I can't fax it to you. I'm being watched. It's going to blow the lid off this story about the death of Special Agent Cruz . . . It's about 6:30 p.m., Wednesday, Nov. 24. I'll be in Versailles about 8 p.m."

He hung up his cell phone and put it into his shirt pocket.

"God, I hope Sam gets the message in time."

The Bears Don't Need Menus

Sam pulled off Interstate 55 in Springfield and drove to a coffee shop for dinner.

"You guys eat, right?" Sam asked.

"Of course we do," Schaumburg responded. "Earth fish and honey are our favorite forms of nourishment."

"I can't take you in there," Sam said. "People will think I am nuts carrying alien teddy bears."

"We could go into a state of suspended hibernation," Leni offered. "It makes us stiff and we look like toy bears. We can wake ourselves from this state, or you can wake us by pressing one of our paws."

"People will still think I'm strange," Sam said. "Now they will see an adult man carrying two teddy bears into a restaurant."

Both Schaumburg and Leni shrugged, not knowing exactly what Sam meant.

"It'll be all right," Schaumburg said. Both the "bears" instantly became stiff, and the light in their eyes seemed to extinguish.

Sam was amazed.

"You guys really do look exactly like teddy bears now," Sam said.

The bears stared back at him blankly, saying nothing.

Sam scooped them up and went inside.

The hostess smiled when she saw the two "bears" dressed in silver pressure suits.

"How cute," she said. "Will they be needing menus too?" she asked.

"No, they're already stuffed," Sam quipped. "Just a table for one in non-smoking. Oh, and could I have two booster chairs for the bears?"

Many people in the restaurant gave Sam a double take when they saw him eating with the bears. Some people asked, "What's with the bears?"

Sam made up stories about how they were for his kids and he was bringing them home. That satisfied most people.

After finishing his meal, Sam requested a to-go order of fish and chips and bought a jar of honey at the cashier's register for the bears.

Back on the road, Schaumburg and Leni awoke and wolfed down their meals.

Sam noticed they ate the honey first.

"On Earth, it is customary to eat dessert after the main meal," Sam said.

"On our home planet of Orisha," Schaumburg said, slurping some honey that dripped onto his chin, "We have a saying—'Life is uncertain. Eat dessert first.'"

Sam, Leni and Schaumburg all laughed.

"So tell me about your planet, Schaumburg," Sam requested.

"We come from a planet called Orisha," Schaumburg said. "The planet orbits around a star which humans call 47 Ursae Majoris in the constellation Ursa Major."

"The Great Bear," Sam mused with a smile. "Figures."

"Our home world is 43 light-years from Earth, and it takes us 23 days to journey to Earth by a hyper-space driven vehicle," Schaumburg continued.

"The planet is covered with lush green forests, fed by our warm sun, underground rivers and streams that nurture the flora and fauna above the ground. We build our homes in the mountainsides, calling them caves. They look very similar to Earth homes, only we use round doors and the roof is the top of a mountain or hill. It constantly rains on our home world, but there are also lots of beautiful rainbows when it stops. The temperature stays steady at about 72 degrees. The atmosphere is thinner than Earth's, with traces of argon and helium. There are many waterfalls and deep green seas as well, teaming with life. We Orishans love to eat all types of seafood, and wild berries that grow all over our planet."

"Sounds like a beautiful paradise," Sam said.

"It is beautiful," Leni said. "And all of our sentient inhabitants look like us, but come in many shapes and colors," Leni offered. "We all live in harmony and most follow the precepts offered by the Mystical Order of the Golden Paw. The masters of that order protect our home world with a powerful spell of love, which surrounds the planet. The shield of love is why the Arjogun has never conquered us. It seems the gray aliens are allergic to love, or something. It makes them violently ill whenever they come near our home world."

"Yes, our planet is safe from their invasion, but not yours," Schaumburg said.

"Who are these Arjogun, you speak of?" Sam asked.

"Didn't you read that fax you were sent from your friend at the FBI?" Schaumburg asked.

"The alien with the hook read us some of the stuff on the Roswell crash, but I haven't looked at the other documents yet," Sam said.

"Let me read you this report," Schaumburg said. "It talks about the Arjogun, and is very accurate regarding those gray aliens."

Sam took one hand off the wheel and pulled out the faxes from his shirt pocket, handing them to Schaumburg. Schaumburg read Armando's report out loud:

Oct. 6, 1997
16:00:00
Report on Project Unicorn
By Armando Cruz, special agent

What you are about to read will shock you, but it is all true. I have been gathering this evidence for two years now, and am on my way out to Africa to infiltrate an alien project to control the weather.

Overview:
A top secret government research organization formed in 1952 to investigate and gather data related to unidentified flying objects, which are being sighted on Earth. The staff members are former military personnel

who have been associated with intelligence activities. They have knowledge of the United States government's black operations concerning UFOs.

The United States started a project in the late 1940s called Project Unicorn. The U.S. Government has in its possession many spacecraft manufactured on other worlds, mostly from Arjogonia, known to inhabitants of Earth as Zeta Reticuli. The natives of Zeta Reticuli call themselves the Arjogun. Members of Project Unicorn refer to them as the grays.

Communication between the United States government secret project members and the Arjogun has been going on since 1964.

The trade agreement:

The Arjogun, as their part of a special trade agreement between our two worlds, are to provide the Project Unicorn people with advanced technology to control the world's weather. In exchange, the Arjogun are provided with bases of operation on the planet Earth.

The aliens are allowed to abduct human beings for experimental medical, psychological and genetic research at the Arjogun bases. These experiments are fully sanctioned by the United States Government and known only to those members of the government who have Unicorn 23 secret clearance, above CIA and NSA clearances.

The Arjogun are to provide Project Unicorn with the lists of people abducted.

In 1973, an area south of Groom Lake (one of the United State's secret centers in Nevada) was closed and a huge underground facility was built for the Arjogun.

The new base, south of Area 51, is named Unicorn A4, for Unicorn/ Arjogun base, America, fourth base of operations.

One of the promised technological advances for Project Unicorn was advanced space travel.

The Arjogun are physically inferior to humans in many respects, such as being smaller in stature. They average between 3 feet 4 inches to 3 feet 7 inches. They have large, almost insect-like eyes and very tough scaly skin, which can withstand great heat.

They prefer colder climates.

Their home planet of Arjogonia is located 39.5 light-years from Earth.

The Arjogun spacecraft can make the journey from Arjogonia to Earth in 92 days using special warp drive technology.

The Nevada Project Unicorn base is located east of the former Nevada atomic test site. It seems the Arjogun are very interested in America's nuclear technology, which is as powerful as their weapons.

After the agreement with the Arjogun and Project Unicorn was established, the new weather control technology began to be constructed in Nevada for later transport to a new secret base off the coast of Africa. This will be the site where the weather weapon will be deployed. I say weather weapon because whoever controls the weather on Earth, controls the Earth. The members of Project Unicorn mean to use it to enslave all of mankind and have betrayed innocent people on this planet to gain this technology.

But, in late 1979 things started to go wrong for Project Unicorn.

Project Unicorn members learned that the Arjogun were starting to implant a tiny probe, 3 mm. in size, into the bodies of certain abductees before releasing them.

Project Unicorn investigators determined that the probe could be used to hypnotically and telepathically program and monitor the person.

Mind control:

Project Unicorn officers tried to reverse the process on some of those with the implants using hypnosis. This only caused the brains of the subjects to "self-destruct." For this reason, Project Unicorn was unable to determine for what purpose the abductees were being "programmed."

The discovery of the aliens abusing their contract with the government caused a change in direction for Project Unicorn. Instead of just working with the aliens, the government decided to secretly work against them at the same time.

In 1980, Lt. General Samuel Grant, an analyst for the Department of Defense and member of Project Unicorn, made the following statement in a report for Project Unicorn:

"We need to use skills we have that the Arjogun cannot duplicate," Grant wrote. "We need to stop competing with the Arjogun. We can't win by competing with their advanced technology. But we must invest our resources in areas where we have the advantage."

In the 1980s, President Ronald Reagan authorized and adamantly supported his Strategic Defense Initiative, or Star Wars program.

This program included the deployment of a satellite in space, which could be used to direct laser weapons on ground targets and on targets approaching the Earth from space.

In 1984, President Reagan said in a public address that the world may, "Someday unite to face a threat from outer space." Reagan made it very clear to the people of Earth that his Star Wars program was in part to defend the Earth from attacks by such beings as the alien grays.

At the same time, General Grant was hedging his bets. He created a subgroup within Project Unicorn, known as the "Protectors." These special members of the project were to continue working directly with the Arjogun, and make them believe the Americans were still willing to cooperate with the aliens.

They continued to work with the Arjogun on the weather station off the coast of Africa because Grant believed this was a weapon America needed to prevent its enemies from attacking it on Earth.

It is obvious from my research that General Grant has been deceiving the Arjogun as much as the Arjogun have been deceiving the Americans.

I do not know if the Arjogun are fully aware of Grant's double-cross, or what the aliens are doing with their implants in the abductees.

Conclusion:

Only a few people on the planet knew Reagan was referring to the Arjogun threat. The people of this country deserve to know how they have been lied to by its government all these years about UFOs and how it allows the aliens to abduct people with impunity just to obtain the aliens' technologies.

I intend to go public with this report, as soon as I return from Africa with further evidence. I feel it is my duty as an American, as a special agent for the FBI, and as a member of the human race to go public with this information.

After reading the Armando Cruz report to Sam, all three were silent for a few minutes in the car as it continued to speed toward St. Louis.

Finally, Sam broke the silence with, "We've got to finish Armando Cruz's work. We've got to stop the Arjogun."

"Leni, I think we came to the right human," Schaumburg said. "Your magic must have known exactly who and when to send us to after our crash. Sam, that's exactly what our mission here on Earth is."

CHAPTER 7

A CHANGE IN ASSIGNMENT

As Sam parked his car near the Gateway Arch in St. Louis, the Orishans reverted to a state of suspended hibernation, now looking stiff and lifeless like toy teddy bears.

He picked them up and proceeded to the arch.

The Arch in St. Louis requires people to walk downstairs to get to the entrance. After people purchase the tickets, tourists ride up a tiny pod, which ratchets its way to the top, 630 feet above the metropolis of St. Louis.

Sam carried the aliens up in his arms, watching as people gave him and his bears strange looks as he stood in line.

"I'm glad there are no X-ray machines at the entrance," Sam thought to himself. If X-rayed, the bears would be revealed to be living beings, not toys. How could he have explained their internal organs to the Arch security guards?

A cramped pod took Sam and his "teddy bears" to the top of the arch in about 20 minutes. Sam at 5-foot 7-inches could barely stand erect in the pod. Once at the top observation level, Sam carried his two charges into the area, which contained windows for people to look at the city below.

"There is a secret door on the sign which says '190m, 630 feet, Gateway Arch, St. Louis,'" Schaumburg had instructed Sam previously.

"Press the letters in the following order and the door will open. Place us inside and close the door. We'll meet you downstairs later in the gift shop."

Sam chose a moment when all the visitors looked out the windows and pressed the letters in the order Schaumburg had instructed. The door popped open slightly. Sam furtively placed both Schaumburg and Leni inside the door—then closed it.

At that moment, a security guard became suspicious.

"Hey, stay away from that sign," the guard said. "Don't be putting your grimy fingers on it."

"Yes sir, sorry," Sam said.

Then he quickly left the observation deck, hopped into the next pod to descend to the bottom again and walked to the gift shop to wait for the two bears.

Meanwhile, at the secret headquarters of the Better Bear Bureau, Schaumburg and Leni awoke from their state of suspended hibernation and were greeted with blinking lights, computer screens, Orishans flitting about, talking on micro headsets, and tapping away on huge keyboards, specially designed to fit an Orishan's paws.

A small Orishan, standing about 12 inches tall, slowly waddled up to Leni and Schaumburg.

"It can't be," the small Orishan said, sizing up the two newcomers. "You look like you haven't aged a day since you left, Schaumburg."

Schaumburg and Leni said nothing.

"Did your ship fall into some sort of time warp or something?"

At that moment, in walked a female Orishan wearing a white lab coat.

"Director Vil, I need your signature on these orders," she said, shoving a clipboard into the smaller Orishan's face. Vil, a honey-colored Orishan, stood much shorter than most. Schaumburg believed his short stature made Vil so nasty, as if he had something to prove to other Orishans merely because he was smaller.

"Director Vil?" Schaumburg asked. "Frank? Frank E. Vil? You're the director of the BBB?"

"Of course, dear boy," Vil said, smiling warmly at Leni and Schaumburg.

"A lot's changed since our fateful missions back in 1947."

"I bet," Leni said, suspicious of Vil. "Like you moving the B.B.B. HQ from Pawtropolis to a secret compartment here in this arch."

"That was done by the Orishan High Command years before I

became director here," Vil responded. "I had nothing to do with that decision . . . Tut, tut, where are my manners. You two need to be briefed and given new missions. We thought you were dead, you know . . . Miss Montgomery," Vil said to the female Orishan in the white lab coat. "Fetch me the assignment roster. We have to give these two new missions."

Then Vil turned to Schaumburg and Leni. "Did the rest of your Hug survive as well?"

"Chocolate and Louis are fine," Schaumburg said. "We all survived the crash. What do you mean, 'new missions'?"

"My dear Schaumburg, we are no longer enemies with the Arjogun," Vil said as he picked up an Arjogun sword he had hanging on his office wall. "Orisha and Arjogonia signed a peace treaty 20 years ago. Now we have a common enemy—the humans."

Schaumburg and Leni looked at each other in shock and grew concerned about the way Vil waved around the sword.

"It's like I told you all those years ago," Vil said. "The humans can't be trusted. We are working together now, the Arjogun and the Orisha, to spy on the humans. I am in charge of all intelligence gathering."

At that point, Miss Montgomery returned with a brown file folder and handed it to Vil who placed the sword down on his desk, much to Schaumburg and Leni's relief.

"Here, please sit down in this office," Vil directed them, asking them to sit at a round table, sized for natives of their planet.

"So, tell me," Vil continued. "Have you met any humans yet? Befriended any?"

"Why yes, as a matter of fact," Schaumburg said.

"We have made friends with a human who works for a newspaper," Leni said.

"Excellent!" Vil said, slapping Schaumburg on the back hard, just like he did more than 50 years ago.

"Ow!," Schaumburg said.

"Now, here is your assignment," Vil said, handing Schaumburg and Leni a printed sheet.

Top Secret:

BETTER BEAR BUREAU ASSIGNMENT:
INFILTRATE HUMAN SOCIETY.
FIND OUT ANYTHING THAT CAN BE
LEARNED ABOUT THEM, ESPECIALLY
IN MATTERS RELATED TO NUCLEAR
ENERGY, MILITARY DEVELOPMENTS,
AND MILITARY EQUIPMENT.
    REPORT ANY AND ALL FINDINGS TO
DIRECTOR VIL ON A WEEKLY BASIS.

"How will we communicate with you?" Schaumburg asked.

Vil handed Leni and Schaumburg four gold pins, shaped like the Gateway Arch.

"These are your communicator pins. Tap them once, and you will be in direct contact with our switchboard. We will also expect written reports weekly via Orishan electronic mail. I suggest you find Pawtropolis and get jobs there, as we cannot provide you with any support. All agents must fend for themselves. That will be all. Report back in a week."

Just as Vil got up from his chair to leave, Schaumburg put his paw on Vil's shoulder. Vil sneered menacingly at Schaumburg. Apparently, Vil did not like being touched in that manner.

"I have something else to tell you," Schaumburg said. "I have discovered that by eating chocolate, I have super strength, X-ray vision, and the ability to fly. My H.A.R.V.E.Y. unit believes it is because of some unique combinations of the chocolate, my Orishan command power ring, and my own unique physiology."

This information intrigued Vil.

"You still have a H.A.R.V.E.Y. unit?" Vil said. "Throw it away. They are almost useless technology now . . . Super powers, you say," he said, stroking his furry chin. "That's amazing. Can you demonstrate?"

Schaumburg took out a piece of chocolate and ate it. Then he floated up out of his chair, and began soaring around the room.

All the Orishans at the headquarters stopped to watch in amazement.

Then Schaumburg softly landed next to a metal safe. He easily ripped open the safe, but not before describing its contents for Vil in exact detail.

"Everyone who has just seen this demonstration—it did not happen, do you understand?" Vil ordered. All the other Orishans immediately got back to work.

Vil leaned over to Schaumburg, and in hushed tones, said, "You have to keep these powers secret. Get a job and disguise yourself somehow so people don't recognize you."

Then Vil got up to leave again.

"Is that all?" Leni asked.

"Oh, and don't ever use those powers. You are forbidden from using them. Understood?"

Then Vil walked away, leaving Leni and Schaumburg alone, shocked by what they had just heard.

After Schaumburg and Leni left to go meet Sam, Vil made a call using a special computer communications device.

"Schaumburg is alive and well, sir," Vil said. "And he has super powers, just as we predicted. Soon he will join his brother. I have instructed Schaumburg to never use his powers. I doubt the idiot will obey. I fear we will have to eliminate him to carry out our plans here on Earth. His brother is under my power and will assist us in that endeavor. I never trusted Schaumburg anyway. Director Vil out."

A Little Help From a Wizard

While Sam, Schaumy and Leni started back from St. Louis, Chocolate and Louis enjoyed the hospitality of Nerwonduh.

Nerwonduh led Chocolate and Louis away down the alley to a hole in an abandoned building's wall. The building, a former factory, still contained some furniture, such as a room full of beds, formerly housing a medical unit in the factory.

Nerwonduh led them to one of the beds, and they all instantly transported, via the Teddy Bear Zone, to Nerwonduh's castle.

"I've always been amazed at how that thing transports us," Louis said.

"It is not magic. It is science," Nerwonduh said. "The Teddy Bear Zone works as a displacement device in a similar fashion to the H.A.R.V.E.Y. unit that can phase in and out. The zone acts as a portal, which changes the vibration of the being that is being transported. The city of Pawtropolis and surrounding suburbs, such as the location of this castle, exist in the same time and space as regular Earth cities and rural areas. Only they vibrate at a different rate, so Pawtropolis and its suburbs cannot be seen by the Earth creatures, including humans."

As Nerwonduh led the Orishans through the castle, they noted how torches lit the dark stone walls, and twisted staircases led to locked rooms.

"Your place is very low tech," Louis offered.

"We Wizards prefer to use simple technology whenever possible," Nerwonduh said. "It keeps us grounded in our magical arts."

The Wizard led the two "bears" to a library filled with walls of ancient texts.

At the center of the library was a large table. Off to one corner of the library was a clothing rack containing all manner of costumes.

Nerwonduh pulled down several outfits.

"Here, Louis," Nerwonduh said. "This pirate captain outfit will fit your personality and the cutlass sword matches your golden hook."

He pulled down a lime green dress for Chocolate, which matched her green crown.

"These two are for Schaumburg. The black suit, fedora and brown trench coat are for his everyday attire, and the costume with the cape is for when he is fighting crime as the Paw. The Wizard robes are for Leni."

Chocolate and Louis noticed there was a press pass sticking out of the fedora.

"What makes you think Schaumburg will be a reporter?" Louis asked.

"Excellent question, young Orishan," Nerwonduh said, smiling at Louis. "Let us just say for now that I have foreseen his need for these costumes."

"What's that other costume for?" Chocolate asked, eyeing a green and purple outfit with a mask and cape.

"Not now, little Chocolate," Nerwonduh said. "We have much to go over and little time. Just take it to Schaumburg. You will know what to do with it when the time comes."

"Thank you for the clothing," Louis said. "I guess we should be getting back to Sam's apartment now."

"Wait," Nerwonduh said. "I have some information for you."

Nerwonduh pulled down a large dusty book from one shelf, opening it to a particular page marked "B.B.B."

"Things are not what they were when you left for your mission 52 years ago," Nerwonduh began. "A lot has changed. For example, Frank E. Vil is now in charge of the Better Bear Bureau in St. Louis."

"What?" Louis and Chocolate indignantly exclaimed at the same time.

"That slime!" Louis said. "How did he end up in charge?"

"The universe works in mysterious ways," Nerwonduh said. "It is imperative that you defy all orders given to you from the B.B.B. Question everything and everyone. Vil has made a pact with the Arjogun here on Earth, and together they are plotting the destruction of mankind."

This stunned Chocolate and Louis into silence. The H.A.R.V.E.Y. unit on Louis' belt instantly activated. "Vil is an idiot!" the unit said.

"Ah, I see you still have your H.A.R.V.E.Y. unit," Nerwonduh said. "I must implore you to never give up your H.A.R.V.E.Y. unit. They are no longer being issued by the B.B.B. and are considered obsolete. However, the real reason they have been deemed redundant by new technology will become clear to you all later. Do not allow the B.B.B. to confiscate it. Be sure you relay this instruction to Schaumburg and Leni."

"Yes, sir," Chocolate said.

"Why should we trust what you are telling us?" Louis asked.

"A fair question, my young friend," Nerwonduh said. "As I said before, you must question everything and everyone. Therefore, I suggest you verify what I have told you yourselves. In the meantime, remember to hang onto that H.A.R.V.E.Y. unit."

After giving Chocolate and Louis some more instruction, he advised they obtain jobs in Pawtropolis, and suggested that Schaumburg seek work as a reporter for *The Daily Times*.

"I will be leaving for my home planet tonight," Nerwonduh said. "I will not return here for awhile. But when you use the Sword of George Washington for its intended purpose, I will return."

Louis and Chocolate looked at each other with puzzled looks on their faces.

"Remember what I have told you," Nerwonduh said. "I will see you again when your original mission has been accomplished."

* * *

At that very moment, in Versailles, Fred arrived at Sam's office. A light snow blanketed the area. He stepped out of his car to find the lights out and the closed sign on the Versailles Bureau.

Fred peered into the glass door, to make sure Sam was not hiding in the dark.

At that moment, Cheryl Cruz sauntered up to Fred.

"What are you doing?" she asked, suspicious of Fred.

"I'm supposed to meet Sam Arctophile, the reporter, here," Fred said, honestly.

"Looks like he's not here," she said. "I'm Cheryl Cruz, the curator of the Versailles George Washington Museum."

Fred's jaw dropped.

"You're Armando Cruz's wife," Fred stammered.

"Yes," Cheryl said. "How do you know about Armando?"

"I'm Fred Steinfeld. I work as a research assistant at the Chicago District office of the FBI. I just faxed a report to Sam about Armando's research on Project Unicorn."

At that moment, fear filled Cheryl's large brown eyes, and she pulled Fred across the street, toward the museum.

"Wait," Fred protested.

"Shhhhhhh!" Cheryl responded. She unlocked the museum and escorted Fred upstairs to her apartment.

"You are in danger," she said.

"I know. So is Sam. That's why I'm here. To warn him."

"No. I will warn him. You must leave Versailles immediately. I am being watched."

"I'm not sure what to make of this beautiful woman," Fred said to himself. Aloud, he stammered, "Uh . . . Okay. I'll go. Are you gonna be all right?"

"I can take care of myself. My husband taught me not to be a damsel in distress."

"Right. Okay. I'll be going now."

Fred left the museum and walked the half a block to the parking lot in front of Sam's office. He got in his car but did not start the engine. Fred noticed disturbed snow on the hood of his car, indicating it had been opened since he parked his car.

When checking under the hood, he saw, to his shock and horror, a bomb attached to the ignition. Then Fred heard gunfire in the distance, and heard a bullet whiz past his left ear.

He bolted from his car, his heart racing in a dead panic. Fred slipped and fell on some new snow. Shots continued to zoom past him, narrowly missing him.

He ducked behind a building, and the shooting stopped. A moment later, he saw two men in dark suits run past his location. He had evaded them, for now. But where would he go?

"Sam's place," he thought to himself. "I have to get myself to Streator."

Scoop Schaumburg, the Paw, Both Get Big Breaks On First Day Out

The next day after Sam arrived back home in Streator with Leni and Schaumburg, Louis and Chocolate greeted them in their new outfits. Leni and Schaumy seemed delighted to receive new clothing themselves.

Louis and Chocolate briefed them on Nerwonduh's instructions. Schaumburg and Leni verified Vil now commanded the Better Bear Bureau.

The Orishans and Sam gathered in Sam's bedroom, preparing to use the Teddy Bear Zone to transport to Pawtropolis.

"Sam, we'll be away for awhile," Schaumburg said to his new human friend. "We have to establish ourselves in Pawtropolis, get jobs and the like. It sounds like I might be a journalist, too."

Nerwonduh the Wise Wizard

Nerwonduh, the wise Wizard, is a member of the Mystical Order of the Golden Paw.

"Couldn't pick a more exciting or rewarding career," Sam said, shaking Schaumburg's paw. Schaumburg was now dressed in a black suit vest and tie, complete with dress white shirt. He also wore a tan trench coat and donned a black fedora with a press pass just like Sam's. Schaumburg cocked the hat ace-deuce (strategically dipped below one eye).

"Won't somebody recognize you as the Paw?" Sam asked. "Shouldn't you wear glasses or something?"

"Leni has agreed to cast a magical spell on me," Schaumburg said. "Whenever anyone sees me as the Paw, they will automatically think I am a different Orishan from Schaumburg. Don't ask me to explain it. It's magic. Besides, the glasses idea is pretty lame. How can a pair of glasses really disguise your identity?"

Then Schaumburg turned up his right cuff to reveal the red leggings of his super hero costume.

"I've got it on just in case I need to switch identities in a hurry."

"You've been watching too many Super Guy movies," Sam said. "But you look very distinguished, Schaumburg."

"Thank you, Sam."

The two hugged. Then Sam hugged all three of the other Orishans individually. They were quickly becoming close friends.

"What are you going to do while we're gone?" Leni asked him.

"I'm going to try and track down Fred," Sam answered. "His message on the answering machine sounded urgent. I'll try his parents' home in Kankakee first. I'm still on vacation so I have some time to kill. And my boss said I should stay away from my apartment for now, anyway."

"Right, Sam," Schaumburg said. "We'll see you in a while. I'll phone you and leave a message to let you know when we are coming back."

Then the four Orishans scampered under Sam's bed, and were gone in an instant.

Sam picked up the bedspread and looked under the bed, seeing nothing but dust and an old sock.

"This is just amazing," Sam said out loud to himself.

The four Orishans in Schaumburg's Hug emerged from the Teddy Bear Zone in downtown Pawtropolis.

The city bustled with cars that were about the third of the size of cars used for humans. The doors in the buildings and many of the windows were round, rather than square, in keeping with the architectural style of their native planet.

"I'll report to the newspaper office to find a job," Schaumburg said. "You guys see what type of work you can dig up. Let's meet back here at lunch."

Schaumburg entered the revolving round glass doors of *The Daily Times* building. He entered what he thought to be an elevator. The letters B.A.R.T (for Bear Area Rapid Transit) hung above the "elevator" door.

A plaque above the door said:

UNLIKE AN ELEVATOR IN HUMAN BUILDINGS, B.A.R.T.S ARE KNOWN AS BEARAVATORS. A BEARAVATOR GOES UP DOWN, SIDEWAYS LEFT AND RIGHT, AND ALSO GOES DIAGONALLY THROUGH THE BUILDING. IT ALSO TRAVELS LIKE A BULLET AT BLINDING SPEEDS. BARTHOLOMEW, THE SAME ORISHAN WHO BEFRIENDED GEORGE WASHINGTON, INVENTED THE BEARAVATOR. BARTHOLOMEW, A GENIUS, SEEMED ALSO SLIGHTLY TOUCHED IN THE HEAD, ACCORDING TO ORISHAN FOLK TALES. LEGENDS INDICATE THAT BARTHOLOMEW'S BEARAVATOR IS HIS JOKE ON ORISHANS WHO TRAVEL TO EARTH.

Schaumburg knew nothing about such a contrivance.

When he pressed the newsroom button (the 32nd floor) the device raised him off the ground and he stayed suspended in mid-air for a moment. The sensation shocked Schaumburg. The B.A.R.T. car slammed him almost against one side as it screamed toward the location, zigging and zagging to and fro, and tossing him all about the inside. Except Schaumburg never hit one side or another of the bearavator car. He continued to stay suspended away from all four walls plus the ceiling and floor at all times, spinning wildly as the bearavator made its journey through *The Daily Times* office building. It started to make Schaumburg dizzy. Fortunately the wild ride did not last long.

The device dumped him indignantly onto the newsroom floor, where he tumbled out and landed on his face.

He glanced around the newsroom with desks and computer terminals. Orishans banged out stories for that day's edition.

One young Orishan, a cub really, bounced up to Schaumburg.

"First time on a B.A.R.T.?" he asked Schaumburg, straightening out Schaumburg's collar and dusting Schaumburg off.

"Yes," Schaumburg said, somewhat shaken. "Thank you, young one . . . Can you help me? I need to see the editor about a reporting job."

"Perry's office is at the end of the aisle," the young Orishan said. Then he stuck out a paw to shake with Schaumburg.

"My name's Andy," he said. "I'm a cub reporter, too. And photographer. Just started here yesterday."

Then Andy scooted along, handing a piece of paper to one of the other reporters, letting Schaumburg fend for himself.

Schaumburg walked through the newsroom, feeling the blood rush to his head as the other reporters stared at him.

He knocked on the editor's glass door and stepped in.

"Ah, you must be Schaumburg," the editor said. "I'm Perry Purple. I received a note from the Bengalian, Nerwonduh, that you were coming in to apply for a job here."

"He notified you I was coming?" Schaumburg asked, surprised.

"Those Wizards take care of everything," Perry said. "Say, don't I know you?"

Suddenly, recognition dawned on Perry's face as he thought back to more than 50 years ago when he worked as a correspondent for the paper.

"I'm the reporter who rescued your Hug after the ship crashed,"

Perry said. "It's you! And you look exactly the same age you did more than 50 years ago! How did you manage that one?"

Schaumburg looked outside into the newsroom. Even though he knew none of the reporters outside Perry's office could hear them, he still lowered his voice.

"Perry, Leni's magic transport spell dropped us two days ago in the apartment of a human reporter," Schaumburg said. "For me, the crash was just days ago. For you and everyone else, apparently, it was 52 years ago."

"Don't you worry, Schaumburg," Perry said kindly. "We'll fix you up with a job here. Can you type?"

"Yup!" Schaumburg said. "But I've never been a reporter before."

"No problem," Perry said. "I'll team you up with young Andy. He'll show you the ropes."

A few minutes later, as Andy gave Schaumburg a quick tour of the newsroom, the police scanner started squawking about a fire a few blocks from the newspaper office.

Perry rushed out of his office.

"Andy, Schaumburg, you're on that fire! And take a camera, Andy!"

Minutes later at the scene of the fire, Andy started snapping pictures. Schaumburg scanned the scene, a 12-story apartment building, with smoke and flames coming out of the tenth floor. Schaumburg noticed Louis, already working as a firefighter with the Pawtropolis Fire Department.

"Lou, what's happening?" Schaumburg inquired.

Some passersby looked up at the smoking structure.

"There's someone up there," one of the Orishans in the crowd below called out.

A female Orishan with tears streaming down her eyes rushed to Louis and Schaumburg. She grabbed Louis' fire coat.

"Please, my cub," she implored Louis. "She's up there in my apartment! On the tenth floor! Somebody save her!"

"We'll do what we can, miss," Louis said to her. "Now please step back behind the fire trucks."

Then Louis spoke to Schaumburg in hushed tones.

"Schaumburg, we can't get to that little cub on time. But you can. Quick, change inside the ambulance over there."

Schaumburg peered over to the ambulance and noticed his sister Chocolate working as an emergency medical technician (EMT).

Seconds later, a blur of mostly red, some blue and yellow streaked up to the tenth floor, crashed through a window, then quickly emerged with a form wrapped in a blanket to shield it from the flames.

"My cub!" the female on the ground cried as she saw Schaumburg, now dressed as the Paw, drift down to the ground safely cradling the girl cub in his arms.

Andy on the ground snapped pictures of the new hero in Pawtropolis.

"Wow! This is gonna be front page!" Andy said. "Where's Schaumburg? He'll get his first byline in tonight's edition!"

*   *   *

"Great job on that, Scoop," Perry said to Schaumburg, affectionately patting him on the back after Andy and Schaumburg returned to the newsroom and filed their story and pictures. "Your first big story."

He held up the afternoon's edition with the blazing headline:

Mysterious Hero Saves Cub From Burning Building

BY SCOOP SCHAUMBURG

"And I like the name, Scoop Schaumburg," Perry continued. "It looks great on a byline."

All the Orishans in the newsroom cheered and applauded Schaumburg on his first big story.

Perry motioned for them to stop applauding.

"That's enough," he said. "Let's not let it go to this young reporter's head, now. This was the first-day story. Now we go for the second-day story. Find out all you can about this mysterious super-powered Orishan! Who is he? What's his name? Where does he live? Why does he have those powers? Is he from Orisha? Is he from Earth? Does he have any weaknesses? Does he have a girlfriend? Is he married? Any kids? What's his favorite book? What color underwear does he wear?"

Then Perry paused for a minute.

"Scratch that last question," Perry said. "We already know what color underwear he wears! It's his costume!"

The entire newsroom burst out in laughter.

"Find out everything you can!"

"Right, boss," Schaumburg said, grabbing his coat from his desk chair. "Let's go, Andy."

After Andy and Schaumburg left the newsroom, Perry looked at the other reporters who stood staring at Perry.

"What are you guys looking at? This doesn't have to be a Scoop Schaumburg exclusive. I want you all on this story. Find out about that super Orishan! I want lots of follow-ups in tomorrow's issue!"

Immediately, the reporters started making phone calls, some grabbed their trench coats, fedoras and reporter's notebooks and stepped out of the newsroom. Others began doing research by looking up information in the newsroom library. They all had ideas on angles to publicize the new hero of Pawtropolis.

CHAPTER 8

THE BIRTH OF MARDI GRAS

Corn and soybean fields surround the city of Pawtropolis. However, unlike Central Illinois where the humans live, this part of Illinois that vibrates to the Orishan's frequency (and therefore invisible to humans) contains hills lush with trees of all shapes and sizes. Flowers in gardens sprinkle the area with bright colors.

Leni, preferring to live in the country, makes her residence on a small farm where she grows herbs. She also plays with unicorns, trains her pet dragon, Scorch, to control his flame as a chef, has two trained owls named Hoot and Nanny, and a pet Arctic seal, named Iggy.

Her farm, called Toleni, lies a few miles southwest of Pawtropolis. The farm includes an apothecary shop called "Hocus Potions" where Leni makes homemade potions to sell to Orishans from the city.

Her farmhouse also contains special apartments for Louis and Chocolate.

The home's architecture is a cottage structure with a thatched roof, a round door, looking like a home fit for a Wizard of Leni's caliber. Some of the windows are round as well.

Her home turned out to be just one of several structures on her farm, which she established in December 1999.

"I need a hideout where you can keep in touch with me and also have access to information," Schaumburg told Leni. "My Paw Cave."

"We can build you a special cave with computers and all the high-tech nerdy stuff you boys like," she said.

"Yes, that's it!" Schaumburg said.

"You can keep your Pawmobile there too."

"I guess I'll need a car, won't I," Schaumburg said. "I can't fly around everywhere since my powers only last 20 minutes at a time."

"We'll carve your cave out of the side of that small mountain on the east end of my farm," Leni said. "Scorch, my pet dragon, can burn the hole for your cave. And I'll build a B.A.R.T. bearavator between my house and your cave."

"No way!" Schaumburg said. "It's bad enough I have to take one of those monstrous devices into my office at *The Daily Times*. I'll just build a secret passage between your farm and the cave."

Louis offered to help Schaumburg build his fortress.

Leni's unicorns lent a hoof or two as well by levitating some of the heavier pieces of equipment, which Schaumburg placed inside, such as his huge computer monitor with a screen larger than five Orishans.

And Scorch helped weld metal joints, using his fire in a controlled manner. Scorch created the cave by melting a hole in the side of the mountain.

One Tuesday night in January, after having completed construction on the Paw Cave (Schaumburg had already purchased his Pawmobile by then), Schaumburg invited Andy over for dinner.

Leni cooked a fine feast with Scorch's help including fresh fish Iggy caught in a nearby stream. Whenever Scorch liked an Orishan, he would give the Orishan a verbal "raspberry." That's how dragons say "hi."

At first the Orishans thought the dragon did not like them, but soon learned this was a sign of affection.

Andy and Schaumburg had worked together for more than a month already. Andy grew quite fond of Schaumburg. However, Andy wondered how Schaumburg miraculously scooped all the other reporters with firsthand accounts of the Paw's exploits. Somehow, Schaumburg knew just where the Paw would be when someone needed rescuing, or some super feat was needed (or a super solution to a problem) for the inhabitants of Pawtropolis. And Andy's superb photographs complimented Schaumburg's yarns, which always appeared on page one of *The Daily Times*. The Paw became big news in Pawtropolis, the likes of which the town had never seen before in its 98-year existence. Andy and Schaumburg became fast celebrities in their own right.

After the feast, Louis, Leni, Schaumburg and Chocolate all sat together in Leni's sumptuous living room, watching Scorch and Iggy play with each other. Scorch and Iggy, still both babies, loved each other. Scorch would fly Iggy around the room to Iggy's delight.

Andy watched the others as they laughed and applauded the feats of the pets.

"How nice it must be to be a part of a family like this," he thought to himself.

"C'mon, Andy," Schaumburg said. "Join the fun."

"I'll be right there, Schaumburg," Andy said. "I think I'd like to take a short walk outside for a few minutes first."

"Excellent idea," Schaumburg said. "You can watch the scarlet sunset over the hills with the unicorns. They love to watch sunsets."

While the other Orishans remained entertained by the pets inside, Andy walked out the round front door, greeted by several white and pink unicorns. Unicorns only approach pure beings, and they liked Andy very much. They began to dance in delight that someone had come to play with them. They spun around Andy, making dazzling sparkles with their horns that made Andy very happy. They almost put Andy into a trance with their magic.

The unicorns seemed to be steering Andy toward the round storm shelter door around the side of Leni's house.

One pink unicorn, a male called Dreamwalker, led the other unicorns. He touched his purple horn to the lock on the shelter door and it miraculously fell down, opening the door for Andy.

Andy slipped into the dark shelter room, walking down the steps into the dampness below.

Dreamwalker led Andy and his horn lit a path for them.

The unicorn and Andy strolled through a swirling darkened cave, which ended in a black rock wall. Then Dreamwalker touched his horn on the wall, and the wall magically dissolved to reveal the secret Paw Cave.

The site of the cave shocked Andy, seeming to wake him from

Dreamwalker's trance. He saw a couple of spare Paw costumes hanging inside a locked glass case on the right side of the room. Andy saw another costume beside the Paw costumes, but he did not recognize that one. This second costume case held an outfit that included a sparkling green and purple cape and a purple facemask with stars. Andy thought to himself how cool it would be if he were a super hero like the Paw wearing that second costume.

Then Andy suddenly realized who the Paw was.

"Is that how Schaumburg gets all those scoops? Because he is really the Paw?" Andy said to himself. "Of course! What a rascal that Schaumburg is!"

The huge Paw computer dominated the center of the cave with its round screen, Orishan writing and controls all around it. The screen remained darkened and without power. The Pawmobile stood sleekly in one corner waiting for someone to jump in and race to adventure.

Andy slid his paw admiringly across the Pawmobile's shiny hood. Its red, blue and yellow colors combined with the glistening chrome, the same colors as the Paw's costume. He sat behind the driver's seat, pretending to be a crime fighter like the Paw.

He punched open the glove compartment, and out popped several Nestles' Crunch bars.

He laughed with delight and opened one up, starting to wolf it down.

After eating the bar, Dreamwalker nudged him out of the car and led Andy to the glass case with the unknown costume he admired earlier—not the Paw's but some other hero's. Dreamwalker magically opened the glass case for Andy.

Andy tried it on, surprised that it fit very well, as if custom-tailored for him.

"I am Mardi Gras, the party dude!" he said out loud, joking around. Then he pointed one paw in the air, just like he'd seen the Paw do, and sprang up, pretending to fly. Only, he wasn't pretending. He really flew.

Shocked, he stumbled to the ground quickly.

"What gives?" he thought. "Is it the costume that gives the Paw his powers?"

At that instant, Dreamwalker started stamping the ground and nudging Andy around to face the entrance to the Paw Cave.

Schaumburg stood at the entrance, looking strangely happy. He peeled off his outer clothing to reveal a Paw costume underneath.

"So you want to be a super hero, eh?" Schaumburg said.

He walked over to the Pawmobile and ate the rest of the chocolate bar Andy started.

Then he grabbed Mardi Gras' paw and they both flew out of the Paw cave into the dusky outside air, flying against the red sunset. Dreamwalker followed them out and all the unicorns danced below, shooting flashes of light at them in all the colors of the rainbow.

Leni, Louis and Chocolate all came outside, followed by Scorch and Iggy to watch the show.

Scorch and Iggy took flight too, chasing the two super "bears" around the sky, and chasing after the sparking colors the unicorns created. Iggy clung gleefully to Scorch's leg.

"Wow!" Andy said. "What a rush! We can fly!"

*   *   *

Later that night, the five Orishans all sat around Leni's round kitchen table and discussed the new development of Andy having the same strange super powers as Schaumburg.

"Do you think it's the costumes?" Andy asked.

"It's the chocolate," Leni said. "But so far, you two seem to be the only ones who can eat chocolate and gain those powers."

"I thought it might have been connected to Schaumburg's command power ring as well," Louis said. "Only Andy is not the commander of an Orishan Hug."

Shocked, Andy pulled out a power ring he wore on a necklace underneath his shirt.

"Where did you get that?" Leni asked, knowing how powerful those rings were, and how only commanders of Orishan space vessels were issued them.

"I don't know," Andy said, shrugging his shoulders.

Leni, Schaumburg, Louis and Chocolate all looked at Andy suspiciously.

"No, I really don't know," Andy continued. "As a matter of fact, I don't know too much about myself at all. I don't even know how I got to Earth and don't remember ever being a part of a space mission. I can't remember much of anything past a few months ago, just before I started working for *The Daily Times* . . . I stumbled into the newsroom much the same way Schaumburg did and Perry gave me a job right away."

"Why did you go there looking for a job to begin with?" Schaumburg asked.

"This Wizard named Nerwonduh pointed me toward *The Daily Times*," Andy said. "He said they were hiring cub reporters and I should apply."

Louis, Leni, Chocolate and Schaumburg gave each other surprised looks.

"Leni, just what do we know about this Wizard Nerwonduh?"

"I have heard of him," Leni said. "Let's look him up in 'Wizards of the Universe.'"

Leni left the table to retrieve a huge, musty tome from her library, a room filled to the brim with old books.

She slammed the book on the table and dust floated up.

The yellowed pages were brittle to Leni's paw as she turned to the letter N.

"Here it is," she said. "'Nerwonduh, a Master Wizard of the Mystical Order of the Golden Paw. Powerful Wizard who sometimes works with Orisha to fight the Arjogun.'"

"It says his planet, Bengali, was once a slave world to the Arjogun and Nerwonduh led a revolt which freed his world," she said. "An Orishan named Bartholomew, who later traveled to Earth in the 1700s, assisted him in the revolt. It also said that in Bartholomew's time, very few Orishans were on Earth, unlike today."

"How old does that make Nerwonduh?" Schaumburg asked, realizing that this revolt must have taken place more than 300 years ago.

"It says his species is very long-lived," Leni said. "The entry says nothing more."

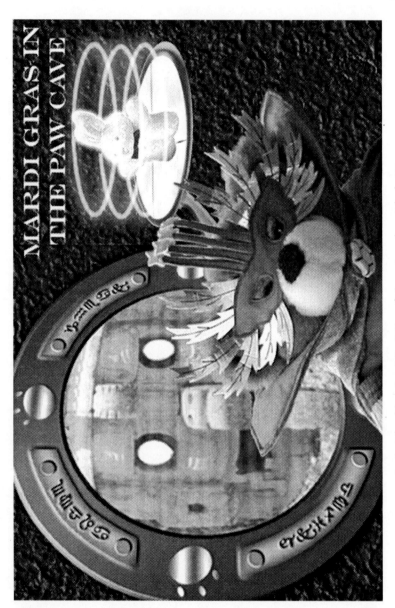

Andy Adorable, a.k.a. Mardi Gras, fights crime alongside the Paw.

"Well, I guess we can trust what Nerwonduh told us," Schaumburg said to Lou and Chocolate.

"You guys know this Wizard?" Andy asked.

"He is the one who left us your Mardi Gras costume," Schaumburg said. All five were now mystified and awestruck at the kind of foreknowledge Nerwonduh must possess.

"Well, enough of this Wizard talk," Schaumburg said. "It's time to start your super hero training, Andy."

Leni still leafed through her book.

"Say, Schaumburg. Look at what this book says about Project Unicorn."

Schaumburg's eyes showed terror.

"That book has an entry on Project Unicorn?" Schaumburg said. "The human contract between Earth and the Arjogun?"

"Yes," Leni responded. "It's under an entry for a being known as the Frown."

The Knights in Blue Satin

The next day, in the newsroom at *The Daily Times* in Pawtropolis, Scoop Schaumburg banged out a story on his special Orishan computer.

Andy approached Schaumburg with a note.

"Schaumburg, this came for you by special messenger today," Andy said, holding a large blue envelope with "Schaumburg" written in delicate calligraphy on the front.

On the back, the envelope contained a wax seal depicting a snake eating its own tail forming a circle, and wearing a crown. Inside the snake circle three rings shined in gold, each with crowns. The snake sparkled in golden hues, but each crown on the rings contained a band of different colors—one red, one green, and one blue.

Schaumburg opened the envelope.

Inside was a blue card, written in beautiful Orishan calligraphy, just like the script on the outside of the envelope. The note said:

DEAREST SCHAUMBURG,
    YOU ARE CORDIALLY INVITED
TO A MEETING OF THE KNIGHTS IN

BLUE SATIN. WE ARE A GROUP OF ORISHANS DEDICATED TO THE IDEALS OF THE MYSTICAL ORDER OF THE GOLDEN PAW. WE ARE NOT WIZARDS, BUT SERVE THE CAUSE OF THE MYSTICAL ORDER.

PLEASE ACCEPT THIS INVITATION TO OUR DINNER MEETING TONIGHT, 6 P.M. WE SUGGEST YOU ALSO BRING ANDY ADORABLE, YOUR PARTNER AND PHOTOGRAPHER, AS A GUEST. WE ARE MEETING IN *THE DAILY TIMES* BUILDING, 23RD FLOOR, ROOM 23.

Schaumburg handed the note to Andy. Both Orishans scratched their heads in confusion.

Schaumburg decided to speak to Perry Purple about it.

In the managing editor's office, he handed the note to Perry.

"Ah!" Perry exclaimed. "You have been invited to join the Knights. Great! I'll see you there tonight."

"But Perry, who are these guys?" Schaumburg asked. "I've never heard of them."

"All will become clear to you tonight. This recent incarnation of the secret society formed in response to the B.B.B. being taken over by a faction of Orishans, led by Frank Vil, who wished to make 'peace' with the Arjogun. We are secretly fighting Vil's agenda."

Schaumburg phoned Leni after getting a bite to eat for lunch.

"What do you think, Leni?" Schaumburg said.

"I'll do some research on these Knights in Blue Satin and get back to you," Leni said. "I'll see what I can find on that seal with the snake as well."

Later, Leni called Schaumburg back.

"Here's what I found out," Leni said. "The Knights in Blue Satin *are* affiliated with the Mystical Order of the Golden Paw. They seem to be the counterpart to the Better Bear Bureau, which my Order now believes has been corrupted by Arjogun spies."

"Geez Louise, Leni," Schaumburg said. "What's happening to Orishans on this planet? There are conspiracies everywhere."

"There's more," Leni said. "I did some research on that symbol of the snake. In my Order, that snake symbol stands for infinity. The three rings represent the three planets that adhere to the Mystical Order of the Golden Paw, Orisha (green), Bengali (red) and one other planet (blue). I have not been able to verify what the third planet is yet. But I think it might be Earth!"

That evening, Andy and Schaumburg went to the secret meeting of the Knights in Blue Satin. Inside were Perry Purple and many other members of the newsroom staff. There were also Orishans whom Schaumburg recognized such as Fatima Furbulous, the television reporter, and various government officials in Pawtropolis. Schaumburg and Andy sat next to a chocolate brown Orishan dressed in an Asian martial arts costume.

"Hi, I'm Champ," the brown Orishan said, extending his paw to Schaumburg and Andy. His English was tinged with a Serbian accent. "I just arrived from Serbia."

After a few minutes, Perry Purple walked up to a podium at the front of the room.

A large screen stood behind him. The lights were turned down, and a slide viewer projected the symbol of the snake and three crowned rings.

"For those of you who don't know, this is the symbol of infinity," Purple said. "Our secret organization has adopted it as the way to identify members to each other. If you are handed a blue envelope with this seal on it, you will know it comes from the Knights in Blue Satin."

A hushed murmur swept the room.

"Settle down, people," Perry said. "I know some of you have never heard of us. We have been secretly plotting to overthrow Vil's rule in the B.B.B. ever since he took over five years ago. We also know of Schaumburg's mission to Earth, and will be assisting him in that endeavor."

Schaumburg's jaw dropped and so did Andy's.

"I know this comes as a surprise, Schaumburg, but we here in the Knights believe you and your Hug are the 'wild card' mentioned in the ancient stone texts written 4,000 years ago by the founders of the Mystical Order of the Golden Paw. You, your Hug, and now Andy, are all part of a grand conspiracy of good beings on three different planets who must collaborate to meet the threat of the Arjogun here on Earth."

Then the slide changed on the screen projector. The new image was one of Andy's photographs of the Paw flying over the city of Pawtropolis.

Schaumburg turned beet red when he saw the photograph.

Andy was a bit surprised too.

"This is the Paw," Purple continued.

"He is also a key player in our plan. He has powers that we do not comprehend. Schaumburg, we want you to contact him and this Mardi Gras person and ask them to help us in our cause."

"The Paw will refuse to become a hired gun," Schaumburg said.

"Then you misunderstand our purpose here," Purple said. "We are not asking for his help to overtly overthrow Vil and his ilk. Information is our most valuable weapon right now. We have *some* information handed down to us from hundreds of years ago that speaks about a defensive weapon here on Earth. And the key to activate those defenses is something called the Sword of George Washington. Our archeologists are working 'round the clock to interpret the passages that refer to this defensive weapon. But we believe that it is all tied to the future of this planet and its inhabitants, Orishan, human and, unknown to most, the Arjogun. We think the Paw can retrieve this key for us."

The slide projector showed a new image: a beautiful silver sword with elaborate carvings in a blue velvet case.

"This is the Sword of George Washington," Purple said. "It is mentioned in the old Orishan texts as the key to the defense of the Earth. It is sized for an Orishan, about nine Earth inches long. We need the Paw's help to dig up information about the sword and to find it. We need his help to figure out how to use it to protect the Earth. It is rumored that the Paw has a vast library of information on computers hidden in his Paw cave."

"Protect the Earth from what?" Schaumburg asked.

"From its destruction by the Arjogun on May 5, in about three years."

Schaumburg's jaws dropped in shock and disbelief. So did Andy's. Schaumburg thought to himself, "How do they know the date? Where did it come from? Who are these Knights in Blue Satin?"

"So exactly what do you want me to do?" Schaumburg quiried.

"Contact the Paw," Purple said. "Tell him about our organization and ask him if he will help. Are you with us, Schaumburg, Andy?"

"I'll contact the Paw," Schaumburg responded.

"I guess I'm with you guys too," Andy responded, somewhat unsure of all this.

"Good," Purple said. "Report to me what the Paw's response is."

"Okay," Schaumburg said. "Now why do you call yourselves the Knights in Blue Satin? Wouldn't knights slip off their horses if they were wearing satin?"

The Orishans in the room all laughed at Schaumburg's statement.

"Forgive us, Schaumburg," Purple said. "The name is actually taken from a passage in our ancient texts. The line says:

The Knights in Blue Satin will ride out on winged horses, one black, two with wind-wings, creating a windstorm to save Earth from the Arjogun's fire.

"That is the only reference to us in the texts."

"What does it mean?" Andy asked.

"It means we have to stop the Arjogun from destroying this planet," Purple said. "Some of our experts also believe it is also a veiled reference to the Paw."

A new slide showed up on the screen. This time, it showed an F-117A, tail number 806: a stealth fighter jet, United States Air Force.

"This is the Americans' stealth fighter. This particular plane was first flown Aug. 20, 1984. It flew 39 combat missions but fell into enemy hands on the night of March 27-28, 1999, 40 miles from Belgrade while participating in the American Operation Allied Force. The American forces rescued the human pilot. All other details remain classified by the American government. This is the black winged horse of the prophecy. We need a plane of this type to carry out our main mission to stop the Arjogun. These aircraft cost Americans more than $40 million apiece to build. We don't have those kinds of resources. This is the only stealth fighter that is available to us which the Americans will not miss if we procure it," Purple said.

"You mean steal it," Schaumburg said.

The Orishans in the room laughed out loud at Schaumburg's translation of Perry's words.

Purple ignored Schaumburg.

"Our mission is to retrieve that aircraft. We plan to enhance its

technology so it can fly for many thousand of miles without needing to
be refueled and some other gizmos our Orishan scientists have cooked
up. This plane is our 'winged horse.'"

Perry Purple outlined an elaborate scheme involving a small
commando group of Orishans who will infiltrate the Serbian forces
and steal the plane that Americans lost, and fly it back to America.

"Sounds like a great plan," Schaumburg said sarcastically. "Who
are the fools who are going to steal that F-117A on that suicide mission?"

"Why you and your Hug, of course," Purple said.

"Hold on a minute, Perry," Schaumburg said. "I have no problem
contacting the Paw for you. But I'm not agreeing to any covert suicide
missions to steal a downed American stealth fighter."

"Don't worry, Schaumburg," Purple continued. "We'll give you all
the support you need, including an Orishan on the inside where the
fighter is being held."

"Where is it being held?" Schaumburg asked.

"In Serbia," Champ answered. "I'm the Orishan inside." He smiled
broadly at Schaumburg and Andy.

"I'll have to discuss this with my Hug," Schaumburg said.

"Get back to me as soon as possible on your Hug's decision about
the mission to Serbia."

Perry gave a thick blue envelope to Schaumburg containing the
same snake seal on the back.

"Details of the mission to retrieve the plane," Purple explained.

*   *   *

Memo

To: Captain Schaumburg Harmony
From: Frank Vil, B.B.B. HQ
Re: Status reports
Earth Date: January 3, 2000

*Captain Schaumburg, you have been very lax in your weekly
reports on your infiltration of the humans. We have learned that you
frequently go to work with the journalist you have become associated*

with. We are happy that you are forming ties to this Earthling, but we must warn you not to get too close to the inhabitants of this planet. Do not trust them. You always did have a soft spot in your heart for aliens of all types.

Also, please send us your reports on a more frequent basis. We need any data, on a weekly basis at least. If you cannot carry out these simple orders, perhaps we should relieve you of your command.

Thank you for your attention to this matter.

Frank Vil
Better Bear Bureau
St. Louis, MO

Memo

To: Frank Vil
From: Captain Schaumburg Harmony
Re: Weekly reports
Earth date: January 5, 2000

Dear Mr. Vil,

Thank you for your concern about my Hug of Orisha and me. I believe I missed one week's report to you, but I will be more careful in the future.

Here is my report for this week:

The human journalist Samuel Arctophile is investigating the mysterious "death" of a human federal agent named Armando Cruz, and seems to be in danger himself.

I am also endangering his position on his job, as the woman who lives in the apartment above the Versailles Bureau complained to the landlord that Sam has been yelling at his "teddy bear," and she believes Sam to be mentally unstable.

Sam has been taking us everywhere with him. Most people believe we are just toys. That is okay, except that some people believe adult humans should not be carrying toys around with them. I am frankly baffled by their attitude. Orishan adults often carry toys with them to relieve stress on dangerous missions.

But we are Orisha, not humans. And I am learning very quickly there are many differences between our species.

You mentioned that I have always been "soft" on alien beings. If you are referring to the now famous incident among B.B.B. agents of the time I saved an Arjogun officer on the planet Serena, I would simply state, once again for the record, that the Mystical Order of the Golden Paw believed our actions were absolutely correct, even though we failed to carry out our primary mission because we stopped to save the Arjogun.

Further, I would like to remind you, sir, that we still must adhere to the laws of the Mystical Order of the Golden Paw, which means we should show mercy to all—humans, Arjogun, or whatever species you care to fill in the blank.

But since you are concerned about our safety, I suggest you issue Louis and I Attitude-Adjuster-Sleeper-Blasters (A.A.S.B.s) to defend ourselves in the event we run into hostile humans.

The crash of our ship in the Earth year 1947 resulted in the destruction of our original set of A.A.S.B.s.

Finally, please report to Orisha High Command that we have uncovered some additional information regarding a human endeavor, Project Unicorn. We believe Armando Cruz's original conclusions may be flawed. He said he thought humans and Arjogun are working together to create a weapon to control the weather. Do you have any data on this?

Thanking you in Advance.

Sincerely,
Captain Schaumburg Harmony
Pawtropolis, IL

Memo

To: *Captain Schaumburg Harmony*
From: *Frank E. Vil, B.B.B. HQ*
Re: *Response to request for blasters and information about Project*
   Unicorn
Earth date: *January 7, 2000*

Dear Schaumburg,
   We will be shipping two A.A.S.B.s for yourself and Captain Louis LaHug. They are, as you know, defensive weapons, and will put aliens to sleep. The Aliens will wake up in a very pleasant mood.
   As for your request for information regarding Project Unicorn, I'm afraid that project, since it involves the Arjogun, is now classified, and beyond your scope on this mission. Therefore, I would suggest you convince this human journalist to stop sticking his snoopy nose where it does not belong. There will be no more discussion of Project Unicorn from this office, is that understood?
   I remind you that your mission has changed from spying on the Arjogun to spying on the humans.
   Please concentrate on your new mission.

> *Thank you.*
> *Frank E. Vil*
> *Better Bear Bureau*
> *St. Louis, MO*

CHAPTER 9

SCHAUMBURG'S RAIDERS

Two months later, after receiving two attitude adjusters (blasters) from Vil, in the Paw Cave, Schaumburg read his Hug of Orishans the following:

Standing Orders for Commando units assigned by the Knights in Blue Satin. These are based on Ancient American Army commando rules:

1. *Don't forget anything. Write down all details.*
2. *Have your Orishan A.A.S.B.s kept clean as a whistle at all times. These weapons are used in defense only, and can stun humans or Arjogun enemy soldiers, putting them to sleep. They wake up with mellow attitudes. Also, all raiders must carry with them their assigned H.A.R.V.E.Y. units. These units can detect enemy Arjogun soldiers. Keep these units with you at all times. Report any damage to the unit to Knights Headquarters in Pawtropolis.*
3. *Be ready to march at a moment's notice. Keep all blaster ammunition in a safe place.*
4. *When on a march, act the way you would if you were sneaking up on a deer. Blend in with the surrounding terrain. Walk silently. See the enemy first.*
5. *Always report honestly to the commanders what you do and see. The Knights in Blue Satin are depending on you for correct information.*
6. *Take no unnecessary chances.*

7. When camping, half the party stays awake while the other half sleeps.
8. Don't ever march home the same way. Take a different route so you won't be ambushed.
9. Each commando unit has to keep a scout at least 20 yards on each flank and two yards in the rear so the main body can't be surprised.
10. Don't sit to eat without posting sentries.
11. If you are being trailed, make a circle and come back onto your own tracks, then ambush those trailing you.
12. When the enemy is coming against you, use the environment to hide yourself. Don't take main roads. Stay hidden in the trees, forests.
13. Let the enemy come until he's close enough to see his eyes. Then blast him.

"These Knights in Blue Satin mean business," Louis said. "Those are based on Major Robert Rogers, an original American Ranger who fought in the Revolutionary War."

"How do you know that?" Andy asked.

"Louis is a big human history buff," Schaumburg said.

"So do we take on this suicide mission?" Chocolate asked.

"You can count me in," Andy said.

"Hold on," Schaumburg said. "You aren't even officially part of my Hug. Besides, we can't all go."

"Schaumy's right," Leni said. "We need someone to stay here as a point of contact."

"According to these instructions, the Knights in Blue Satin want me to ask the Paw if he will agree to keep the stolen F-117A in his Paw Cave," Schaumburg said. "Do you think they suspect I am the Paw?"

"Naw," Louis said. "For some reason, nobody recognizes you with that trench coat and fedora you wear now as Scoop Schaumburg."

"That's because of a simple two-plus-two-does-not-equal-four spell," Leni said. "They teach us that spell in our third year at the Wizard University on Orisha. I cast one on Schaumy so people will think Scoop Schaumburg and the Paw are actually two separate Orishans, even though they look exactly alike, save for their outfits. It's pretty amazing. Fooled you, Andy, before you discovered the truth."

Andy said nothing, feeling a little foolish.

"I'd like some more time to think about this mission," Schaumburg said. "This could be beary dangerous."

"Yeah, and Nerwonduh told us to question everything and everyone," Chocolate added.

"Right you are," Leni said. "I'll do some more digging on this Knights in Blue Satin group, and on Perry Purple as well. It is strange that he was on the scene of our crash before anyone else. How did he find out about it? Did he sabotage our space ship?"

"Perry saved us," Schaumburg complained, not wishing to believe his boss at the paper was connected to a plot against him.

"Question everyone and everything," Louis said, repeating Nerwonduh's warning.

"Sometimes I wish this war with Arjogunia was over," Schaumburg said. After a long pause, he said, "This is going to take place in the human world. I think it's time we contacted our human friend, Sam."

*   *   *

Captain's Log
Earth Date: March 10, 2000
Captain Schaumburg Harmony, reporting.

We have been contacted by a secret group of Orishans here on Earth that calls itself the Knights in Blue Satin. They have given me and my Hug an assignment to retrieve an Earth aircraft, which they plan to use in their fight against the Arjogun.

As commander of our Hug, I decided that if we are going to attempt this mission, we should not only have Orishan help, but human help as well.

So we enlisted the aid of our human companion, Samuel Arctophile, a human who works as a newspaperman.

We have determined that we can trust the Knights in Blue Satin. Millennium contacted her mentor on Orisha and explained our situation—how we were whisked into the future 52 years and still charged with carrying out our original assignment.

He verified for us that Perry Purple could be trusted and said that Vil is now an enemy of the Mystical Order because of his ties to the Arjogun.

As you know, the Arjogun prefer to fight with swords when the battle is hand-to-hand in close quarters. Leni and I saw several Arjogun swords hanging on display in Vil's office, which surprised us. All Orishan agents in the space command learn to swordfight, but Orishans rarely display Arjogun swords the way Vil does.

We hope to travel with Sam to Europe to retrieve the F-117A stealth fighter for the Knights in Blue Satin.

Louis learned how to fly the Earth planes by studying them on the Internet. Sam also took us to an Air Force Base in St. Louis, where we were able to learn first-hand more details about the stealth fighter.

Sam took Louis to the base, disguised as a toy teddy bear, asking a list of prepared questions we gave Sam. Sam's credentials as a journalist helped us obtain much more information than civilians would have been able to retrieve from the human military.

We have practiced our mission in simulations at my wife's farm, Toleni.

All four of us are ready for action.

We have also made contact with Champ, the Knights' operative in Serbia where the F-117A is being held. The Serbian Army is repairing the downed jet, which is virtually undamaged, and plans to use it in its own war effort.

We will leave for Europe tomorrow. We have a few extra tricks up our sleeve that even the Knights in Blue Satin are not aware of.

I am confident we will succeed, however I also know that on missions such as this, not every contingency can be anticipated. Vil has been hassling us for information about the humans. I have been pacifying him at B.B.B. headquarters with as little information about humans as I can without raising too much suspicion. But I do not know if we are fooling Vil. Vil, a small individual by Orishan standards, seems to have what humans call a "Napoleon complex" and tries to throw his weight around.

I just hope the B.B.B. does not interfere with our mission in Serbia.

Andy, the latest addition to our Hug, will remain in Pawtropolis, coordinating our efforts with the Knights in Blue Satin. We will be in a communication blackout until we are free of Serbian air space. We plan to land the F-117A on a secret Orishan base in Greece. We will radio Andy when we escape from Serbia via our H.A.R.V.E.Y. unit.

The H.A.R.V.E.Y. unit is still acting up, once in a while. I think the electromagnetic pulse that hit our ship may have fried some of his circuits. Louis is working on repairing the unit.

That is all for now.

Captain Schaumburg Harmony, reporting from the planet Earth.

The Mission to Serbia

In Sam's Versailles Bureau of *The Daily Press*, Scoop Schaumburg, dressed in his trench coat, fedora, and black three-piece suit, implored Sam to help the Orishans with their mission to "procure" a downed F-117A Stealth Fighter.

"Are you nuts?" Sam said. "I'm a reporter, not a spy! Use your super powers and just fly it out of there!"

"My powers only last twenty minutes at a time," Schaumburg said. "Besides, we would still need your help. We can't get into Serbia without you. We have contacted a dissident scientist in Serbia. Our friend Champ convinced him to help us. We have several agents on the inside. This will work, Sam."

"All I have to do is drive you guys into Serbia with a truck and pretend I'm a toy salesman?"

"Please Sam. You are our only human contact here in America."

Sam rubbed his chin in discomfort, thinking over Schaumburg's proposal.

"And I get to leave as soon as I drop you four off inside Serbia, right?"

"Yes, and you can come back here. You will only be gone for a few days. You have vacation time coming, right?"

"Oy, why am I mixed up with you aliens anyway?" Sam said, striking himself on the forehead. "I just hope we don't wind up dead!"

* * *

Sam purchased a special leather shoulder bag that accommodated Schaumburg, Louis, Leni and Chocolate, and then placed it on wheels so he could easily transport them around at the airports as well as to and from motor vehicles. Scorch also rode along for the mission, hidden inside the bag.

The Knights in Blue Satin created special passports for Sam so he could pose as a different person inside Serbia.

On the airliner from Chicago to Europe, Sam sat with the four "bears" who all rode in an empty seat, stiff like toy teddy bears.

The stewardesses all fawned over Sam, telling him how cute the "teddy bears" were.

Sam pretended to be a toy salesman, but cautioned that these samples were not for sale.

After an uneventful flight to Sarajevo, Sam rented a truck, and put the bears in the front seat next to him.

They had a long road trip to Serbia. The bears woke from their suspended hibernation to converse with their human driver.

"Leni, I've been meaning to ask you something," he said, noting she wore her Wizard robes.

"How come, if you are a female, you call yourself a Wizard, instead of a witch?"

"On Orisha, male or female, we are known as Wizards," Leni responded indignantly.

"It's just that on Earth, the magical women are called witches," Sam said.

"Witches on Earth are different, from what I understand," Leni said. "Wizards are all part of the Mystical Order of the Golden Paw. Witches, I believe, are associated with many pagan religions on Earth."

"Yes, Leni," Sam agreed. "What kind of beliefs does your magical order practice?"

"They are not beliefs," Leni said. "They are laws—universal laws discovered by Orishans and other beings, such as the Bengali, over a period of centuries by trial and error."

"Such as?"

"Such as the prime rule," the Paw interjected. Schaumburg was dressed in his Paw outfit. "Treat all beings as you would have them treat you."

"What else," Sam asked.

"We are all atoms of the creator, containing in miniature all of his attributes," Louis said, dressed in his pirate outfit complete with A.A.S.B. and miniature cutlass sword.

Sam looked at Lou's pirate outfit, and Lou's statement made him laugh.

"We must develop our spirit of self-sacrifice for our fellow beings," said the Paw. Sam believed that sentiment was appropriate coming from a super hero.

"All beings yearn to become one with the creator," Chocolate added. Chocolate specialized in discerning what people desire. Chocolate wore her Miss Libearty outfit.

"And finally, the work of a Wizard of the Mystical Order of the Golden Paw is to unite your body, mind and spirit so you become an instrument of the Divine," Leni added.

"Sounds pretty deep," Sam said, thoughtfully.

At that moment, Sam noticed they approached the entrance to Serbia. A checkpoint guardhouse stood at the entrance, requiring Sam to show his identification papers before entering the country.

"Schaumburg, I just realized, I can't speak this language," Sam said in a panic.

"H.A.R.V.E.Y. will translate for us," Schaumburg said, brandishing his tiny white rabbit attached to his left paw.

At the checkpoint, the security guard asked for Sam's papers.

To Sam, the guard seemed to actually speak to him in English because of the translation power of the H.A.R.V.E.Y. unit.

The guard reviewed his papers.

"You are a toy salesman?" the guard asked.

"Yes, I sell teddy bears," he said, indicating the four Orishans who were now stiff in a state of suspended hibernation. Scorch hid inside Sam's special bag.

"I like the super hero one," the guard said. "How much does he cost?"

"$175 American," Sam replied, hoping it was too much for this guard to pay.

"Ach! That is too much! I doubt very much you will sell your teddy bears in this country."

With that he waved Sam on and Sam gunned the fuel pedal of his rented truck.

"We have to contact Professor Verity next," Schaumburg said; awake once again from his hibernation.

Sam started sweating and seemed visibly shaken.

Chocolate took out a cloth and gently dabbed his brow dry.

"We will be okay, Mr. Arctophile," Chocolate said. "Do not be concerned. My big brother Schaumburg will get us through this."

"I know the Paw is powerful, but these guys mean business," Sam said. "And you guys plan to steal a military weapon from them. You are suicidal!"

"Stop it Sam," the Paw said. "Just drive us to Professor Verity and you can go back home. We'll . . ."

But the Paw could not complete his sentence.

Up ahead on the road was an upturned military vehicle with four armed soldiers pointing their weapons toward Sam and the Orishans.

Sam immediately started to slow down.

"Schaumy, use H.A.R.V.E.Y. to turn invisible and disarm those troops," Leni said.

Schaumburg grabbed a chocolate bar, gulped it down, pressed one of H.A.R.V.E.Y.'s paws and vanished. Sam stopped the truck 100 yards away from the soldiers. However, when Sam stopped the truck, that alarmed the soldiers.

Then, one of the soldier's rifles flew away from him and floated about 10 feet above the soldier's head. The gun began to collapse onto itself in mid-air by an unseen force. Ruined, the rifle flew away. The same thing happened to a second soldier's rifle.

The remaining two soldiers looked at each other in fear, threw down their arms and ran off in different directions, followed by the two soldiers Schaumburg had disarmed before.

Sam started driving again, turning off to the side of the road to avoid the upturned military vehicle.

Sweat beaded up on Sam's forehead again. When Schaumburg popped back into sight inside the truck cab, Sam jumped in fright.

Chocolate tried to sooth Sam again.

Chocolate Harmony, the counselor bear, a.k.a. Miss Libearty. She is also ship's science officer and ship's surgeon for the Schaumburg Hug of Orishans.

"See, I told you Schaumy would save us," Chocolate said.

Louis laughed out loud, pounding his fist on the seat.

"Did you see those soldiers run in terror?" Louis asked. "That was the funniest thing I ever saw."

"Turn left at this next road," Leni commanded. "We are almost at Professor Verity's village."

A Change in Plans

As Sam entered the tiny village of Anastasia, he pulled up to an Inn.

Leaving the bears inside the vehicle, he inquired about the location of Professor Maximilian Verity's residence.

Professor Verity walked up to the truck and woke the Orishans by pressing their paws.

"Quick, where's the driver?" the professor asked.

"He's inside looking for your house," Lou answered. The Orishans recognized the gray-bearded scientist from a picture provided by the Knights in Blue Satin. Verity climbed inside the truck and Sam came out of the Inn.

"I can't seem to communicate too well with the natives," Sam said. "Perhaps we should take in your translation unit . . ." But before Sam could finish he noticed the professor sitting in the truck on the far passenger side, the Orishans to his side.

"Get in and drive," the professor said.

"Who are you?"

"He's the aviation scientist we are looking for," Schaumburg said. "Let's go."

"Wait," Sam said. "I'm supposed to just drop off the bears here with you."

"Drive before someone suspects us of something," Verity said gruffly.

Reluctantly, Sam started the engine and spun away on the dirt road, following Verity's directions to his home.

As Sam, Verity and the Orishans arrived at Verity's home, two airfield security police greeted them, making an unannounced security inspection.

The "bears" had to quickly revert back to suspended hibernation, and Verity was hard-pressed to explain that these were toys for his niece in America. One of the guards picked up Chocolate, dressed as Miss Libearty.

"This is an American symbol," one guard said. "We will have to confiscate this one as being unpatriotic, Professor Verity."

"But wait," Verity said.

"If you resist, I will have no choice but to report you to the Air Field commander, and arrest your American toy salesman.

This upset Sam, but the security policemen left with Chocolate anyway. Verity rushed all inside, helping to carry some of the Orishans. Sam carried the bag in with Scorch, who remained very quiet inside.

Once awake again, Lou protested the guard taking Chocolate.

"We have to go after her," Lou insisted.

"The guards' quarters are at the air field," Verity said. "We will be able to rescue her when you procure the F-117A."

"We will have to alter our plans slightly," Verity said. "You, Sam, will be posing as a milk delivery man and deliver your load first thing tomorrow morning. I will have your papers ready."

"But I thought you were going to take the Orishans in?" Sam protested. "My part of this escape was supposed to be over now. I'm no secret agent!"

"They changed the security protocols just two days ago," Verity said. "Champ is hiding there near the F-117A, preparing for your extraction of the plane tomorrow."

Verity pulled out a crudely drawn map showing the layout of the airfield.

"Here is the hangar where the F-117A is being kept. It is fully fueled and operational, although it has no missiles on board," Verity said, pointing to one of the hangers on the map.

"This is where the air security headquarters are located. Those guards will still be sleeping because they will have finished tonight's shift at midnight. They begin tomorrow's shift at 2 p.m. I suspect Chocolate is not being turned in, but will be a gift for the guard's daughter or son. Here is where Champ is hiding. He will be providing the distraction, which will allow you to steal the airplane. You will need to dig your tunnel from outside the fence in this grove of trees to remain undetected by their perimeter alarms. Sam will drop you off outside, and then deliver his 'load' inside at precisely 5:30 a.m. That is the exact time of their milk delivery each day. You must not be early or late. This is very important."

"I don't get it," Sam said. "What's so important about this milk delivery?"

"It is the equipment Champ will need to create an electronic supersonic pulse. Champ will deploy the pulse just before Schaumburg and his team enters the hangar to retrieve the plane. The only catch is that the Orishans will only have three minutes before all the humans in the hangar wake up. You will need to wear these special earmuffs, or else you will be knocked out too. The Orishans are immune to the effects of the pulse. The timing on this is very important. I will have to contact Champ tonight with your H.A.R.V.E.Y. unit so that he knows not to set the sonic pulse off before you liberate Chocolate."

"You." Sam said. "You mean me? Oh, no. I'm doing no such thing."

"I'm going with Sam," Lou said. "I'll be able to help him."

"Good thinking Lou," the Paw said. "Leni and I will be digging through with Scorch's fire breath. She has been training him to be able to concentrate his dragon flame."

"He's a beary fast learner," Leni said of her pet dragon, proudly. Scorch the dragon, who was colored a smokey purple, seemed to blush at Leni's praise, then flapped his reddish-gold wings in a happy fashion. The baby dragon stood about 10 inches tall.

"Buck up, Sam," Lou said. "We'll be fine. And we'll get Chocolate back."

"Sam, you will be required to ride back in the F-117A with the Orishans and dragon," Verity said. "You cannot risk driving back from the airfield after they steal the plane. You would be stopped and questioned, possibly thrown in prison as a spy."

"Great!" Sam said. "I guess I am James Bond, after all. So why are you helping these aliens and an American steal this stealth fighter from your own country?"

"The Serbs threatened to murder my family if I did not work as a scientist in their reverse engineering laboratory," Verity said.

"Where is your family?" Sam asked.

"They are in a prison camp. You see, I am a Muslim. The Serbs hate us. So to spare my wife and children, I work for those monsters. Soon, my family and I will escape with Champ's help . . . Now, let us get some rest. We have to rise early and have much to do tomorrow."

Meanwhile, Chocolate sat in the security police officer's vehicle until he arrived back at the base. The guard put her on his dresser when he retired for the night.

As soon as she heard him snoring, she snuck down from the dresser and immediately climbed under his bed to transport to Pawtropolis via the Teddy Bear Zone. Then she contacted Perry Purple and explained their current status to him.

Purple said he could not contact her Hug yet because of the communication blackout during the mission.

"But we have to tell them I'm all right," Chocolate insisted. "They may not get my message."

"They'll figure it out," Perry told her, compassionately. "Go back to Toleni to be with Andy and see if they contact you there."

Early the next morning, Leni, Scorch, the Paw and Lou prepared with Sam to ride out to the airfield in the milk truck. The truck had been stashed under some trees behind Verity's home.

Sam stopped the truck before rounding a corner in the road that led to the airfield.

"Sam, remember, as soon as you and Lou drop the package and rescue Chocolate, hightail it back to this tunnel and meet us in the hangar," the Paw said to Sam. "We have very little time."

Sam nodded to Schaumburg. Leni hugged Sam and Lou. Schaumburg, Leni and Scorch got out of the truck and waddled quickly to the field of trees to begin "burning" the access tunnel. The hangar stood close to the outside fence; the tunnel they needed would only be a few feet long.

Sam continued to round the corner and on to the front gate, showing his papers to the guard and being passed on without incident. Lou was hidden under the dashboard in the truck.

Sweat began to bead up on Sam's forehead again.

Sam stopped in front of the mess building, and delivered the milk. One of the bottles contained the sonic pulse device. Sam saw Champ, whom he had never met, dressed in a martial arts outfit, scamper out to retrieve the device and move quickly back into the shadows.

Sam pulled up to the security guard's quarters.

Sam got out, but Lou exited later, unseen, and followed Sam into the building.

They arrived at the room where the guards slept, and Sam knocked on the door.

The sleepy guard who had taken Chocolate answered the door, recognizing Sam as the man who had "teddy bears."

"I will pay $300 American for the teddy bear," Sam said in Serbian with a thick accent, flashing the bills to the guard.

As the guard was focusing his attention on the cash, Lou climbed onto a case next to the door, then applied pressure on the guard's brachial plexus nerve found at the base of the neck, directly above the collarbone. As Lou applied his paw pressure, the guard fell down unconscious.

This surprised Sam.

"Vulcan nerve pinch," Lou said. "I saw it at your house on a 'Star Trek' television show."

Sam raised an eyebrow in puzzlement. Sam and Lou slipped into the room, pulling the guard back on the bed and closing the door.

"Chocolate, where are you?" Lou said in hushed tones. After a few minutes of fruitless searching by Lou and Sam, Lou suddenly came to a realization.

"The bed," Lou said.

"She's in the bed?" Sam asked.

"No, silly," Lou replied. "She must have used the Teddy Bear Zone to escape. She's probably been home all night."

"Are you sure?" Sam asked.

"She wrote it in the dust on the guard's dresser."

Sam saw strange writing, which looked like gibberish on the dresser.

"Let's get out of here and get to the tunnel," Sam said.

Captain Louis LaHug fires his Attitude-Adjuster-Sleeper-Blaster to stop a Serbian guard as Sam races to reach the tunnel while he carries Louis over his shoulder.

In the tunnel, Schaumburg and Leni watched as Scorch burned their tunnel toward the Serbian hangar.

Leni noticed an aura of worry on Schaumburg's furry face.

"Don't worry, husband," she said affectionately. "Sam and Lou will be back with Chocolate in a jiffy."

"Time is running out, Leni," he said to her. They hugged tightly. Scorch continued to burn the tunnel.

Sam picked up Lou and moved quietly out of the guards' quarters toward the entrance of the tunnel Scorch worked to create.

A Serbian guard spotted Sam, shouting "Halt!"

Sam ducked behind a stack of boxes.

Lou took out his A.A.S.B. "Sam, we've got to get out of here," Lou said.

"Duh!" Sam said.

"No, I mean from behind these boxes," Lou said.

"Why?" Sam asked.

"Because they are filled with munitions," Lou explained. "One strike from that guard's gun and we will all blow into billions of pieces."

"Cover me with your blaster," Sam said. He picked up Lou, holding him close to his chest like a small child. Lou could peer over Sam's shoulder, and aimed at the guard with the A.A.S.B. as Sam made a run for the cave. Lou shot the A.A.S.B. at the guard, but missed.

The guard fired back, shooting the blaster out of Lou's paw. Another guard spotted Sam running for the tunnel.

"I knew going back for Chocolate was gonna cause trouble," Sam said. "I only hope she's having better luck than we are."

Dragons Come In Handy

Champ prepared the sonic device in the hangar where the Serbs stored the F-117A, hiding behind some barrels of oil. He set the device to go off at a precise moment when the Orishans would be ready to emerge from the tunnel.

Inside the tunnel . . .

"Where did you get that thing, anyway?" Schaumburg asked Leni. "Did you conjure it up with your magic? Aren't dragons dangerous?"

"My dragon, with reddish-gold wings and soft purple scales, does not come from Earth or Orisha," Leni said to Schaumburg. "The animal hails from a planet in the Draconis star system. The dragons exist mostly in the same time phase as Pawtropolis and other Orishan settlements. I found Scorch around my farm soon after I established it, and we became friends. The unicorns have taught him to pop corn, and they play a popcorn catch game with him. They also play a bagel toss game, catching with their horns the bagels Scorch toasts in mid-air. With my influence and the influence of the unicorns, the dragon is growing up in a very different environment than he would normally, becoming a staunch ally of both the Orishans and the unicorns."

Schaumburg told Scorch to stop when he reached the point just before breaking through the hangar floor.

Just at that moment, the guard who spotted Sam and Lou sounded the alarm. Klaxons blared all over the compound.

Sam and Lou tumbled into the open end of the tunnel, but the guard ran close behind and continued shooting at them.

Schaumburg threw his A.A.S.B. to Lou who popped his furry head out of the tunnel to blast the guard outside to sleep.

Meanwhile, underground, Scorch, with Leni's help, started to burn the final access to the hangar floor.

"Where's Chocolate?" Schaumburg asked.

"She must have gone through the Teddy Bear Zone," Lou shouted back. "She left a note written in the thick dust on the guard's dresser."

"Clever girl," Leni said.

"Can't that thing burn any faster?" Sam asked nervously, as Lou continued to blast guards that tried to get near the tunnel.

"He's only a baby you know," Leni said, defending her pet. Schaumburg looked at his watch.

Lou finally entered the tunnel, running toward the others. He handed the A.A.S.B. to Leni, absentmindedly. Leni tucked it into her Wizard's robes. "This could come in handy," she thought to herself.

"Champ will be setting off the sonic device in just a few seconds," Schaumburg said. "We have to wait until after the humans are asleep. Sam, put on your earmuffs."

Inside the hangar, Champ watched the second hand on his watch, determining to set off the sonic device at precisely the prearranged time. In a few seconds, he punched the large red button on the Orishan sonic device. A strong, whining vibration shook the hangar. At first the humans slapped their hands to their heads in pain. In an instant, all the humans in the hangar and the guards outside simply dropped unconscious to the ground with loud thuds, some face down.

Unseen by Champ, an Arjogun agent (who was unaffected by the sonic blast) realized something was wrong as he heard the alarm then watched the humans drop before his eyes. The Arjogun guessed some Orishans might be trying to take the F-117A and scrambled onboard unseen by Champ. The Arjogun climbed gingerly inside the cockpit squeezing himself into a storage compartment.

"Ooo," Champ said to himself. "That must hurt," he added as he saw one aviation worker in a jumpsuit fall flat on his face hard, smashing his nose on the cement floor.

At that moment, Scorch broke through the floor, and the Orishans, Sam and Scorch clambered into the hangar.

"The plane's ready to go," Champ called to Schaumburg and friends. "Hurry! The humans will wake soon."

The sleek, black-skinned ship gleamed in the hangar lights like a dark demon. Schaumburg, Lou, Leni, and Sam all climbed the side-ladder leading to the F-117A cockpit.

Lou and Schaumburg began powering up the jet as Leni helped Sam squeeze into a corner in the cockpit out of the way. Because the plane designers made it for a human pilot, Lou took the stick while Schaumburg helped with some of the computer electronics and avionics. Both had trained long and hard, and knew precisely how to fly the plane in tandem. Leni kept a lookout, watching to be sure the humans in the hangar still slept.

Champ opened the hangar door and waved the crew off as the engine roared to life. The plane taxied out of the hangar. The black jet soared gracefully into the morning sky.

"Looks like we're home free," Lou said.

"Not yet," Leni said. "A Mig is scrambling to intercept us. The humans are awake and must have realized we took the plane."

"We're going to be shot down," Sam said in a panic.

"Relax, Sam," Schaumburg said. "Lou and I know a few tricks."

Lou first flew straight up, throwing the occupants against the back of the cockpit. The jet screamed against both gravity and friction in the air.

"Okay, Lou," Schaumburg said. "That's high enough—15,000 feet."

The Mig climbed after the Orishans.

Lou leveled out the plane then turned down to an inverted nosedive. The air around the plane screamed as if in pain.

The Mig pilot followed Lou straight down.

"The Mig is right behind us," Leni said, looking out the tinted cockpit window and hanging on so she would not fall to the bottom of the cockpit as the plane continued to descend.

"That's okay," Lou said.

Sam grabbed hold of the pilot's chair and hugged it in fear.

"We're gonna crash," he said.

Sam could see Lou continuing to bear down on the control stick of the jet. Seconds before slamming into the ground, Lou strained to yank back on the stick to climb again. But the stick was resisting. Schaumburg moved to assist Lou. Sam got up and assisted too. Between the three of them, they managed to turn the plane around and climb again. The jet soared high and fast, like a bullet shot from a rifle.

Sam sat back and relaxed. Leni looked outside.

"The Mig's still following," she said.

"We're at 15,000 feet again," Schaumburg said, watching the altimeter.

"Now, watch this," Lou said, a bit cocky. Lou moved the plane level again and it looked to the Mig pilot like Lou was about to dive again.

The Mig pilot started to follow the F-117A down again. Only this time, Lou veered sharply to the left. The Mig went into an uncontrollable spin.

Lou hit the throttle and sped off, zooming away too fast for the Mig to pursue at this point.

Leni watched as the Mig pilot struggled to regain control and became smaller and smaller in the cockpit window.

"You did it," Sam said, looking out the window with Leni.

Scorch jumped up and down in the cockpit, excited.

The Arjogun determined this could be a good time to make his move since the plane no longer forced him from one side to another inside the compartment due to strenuous G-forces. He slowly cracked the compartment door open, but remained unnoticed.

"Head for the Greek islands," Schaumburg said. "There's an Orishan settlement on Crete called August that is hidden to humans using a phase shift just like in Pawtropolis. I will attach H.A.R.V.E.Y. to the ship's computer to shift us into phase with August when we arrive."

Lou continued to fly the fighter toward Greece, thinking they were safe.

At that moment, the Arjogun burst out of the storage compartment, gun pointed at Leni's head. Sam peered out a window and did not notice the Arjogun.

Startled and taken by surprise, the Orishans raised their paws in the air. The Arjogun officer shot the H.A.R.V.E.Y. unit, knowing it was a danger to him. The H.A.R.V.E.Y. unit sparked and sputtered.

"This is not right," H.A.R.V.E.Y. said, in a slow voice. Sparks continued to fly from his head—wires protruded from his fur.

The Arjogun put his gun into Sam's back.

"Stop goofing around, Schaumburg," Sam said. Sam's reaction puzzled the Arjogun.

Sam knocked the weapon out of the Arjogun's hand without even turning around. Then, by accident, he elbowed the gray alien in the jaw, knocking it down.

Sam still peered out the window. This gave the Orishans their chance.

Schaumburg and the Arjogun scrambled for the gun. Leni stood off to the side. Lou continued to fly the plane. Sam turned around, surprised to see Schaumburg and the Arjogun struggling over the weapon.

Leni pointed her paw at the Arjogun and said, "Nap time!" The gray alien fell to the floor of the cockpit, fast asleep.

"A new trick I learned," Leni said, smiling.

Schaumburg grabbed some spare wires and tied up the Arjogun.

"Thanks for your help," Schaumburg said to Sam. The alien stood no more than three feet tall.

The Arjogun's appearance caused Sam to recoil. The Arjogun looked more like a lizard than a sentient being with its huge eyes dominating an angular face, which had two holes for a nose and a large mouth, but no eyebrows or hair. The Arjogun's skin seemed to be lined with scales like a reptile.

Schaumburg handed the Arjogun's weapon to Sam.

"You keep on eye on our stowaway," Schaumburg said to Sam.

"Uh, yeah, right," Sam replied.

Scorch fused the wires around the Arjogun with a small, concentrated flame so they would not come undone.

Leni and Sam looked at each other.

"He's an Arjogun," Leni said to Sam. "He is one of the creatures trying to enslave your world. He must be working with the Serbians."

Sam said nothing. He looked back at the Arjogun, who looked mean, even in sleep. Sam noticed the symbol on the Arjogun's space suit—a paw symbol with a circle around it and a slash mark across it.

H.A.R.V.E.Y. Unit
Damaged

The H.A.R.V.E.Y. unit sustained major damage during the mission to Serbia.

CHAPTER 10

CAREER CHOICE

Sam arrived at the Versailles Bureau Monday morning, affectionately carrying Schaumburg against his shoulder like a child, and opened the door to the Bureau office. By this time, mid-spring, 2000, Sam took Schaumburg to work with him almost every day. At night, Schaumburg traveled via the Teddy Bear Zone to Pawtropolis to work at his Orishan newspaper.

On the floor inside Sam's office Sam saw a note marked: "Urgent."

He placed Schaumburg by his Power Mac G-3 computer and opened the envelope. The note read:

I have more information for you on the alien conspiracy. Come to the George Washington Museum Gift Shop at 8 p.m. And come alone. You will know me by my white carnation.

No signature accompanied the note.

"What is it," Schaumburg asked.

"Could be nothing," Sam replied. "Then again, this could be the biggest story of my career. It's probably that kook who runs that museum. She has been spouting alien conspiracy theories."

"I have found, in my short time here on your planet, that humans tend to string together unrelated events and try to make sense of them . . . try to find patterns where none exist," Schaumburg said.

"You could be right," Sam said, sighing. "This will likely turn out to be nothing."

Then Sam's face suddenly blanched a pale white.

"Maybe this is Fred finally contacting me," Sam said. "I haven't heard from him in months. He's disappeared."

"You mean you still haven't found out what happened to him?" Schaumburg asked, now concerned.

"I did a story about a shooting and a blown up car across the street a few months ago," Sam said. "But I did not connect it to Fred then. Hold on a minute! I just realized. That car was the same make, model and year as Fred's and was blown up the day he was supposed to meet me here. We were down in St. Louis at the time so you could meet with the Better Bear Bureau. Remember?"

Schaumburg grew more alarmed.

"Didn't you have your fill of cloak and dagger stuff from our recent trip to Serbia?" Schaumburg asked.

"What did you ever do with that alien Arjogun stowaway, anyway?" Sam asked.

"The Knights in Blue Satin have him," Schaumburg said. "They are trying to convince him to switch sides and be a double agent. I doubt they will be successful. These Arjogun are very loyal to their leader. And they despise the Orisha."

"Come to think of it, it can't be Fred," Sam said. "Fred would not need to wear a white carnation for me to recognize him. Unless he's changed the way he looks."

Suddenly, the phone rang.

"*Daily Press*, Sam Arctophile speaking," he said.

"Sam, this is Izzie. Let's meet for lunch. We need to talk."

"Gotcha! How about McDonald's in Montreal?"

"I'll see you at 1 p.m."

After hanging up the phone, Schaumburg noticed Sam looked concerned.

"This is not good," Sam said. "The managing editor rarely asks me to lunch. I've been working at the paper for 10 years."

"Don't be so glum," Schaumburg replied. "Maybe it's a promotion or raise."

The glass door to the bureau office slid open, and a woman in her late 20s gracefully waltzed over the threshold. Her skin seemed naturally tanned a deep bronze—her hair dark brown, large eyes the same color.

She wore a dark, short skirt showing off shapely long legs and taking advantage of the warm April day.

Schaumburg immediately froze into suspended hibernation, perched next to Sam's computer and facing away from her. He wore his reporter's trench coat and black fedora with press pass attached.

"Oh, what a cute teddy bear," she said.

"Mrs. Cruz," Sam greeted her, nervously. "God, she's gorgeous," he thought to himself.

"Can you put this letter to the editor in for me?" she asked.

"Sure," Sam replied, tripping over the chair on his way up to the counter.

Cheryl covered her mouth so Sam could not see her chuckling at him. "Can I see the teddy bear?" she asked.

He picked up Schaumburg, and said, "He likes hugs," as he offered the stiff-Orishan to her.

She hugged Schaumburg.

She noticed a small white bunny banded to the "bear's" left paw.

"What's with the little bunny?" she asked as Sam read over the letter.

"That's Harvey, his invisible rabbit," Sam replied, honestly, not telling her that he was actually a hand-held computer unit. H.A.R.V.E.Y. had to be repaired extensively after the Arjogun agent shot the him on board the F-117A.

Cheryl warmly smiled, recognizing the "Harvey" joke related to the famous story of Elwood P. Dowd and his invisible white rabbit. The play became a movie starring Jimmy Stewart in the early 1950s.

"'Harvey' is one of my favorite movies," she said.

"Figures," Sam said sarcastically, under his breath, still reading the letter.

"What?" she said handing Schaumburg back to Sam.

"Oh, nothing," Sam quickly replied. Wishing to change the subject, he said, "What's your phone number? They will need it in case the editors have questions."

She jotted down her phone number on the letter.

The letter contained a plea to anyone who had information about her missing husband, Armando Cruz.

"Do you really think he's alive?" Sam asked, trying to be as compassionate as possible.

She did not answer.

"Thank you for getting this to your editor. I have to go now," she said and flitted out the door.

As soon as the glass door closed shut, Sam pressed Schaumburg's left paw.

The Orishan seemed to take a deep breath. His amber eyes, which looked like cold glass a moment ago, seemed to come alive with a soul inside.

"You love her," Schaumburg said.

"What??!!!" Sam asked, shocked.

"I can tell. It's in your eyes. They dilate every time she walks anywhere near you."

"You're imagining things," Sam countered and went to his computer to write the day's stories.

At 1 p.m., he sat down with his boss for lunch. He placed the now-stiffened Schaumburg on the seat next to him.

Izzie looked disgusted.

"I'm glad you brought the teddy bear," Izzie said while he unwrapped a Big Mac. "That bear and your career here at *The Daily Press* are the reasons we're meeting."

"Really?" Sam said, sipping his Sprite.

"You've got to get rid of that thing, Sam.," Izzie said. "It's hurting your credibility as a journalist and tarnishing the image of the newspaper . . . I have decided that either you lose the bear or you lose your job!"

Sam's jaw dropped in disbelief.

Love and Hate Are In The Air

After his lunch meeting with Izzie, Sam wandered a little dazed into the Montreal newsroom with Schaumburg tucked under his arm. Izzie had not yet returned to work.

"Hey, Tiger, why the long face?" Sam heard a female voice call out.

"Amy Sampson!" Sam said. "Hi!" Sam looked in Amy's bright blue eyes and watched as her mouth formed a warm grin.

"I forgot how pretty your smile is," Sam said.

"Idle flattery will get you everywhere," Amy said, flipping blonde bangs away from her eyes. "You know, Tiger, I can turn that frown on your face upside down, if you like."

"Amy, I don't think I'm right for you," Sam said.

"I'm not asking you to marry me, dopey!" Amy responded. "I just thought maybe you might like to spend an evening together some time. Just because we broke off our five-year courtship doesn't mean we can't be friends, does it?"

"You wouldn't mind that?" Sam asked.

"Of course not!" Amy said. "I still care about you! Now what's eating you?"

"Izzie told me to get rid of my teddy bear," Sam said, not making eye contact with her. "He thinks it's affecting my reputation as a professional reporter."

"So, Izzie is afraid of a teddy bear, huh?" Amy said, slapping Sam on the back, good-naturedly. "Must be a pretty scary teddy bear. Let me see him."

Sam handed Schaumburg to Amy. She gave him a warm hug. Sam smiled, knowing Amy was hugging more than just a teddy bear.

"So tell me, Tiger," Amy said.

"Yes?"

"You don't sleep with this little guy, do you?"

"He's married," Sam replied.

Sam's response stunned Amy.

"I certainly didn't see that one coming," Amy said, almost to herself.

"Here you go, Tiger," she said handing Schaumburg back. "Don't let Izzie get to you. A teddy bear doesn't affect your skills as an ace reporter."

Sam left the newsroom and headed for Versailles with a little bit more bounce in his step.

*   *   *

Later that evening, Sam waited outside the George Washington Museum for a man or woman wearing a white carnation to show.

Schaumburg stayed in Toleni with the other Orishans.

At precisely 8 p.m., a graying man in his middle 60s approached Sam. He wore a black suit with a white carnation stuck in his lapel.

He also wore a black fedora and tan trench coat, looking very similar to Scoop Schaumburg, Sam thought.

"Samuel Arctophile?" the man asked, extending a hand to shake Sam's in greeting.

Sam extended his hand to the stranger.

"Good evening," the stranger said. "I believe we have a mutual acquaintance, Fred Steinfeld."

"Let's talk on the park bench over there," Sam said, motioning to a bench at the George Washington Park adjacent to the museum.

"Fred wanted me to tell you he is fine, but in hiding," the stranger went on.

"And just why should I trust what you are telling me?" Sam asked. "Who are you, anyway?"

"Let's just say I am a protector. I am a former federal operative who had the highest security clearance," the stranger said. "I worked for several years on Project Unicorn. And I know you are harboring Orishans."

This grabbed Sam's attention. Other than the Armando Cruz report, he had never heard of this secret government project before.

"I have been a deep undercover source for Fred and you, indirectly, for many years only you never knew it," the stranger continued. "How do you think Fred has always been able to obtain government documents for you? Do you think he just happened upon them? I have been associated with Fred for many years since I tried to blow the whistle on Project Unicorn in the 1970s. His father was a family friend, and when Fred started working for the FBI, I used to channel documents to him which I knew he would leak to his friends in the news media, like you and Amy Sampson."

Sam remained skeptical.

"I thought the FBI put their agents through all sorts of tests to make sure they aren't the sort of people who would reveal government secrets," Sam said.

"The tests are not perfect," the stranger said.

"You wouldn't want to tell me your name would you?" Sam asked.

"Let's just refer to me from now on as Commander Black," he said.

"Okay, Commander," Sam said. "Let's assume what you are telling me is true. What can you tell me about Armando Cruz and his report on Project Unicorn? Is he alive? Was he on to something?"

Commander Black's eyes grew sad for a moment.

"I'm afraid Mrs. Cruz is going to have to depend on your investigative skills to determine his fate," Mr. Black said. "As for Project Unicorn, Armando's report is partly correct. But it is missing a key piece of information that even General Grant is unaware of."

"What's that?" Sam asked.

Just then Sam heard a popping sound, and suddenly . . . thud! Then he sensed nothing but blackness.

Sam woke up the next morning with an aching head. He felt a bump on his head. He realized where he was; still on the park bench only it was morning. He sat up, and saw spots of crimson gleaming in the morning sunlight where Commander Black had been sitting.

"Oh, my God!" Sam said horrified.

Sam darted his eyes around the scene in downtown Versailles, trying to discover what happened to him, still in a daze.

Sam's heart raced. He scrambled to his feet. He rushed over to the nearby police station, and banged violently on the dispatcher's glass window.

"Somebody help," Sam yelled to the dispatcher. "Someone may have been shot, or kidnapped, or both—in the park."

*   *   *

After hours of questioning by Versailles police, Sam crawled into his car and drove home to Streator. He intended to write a story the next day on the mysterious events of the night before.

Upon arriving at the newspaper bureau the next day with Schaumburg, Sam began writing what he knew about the circumstances surrounding Commander Black for that day's paper.

He phoned Izzie at the Montreal office to let him know he had a big crime story for page one that day.

"Forget it," Izzie said. "We can't print anything about that stranger in Versailles."

"What???!!!" Sam yelled.

"Just forget about it, Sam," Izzie continued.

Sam could not believe what he was hearing.

"But Izzie, I am a witness to a crime," Sam said. "How often do we get that close to a story?"

"We will not be printing anything in our newspaper about it, and that's final." Then Izzie hung up.

"What do you suppose that was all about?" Sam asked Schaumburg.

"I suggest you contact Mrs. Cruz about it," Schaumburg said. "You told me the stranger did not say what happened to her husband. But from your description, it sounds like this stranger knew what happened to Armando."

"I can't talk to her," Sam said. "She makes me nervous."

"She needs to know about what happened, Sam," Schaumburg said. "Besides, you'll get over your shyness with her."

"Now, stop it Schaumburg," Sam said. "I tell you I am not in love with her."

Schaumburg grinned mischievously. "Me thinks thou dost protest too much," Schaumburg said.

Disgusted, Sam picked up the phone and dialed Mrs. Cruz.

"Cheryl, this is Sam with *The Daily Press*," he said.

"Yes, Sam," she said, hope in her voice.

"Something terrible happened here in town the other night and I think it is connected to your husband," Sam said. "Can we meet and talk someplace . . . A place out in the open, but in a crowd?"

"How about we meet for lunch at the Washington Mansion?"

The Washington Mansion included a bed and breakfast establishment designed to look exactly like the Washington home, Mt. Vernon, and included a posh eatery on the Illinois River. Sam did not usually eat there, as the place tended to be a bit pricey. But he liked the colonial atmosphere and the excellent food.

"I'll meet you there at 11:30 a.m.," Sam said. "I'll reserve us a table out on the balcony overlooking the river. It's a nice day today."

Later, seated at the restaurant, Sam told the story of the stranger to

Cheryl. Cheryl's large brown eyes grew wide with horror. Sam had brought Schaumburg with him, giving him a separate chair to sit on. Schaumburg remained in suspended hibernation, but could hear the conversation.

"Oh, Sam," Cheryl said. "Somebody is trying to prevent us from knowing what's going on."

Sam paid the bill.

"Let's go for a walk," Sam suggested, picking up Schaumburg and pulling him close to his shoulder.

Walking very close down the lush path between the restaurant and the museum, Sam could smell a hint of patchouli spice in her long, brown curls that draped over her bare shoulders. Cheryl wore a dark sleeveless blouse fit for the warm spring air. Her pleated powder blue skirt fluttered in the warm breeze, showing more of Cheryl's shapely legs to Sam as they walked slowly.

"Sam, I'm frightened," she said, grabbing hold of Sam's arm. The small token of affection shot Sam's heart racing. He did not think about the danger she and he may be facing as he investigated the mysterious circumstances surrounding her husband's aircraft accident two years ago. He thought instead about how much his heart ached to tell this married woman how much he adored her.

They reached the museum entrance.

"Let's sit down for a moment," Cheryl suggested.

They sat together on a bench inside the museum entranceway. The entrance consisted of a long hall greeting visitors just before they paid a nominal admission fee. Elegant painted portraits of George Washington at various stages of his life lined the entranceway walls.

Cheryl sat very close to Sam on his right. Sam placed Schaumburg on his left. He could feel her soft hips brushing against his side.

She looked at him, tears welling up in her large brown eyes, streaming down her dark brown cheeks. Her eye makeup began to run, creating a black streak down her left cheek.

Schaumburg woke himself up from his state of suspended hibernation.

"Yo te amo," Schaumburg said.

"What?" Cheryl said.

Sam nudged Schaumburg, to try and get him to shut up.

"Oh, nothing," Sam said.

"I thought you said 'Yo te amo,' to me," Cheryl said. "That means 'I love you,' in Spanish."

"No, I was just coughing," Sam said, awkwardly.

Cheryl stopped crying and smiled softly at Sam.

"Cheryl, what if I discover Armando really is dead?" Sam said, softly, trying to change the subject.

"Why won't anyone believe me," Cheryl said, now angry. "He can't be dead, he can't be." As she screamed the words, she began thumping on Sam's chest with her fists. Then she slumped onto Sam's shoulder and sobbed.

"Oh, Sam," she said. "What are we going to do?"

Sam gingerly lifted Cheryl's head so he could look into her eyes. She looked back, boring deep into Sam's soul with her gaze.

Then Sam moved in to kiss her, and she moved in as well. They kissed gently.

Cheryl pulled herself away.

"Stop it!" Cheryl said. "I am a married woman! What are you doing? Get out of here!"

Sam, confused, got up, grabbed Schaumburg, and left the museum rapidly, saying nothing to her.

He brought Schaumburg inside the Versailles Bureau office.

"You should never have said that," Sam yelled at Schaumburg. Schaumburg became visibly shaken at Sam's angry tone.

"Yo te amo? What do you think you are, some sort of alien yenta?" Sam continued, now ranting.

A tear began to stream down Schaumburg's face as his furry chin trembled.

Sam realized he was being mean to Schaumburg and he bent down to hug the Orishan.

"I'm sorry Schaumburg," Sam said. "I should not have yelled at you. But you should not have interfered, either. Now look what you've done. She hates me."

Schaumburg was silent for a long moment.

"I'm sorry too," he said to Sam. "Humans are not like Orishans,"

Schaumburg said. "But I have learned a few things about humans in my few months on your planet. And you are in love with her."

"I should never have kissed her," Sam said.

"She feels guilty and believes her husband may still be alive," Schaumburg guessed. "If I were you, I would concentrate on learning the truth about Armando Cruz's fate. Either you will restore him to his wife, or you will free her to fall in love with you, depending on what you discover. If you are not meant to be with Cheryl, perhaps there is another."

"Schaumburg, to tell you the truth, I don't want to know if Armando is still alive," Sam said, sitting back down in his chair and putting Schaumburg down on the desk. "If he's still alive, I don't think I could bear to bring them back together. And I feel guilty about that, but that's how I really feel. I've always been so alone."

"Perhaps you have created your own loneliness," Schaumburg said. "You have chosen to fall in love with a woman who believes she is still married. It's almost as if you went out of your way to set yourself up to fail in this relationship."

Sam said nothing.

"Perhaps you are running away from a commitment to real love?" Schaumburg asked.

At that instant, something snapped in Sam's brain.

"That's exactly what Amy said when I broke up with her a year ago," Sam said. "She started talking about wanting to get married and having children. That scared the heck out of me."

"Who's Amy?" Schaumburg said.

"You just met her, remember?" Sam said, now grinning. "She's the hot blonde who works in the newsroom in Montreal."

Schaumburg noticed Sam's pupils dilated as he spoke of Amy.

Spy For Me

While Schaumburg worked with Sam in his quest to discover what really happened to Armando Cruz, Andy busied himself with his boss Perry Purple and the Knights in Blue Satin.

At a secret room inside *The Daily Times* skyscraper in Pawtropolis,

Perry talked with the Arjogun whom Schaumburg, Louis, Leni and Sam had captured when the Arjogun stowed away onboard the F-117A as the team of Orishans "acquired" the airplane from Serbia.

The Orishans had tied the Arjogun to a chair. Perry and Andy peppered the alien gray with questions.

"My name is Gobador," the alien said. "I was originally assigned to attack the Orishans who were guarding the Planet Serena more than 50 earth years ago. Orishans saved my life by healing my wounds. The Arjogun command decided to transfer me to Earth. I have been here ever since, working with the humans on Project Unicorn."

"You say you were saved by Orishans on the Planet Serena?" Perry asked.

"Yes," the Arjogun answered, almost spitting out his words. "You foolish Orishans believe in kindness and mercy. That Orishan commander should have killed me as a spy! Instead, he has his wife, a Wizard, heal my wounds, and let me go. We would have shot one of our agents if he showed that kind of foolish mercy to Orishans."

The Arjogun's attitude shocked Andy.

"Your beliefs go against everything the Mystical Order of the Golden Paw teaches," Andy said.

"Don't even try to reason with this one," Perry said. "He's an Arjogun! They only believe in hate. Look at the symbols they wear on their uniform."

Andy noticed his uniform had a paw within a circle and slash mark across the paw. In other words, a symbol for no paw, or no Orishans. This did not convince Andy.

"Perry, wait," Andy said. "Give Gobador a chance." Andy turned to the Arjogun agent again.

"Why did you stow aboard the F-117A?" Andy asked. "Were you trying to sabotage Schaumburg's mission?"

"Schaumburg!" the Arjogun snarled. "That was the name of the Orishan commander who spared my life on Serena! Are they related?" The Orishans did not respond to Gobador's question. After a few minutes, Gobador started speaking again.

"That can't be the same Orishan! That was 53 Earth years ago! That Orishan would look much older and grayer by now."

Perry and Andy looked at each other, puzzled. Then Perry remembered that Schaumburg crash-landed in Earth in 1947 but transported more than 50 years into the future through Leni's magic spell. Andy could tell Perry was deep in thought. Gobador seemed curious about what Perry was thinking.

Perry thought Andy might be correct about this Arjogun agent.

"You know, Andy, you might be on to something," Perry said. "This is no ordinary Arjogun agent. He seems to actually feel some compassion for the Orisha."

With that statement, the Arjogun became violent, straining at his bonds, and cursing Andy and Perry.

"Do you see this symbol on my uniform?" Gobador asked. "It means we hate the Orisha! Do you hear me? We hate you and all you stand for!"

Gobador spat at Perry's face. The thick saliva stuck on Perry's fur like syrup. Perry grabbed a napkin to clean it off.

"Yes, Andy. I think we may be on to something, indeed."

Andy looked at Perry, beary confused. Gobador looked exasperated.

*   *   *

Meanwhile, aboard an Arjogun spacecraft, the Arjogun interrogated Commander Black. An Arjogun agent named Snopple asked questions while another named Polaris stood by. The Arjogunians had tied Black at hands and feet to a chair facing the two Arjogun across a steel table. His face showed bruises from repeated beatings.

"Black, your pitiful band of agents known as the Protectors will soon be drawn out and destroyed," Snopple said. "So you might as well tell us who they are now and save yourself a painful death."

"Snopple, you are a fool!" Black said. "Before you can finish questioning me, I will be free of you and your horrid stench!" Black spotted Fred lurking behind the two Arjogun. The aliens did not notice the intruder. Fred had been following Black since the Arjogun abducted Black in Versailles.

"You humans are so arrogant," Snopple said.

"Ha!" Black yelled back at Snopple. "You conquer those who are weaker than you, and destroy those who are not. And you call us arrogant?"

Snopple and Polaris looked at each other, puzzled. But before they could ask another question, they felt hard thuds against the back of their heads.

Fred quickly untied the commander.

"Hurry, Commander," Fred said. "We have a helicopter waiting not far from here. We can sneak out of the saucer from the docking port on the bottom." Fred assisted the elderly commander, who was weakened from the Arjogun beating and torture.

The docking port flipped open, and Fred radioed the helicopter to fly in for the pickup.

"Hurry, before we're discovered," Fred shouted into his radio. A Ch-47 Chinook helicopter zoomed up to them. Fred started to lower Black down to a waiting pair of hands. But before Commander Black could leave the Arjogun aircraft, two gray hands pulled him back.

Gobador is an Arjogun soldier captured by Schaumburg's Hug.

CHAPTER 11

HEADING FOR A HEADSHRINKER

Sam reported to the Montreal office for a staff meeting the following Monday. He enjoyed the meetings because he had a chance to meet with the other reporters and catch up on some of the latest scoops they all investigated.

After the staff meeting, Izzie pulled Sam aside.

"Sam, can we talk in my office for a few minutes," Izzie said.

"Sure, boss," Sam replied.

Inside the glass cubicle, Izzie closed the door after Sam came inside.

"Have a seat, son," Izzie said.

"What's up?" Sam asked.

"I suppose you are wondering why we would not let you do a story on that strange situation with the man, the park bench and all," Izzie said.

"Yeah, I was kind of curious," Sam said. "But I've been here long enough to know when your decision is final. You're the editor."

"That wasn't my decision, Sam," Izzie said. "The Old Lady called me up that day."

Sam grew nervous at the mention of "The Old Lady." Nancy Jo Mason, the owner of the newspaper chain, acted as publisher of *The Daily Press*. She inherited the mantle of the business after her husband, Herbert Mason, died of a heart attack at the age of 55. There are seven daily and four weekly newspapers in the chain, all in north central Illinois towns.

When The Old Lady called, it meant trouble.

"What did she say?" Sam asked.

"She said she was called by the President of the United States," Izzie said.

"What the heck would Bill Clinton want with her?"

"Clinton specifically asked about you," Izzie said. "He wanted to know what story you were chasing and what story the paper would be publishing regarding a certain Project Unicorn and an FBI agent named Armando Cruz."

"Wow!" Sam said. "I must really be on to something if the President is involved."

"That's just it," Izzie said. "The President asked The Old Lady to kill the story, for national security reasons."

Izzie paused for a moment to gauge Sam's reaction. Sam remained pensive.

"What did The Old Lady tell you she decided to do?"

"Well, you know she's a Republican and hates Clinton," Izzie said. "She said to lay off the story for a few weeks, but then to . . . and I quote, 'Give Clinton Hell!'"

Sam and Izzie both laughed. Sam had worked for Izzie for more than a decade and knew Izzie would not run away from a good story, especially if the government warned the paper off. However, Sam grew suspicious of his boss.

."You must have struck a nerve, son," Izzie continued. "I'm taking you off the Bureau assignment. I will have Hobson cover your stories from our office. I want you to work on this story exclusively. The Old Lady has given us all the money we need. You are officially investigating Mr. Cruz's accident. I want you to go to Nevada and interview people at the National Transportation Safety Board. Use the Freedom of Information Act to get what you can on Project Unicorn. We're pulling out all the stops. And I am to assist you in any way I can."

Sam seemed very pleased with his bosses' support. He stood up and shook Izzie's hand.

"I knew you wouldn't let me drop this story," Sam said, as he was about to leave.

"There's one more thing son," Izzie said.

"What's that?" Sam asked.

"The Old Lady is growing more and more concerned about this teddy bear thing," Izzie said. "I know," he added, stopping Sam from saying anything. "I told her you were just playing around, and that it was harmless. She thinks a grown man should not be playing with teddy bears and wants you to see a counselor."

Sam sat back down, now shocked.

"She said the company will pay for the bill, 100 percent," Izzie went on. "We have already made an appointment for you. You are to report to Montreal Behavioral Center at 3 p.m. today for your initial interview."

Izzie waited a few minutes before going on. Sam said nothing.

"Don't worry, son," Izzie said. "I know you're not crazy. But one of the things the government will try to do is discredit you if you really dig up something. Your habit of carrying around teddy bears has not helped, either. I told you it would cause problems. We need to have documented proof you aren't looney tunes."

That made Sam feel more comfortable.

"Okay, boss," Sam said. "Whatever you say. I'll go see the headshrinker."

"You know Sam, you really should get rid of those bears," Izzie continued. "I had a teddy bear once, when I was a young boy. My father traded it in for a baseball bat and glove. It didn't hurt me, now did it?"

"You weren't upset that your father got rid of your teddy bear?" Sam asked.

"My father was a very rational man," Izzie said, now looking deep into his past to remember that fateful day when his bear "Joey" was taken from him.

"He was a doctor," Izzie continued. "He took my bear on the pretense that he was giving the bear a medical exam. I never saw Joey again."

"You've never forgiven your father for that, have you?" Sam asked.

"Nonsense!" Izzie said. Suddenly, Izzie's eyes became glazed over.

"Teddy bears are dangerous to children," he said, as if in a trance. "They will fool you into thinking they are your friend, then betray you when you least expect it! Don't trust them."

Then Izzie said nothing.

"Boss?" Sam asked.

Izzie gave no response. Sam thought perhaps Izzie was lost in his memories.

After Sam left Izzie's office, Izzie picked up the phone. "Get me the city desk!" he bellowed. "I want a story about how dangerous teddy bears are to children. Focus on that angle of the germs they carry when kids play with them . . . What? No, I want it for page one tomorrow!" Izzie hung up the phone.

*　　*　　*

Sam reported to Montreal Behavioral Center for his appointment, with Schaumburg in tow.

The receptionist smiled broadly at Schaumburg when she saw him. "How cute," she said. "Oh, and he's a reporter teddy bear!"

"He's my bud," Sam said. "He goes with me wherever I do."

"Mr. Arctophile, Dr. Daniels is expecting you. Go right in."

Sam and Schaumburg entered Dr. Daniels' office. The doctor, a slight man, red hair with red beard, and no mustache, looked like an elf without the pointy ears.

"Good afternoon Mr. Arctophile," he said, extending his hand to shake Sam's. "And who might this be?"

"This is Schaumburg," Sam said. "He's my bud. He goes with me everywhere."

"Aren't you a little old to be carrying around a teddy bear?"

"I work alone in the newspaper's Versailles Bureau office," Sam replied. "He keeps me company there."

"Do you talk to the bear?"

"Yes," Sam answered, honestly.

"Does he talk back?"

Sam stayed silent for a minute. "What do you think?" Sam asked.

Dr. Daniels said nothing in response.

"Mr. Feinberg, your editor, said you are about to work exclusively on a story which could be dangerous," Daniels finally said. "How does that make you feel?"

"How does that make me feel?" Sam replied. "I've had to work on dangerous stories before. I once did a series of investigative pieces on the Chicago Mob infiltrating the Versailles real estate market to legitimize their drug business. They tried to kill me by putting a bomb in my car. I found the bomb before I started the engine, fortunately."

"So, do you think of yourself as a sort of James Bond?" Daniels asked.

"No, I think of myself as a sort of investigative reporter," Sam replied, now disgusted.

"Why is your bear dressed as a reporter?" Daniels asked.

"Because he is," Sam said, without thinking. "I mean, he works with me in the Versailles Bureau. I mean he doesn't work. He just keeps me company."

"So which is it?" Daniels said. "Is he a reporter or just a teddy bear?"

"What do you want me to tell you, doctor?" Sam asked, growing frustrated. "Do you want me to tell you this is not really a teddy bear, but a strange alien creature from another planet? He comes from a planet that orbits a star in the constellation Ursa Major, also known as the Great Bear. And he was sent to Earth to save our planet."

"There's no need for you to be a smart alec, young man," Daniels said, not realizing that Sam was actually telling him the truth. "I do find it curious that a grown man would find it necessary to carry a teddy bear around with him," Daniels added.

"I've had enough of this," Sam said. "I'm not a nut ball, okay? Just sign the paper and tell my boss I'm perfectly healthy. I'm getting out of here."

Daniels rose and pressed a button on his desk.

"Please remain seated, Mr. Arctophile," Daniels said.

Two large men in white jumpsuits came into the room.

"Take Mr. Arctophile to the 'quiet' room," Daniels said. "I want him transferred to the sanitarium for observation."

"What?" Sam said in protest.

One of the large men took Schaumburg from Sam.

"Hey, give me back my bear!" Sam yelled.

"Let him keep it, for now," Daniels said. "We will test his separation

anxiety later." The man gave Schaumburg back to Sam, and then
escorted Sam and Schaumburg to a large room with glass mirrors on
one side. They locked Sam in the room alone. The room contained a
couch, a bed and a chair—nothing more. Sam guessed the mirror
allowed doctors to observe him while he could not see them. He knew
it could be dangerous to talk to Schaumburg, but had no choice.

"Schaumburg, don't awaken," he told the Orishan, who stayed still
in a state of suspended hibernation. "I know you can hear me. I want
you to get out of here by using the bed. Then go for help and spring me
from this looney bin."

Sam thought if he were being recorded, they would think he was
being delusional, or something. He placed Schaumburg under the bed
where Schaumburg safely transported unseen to Pawtropolis.

A few minutes later, Daniels came into the room.

"Mr. Arctophile, you will remain here for 24 hours. We will provide
you with meals, and there is a restroom off to the side there behind
that door. But you are not to watch television, listen to the radio, or
read anything. You will be observed the whole time. Now, I would ask
that you give me the bear."

"What bear?" Sam said.

"Your bear," Daniels said. "The one dressed in the trench coat
and fedora."

"I don't see any bear, do you?"

"I saw you put him under the bed," Daniels said.

"You're welcome to look under the bed, doctor."

Daniels, somewhat miffed, bent down to look under the bed only
to find nothing.

"Where is it?"

"Where is what?" Sam said.

"Don't be funny, young man," Daniels said now growing angry.
"Where is the teddy bear?"

"Dr. Daniels, are you okay?"

Daniels' face began to turn almost as red as his hair.

"I assure you, young man, we will find that teddy bear," Daniels
said. "You are to be deprived of the bear for 24 hours during this
examination."

"Why don't you get those two goons in white jumpsuits to search for this alleged bear?" Sam asked.

"Humph!" Daniels said, disturbed by the missing teddy bear. He motioned in front of the mirrors, and shortly, the two large men came in.

"Find that bear!" Daniels said.

Of course, their search turned up nothing.

This made Daniels even angrier.

"Mr. Arctophile, I don't know what your game is, but if you continue to be belligerent, I will be forced to prolong your stay at the sanitarium," Daniels said.

Sam started to worry now.

You're Just Jealous

Dr. Daniels sat reviewing a tape of his patient, Samuel Arctophile. On the tape, Dr. Daniels asked Sam a question.

"So, where is this teddy bear?" Daniels asked calmly.

At first, Sam did not answer. Then he looked up and smiled wryly at the doctor.

"You're just jealous because the voices only talk to me," Sam said. Then Sam started laughing out loud.

Dr. Daniels turned off the tape machine. Nurse Muriel Johnson walked into his office.

"It's been two months since we placed Mr. Arctophile under observation doctor," Nurse Johnson said to Dr. Daniels. Dr. Daniels got up from the desk and went to the observation window. Both Nurse Johnson and Daniels observed Sam through a two-way mirror. Sam sat strapped into a straight jacket, mumbling to himself. Sam's eyes had dark shadows beneath them.

"We have been observing him with surveillance cameras as well as live observation," Daniels said. "Why can't we find that teddy bear? I know he had it. He has been observed with the bear many times by co-workers and other eyewitnesses. What kind of magician are we dealing with here?"

"Have you tried using a truth drug?" she asked him.

"I have been refraining from using drugs just yet, so as not to damage his natural reactions to my tests and observations," Daniels said. "But perhaps you are right. Nurse, get me my medical bag. We'll get to the bottom of this."

A few minutes later, Dr. Daniels and the nurse came into Sam's room and administered the drug to him.

"Now, Mr. Arctophile, suppose you tell me the truth this time," Daniels said a few minutes later, as he checked Sam's eyes with a tiny flashlight to be sure the drug was working.

"Truth about what?" Sam said, groggy.

"About that teddy bear?" Daniels said.

"What teddy bear?" Sam said.

"The one you were carrying when you came to me two months ago," Daniels said.

Sam said nothing.

"I believe he is called Schaumburg?" Daniels said.

"What about Schaumburg?" Sam said, his eyes drooping.

"Ah ha!" Daniels said. "Now we're getting somewhere. Where is Schaumburg?"

"I don't know," Sam said.

"What do you mean, you 'don't know'?" Daniels said, frustrated.

"I don't know where Schaumburg is," Arctophile answered.

"We're getting nowhere here," Daniels said. "Look you pipsqueak," Daniels said. "Tell me how you made that teddy bear disappear!"

"What teddy bear?" Sam asked.

"Schaumburg!" Daniels said.

"Schaumburg is not a teddy bear," Sam said.

"What?"

"Schaumburg is not a teddy bear," Sam said again.

"I heard you," Daniels said. "If Schaumburg is not a teddy bear, what is he?"

"He is an Orishan."

Nurse Johnson and Daniels looked at each other, puzzled.

"What's an obershan?" Daniels said.

"Not obershan, Orishan," Sam said.

"What is an Orishan? Is that a brand of teddy bear?"

"Orishans are aliens from the planet Orisha," Sam said.

"His psychosis is deeper than I imagined," Daniels muttered to himself. "Tell me more about this planet."

"I don't know too much about it," Sam answered. "You should ask Schaumburg. He could explain it better. His planet is in the constellation Ursa Major, but I don't remember too much more."

"Did you say, 'ask Schaumburg'?" Daniels asked.

"Yes."

"You talk to your teddy bear?"

"What teddy bear?"

Just as Daniels was about to become exasperated again, a short, lanky man dressed in black with sunglasses and a black fedora walked into the room. Before Daniels could protest, a gun seemed to protrude by itself from behind the center of the man's buttoned blazer. The gun emitted a lime green light toward Daniels. He slumped to the floor asleep. A repeat of the green light hit Nurse Johnson, who also slumped down asleep.

The man went behind Sam, still seated in the chair in the center of the room. Several furry "hands" began untying the straight jacket, freeing Sam.

"What's happening, Schaumburg?" Sam said, a little giddy at the sight of the doctor and nurse falling asleep.

"Nighty night," he said to them, his hand now free. Then he waved at them. "They must be real tired."

"Shhh!!!" the stranger hissed, trying to keep Sam quiet as he escorted the drugged reporter out the front door of the clinic.

Waiting on the lawn of the clinic was the same F-117A that Sam helped Schaumburg and company steal from Serbia a few months earlier.

The man suddenly began to fall apart as he revealed to Sam four Orishans standing on top of each other's shoulders (Schaumburg, Louis, Leni and Chocolate). Schaumburg stood on top and hopped onto the top of the ladder and climbed aboard the jet.

"C'mon, hurry," Schaumburg hissed in hushed tones. "We don't know if there are other orderlies in there we did not zap with the A.A.S.B."

Louis, Chocolate, Leni and Schaumburg all climbed aboard, pulling up Sam, who seemed to be having a great deal of fun.

"We gonna go flying, Schaumy?" he asked, still loopy from the truth drug.

"Will you shut him up?" Louis said as he fired up the jet.

"Hey, he's been drugged," Chocolate said. "He can't help himself."

"I don't do drugs," Sam said, very loudly, with confidence.

"Never mind, Sam," Schaumburg said. "Just get in so we can close the canopy."

As the Orishans were preparing the jet for takeoff, Andy's voice came over the intercom.

"We just picked up an alert on our Paw Scanner," Andy said. "The military heard there was an F-117A flying around downtown Montreal. The jig is up, people. Fly that thing out of there."

"We're leaving, Mardi Gras," Schaumburg said, helping Lou with the controls.

Suddenly, they could hear gunfire coming from a security guard at the clinic.

"Somebody's trying to stop us," Leni said. "I'll obscure their view."

She cast a spell to create a cloud of smoke around the F-117A as it ascended and soared away safely.

Onboard, Sam began to wake out of his drugged state.

"What's happening?" he asked.

Chocolate hugged Sam.

"It's okay, Sam," she said. "You're no longer in that awful place anymore. We're taking you home."

A short time later, Daniels woke up from his blaster-induced sleep.

"Somehow, I don't feel angry anymore," Daniels said to himself. "Where did Mr. Arctophile go?"

Nurse Johnson awoke too, and suggested they review the security videotape to see what happened.

They reviewed the tape, seeing the short man in black enter the room.

"There, stop that frame and enhance," Daniels said. "I want to see the face of this strange man in black who abducted our patient."

After clicking the computer keyboard and directing that the image be enhanced, the face of the "man" seemed to look remarkably like the face of the teddy bear which Sam brought in with him at his original meeting with Dr. Daniels two months earlier.

"I think I need a vacation," Daniels said.

Motivations

The next day in the office of Nancy Jo Mason, publisher of *The Daily Press* of Montreal, Illinois

Dr. Daniels knocked nervously on her door.

Mrs. Mason, a frail, thin woman in her late 80s, answered the door.

"Come in Dr. Daniels," she said. "I trust you brought the tapes of Mr. Arctophile with you?"

"Yes, Mrs. Mason," Daniels said, nervously. This woman intimidated him. Then he noticed another man in the room with them, standing silently in the corner.

"Well then, play them for me," she said.

"Who is he?" Daniels asked of the other man.

"Oh, pardon my rudeness," Mrs. Mason said. "This is my personal physician and a member of the paper's board of directors, Dr. Xavier Montalvo. He will be giving me his medical opinion of Mr. Arctophile's condition."

"It will be obvious that this reporter, Samuel Arctophile, is a menace to himself and to the rest of society," Daniels said. "Your own managing editor, Izzie Feinberg, agrees with my diagnosis and wants to keep Arctophile institutionalized as well."

"We will make our own determination, Dr. Daniels," Mrs. Mason said sternly. "Mr. Feinberg was acting against my express orders by keeping Arctophile in your institution for two months."

"But Mrs. Mason . . ." Daniels started.

"Just play the tapes," Mrs. Mason insisted.

They reviewed the tapes showing Sam drugged and talking about the aliens that look like teddy bears, then the tape showing a strange creature that looked like a short, skinny man abducting Sam from the clinic.

"There, you see?" Daniels said. "This man is obviously delusional! Please release him back into my custody."

For the first time since Daniels came in the room, Dr. Montalvo spoke.

"What makes you think Arctophile is insane?" Montalvo asked.

"Are you nuts?" Daniels asked, now agitated.

"I thought we were talking about Mr. Arctophile's sanity," Montalvo said.

"Oh, I'm sorry sir," Daniels said. "What I mean to say is, Mr. Arctophile has developed the illusion that his teddy bears are living breathing beings and that they are here on Earth to stop some other aliens from destroying the planet. Don't you see? It's a typical paranoid delusion made up by a man with schizophrenia."

"Show him the picture, Xavier," Mrs. Mason ordered.

Montalvo opened a manila envelope and showed Daniels an 8 by 10 inch black and white glossy photo of Ronald Reagan talking to an alien gray.

"What is this, a picture from one of those supermarket tabloids?" Daniels said, laughing. However, Montalvo and Mason did not show the same amusement.

Montalvo took out another photo. This time it showed the crash site at Roswell, New Mexico with four "teddy bears" sprawled over the desert at night.

"This picture of the crash was taken by a being known as an Orishan," Montalvo said. "It was given to us by the being who shot it more than 50 years ago in Roswell, New Mexico."

"Don't tell me you two believe in this alien garbage, too!" Daniels said.

"Dr. Daniels, Dr. Montalvo and I are part of a group of secret government operatives called the Protectors. We are working with the Orishans to find out the truth behind what the alien grays are plotting. We already know the grays are conducting nefarious medical experiments on humans, with government sanctions. Sam was investigating the disappearance of an FBI agent named Armando Cruz. We want to find Cruz, too, and are giving Sam all the help he needs in locating him. This conspiracy between our government and the alien grays has national and worldwide implications. We will allow Mr. Arctophile back on the job, and if you or anyone in your clinic ever speaks about Mr. Arctophile's assignment to anyone, we will sue your clinic for slander and have you arrested for interfering with a criminal investigation. Is that understood?" This stunned Dr. Daniels. "But Izzie Feinberg specifically told me Arctophile was nuts!"

"You may leave now," Mrs. Mason said.

Daniels picked up his videotapes and scrambled for the door. But before leaving the office, he turned to both of them, saying, "This is not over. I will have that man Arctophile committed to a mental institution. Mark my words."

After Daniels left, Mason turned to Montalvo. "Can we pull his medical license, have him discredited?"

"The Protectors don't work that way," Montalvo said. "We are not the NSA or the CIA. No, we will just have to allow Dr. Daniels to make the first move and use that to discredit him. Nobody will believe his ranting. Besides, your video machine has already destroyed his tapes."

"Yes, but he may have made copies."

On the way to the car, Daniels noticed the videotapes started smoking. He dropped them, frightened. He tried to stomp out the fire to no avail. The tapes all self-destructed before his eyes.

"Who are those people?" Daniels asked himself.

*   *   *

Sam sat down on the bench at the George Washington Park, overlooking the museum. Cheryl sat next to him. He looked more rested, but still tired from his experience at the clinic with Dr. Daniels. He planned to start back at the Bureau the following Monday, but on special assignment to help Cheryl find out the truth behind her husband's accident.

Sam and Cheryl hadn't spoken since the night of the inappropriate kiss.

"I've missed you, Sam," Cheryl said. "I'm glad you're back. They told me at the newspaper office you were at the hospital, but did not give me any details."

Sam looked into Cheryl's large brown eyes, admiring her long dark eyelashes.

"Stop looking at me like that, Sam," she said. "It can't be like that."

"I'm sorry, Cheryl . . . I mean Mrs. Cruz," Sam said. "I was out of line. I never should have kissed you."

"No, no," Cheryl said, putting her hand softly on Sam's chest. "It wasn't just you. I kissed you back. We just can't, that's all."

"You are a married woman," Sam said. "I never . . ."

"Stop it, Sam," Cheryl said. "As long as there is a chance Armando is alive, I must stay faithful to him."

"I understand," Sam said, now a little sadder.

"But we will remain good friends, especially now that your paper has agreed to allow you to work exclusively on the story about my husband."

"I promise you, Cheryl, if he is alive, we will find him and rescue him from whatever prison he is in," Sam said.

"I know you will, Sam," she replied, looking deep into his soul with her eyes again.

"Sam, can I ask you a question?"

"Sure."

"Why did you become a journalist?"

"I always liked to write," Sam said. "When I was in grade school, and the teacher asked us to create a story, I loved it. I used to write stories all the time, creating characters and stuff. I enjoyed creating my own heroes for my stories. I read a lot of comic books and stuff, too, which influenced my creative writing. I would write extra stories and turn them into my English teachers, who encouraged me. In my tenth grade at Kankakee High School, the English teacher suggested I take a journalism course. At the time, I had taken a drafting class and thought about going into the field of architecture. I talked it over with my folks. My mom said I would like journalism. She said I was always writing anyway—might as well make a living doing it. So, I dropped my drafting class after one semester and took journalism. There were three of us in the beginning class; Fred Steinfeld and Amy Sampson were the other two students. The rest studied in the intermediate class, already putting out the paper. The teacher, Mr. Gillespie, taught the three of us the basic inverted pyramid structure of a news story, putting the most important information first, answering all the questions—who, what, where, when, why and how. Then I got my first assignment. I was to interview the math teacher, Mrs. Slope, who earned a special teaching award. So I called her up, scheduled an interview and met her for the appointment."

"Yes, what happened?" Cheryl said, seeming very interested.

"I went to her office. She sat behind her desk, a very large woman. I sat down in front of her. She looked at me. I looked at her. She looked at me. I looked at her. This went on for a couple of minutes."

Sam started to laugh.

Cheryl slapped Sam in a friendly manner on the shoulder.

"Go on, silly," she said. Her voice had a lilting quality, almost like laughter, Sam thought.

"Well, after a couple of minutes of us staring at each other, I finally figured out that I should start asking her questions for my story," Sam continued.

"No kidding!" Cheryl said, amused.

"Cheryl, it was just like this conversation we are having right now," Sam responded. "I fell in love with journalism at that moment and I've been hooked on it ever since. I asked questions, she answered, and I wrote down her answers."

"So how did you start in the field?"

"I started working for *The Daily Press* while still in high school," Sam replied. "I covered features and a few board meetings in the outlying areas around Montreal for a buck an inch. That helped pay my way through college at Illinois State University. After graduation, and after working at some other papers, I eventually landed a job at *The Daily Press*. I love this job. It's like a calling to me, not just a job. I get to root out corruption in government by exposing those who abuse their power to the public. I get to shine the light of day on injustices. It's satisfying to see people, for example, come to the aid of a single mom who can't afford to give her children any Christmas presents because the state screwed up and won't give her the child support payments she is due. After that story ran, she was flooded with gifts from people all over La

Salle County. Her three kids had the best Christmas ever that year.
And the state fixed their problems with child support payments to
single parents. Stories like that keep me going."

"I'm glad it's you helping me find out what really happened to
Armando," Cheryl said.

Sam sighed.

"You must be tired, Sam," Cheryl said. "I better let you go home.
You have to rest up to start your work Monday. At least you have the
weekend to rest."

"Cheryl . . . Can we do something this weekend?"

"Okay, I'm game," she replied. "We can take Jose. Want to go to
Chicago or something?"

"Let's take in the Field Museum," Sam said. "We can hop on a
Metra train in Joliet."

"Sounds great!"

"I'll come by Saturday morning, about 10 a.m."

"Okay, Sam," Cheryl said. "I'll see you then."

Then Cheryl kissed Sam on the forehead and got up to walk back
to the museum to go home to her apartment upstairs.

Sam watched her walk gracefully away.

"She's an ethereal vision of angelic grace and loveliness," Sam said
to himself, sighing again.

*   *   *

That Saturday, Cheryl observed Sam and Jose as they rode the
train from Joliet to the Loop in Chicago. Sam brought his teddy bear
with him, which delighted Jose.

"His name is Scoop Schaumburg," Sam said to Jose. "He is a
reporter just like me. And he writes stories for a daily newspaper for
teddy bears."

"Jose is enthralled with these stories Sam is making up," Cheryl
thought to herself. "Look how Jose is gazing at Sam with his adoring
puppy dog eyes. I am glad Sam is around to fill in while Armando is
missing."

In the third floor office of the Montreal *Daily Press*, two reporters sat chatting that same morning outside their boss' glass office door. Kevin Murphy, the new kid in the newsroom, had just finished journalism school and was on the job for two weeks. He hadn't even met Sam yet. He was talking with Amy Sampson, investigative reporter for the paper. Amy towered over the bespectacled Murphy, who stood 5'5." Sampson was taller at 6'2" and she wore short skirts to show off her pleasing, hourglass figure. Even though she bobbed her hair short around the curves of her face, she could pull it off without looking masculine. But the feature that struck Murphy the most about Amy was her ear-to-ear grin surrounded by luscious lips.

Murphy, at the age of 22, sat enthralled by Miss Sampson's beauty.

"Why is the boss all alone in the dark in his office on a Saturday morning?" Murphy asked Amy.

"First off, Kevin, it's not 'the boss,'" she said. "Call him Izzie. He prefers it."

"Izzie. His name is Israel Feinberg. What kind of a name is Izzie?"

"Never mind. And next, he is not to be disturbed when he is in the office by himself in the dark. That's his signal to us that he is sort of— not there."

"Why?"

"He's a little upset," Amy went on. "One of our ace reporters, Samuel Arctophile, has just spent two months in a lunatic hospital and he escaped. The shrink wants him back and Izzie had to fight with the paper's owners about allowing Sam back on the job."

"Is this Sam guy crazy or what?"

"Naw," Amy said. "He just carries teddy bears around with him all the time. That made Izzie think Sam could be a few bricks short of a full load."

"So, is he?"

"Sam?" Sampson said. "Samuel Arctophile is the best investigative reporter I have ever had the pleasure to work with," she said. Her eyes twinkled as she described Sam. "Sam and I went to high school together. I've known him for a long time. He's kind of a jerk with women, though. Izzie and Sam have been an award-winning team for 10 years now. Only Izzie got real upset when Sam starting carrying around those teddy bears all over the place."

"Did you and Sam have a thing going or something?"

"Why did you ask that?" Amy said, blushing.

"When you described Sam, I could see something in your eyes," Murphy said.

"Sam and I have a history," Amy explained. "We started to date once. I think I love the big dope." She turned her bright blue eyes to the window outside, looking winsome. "We should be an item. But Sam is too shy."

"This Sam guy has no idea you love him, does he?" Murphy asked.

Amy said nothing.

Murphy started feeling uncomfortable, and wanted to change the subject.

"What's a grown man doing carrying around teddy bears, anyway?" Murphy asked. "Does he take them with him to interviews and board meetings?"

"Naw, he leaves them buckled in the passenger seat of his car," Sampson said. The two reporters both laughed out loud.

"Does Sam sleep with his teddy bear?"

"He says the bear is married," Amy replied.

Both laughed again.

"Izzie is very disturbed about Sam carrying around that bear all the time," Sampson said in hushed tones now. "He told me once that people in Montreal think Izzie should fire Sam for doing it because it makes the paper look silly. I think Sam has just made too many enemies being a good investigative reporter, that's all. But Izzie needs to get over this teddy bear thing and just let Sam do what he does best, being a good investigative reporter."

Inside the managing editor's office, Izzie spoke on the phone.

"Listen to me," Izzie said. "You have to start acting outside the law. That's the only way you are going to be able to accomplish your mission. Do you honestly think you can stop him through conventional means?"

"He's very powerful," the voice on the other end of the line said. "He has amazing strength when he ingests the human confection chocolate."

"Didn't you say his younger brother has the same powers?"

"We think so, yes," the voice answered.

"Then use his younger brother. Wipe out his memory, or something, and use him to infiltrate the enemy camp. We will not only be able to keep tabs on his movements, but ultimately, we will be able to destroy him by taking advantage of weaknesses we discover."

"Brilliant, sir," the voice said. "However, we have already done that. Andy is posing as this Mardi Gras character. He has no idea who he really is or how he has the same powers as the Paw. We came up with the same plan that you have. It's nice to know you are every bit as diabolical as we are. Are most humans just like you?"

"I'm different," Izzie said. "Ever since I was about four years old, I learned the hard way that you can never trust anyone but yourself."

"We'll continue to execute our plan, sir," the voice on the other end said. "I myself will devise a costume just like the Paw and Mardi Gras to disguise my own identity. That will allow me to act outside the law more easily since nobody will know it's me behind the mask. I will continue to use Andy to infiltrate the Paw's inner circle. We will soon be able to stop the Paw, sir."

"You better," Izzie said. "We don't want anyone preventing the Arjogun from building that weather control device. It is vital to our interests." Then Izzie slammed the phone down.

* * *

Fred and Commander Black lay strapped down to tables onboard the Arjogun ship.

Snopple injected each man with a drug.

"That is an Arjogun truth serum," Snopple said. "Now, with a little help from this chemical, you two will tell me the identities of all involved with the so-called 'Protectors.'"

Fred and Black looked nervously at each other. But before the interrogation could begin, another Arjogun came into the room.

"Leave us," Snopple said. "This is an interrogation. Where is Polaris, my aide?"

The Arjogun said nothing. Instead he pulled out an Orishan A.A.S.B., putting Snopple to sleep.

Then the mysterious Arjogun began untying both Black and Fred. "My name is Gobador," the Arjogun said. "I am working with the Orishans undercover now. I have contacted your rescue helicopter. This time, you will be able to escape. Did Snopple inject you with the serum yet?"

"Yes, both of us," Fred said as he rubbed his wrists.

"That is bad," Gobador said. "I hope you do not have the same reactions other humans have had to the Arjogun truth drug."

"What reaction is that?" Black wanted to know.

"The drug causes a slow and painful death in humans."

Fred and Commander Black were speechless.

"Hurry, we must get you to the rescue helicopter," Gobador said.

CHAPTER 12

SUPER VILLAIN MATCHES WITS WITH THE PAW

BY SCOOP SCHAUMBURG
THE DAILY TIMES OF PAWTROPOLIS

PAWTROPOLIS, IL, Oct. 10, 2000—Just like Superguy has his nemesis, Luther Lexicon, the Paw now has his nemesis—the Frown.

The Frown revealed his existence this week when he threatened to murder hundreds of Orishans working in the Pawtropolis 50-story Capital building downtown. He planted a bomb in the building, and then taunted the Paw to save the Orishans in the building before the bomb exploded.

Instead of telling the Paw where the bomb was, he gave the Paw an enigmatic clue, a riddle, taunting the Paw to figure out the riddle before it was too late. The Paw had one hour to solve the puzzle.

The Frown wrote the following riddle on a piece of paper:

WHAT IS CLEAR, TASTELESS, AND YET MORE PRECIOUS THAN NECTAR OF THE GODS? WHAT KIND OF HOUSE IS SO COLD YOU CAN'T LIVE IN IT YET PROVIDES YOU WITH NOURISHMENT? ANSWER THESE RIDDLES AND YOU

WILL FIND THE PACKAGE THAT IS SLATED TO DESTROY THIS BUILDING IN EXACTLY ONE HOUR.

Along with his trusty sidekick, Mardi Gras, the Paw courageously rounded up all the people in the building with a super feat of strength and speed, scooping them all into a crop harvesting bin used on a farm just outside of town, belonging to a Wizard Orishan.

The Paw and Mardi Gras managed to save all 350 Orishans working in the building, while police and fire crews evacuated nearby office buildings on the block and a bomb squad began searching through the Capital building.

While the action took place, the Frown piped in an image of himself over all the office computers, chastising the Paw for being a "fraud."

While the Paw struggled with the riddle, Mardi Gras seemed to turn on the Paw for a few minutes, actually obstructing the hero from finding the bomb.

"The Frown seemed to have some kind of mind-control device fixed on Mardi Gras," the Paw told *The Daily Times* this morning.

"I do not know why the mind-control only worked on Mardi Gras and did not affect me," the Paw continued.

When asked what the Paw used to solve the Frown's riddle, he said he used the help of an assistant back in his now-famous Paw Cave.

The Daily Times staff was able to observe Mardi Gras and the Paw in action starting just before the mind-control device took over the Paw's sidekick. They were busy working to solve the riddle.

*   *   *

Scoop Schaumburg stopped typing out his story for a minute, trying to remember the events that transpired earlier that day . . .

"Gosh, Paw," Mardi Gras said to the hero. "Could the answer to the first question be plain old ordinary water?"

"Right you are, chum," the Paw replied. "But the second question is trickier. He seems to be referring to a refrigerator, but there's more to it than that."

For a split second, the Paw seemed to be hearing a voice over a radio. "Yes, that's it," the Paw announced. "He's hidden the bomb in one of the office water coolers."

"Of course," Mardi Gras said. "How positively evil! It could be one of hundreds in this high rise office building."

At that moment, Mardi Gras' eyes seemed to glaze over. He slowly walked up to the Paw and held both of the Paw's paws tightly.

"What are you doing," the Paw asked Mardi Gras.

"You-must-not-stop-that-bomb-from-exploding," Mardi Gras said in a monotone voice, as if in a trance.

Both tried using their super strength to break free from each other, but to no avail.

"Stop it Mardi Gras," the Paw said, almost pleading now. "I have to find that bomb before it's too late."

At that instant, the computer monitors in the building all carried the Frown's evil face and menacing cackle.

"Poor Pawsie-wasie," the Frown taunted. "Can't break free of your pal's grip? Perhaps you two will be blown to smithereens instead of the office workers, eh?"

"Mardi Gras," the Paw said. "Snap out of it! It's this evil guy's mind-control on you!"

At that moment, the Paw stared deep into Mardi Gras eyes.

"Yes, I think I can break through," the Paw said to Leni, telepathically listening from his secret Paw Cave.

"Oh, that's good, Paw!" the Frown shouted over the computer monitors. "Keep up the staring contest. That will save your hides for sure! Ha,ha,ha,ha,ha!"

"It's working," the Paw said. Then he started to talk softly to Mardi Gras.

"Listen to the sound of my voice," the Paw said. "It's me, the Paw. I am your friend. The Frown is our enemy. Listen to the sound of my voice."

"The clock's ticking, Paw!" the Frown taunted. "You have less than 10 minutes before you are a dead Orishan. And you still haven't found the right water cooler yet!"

The bomb squad chief found the Paw and Mardi Gras.

"Chief," the Paw said. "I need your help. Can you take out the object in the third left pocket on my utility belt?"

The officer complied, pulling out a supersonic Paw mind-control descrambler.

"Great," the Paw said, still in the vice-like grip of his hypnotized partner. "Now, set the device for anti-mind control, aim it at Mardi Gras' eyes and place it under my chin."

The officer gingerly followed the Paw's orders, then departed.

"Listen to me!" the Paw said. "You have to fight it! You have to listen to the sound of my voice!"

The beam from the descrambler started to make Mardi Gras' furry face glow bright red.

"I think it's working," the Paw said.

At that instant, Mardi Gras relaxed his grip on the Paw's paws and seemed to be himself again. The Paw placed the descrambler back into his utility belt pouch.

"What happened?" Mardi Gras asked, looking confused.

"Never mind," the Paw said. "The bomb's in one of this building's water coolers. We have less than 10 minutes to find it. You take the top 25 stories. I'll take the bottom 25."

*   *   *

Scoop Schaumburg went back to pounding out his story:

The Paw and Mardi Gras had about five minutes of super powers left, but they zoomed around the building at blinding speed, darting from office to office until they located the bomb.

The Paw found it four minutes later, leapt out a window and flew straight up into the sky to allow the bomb to blow up harmlessly over Lake Orisha.

"I had to eat some more chocolate on the way up over the lake before the bomb went off, otherwise I would have been blown up along with the bomb," the Paw told *The Daily Times* later.

And what about Mardi Gras' problem with the Frown's mind-control device?

"It seems that only Mardi Gras was affected by whatever device the Frown was using," the Paw replied.

"We have reason to believe that it is Arjogun technology," the Paw continued. "We still have many questions. In the meantime, I plan to stop this Frown from hurting anyone in the future."

In truth, however, nobody knows who the Frown is. He is an Orishan, but he wears a black facemask over his eyes to hide his identity. He is dressed in a blue cape similar to the Paw's. His fur is colored cream beige. But *The Daily Times* has learned nothing more about him.

The Paw and police authorities are asking anyone who may recognize the Frown's recorded voice on the computer monitors or has any other information leading to his identity to please contact the authorities as soon as possible.

Perry Purple, editor of *The Daily Times*, believed it inevitable that once a super hero like the Paw showed up in Pawtropolis, a super villain would follow.

"But this Frown seems more evil than any of those comic book super villains," Purple said. "He also seemed bent on murdering innocents, as well as killing the Paw. Lucky for the Paw he was able to shake Mardi Gras out of that mind-control spell or the city would be minus one skyscraper and two super heroes."

*   *   *

As Scoop Schaumburg continued to bang out his story for the next edition of *The Daily Times*, Perry Purple, shut away in his office, called up the local television station.

"Yes, can you have Fatima Furbulous come to my office please?" Purple said. "Yes, it's concerning coverage of this villain, the Frown."

A few minutes later, Furbulous drifted into the newsroom, haughtily carrying her nose high as if she could not bear the smell of newspaper reporters.

She knocked on Purple's office door.

"Yes, Mr. Purple," she said in a breathy voice.

"Come in, Miss Furbulous," Purple said. "I'd like to discuss this new villain on the scene, the Frown."

"Why, yes," Fatima said. "Did you see my coverage of the Paw trying to save those people in the capital building?"

"Yes I did, Miss Furbulous," Purple said. "And I wanted to know how you learned that the Frown had Arjogun technology?"

"Why . . . uh . . . the Frown told me," she finally said.

"You interviewed this evil character?"

"Uh . . . er . . . Why of course, Mr. Purple," Fatima said. "Do you think I work for some rag that only covers heroes? We at the television station cover all the news, including the bad guys."

"Don't give me that, Miss Furbulous," Perry pushed. "What do you know about this Frown character? Is he really an Orishan?"

At that moment, Fatima Furbulous jumped up from her chair and angrily pounded her furry fist on Purple's desk.

"What gives you the idea that he is anything but an Orishan?" she screamed at him. "I suppose you think I am not an Orishan as well? How dare you!"

With that, Furbulous stormed out of Purple's office.

"Me thinks thou dost protest too much," Purple said to himself as he watched the beautiful television newscaster rush out of the newsroom and enter a Bearavator.

Test Flight

Toleni farm on the outskirts of Pawtropolis, Illinois, Oct. 15, 2000, 1 p.m.

Captain Louis LaHug worked inside the cockpit of the F-117A, now being held secretly inside the Paw Cave. Chocolate assisted her boyfriend as he worked to modify the interior heads-up display and reconfigure the engines. Chocolate and Louis started dating when they landed on Earth.

"We have to create a platform for the H.A.R.V.E.Y. unit so he can easily be attached for true stealth mode," Louis said as he worked a tool to reconnect some wiring in the cockpit computer electronics. He was lying on his back with his head inside the electronic guts.

"But I thought this plane was already invisible to human radar," Chocolate said as she attached a flat disc to the cockpit. She sat on the floor of the cockpit near Louis.

"No, true stealth," Louis said. "With H.A.R.V.E.Y. on board, we can phase shift so that no humans can ever detect us, visually, or with any of their primitive instruments."

"Why?" Chocolate said.

"When you go flying around a $40 million piece of American hardware, it tends to create suspicion among the humans," Louis said, half-joking.

"Humans are very suspicious as a species," Chocolate said. "They need to learn to trust each other more."

"And we Orishans could learn a little bit from their suspicious nature," Louis said. He pulled himself out of the cockpit electronic wiring and sat up to look at Chocolate. "Remember what Nerwonduh told us?"

"About what?" Chocolate said.

"About not trusting anyone and questioning everything," Louis said.

"Yes, but that is very hard for Orishans to do," Chocolate said.

"That's precisely why Nerwonduh told us to be more suspicious," Louis said. "Look what happened to Andy last week. He was placed under the mind-control of that creep, the Frown."

"What does that have to do with trust?" Chocolate wanted to know.

"Don't you see?" Louis said. "We don't really know who Andy is."

"What are you saying?" Chocolate said, now upset.

"Andy could be a spy for the Arjogun," Louis said.

"Stop that!" Chocolate said, growing very upset. "Andy is our close friend. And he has helped my brother Schaumburg out of plenty of scrapes as Mardi Gras. Nerwonduh knew he would work with us. That's why he gave us Andy's costume. He was supposed to help us and become a part of our Hug."

Louis thought about what Chocolate had said.

"Perhaps you are correct about Andy," Louis said. "But we need to be sure. I should write to Orishan Command to find out more about Andy's background. What do we really know about him? And why does he have super powers and we do not? And why does Andy have a command power ring? Where did he get it? There are too many unanswered questions."

"How much do I really know about you, Louis?" Chocolate said, her eyes sparkling with mischief.

"Okay, what do you want to know?"

"How did you lose your left paw and why do you wear a hook instead?"

Louis started to laugh.

"What's so funny?" Chocolate asked.

Then Louis pulled off his golden hook that revealed a perfectly healthy left paw underneath.

"Louis LaHug, you brat!" Chocolate yelled, batting his arm affectionately.

"I just wear this because it looks cool," Louis said.

Chocolate stayed quiet for a moment.

"I don't like the idea of checking up on our own friends," Chocolate said. "I want to talk to Leni and Schaumburg about this background check on Andy."

"Agreed."

"Then the matter's settled," Chocolate said. "Let's not discuss this anymore." Chocolate leaned over to give Louis a quick peck on the cheek. "Besides, sweetie, we have to get this machine flying soon," she added.

Lou's amber eyes sparkled as he peered into Chocolate's deep brown eyes.

"Have I told you I love you yet today?" he asked her.

"Not yet."

They kissed again, this time longer, and then hugged for a long time.

When they pulled away from each other, still looking into each other's eyes, Louis noticed tears in Chocolate's eyes.

"What is it, love?" Lou asked.

"It's this war with the Arjogun," Chocolate said. "I wish it were all over. I wish we could just enjoy each other's company without building weapons like this airplane."

"I know, love," Louis said, hugging his girlfriend again. "I would rather we were building a pleasure hover craft to enjoy this world. But this is not an offensive weapon any longer. We have modified the electromagnetic field onboard to serve as an invisible shield to human weapons. And now, this baby is built for speed. With the 10,800 lb.-thrust engines replaced with Orishan twin hyperdrives, she will fly from one end of the planet to the other in a fraction of a second. We will need that kind of speed as we approach D-Day."

"That's another thing," Chocolate said. "How come you don't trust Andy, yet we all seem to think this group, the Knights in Blue Satin is okay? How do they know the date when the Arjogun plan to implement their weapon of destruction? Could their sources be wrong?"

"Now you're starting to think more like a suspicious human," Louis said, chiding his girlfriend.

They both laughed, and then got back to work.

Chocolate leaned back and almost fell over, putting out a paw to stop her fall. She almost hit the emergency pilot ejection button.

"Careful, honey," Louis said. "If you hit that button, we'd lose the pilot's seat. It would have smashed through the cockpit roof but would flatten up against the Paw Cave ceiling."

"Sorry, Lou," Chocolate said. "I'll be more careful."

In a few hours, all the modifications to the airplane were complete.

Andy and Schaumburg waited outside the Paw Cave, watching as Louis and Chocolate taxied the human craft outside to test it. The F-117A, with its black color and pointed nose, seemed like an angry bird as it slowly moved out into the open air.

Leni stayed inside monitoring the bird's functions with her crystal ball.

Louis popped open the cockpit and stopped the forward motion of the craft.

The engine's deafening roar required that all wear special ear protection. They communicated through special gold pins shaped like the arch in St. Louis that were connected to headsets for speaking and hearing.

"Test the true stealth mode first on the ground," Schaumburg commanded.

"Roger," Louis said. He closed the cockpit and turned to H.A.R.V.E.Y., now standing on the special platform. Three golden rings of light surrounded the H.A.R.V.E.Y. unit.

"Engage true stealth mode," Louis said.

"Hold on a minute," the H.A.R.V.E.Y. unit complained. "This new connection itches. I gotta scratch."

"The H.A.R.V.E.Y. unit acts even more erratic since the Arjogun shot it a few months ago when we stole the plane from Serbia," Louis said. "I tried to repair him with help from members of the Knights in Blue Satin, but now H.A.R.V.E.Y. seems to be taking on emotions. H.A.R.V.E.Y. questions orders now . . . Any time you are ready, H.A.R.V.E.Y.," Louis said, now disturbed. Chocolate prepared the engines for takeoff.

"Okay, go ahead and flip the switch," H.A.R.V.E.Y. said. At that instant, the huge black bird shimmered into nothingness before Schaumburg and Andy's eyes.

"It's working!" Andy shouted.

"Are you there?" Schaumburg asked.

"Roger," Louis responded. "Can you still see us?"

"Not at all," Schaumburg responded.

"Leni, what does the crystal ball show you?" Schaumburg asked.

"Everything is perfect," Leni said. "They are vibrating at a nutational rate outside both Orishan and human ability to see or detect."

Chocolate touched her communicator button. "What about the Arjogun?" she asked Leni.

"This true stealth mode is outside of their field of vision and instrumentation as well," Leni said.

"Perfect!" Louis said. "H.A.R.V.E.Y., you are to be congratulated."

"Thanks Captain Hook," H.A.R.V.E.Y. said.

"Okay, Louis. Take her up and test the hyperdrives," Schaumburg said.

"Roger," Louis replied to Schaumburg.

Andy and Schaumburg raced back into the Paw Cave to watch the ship's progress on Leni's crystal ball.

"Okay, Chocolate, here goes nothing," Louis said, punching a new button on the computer monitor onboard with a strange Orishan marking.

At first nothing happened. Then Chocolate and Louis heard the quiet murmur of the Orishan hyperdrive engines.

For a couple of seconds, Louis and Chocolate felt like the ship stretched and pulled them from all sides and angles. Then the ship jolted.

"Where are we?" Louis asked Chocolate.

"We're directly over Saudi Arabia," Chocolate responded.

"I have you on my crystal ball," Leni called over the Orishan radio. "Your trip took less than a second!"

"Okay, come on back," Schaumburg said. "Leni's crystal ball is showing us high temperatures inside the H.A.R.V.E.Y. unit."

"Rog . . ." before Louis could finish his word; the H.A.R.V.E.Y. unit began sparking and sputtering. The plane, flying now at an altitude of 14,000 feet, suddenly shimmered back into the vibration that could be seen by the humans on the surface below.

"True stealth mode has failed," Louis said.

"Louis, get back here now," Schaumburg ordered.

Chocolate assisted Louis in rearming the hyperdrives for the return trip.

About one second later, Andy and Schaumburg, rushing outside to pick up the stealth fighter visually, saw the black bird as it slowed down to about 200 miles per hour and soared above Leni's farm in Toleni.

"Bring her down, Louis," Schaumburg said. "It looks like the hyperdrives work great, but we need to work on that true stealth mode."

Louis landed the bird safely and taxied back into the Paw Cave.

When Chocolate and Louis climbed outside the craft, Louis handed the damaged H.A.R.V.E.Y. unit to Schaumburg.

The unit, normally white, showed black burnt spots and revealed burnt circuitry beneath the white fur.

"This is bad," Schaumburg said.

"I'll help you fix him," Andy said to Louis.

"I hope we can fix him this time," Louis said. "He's been through a lot, you know."

Captain Louis LaHug is second in command on Schaumburg's mission to Earth.

CHAPTER 13

THE LEGEND
OF THE KEY

At the Paw Cave, the Paw, Mardi Gras and Leni researched all they could on the Knights in Blue Satin. Leni combed through her library of ancient Orishan books, the Paw used the Paw Computer, and Mardi Gras used the recently repaired H.A.R.V.E.Y. unit.

It had been a month since the initial test flight of the modified F-117A.

"Where are Louis and Chocolate off to?" Mardi Gras wanted to know.

"Louis and Chocolate are on a secret mission I assigned them," the Paw said. Leni and the Paw looked at each other. Mardi Gras seemed confused. Normally the Orishans in Schaumburg's Hug never kept anything from each other.

Mardi Gras shook it off as not important.

"Wow!" the Paw said. "Look at what this entry on the Orishan Internet says about the Knights in Blue Satin!"

Mardi Gras and Leni immediately turned toward the huge Paw Computer screen.

Data streamed across the screen as the Paw began to read:

The Knights In Blue Satin—secret underground spy ring headquartered in Pawtropolis, Illinois on the Planet Earth. Their main mission is to prevent the plot by the Arjogun from destroying the planet Earth.

The Knights in Blue Satin trace their origins to the Mystical Order of the Golden Paw, which began on Earth before it spread to Orisha and

Bengali. Their prime rule, known as the Golden Paw Rule, is to treat all beings as you want them to treat you.

Orishans have been on the Earth for centuries, dating back to prehistoric human times. They are responsible for many Earth legends regarding bears, the constellation Ursa Major and Ursa Minor, and similar myths based in fact. Orishans believe that their ancestors were once large like the grizzly bears of Earth, but evolution on Orisha shrank them to the size of grizzly bear cubs. It is not known if Orishans began on Earth, or if they began on Orisha and migrated to Earth.

The Legend of Alioth

The first Orishan known in Orishan history to visit the planet Earth, Alioth, began the Knights in Blue Satin as a group of grizzly bears and humans. Alioth worked with humans and grizzly bears to help both species survive during the Ice Age.

The legend says that grizzly bears, at that time, did not behave like the animals of today. They walked upright, had the power of speech, hunted with clubs and used their great claws to catch their prey. That is why Orishans believe grizzly bears and Orishans have common origins in the far distant reaches of time.

When Alioth first came to visit Earth, he had crashed there by accident. The grizzly bears saw Alioth as a child bear, not as an alien.

But both the men and bears soon realized Alioth could not be a child. Alioth had Orishan technology as well as magic far ahead of Earth—whose inhabitants had developed primitive stone age knives and such. Earth's inhabitants considered Alioth a great Wizard. He gave bears and humans fire and the wheel, as well as the first written language and the skills to grow crops.

Alioth would often heal the sick and give great lessons in healing arts and sciences to both species (grizzly bears and humans) of Earth. Alioth, for example, showed both bears and humans how to chew bark to cure a headache, the basis for the modern aspirin pill.

Under Alioth's leadership, the Knights in Blue Satin formed the great alliance between Earth and Orisha.

Orishan legends tell of Alioth as a wise prophet.
Here follow some of the teachings of Alioth:

Giving Thanks

"Remember that all creatures deserve their dignity. When a man is hunting to feed his family, he should give thanks to the Creator for his bountiful harvest and for the game he catches on the hunt. Always give one-tenth of your bounty to the poor to thank the universe."

Kindness

"Men and bears must learn to treat all with kindness and gentleness for honey will draw more flies than bread that has no honey."

Prosperity

"Give a man or a bear a fish, you feed him for that day's meal. Teach a man or a bear how to fish, you feed him for a lifetime."

Positive Attitude

"We create our environments and our own happiness. When you look at a vessel of water, what do you see? If you see a vessel half full instead of half empty, you will be happier."

Using The Creator's Gifts

"We are in charge of our own destinies, not the Creator. The Creator has given us all the tools we need to succeed. We must use our minds to solve whatever puzzles and mysteries life offers. Remember, the Creator will never test us beyond our abilities to cope."

These uplifting lessons given to both grizzly bears and humans helped both species to build the first great civilization on Earth known as the nation of Ursa. This civilization flourished hundreds of thousands of years before the current time, and most records of its existence have been lost to the mists of time. Some say the legends of Atlantis and Lemuria were based on the nation of Ursa.

For many thousands of years, the humans and the grizzly bears flourished. The Orishans often visited the planet, and taught the humans and grizzly bears to love one another.

Then one day, when Alioth was old and gray, at the age of 3001, he lay down on his bed to die. He called his friends together, the Knights in Blue Satin, and gave them one last lesson.

"Remember, my children, what I have taught you," Alioth said. "We Orishans will visit you often to check on your progress. Never forget to love each other, and give each other great hugs."

Alioth appointed one grizzly bear, Mehrak, and one human, Alcor, to take over as Wizards after he died. Mehrak and Alcor grew jealous of each other, and soon began to bicker between themselves about how to rule the land of Ursa.

The Tribe of Mehrak

Mehrak decided to take the grizzly bears away with him to form his own nation. This branch founded the Mystical Order of the Golden Paw on Earth, and eventually on Orisha. The grizzly bears made a great exodus from the land of Ursa, traveling by foot to the north. At first they prospered, but a great earthquake shattered their lands, and many grizzly bears perished. Those who survived endured many hardships over many thousands of years. Without the help of their human friends, grizzly bears began to live in the wild.

A great asteroid struck the Earth, causing Orishans to avoid the planet for many years. The tragedy affected both humans and grizzly bears, but had a horrible effect on the bears, which the humans did not suffer. The bears quickly began to lose their powers of speech and writing. It happened over the span of one generation after the asteroid struck the earth.

Orishans lost track of them, and the grizzly bears eventually lost their civilization, reverting to wild beasts. It is said there is still one city on Earth where the bears retain their great civilization, and have the power of speech. But Orishans have never been able to locate this fabled city, known through the ages as Paw. All bears of Earth are the sons and daughters of the tribe of Mehrak, the original inhabitants who befriended the humans many eons ago, but they have forgotten their friendships of old.

That is why today the grizzly bears do not speak or walk upright or hunt with tools like their ancestors. But some day the grizzly bears may learn the power of speech again.

The Tribe of Alcor

Alcor was happy that the grizzly bears left the nation of Ursa and formed an army to attack their enemies in the forests. Sometimes they would attack animals for sport. They forgot many of the teachings of Alioth, and forgot that grizzly bears were once their friends. They began to learn the arts of war. Orishans came to Earth from time to time, trying to teach both the humans and the grizzly bears again. For many thousands of years, the humans were almost as lost as the grizzly bears, but the asteroid did not cause them to lose their powers of speech and language.

Very slowly, the humans climbed back out of the abyss to form civilization again.

Finally in the human year of 1750, an Orishan named Bartholomew came to Earth, and befriended a human farmer named George Washington. (For further notes on Bartholomew, see article on him under his name).

Two Good Friends

Bartholomew renewed the friendship between Orisha and Earth, and helped George Washington and other humans form a new nation, an experiment in democracy. The new nation would help foster some of the ideals Alioth had once taught to humans and grizzly bears alike.

Bartholomew was a great Orishan but he turned his back on the teachings of the Mystical Order of the Golden Paw because of a disaster on a planet the Arjogun destroyed. The Knights in Blue Satin were reinstated, but only in secret. The First Knights, George Washington and Bartholomew, founded the new secret society on Earth, which has nurtured the United States of America in preparation for the time when the Arjogun would attack the Earth. The sons and daughters of Alcor would once again be ready, perhaps 225 years after the founding of the new nation, to defend the Earth from the alien invaders. It is said that the tribe of Mehrak must once again form an alliance with the tribe of Alcor before the aliens can be defeated to save the Earth.

George Washington drew the first Knights in Blue Satin Coat of Arms that contains the snake forming a circle. The snake appears to be about to eat its tail, and the three crowned rings in the center of the circle. The three rings represent Orisha, Earth and Bengali.

The Knights in the End Time

The Arjogun will try to destroy the Earth, fearing that the warlike humans will eventually reach out into space and conquer the Arjogun. On that day the Earth will split apart. The key to stop the doomsday machine can be found by reading the Journal of Bartholomew.

The current incarnation of the Knights in Blue Satin are working to locate the Journal of Bartholomew, find the secret writing, locate the key and stop the Arjogun doomsday machine. The Journal of Bartholomew also contains a map showing the location of the key.

The Paw, Mardi Gras and Leni all looked at each other in amazement. They had never heard of these legends, and had no idea of the connections between Earth, Orisha and Bengali.

"Holy grizzly bear!" Mardi Gras said. "We could be brothers and sisters of the grizzly bears on earth! Those guys are big!"

"We have to find the Sword of George Washington!" the Paw said.

"But where do we start?" Leni asked.

"What do your ancient tomes have on the Sword of George Washington?"

Leni thought for a moment. Then she pulled down a large dusty book from a top shelf. She blew off the dust and showed it to the Paw.

"Let's try this book," Leni said. "Presidents of the United States. It may be a start."

Will the Real Andy Adorable Please Stand Up?

While Leni, the Paw and Mardi Gras researched the legends of the Knights in Blue Satin, Chocolate and Louis set off on a secret mission to discover more about the origins of Andy Adorable, a.k.a. Mardi Gras.

Andy and Schaumburg first met when Schaumburg applied for a job at *The Daily Times* of Pawtropolis, about a year ago. So Louis reasoned they should start with the managing editor of the paper, Perry Purple.

Louis and Chocolate had arranged for a private interview with Perry.

"What can I do for you two today?" Perry asked.

"We'd like to know a little more about Andy Adorable," Louis said.

"Yes," Chocolate added. "When did you hire him?"

"Funny you should ask, Chocolate," Perry said. "We hired him the same week as your older brother, Scoop Schaumburg. Schaumburg and Andy hit it off right away, and soon became friends. They make a terrific reporting team with Schaumburg's snappy prose and Andy's magnificent photographs. I especially like their work on the Paw and Mardi Gras."

Louis and Chocolate gave each other a knowing look, but said nothing to Perry.

"Did you do any reference checks on Andy?" Louis asked.

"Why yes," Perry said, standing up from his desk to pull open a file cabinet drawer. "I have his original employment application and background check right here."

Perry pulled out Andy's file and sat back down at his desk. "Ah," Perry finally said. "Here it is. He was an orphan. His background details can be found at the Pawtropolis Orphanage located a couple of blocks away. Here's the address."

"Thanks, Perry," Louis said, snatching up Andy's file. Louis and Chocolate quickly left Perry's office.

"I wonder what that was all about?" Perry thought to himself, watching as Louis and Chocolate entered the B.A.R.T. at the end of the newsroom. "Hey, you guys can't take our personnel files!"

But it was too late. Louis and Chocolate were long gone.

A few minutes later, Louis and Chocolate entered the lobby of the Pawtropolis Orphanage.

A young female Orishan receptionist greeted them at the information desk. They could hear the joyful squeals of young Orishans playing in some rooms nearby.

"May I help you?" the receptionist asked.

"Yes," Louis said, flashing his Better Bear Bureau badge. "We're here to find out some background information on one of the orphans who left your care recently. His name is Andy Adorable."

"You'll have to go to records," she said. "Their office is on the second floor. Ask for Mrs. Winthrop."

Upstairs, Louis and Chocolate again inquired about Andy. A gray-haired Orishan female in a white lab coat greeted them this time. Her nametag said "S. Winthrop, M.D."

"Yes, Andy was our charge until about a year ago," Mrs. Winthrop said. "We have his file here. But I can't release that information to just anybody."

Louis leaned very close to Mrs. Winthrop. "Andy is part of our Hug of Orishans now," Louis said. "We have been assigned a mission by the Better Bear Bureau to find out what we can on Andy."

"I don't care if you are Mr. Vil himself," Mrs. Winthrop said haughtily. "I cannot release my charge's private files without authorization."

"Louis, let me try," Chocolate said. "Mrs. Winthrop, I am a medical doctor too. I am charged with caring for the members of our Hug here in Earth. Since Andy has become part of our Hug, we need to know his medical history for future reference. You understand."

Mrs. Winthrop's manner changed to an Orishan much less tense now.

"Well, why didn't you say so in the first place," Mrs. Winthrop said. She found Andy's medical file and handed it to Chocolate, even though Louis put out his paw for it first.

"You may take it with you," Mrs. Winthrop said. "You will need it now that Andy is part of your Hug. We are so proud of him here."

"Oh?" Louis asked.

"Why, yes," Mrs. Winthrop said. "We thought he would turn out to be a horrible Orishan at first, with that nasty temper and all. And he is such a marvelous photographer now, shooting pictures of those heroes, the Paw and Mardi Gras."

"Andy was surly when he first came here?" Louis asked.

"He was a terror! We raised him since he was just a cub. He was here for 16 years before taking the job at *The Daily Times*. Poor thing had no visitors or potential parents wishing to adopt him . . . Except one."

"Who wanted to adopt him?" Chocolate asked.

"Why Mr. Vil, of course," Mrs. Winthrop said matter-of-factly.

"What?" both Louis and Chocolate asked in unison.

"Why, didn't you know?" Mrs. Winthrop said. "Frank Vil was

about to adopt the boy two years ago. He even took the boy home to St. Louis for a few weeks, but brought him back, and decided against the adoption. Andy was much better behaved after Mr. Vil brought him back. I have no idea what Mr. Vil did to Andy, but he was a changed Orishan when he returned to the orphanage."

"You say Andy was surly until Mr. Vil brought him home with him for a few weeks, then Vil brought him back, and Andy was sweet and adorable as he is now?" Chocolate said.

"Why yes, exactly," Mrs. Winthrop said. "It was as if Andy had undergone a complete personality transformation. Mr. Vil loved that boy very much. That must be it. Although I never could figure out why he decided against the adoption."

Later, at a popular Pawtropolis restaurant known as The Honey Pot, located on the top of a skyscraper, Louis and Chocolate combed through the files they obtained from both the orphanage and from *The Daily Times*.

"It says here in the Orphanage file that Andy's parents are from Orisha," Chocolate said. "It says his parents lived in the capital city on Orisha. The father was in the Orishan Command, but the mother was a waitress at a restaurant. . . . Hmm . . . My late mother was a waitress at this same restaurant."

"Wasn't Schaumburg's father, Hamburg, in the Orishan Command?"

"Yes," Chocolate said. "Schaumy and I are only half siblings. We share the same mother. His real father died when he was just a boy, and his mom married my father. Then I came onto the scene in the Harmony household. As you know, surnames are different from Earth on our home planet. When a person is born into the older house, like the House of Harmony, the surname remains with the older family even if a new father marries into it. He takes on the older family's surname too."

"Unless the new father is of a more powerful house," Louis said.

"Yes, but Hamburg Harmony's house was older than my father's, so I retained the surname of Harmony."

"And I am glad you did," Louis said with a twinkle in his eye. "Your connection to Harmony House is to my advantage. The LaHug

House and Harmony House have often served together with the Orishan Command on deep space missions. Since I was associated with Schaumburg's Hug, we met and could fall in love"

"Stop flirting, you big dope," Chocolate said, gently slapping Louis on the fake hook. "Let's get back to work."

At that moment, Chocolate spied something in the documents that shocked her.

"What is it, Chocolate?" Louis asked.

"This is incredible," Chocolate said. "Did you know Schaumy had a brother who was kidnapped when just a cub?"

"Yeah, I think I remember Schaumburg mentioning that before."

"I think Andy could be Schaumburg's lost brother."

"What?" Louis asked, now shocked. "Are you sure?"

"There can be no mistake. His father is listed as Hamburg Harmony in this document the orphanage gave us."

Louis looked at the adoption papers again. "Something is very fishy, Chocolate," Louis said. "Why would Vil adopt this boy? Especially if he was kin to Schaumburg? And how did Vil change Andy's personality?"

"Yeah, Frank Vil is not exactly known for his skills in kindness," Chocolate said. "If anything, Vil would more likely change the boy from sweet to surly, not the other way around."

A light seemed to flash inside Lou's eyes.

"Let me see that orphanage file again," Louis said. Chocolate handed it to Louis, who thumbed through the papers.

"Here it is. Look at this record of when he was taken to the orphanage."

Adoption Records,
Andy Adorable Pawtropolis Orphanage

Earth Date, July 12, 1986. The toddler is very sweet and adorable. All we have is a first name Andy, so the doctors at the Orphanage decided to give him the surname of Adorable to match his pleasant personality. I am sure a loving Pawtropolis family will adopt him very soon.

"That's interesting," Chocolate. "Pleasant personality."

"Right! Now look at this entry five years later, after Frank Vil started to show an interest in the boy.

Adoption Records, ### Andy Adorable Pawtropolis Orphanage

Earth Date, January 30, 1991. The boy Andy was sent to live with Frank Vil for one week to see if Vil would be interested in adopting the boy, and see if Andy liked Vil as a father. When Andy came back, he seemed quiet and withdrawn. Then he started acting very rudely to the nurses and doctors on staff. We believe the experience may have been unpleasant for Andy.

"That's the point where Vil first took Andy home," Louis said. "Andy comes back after one week with Vil, and he turns into an instant monster."

"I wouldn't exactly call Andy a 'monster,'" Chocolate said. "But he did show a drastic change in personality after that first week."

Upon examining the records more closely, Chocolate and Louis learned that Andy had many more visits from Vil, and his personality became increasingly worse as time wore on. Then, after the last visit, when Vil decided he did not want Andy as an adopted son, Andy became pleasant once again.

"Why wouldn't Winthrop have noticed this before?" Louis wanted to know.

"It says here Dr. Winthrop only just started at the orphanage the year before Vil decided he did not want to adopt Andy. She never knew him to be sweet until after Vil's decision not to adopt Andy."

"I think we need to pay a secret visit to Vil," Louis said. "Perhaps we should use H.A.R.V.E.Y. so we can spy on Vil unseen. He has a house here in Pawtropolis where he spends his off hours. And Chocolate, don't say anything to Schaumburg about this yet until we know more."

"Understood," she said, now a little frightened about Andy's origins.

"Wait a minute," Louis said. "If you are younger than Andy, how can he be a year younger than you?"

"If Andy is Schaumburg's lost brother, he was actually born two years before me on Orisha," Chocolate said.

"So Andy can't be Schaumburg's brother," Louis said. "We traveled more than 50 years into the future, remember?"

Chocolate said nothing.

A few hours later, now armed with H.A.R.V.E.Y., Louis and Chocolate entered the home of Frank E. Vil. They were invisible by holding onto H.A.R.V.E.Y.'s paws, but there was nobody home anyway.

"I feel like a thief searching through his private house like this," Chocolate said.

"Never mind that," Louis said. "Just start looking."

"What are we looking for?"

"Anything that could shed some light on this mystery of Andy's personality change," Louis said.

Vil's home was a spacious modern ranch, split level on the side of a mountain in a posh residential subdivision of Pawtropolis.

The home was filled with Arjogun artifacts.

"Boy, this guy must be really into those Arjogun aliens," Louis said.

"Yes, it is strange for an Orishan," Chocolate said. "Most Orishans would consider Arjogun artifacts ugly and would never decorate their homes with them."

Shortly, while Louis rifled through a desk drawer, he accidentally triggered a mechanism that opened a secret doorway.

"Hello, what's this?" Louis said. "Chocolate, come quick."

Louis and Chocolate entered the secret doorway, which led to a long, darkened hallway. The two walked for what seemed like ten minutes before arriving at a stone door.

Louis and Chocolate looked at each other in surprise.

"That lock is of Arjogun origin," Louis said. "What's with this guy?"

"Perhaps the answers lie behind that door," Chocolate guessed.

Louis took out some of the Paw's dissolving powder and melted the lock.

The stone doorway opened into a chamber in a castle. Louis recognized it immediately.

"We're in the Frown's castle," Louis said.

At that moment, an alarm sounded.

"We've got to get out of here," Chocolate said.

"Right—back through the hallway."

But as the two invisible Orishans raced back to Vil's home through the secret passage, the H.A.R.V.E.Y. unit malfunctioned, and they turned visible.

As Louis and Chocolate entered Vil's house, Frank Vil greeted them at the secret doorway.

"Seems I have some uninvited guests," Vil said.

The Paw Discovers Vil's Secret Identity

At that instant in the Paw Cave . . .

"It's Chocolate," Leni said to the Paw and Mardi Gras as they continued to explore ancient history of Orishans on Earth via the computer. "She's in trouble."

Leni went to her crystal ball and immediately saw Louis and Chocolate trapped by Vil.

"What's happening?" Mardi Gras asked.

"Get the Pawmobile ready, chum," the Paw said. "Chocolate and Louis need our help."

The Paw and Mardi Gras raced to Vil's house via the Pawmobile.

Meanwhile, back in Vil's house, Vil treated his guests rudely. He pulled out a blaster, but it was not the A.A.S.B.-type normally issued to Better Bear Bureau agents. Vil brandished an Arjogun weapon, capable of killing, not just putting an attacker to sleep.

"Vil, hold on," Louis said. "Don't do anything hasty."

"Quiet, Louis," Vil shouted back at him. "Both of you march back into the secret passage."

Louis and Chocolate looked at each other, puzzled.

"Now!" Vil screamed. Louis and Chocolate complied.

Vil forced Louis and Chocolate to a chamber marked "Torture." He tied up both Louis and Chocolate on two large tables.

Then he pulled down a special machine that looked like a giant telescope, only it pointed down instead of to the heavens.

Louis recognized the device.

"That's an Arjogun sun cannon," Louis said. "It captures a sun's rays and turns them into a beam of power capable of cutting through anything . . . or anyone."

"Very good, Louis," Vil said. He pointed the cannon at Lou's left paw, the one covered by the fake pirate hook.

"Perhaps I should cut off your paw so you will really need that hook?" Vil said.

"Stop it, Vil!" Chocolate shouted. "Don't be such a beast! What is wrong with you?"

"Now, now, my dear Chocolate," Vil said. "So young, so innocent. Schaumburg should never have taken you on such a dangerous mission. You never know what kind of danger you will encounter on a deep space mission."

Vil turned on the beam that pointed about seven inches above Lou's left paw. It began to burn a sizzling line in the table, and moved slowly toward Lou's paw.

"I will return in a moment," Vil said. "Then, perhaps I'll lend you a paw." Vil started chuckling at his sick joke and left the room.

Meanwhile, the beam slowly moved closer to Lou's paw.

"Lou, can you reach my robe pocket?" Chocolate said, in desperate tones.

Lou squirmed in his bonds, and tried to move closer to Chocolate to reach into her pocket.

"What am I looking for?" Lou asked.

"My mirror," Chocolate said.

Louis painfully pulled his right paw free to reach into Chocolate's robe pocket, grabbing the mirror.

"Got it!" he said triumphantly and not a moment too soon. Just as the beam was less than 1/4 of an inch from Lou's left arm ready to sever it from his body, Lou turned the mirror so it reflected the concentrated sunbeam toward the ropes that tied both he and Chocolate.

"Ouch!" Chocolate complained as the beam burning her ropes accidentally charred a small portion of her fur before she was able to get out of harm's way.

"Sorry, Chocolate," Louis said.

"Give me that mirror!" Chocolate demanded, now free of her bonds.

She reflected the beam back at the cannon, causing it to explode, shattering into hundreds of tiny pieces. Fortunately, most of the debris landed away from them on the end of the table, over Louis and Chocolate's heads. Chocolate quickly freed Louis. At that instant, the door to the chamber burst open as the Paw and Mardi Gras came to their rescue.

"Hi, guys," Louis said, now amused. "Glad you could drop by."

"Looks like you didn't need our help after all," the Paw said, hugging Chocolate and Louis.

"This is not over yet, Paw," Louis said. "Vil is here and he is the one who tied us up. I think Vil is really the Frown."

"You could be right," the Paw said. At that moment, the Frown stepped into the room, waving around in the smoke and debris from the exploded sun cannon.

Suddenly, the H.A.R.V.E.Y. unit on Lou's belt began to make a shrieking noise, and kept repeating, "Arjogun spy in proximity, Arjogun spy in proximity, Arjogun spy in proximity, Arjogun spy in . . ."

"So, you think escape is that easy do you?" the Frown asked, pointing a small metal box at Mardi Gras.

"Kill the Paw!" the Frown commanded Mardi Gras. As the Frown said those words to the Paw's young sidekick, Mardi Gras' eyes suddenly glazed over as if he was in a trance.

The Paw gulped down a piece of chocolate.

The Paw used his X-ray vision to examine his sidekick turned would-be attacker. Mardi Gras approached the Paw slowly, his paws outstretched as if he were about to throttle the Paw.

Louis stepped in to prevent Mardi Gras from reaching the Paw.

"It's okay, Louis," the Paw said. "I know what's behind this mind-control now. I can see an implant in Mardi Gras' neck. It's Arjogun technology. We will have to remove it surgically. Lou, use your Vulcan neck pinch on Mardi Gras. We'll take him with us."

Louis complied. The Paw picked up Mardi Gras, now fast asleep. The Paw reached into his utility belt, pulling out a small pellet. He threw the pellets down and huge clouds of smoke covered Louis, Chocolate, and the Paw now carrying Mardi Gras.

Before the Frown could react and the smoke clear, the Paw had whisked Louis, Chocolate and Mardi Gras all away at super speed, returning them to the safety of the Pawmobile.

*   *   *

On an operating table in the Paw Cave, Louis assisted Chocolate as she operated on the unconscious form of Mardi Gras. Chocolate safely removed the chip that had been implanted in his neck by the Frown, a.k.a. Frank E. Vil.

"He's okay," Chocolate announced, as she handed Louis the tiny chip.

"He'll be fine after this," Chocolate continued, speaking to the Paw and Leni by microphone outside the operating room. Glass walls surrounded the room.

"He's not an Arjogun agent surgically altered to look like an Orishan, is he?" the Paw asked.

"No, and I did not expect he was," Chocolate said. "From what Louis and I have been able to determine, he is an orphan from Orisha. Vil/the Frown must have implanted this chip when he first stayed at Vil's home in preparation for an adoption. It was all a scheme to use this mind-control device on him."

"Is that what the H.A.R.V.E.Y. unit meant by an Arjogun spy or was it referring to Vil?" Chocolate asked.

"Let's ask him," the Paw said, activating his H.A.R.V.E.Y. unit.

"So, who was the Arjogun spy in proximity to us in the Frown's castle?" the Paw asked.

The H.A.R.V.E.Y. unit sputtered and sparked. "It is Frank E. Vil, a . . . dwarf Arjogun . . . surgically altered to look like . . . an Orishan," the unit said.

"I knew it," the Paw said. "I never did trust that shrimp! He's small even for an Orishan!"

"That must have been why Nerwonduh told us not to let go of our

H.A.R.V.E.Y. unit and why Vil told us to get rid of it," Louis said. "The Mystical Order of the Golden Paw designed the units to detect Arjogun spies in our midst."

"Yes," Leni said. "There have been instances in the past of surgically altered Arjogun trying to pass themselves off as Orishans. They usually perform surgery on the Arjogun dwarfs. Vil can't be more than 12 inches tall."

"It explains a lot," Chocolate said. "But didn't you tell Vil when you met with him at the B.B.B. headquarters that you had super powers after eating chocolate bars?"

"So we know he is the Frown and he knows I am the Paw," the Paw said. "But we also know that he is an Arjogun, surgically altered to look like us. But he doesn't know that we know."

"Are we confused yet?" Louis said, half-joking.

"And more importantly," Chocolate said. "I know who Andy really is."

All eyes were on Chocolate now, amazed at her statement.

"What do you mean?" the Paw said.

"Schaumburg, remember mother telling us about the boy born after you who was kidnapped as a baby?"

"You can't mean . . ." the Paw said.

"Don't you see, Schaumy," Chocolate went on. "It makes sense. After the research Louis and I did, we discovered he was an orphan and traced his natural parents back to Orisha. Andy is our lost brother."

"That explains why only you and he can use the chocolate super powers," Leni said. "Your genetic make-up must be close enough that the confection reacts with both your body systems in the exact same manner."

"And Chocolate, born of a different father, would not have the same genetic makeup," the Paw said. "Of course."

"Vil must have known of his origins and planned to use him against you all along," Louis said. "We learned of his plans to adopt Andy. Now we have proof that he implanted this mind-control device on him."

"But how did he know we would turn up 50 years later?" the Paw asked.

"I can . . . answer that," sputtered the H.A.R.V.E.Y. unit. "Vil, as . . . an Arjogun has . . . access to temporal telemetry which he was able to read when Leni cast her spell, transporting . . . the four of you to the future."

"Yes, of course," the Paw said. "The old 'Arjogun Temporal Tracking Device Trick.' I should have known."

"Vil must have stolen Andy in the past and arranged for Andy to wind up in the orphanage years before we would transport to Sam's apartment in Streator," Chocolate said.

CHAPTER 14

BARTHOLOMEW AND GEORGE WASHINGTON

Sept. 4, 2001, the George Washington Museum, Versailles, Illinois. 7 p.m.

Sam and Cheryl combed through some ancient letters from George Washington.

"I have to catalogue these letters and then set them up for display in the museum," Cheryl told Sam. Visiting hours at the museum had ended.

"Where did they come from?" Sam asked.

"They were donated by a strange man from Streator," Cheryl said.

"Oh really?" Sam said, now curious. "What do you mean 'strange'?"

"He was dressed in black, wore sunglasses, and appeared to have a very thick beard," Cheryl said. "He was very skinny, but his head was sort of small. He was not too tall either."

"The Orishans!" Sam said to himself, remembering how ridiculous they looked when they stood on top of each other and put on a human black suit to appear as one human being.

"What was that?" Cheryl wanted to know.

"Oh, nothing," Sam said. "May I see the letters?"

"Sure," Cheryl said. "They are all addressed to the same man. His name is Bartholomew. He must have been very close to Washington."

"Ah, Bartholomew," Sam said.

"What?" Cheryl said, surprised. "You know about this Bartholomew?"

"Let's just say my teddy bear told me about him."

"Tell me the truth," Cheryl said.

Cheryl looked deep into Sam's eyes. "Look, Mr. Arctophile. We have known each other for almost two years now. We have become close friends. I know you like to take teddy bears to work with you. But how could you possibly know about Bartholomew? I am one of the world's foremost experts on George Washington, and until I was given these letters (which have only recently been authenticated as from the first president himself), I had never heard of this man."

"I am telling you the truth, Cheryl," Sam said, innocently.

"Okay, Sam," Cheryl said, now disgusted. "I thought we trusted each other. But if you wish to keep secrets from me, that is your choice. Now give me those letters."

"Wait, Cheryl," Sam pleaded. "Look. I'm sorry. We've been through so much together. Why are you being like this? Can you please just trust me on this? I can't tell you how I know about Bartholomew . . . yet. But I promise, when the time is right, I will tell you everything. As a matter of fact, I believe Bartholomew and his friendship with George Washington is actually connected to your husband's strange 'accident.'"

That grabbed Cheryl's attention. Every time Sam discovered an eyewitness who claimed to have knowledge of one of the Arjogun work sites, or had been implanted by an Arjogun device, the witness clammed up or vanished from the face of the Earth.

The frustrating search, which Cheryl had helped Sam with, resulted in both taking a break from the investigation.

Sam took a vacation and volunteered to assist Cheryl with the archiving of new letters at the museum.

Schaumburg and Leni told Sam in the first few weeks they met that Bartholomew was a "legend" on the planet Orisha and helped Washington "form a new independent state, namely the United States."

Sam wondered what kind of influence on the evolution of mankind these Orishans had, and if the Bartholomew was connected to the current threat from Arjogun. Would he find clues to this Project Unicorn among Washington's letters to Bartholomew?

But he could not confide all that to Cheryl. Mrs. Cruz would think him a kook.

"Now, isn't that ironic?" Sam thought to himself. "If I tell Cheryl

Cruz that I am harboring aliens that look like teddy bears, she will think I am nuts. She being the most ardent alien conspiracy nut I have ever known."

Cheryl had been watching the strange expressions on Sam's face. Then Sam started laughing to himself.

"What's so funny?" Cheryl wanted to know.

"It's just that our positions seemed to have reversed themselves," Sam said.

"What do you mean?" Cheryl inquired.

"Well, when we first met two years ago, you were the alien conspiracy nut who wanted to find out what happened to your husband."

"Yes."

"Now, I am the one absolutely convinced there is an alien conspiracy here on Earth, and you are becoming more and more skeptical."

"Sam, I just wanted to find out what happened to my husband," Cheryl said. "After all, Jose needs his father."

"Well, I have something that might perk you up," Sam said, handing one of the letters to Cheryl.

She began to read the letter:

Jan. 2, 1754

Dearest Bartholomew,

It has been two years since you gave me your sword. You advised me to lead a military foray into the Ohio Valley. But I fear battling the French will be too risky. They are really French Ambassadors under diplomatic immunity. I am not concerned that I could be in great danger. That magic sword may be enough to get me out of physical harm. But what concerns me is the French reaction to this little endeavor.

Cheryl put the letter down, now stunned.

"My God, Sam," Cheryl said. "Do you realize what this letter means?"

Sam shrugged, not knowing what Cheryl meant.

"This proves my theory that George Washington may have instigated the revolution in the British colonies."

"Wow!" Sam said. "Talk about conspiracy theories."

"Sam, Washington scholars have debated for years whether or not George Washington actually started the American Revolution."

"I was actually wishing you to note the part about the magic sword," Sam said, sheepishly.

"Yes, yes, that is interesting too," Cheryl said, now very excited. "We'll get to the so-called magic sword later. First, let me explain something. George Washington in 1754 took some British troops out into the Ohio Valley. His troops fired on French soldiers. The French claimed that the soldiers were ambassadors with diplomatic immunity. Washington dismissed the French claim."

"I don't get it," Sam said, perplexed. "What does that have to do with the Revolutionary War?"

"I'm getting to that," Cheryl said. "After Washington attacked the French troops in the Ohio Valley, French retaliatory action forced Washington's surrender at Necessity, Pennsylvania. That incident turned frontier tension into the French and Indian War, which also spread to Europe as the Seven Years War."

"Then Washington is responsible for the French and Indian War, not the Revolutionary War," Sam said.

"Stop jumping to conclusions," Cheryl said, as if she were teaching Sam a lesson in school. "Now listen. Washington's causing the French and Indian War drained Great Britain's economy, forcing the British Parliament to saddle the American Colonies with the cost of the war."

"Don't tell me," Sam stopped her. "They taxed us?"

"Exactly," Cheryl said. "Taxation without representation was a key issue in the Revolutionary War and it all stems back to this attack by Washington on those French soldiers whom France claims had diplomatic immunity."

"So, let me get this straight," Sam said. "First, Washington is advised by this mysterious Bartholomew to attack the French soldiers. He does, and it escalates into the French and Indian War which drains British finances which forces Great Britain to tax the heck out of the American Colonies, thus starting the American Revolution."

Sam thought to himself that this Bartholomew, whom he knew to be an Orishan, seemed to operate differently from Schaumburg. He seemed to be encouraging Washington to start a war.

"Exactly," Cheryl said. "Scholars have been searching for this kind of proof for more than two centuries. This letter proves Washington knew about the French. He knew they had diplomatic immunity."

"That may prove he was just foolhardy, but does not prove he engineered the Revolutionary War," Sam said, defending his boyhood hero.

"No? Read on," Cheryl retorted.

> *We know that a war against France will greatly drain Britain's finances. But there is no guarantee that England will tax the American Colonies the way you have predicted. We need those taxes to rally the people.*
>
> *But I have never been steered wrong by you before. I have known you for four years now. You have always guided me in the right direction, my dear Bartholomew. If you weren't so short, I would say you are the tallest being I have ever known. In any case, great men will stand on your short shoulders as we form a new nation here in the new world.*
>
> *I will see you later this year.*
>
> *Sincerely,*
> *Your Friend,*
> *G. Washington*

"This is it!" Cheryl said, standing up excitedly and grasping the letter. "I can finally prove my theory!"

"Okay," Sam said. "So what is it you were going to tell me about this magic sword?"

"Well, it's really more like a letter opener," Cheryl said.

"A letter opener?" Sam asked, now really confused.

"Yeah, Washington was into all sorts of weird mystical stuff," Cheryl said. "He was a Freemason at the age of 20, you know."

She pulled a book off a shelf and showed Sam a photo of George Washington in Masonic Apron performing a ceremony at a Masonic temple.

"This sword is the stuff of legends," Cheryl said. "It is said that he was given the sword by a friend as a gift, a kind of magical amulet that protected Washington in battle. There is documented history that shows

Washington's horse was shot right out from under him in battle many times, and he never, never ever was hit by a bullet. There is a story about how Washington's coat was found to be full of bullet holes after one battle, but Washington never had a scratch on him."

"Maybe he wore a bullet-proof vest," Sam offered.

"That would certainly be more reasonable than a magic sword the size of a letter opener," Cheryl said.

"Wait a minute," Sam said. "The size of a letter opener. About seven or eight inches long?"

"Why yes, that should be about right," Cheryl said. "Why?"

"That's exactly the size a sword would be if it belonged to a being who stood less than two feet tall."

"Are you thinking aliens?" Cheryl said, following Sam's line of thought.

Feinman 175...

Bartholomew, the Orishan who visited the Earth in the mid-1700s, modeled for a painting by a famous Romanian artist, Anton Feinman, in 1753.

Forging a New Nation

As Cheryl and Sam continued to sift through the letters from an anonymous source, they failed to notice somebody walk into the museum.

Suddenly, Fred stood before the two, dressed in rags and looking like he hadn't eaten for days.

"Fred!" Sam said suddenly, shocked to see him. "Where have you been? What's happened to you?"

"I have news for you both . . ." Fred replied, then slumped down and fainted.

*   *   *

Fred awoke on Cheryl's bed a few hours later, Cheryl bending over him with a wet cloth on his forehead.

"Here, drink some of this orange juice," she said to him.

He gulped it down.

"Hey, take it easy," Cheryl advised Fred.

Fred sat up in the bed.

"Thank you, Mrs. Cruz," Fred said. "I haven't been able to eat for days. I've been on the run from some government goons. I think they are NSA."

At that moment, Sam came into the room.

"Did you say NSA?" Sam asked. "The No Such Agency?"

Fred laughed at the nickname given to the National Security Agency by the Federal Bureau of Investigation, then started to cough.

"We are all in grave danger, Sam," Fred said.

"What have you learned?" Cheryl asked.

Fred looked at Cheryl as sadness entered his eyes. Fred was a short man, about 33 years old. Because of his dark skin many people mistook him for an Italian or an Arab, which is ironic since he was the son of Eastern European Jewish immigrants.

Tears began to form within Fred's eyes, which contained a deep, almost smoldering blue color.

"I think I know what happened to your husband," Fred said.

Sam sat down on the bed next to Cheryl, prepared to comfort her if need be.

"He has been kept in a secret prison on an outpost somewhere off the coast of Mozambique, Africa, I think. My contact, Commander Black, helped me discover Armando's fate."

"We have been searching for clues to Armando's whereabouts for several months with no success," Sam said.

Fred said nothing at first, looking at both Cheryl and Sam.

"Listen, Sam," Fred said. "I know I can trust you. So what I am about to tell you, you have to take in with an open mind."

"Agreed," Sam said. "I trust you Fred. We go back a long ways."

Fred reached into his pocket and pulled out a small wooden box, the type a jeweler would sell to hold a ring. He opened it.

Inside was a ring made of pure gold, but not for a human finger. It was almost large enough for a bracelet, only not quite.

There was a symbol on the ring: a snake in a circle with its tail about to enter its mouth. Within the circle were three rings, all crowned.

"This is the symbol of a group of beings that are helping humans," Fred said. "They gave Commander Black a lot of information."

"Commander Black and I were about to leave on a steamship bound for Mozambique when we received word from this group of beings. They call themselves the Knights in Blue Satin. They said they knew about you and Sam, and your efforts to locate Armando. They knew a lot about the aliens, too."

At that moment, Fred winced in pain.

"Fred, what happened to you?" Sam asked.

"Commander Black and I were abducted by the alien grays," Fred said. "They injected the Commander and me with some drug or something. A spy Arjogun working for the Knights in Blue Satin rescued me. The Commander and I were separated. I made it back to Illinois by hitchhiking and walking most of the way. Our Arjogun abductors gave us some sort of experimental drug, knowing it might kill us. The Knights said it was Arjogun truth serum, whatever that is. They told me it was used by the Aliens to secure information from their enemies. But it can be poison to humans."

Cheryl looked deep into Fred's eyes. "What did they do to my Armando?" she said, now angry.

"We think he is being kept in prison because he was about to blow the whistle on the government's weather control program," Fred said. "It's called Project Unicorn. I believe you two already know about it."

"Go on," she said, growing angrier.

"Armando was about to go public when the government caught up with him and sent him to a work camp off the coast of Africa somewhere. I haven't determined exactly where yet. There, he was forced to work as a slave in the alien weather control station, buried deep underground. Commander Black learned that this is all linked to some secret documents written by George Washington. Commander Black said there is a secret message written on one of the letters from Washington. I was told by Commander Black you recently acquired the letters."

Cheryl and Sam both looked at each other surprised now. How did Fred know about those letters that she just received not more than two days ago?

"Which letter? What secret writing?" Sam asked.

"Washington used invisible ink on his letters to hide secret messages," Cheryl said. "Of course. There must be something in those letters."

"Look at the letter dated July 10, 1776," Fred instructed, then winced in pain again.

"Fred, we've got to get you to a hospital," Sam said.

Fred began to cough. "No, listen to me, Sam," Fred said. "There is a spy working at your paper, Sam. You have to be very careful whom you trust now."

Fred began to cough again.

"I'm calling 9-1-1," Sam said.

"No!" Fred yelled violently. "Just go get the letter."

Cheryl and Sam looked at each other in surprise.

Cheryl got up and fished through the letters, finding the one dated July 10, 1776. It was addressed to Bartholomew.

"Now, get a match or cigarette lighter," Fred instructed.

"I know what you want me to do," Cheryl said. "In ancient times, spies wrote secret messages in invisible inks made from lemon juice or onion juice. Heating the letter, sort of burning the invisible ink visible, could then allow a person to see the secret writing."

She heated the letter with a match and the burnt writing started to appear on the letter.

She read it out loud.

Dearest George,

This is Bartholomew. I am writing this on your own letter in invisible ink so nobody else can know the truth behind the events in Philadelphia on July 4, 1776.

The patriots in Philadelphia were not going to sign the Declaration of Independence. They had to be persuaded. As the debate to forge a new nation engrossed the Continental Congress, it began to reach a heated climax on July 4. At that moment, I entered the room.

I was dressed in a dark cloak. Since I only stand about 18 inches tall, my strange appearance and stature startled the assembly.

Many of the patriots hesitated to sign the Declaration of Independence. I stood before these great men from all the colonies, and convinced them all that they must do their part to forge a new nation from their own blood and sweat. I told them that many may lose their lives and property in a war against Mother England, but in the end, they would be free of England's stranglehold over them.

I told them of how they had a chance to start as a new nation in the new world, to help all men live free in a democratic nation ruled by law, not by aristocrats.

I told them that one day this would be the mightiest nation on the planet, and that England would one day ask America for help in keeping the world safe for free men.

My speech spellbound and transfixed them.

I ended my speech with "God has given America to be a free nation!" and, amid cheers filled with intense emotions, every member of the Congress raced forward to sign the document. Then I swiftly left the room and returned to the city of Paw. I will return to you soon. Please know that all we have worked for has started to come to pass. America will become a great nation on this planet. I promise you that. And the Knights in Blue Satin will always be here to help mankind

*against the forces of evil. Stay in good cheer. Inspire your men. You have
a nation to win!"*

"These Knights in Blue Satin have been on Earth for a long time,"
Fred said. "They helped form the American nation because it would be
needed in the coming days when the aliens try to destroy our planet."

"Destroy our planet?" Sam said. "What do you mean? I thought
they just wanted to . . ."

"The aliens have duped our government officials into thinking
they were building a weather control station off the coast of Africa,"
Fred said. "It is not a weather station. They are building a giant machine
that reaches deep into the Earth's core. Its purpose is to blow this
planet to pieces."

"I suppose these Knights in pajamas told you this?" Sam asked,
now suspicious.

"Knights in Blue Satin," Fred said. "Don't mock them. They may
be small and furry, but they are very wise beings."

"Wait a minute," Sam said. "Did you say small and furry? Like
teddy bears?"

"Exactly," Fred said. He began to cough violently again.

"Sam, these beings, the Knights in Blue Satin, they are working as
slaves alongside Armando Cruz in Africa," Fred continued.

Fred coughed violently.

"You and Cheryl cannot let on that you know any of this," Fred
sputtered. "Sam has to continue to work at *The Daily Press* to smoke
out the spy working there. And Mrs. Cruz, you must continue to sift
through those letters from George Washington. There is more secret
writing. Find the letter with the map. It will lead you to the keys that
eventually will take you to the alien encampment where Armando is
being held."

Fred continued to cough.

"I'm calling 9-1-1," Sam said. He picked up the phone. Fred began
to choke. Cheryl picked him up to try and clear his windpipe. Fred
gasped, trying to breathe.

"Hello, this is Samuel Arctophile. I'm at the apartment above the
George Washington Museum. Please send an ambulance right away!"

Powdered Sugar Blankets Streator

Report to Orishan Command from Captain Schaumburg Harmony
Earth Date: Jan. 19, 2002

Dear Commander,

We have spent a lot of time with our human charges, Samuel Arctophile and his friend, Mrs. Cheryl Cruz.

We are also learning much about these humans and their strange planet. But what surprises us the most is the strange white powered sugar that blankets the area in their winter.

They call it snow.

The other day, Cheryl was attacked by a vicious telephone pole on the way home from Montreal to Versailles. The mysterious white powdered sugar began falling onto Versailles, Ottawa and Streator about 11 a.m. that day and continued throughout the afternoon.

The Better Bear Bureau officials have reported to us that the white powder may have something to do with the wild telephone pole coming to life.

Cheryl piloted her land ship called a 1974 Pinto station wagon when the pole jumped out from the side of the road and struck her vehicle.

She had to be transported to the hospital in Montreal. Sam has been spending a lot of time at the hospital lately, hoping she will recover.

The accident knocked out one of the vehicle's eyes and the bulkhead was rubbing against the ship's landing gear.

Sam took Cheryl's ship to a place called Dan's shipyard, or some such name, in Streator. Dan sawed a piece of the bulkhead off so it would not rub when the ship was moving.

Dan saw me sitting in the cockpit and asked if I was the one piloting the ship at the time of the accident.

Sam answered that Cheryl was the pilot, defending my honor.

Then Sam went to see what he called an assurance man. Sam said his name was Tom Smith (an obvious alias). The assurance man on Earth assures the owner of the ship that if he is paid lots of money each month, the assurance man will pay for repairs in case the ship is damaged in transit. Sounds like a scam to me. The Better Bear Bureau is investigating. More on that later.

Meanwhile, Tom Smith said to Sam that he was glad Cheryl was taken quickly to the hospital and hopes she is okay. Smith also said "it was a real bummer when those poles take so long to cross the street."

This pole thing must be more common than we Orishans realize. However, I have never heard of any other incidents of poles coming to life on this planet. It could be magic, but Leni said she is unaware of any spells that would make a pole run across a street.

Cheryl is in the intensive care unit at the hospital, not too far from where Fred has been for many months since his escape from the Arjogun. He has been in a coma.

Sam told me that the Arjogun agents slipped Fred some Arjogun truth serum. Chocolate has been trying to develop a counter agent that would help the human heal.

Now Sam's best friends, Fred and Cheryl, are both hospitalized. Sam is beside himself with grief and concern.

Sam and Cheryl have been doing research on the letters your office instructed us to give to her. They discovered Bartholomew's secret writing and have also managed to piece together a map. Did you guys know about Bartholomew's secret writing? The map seems to show the location of where Washington buried the sword. The Knights in Blue Satin have never explained exactly what the sword is for, only that it is a key to saving the planet.

Sam said as soon as Fred and Cheryl recover, he would set out on an expedition to recover the Sword of George Washington.

Meanwhile, Sam has begun to befriend Jose Cruz, Cheryl's son. There is nobody to care for the boy now that Cheryl is being hospitalized. Cheryl's family lives in California. Sam has contacted them, but it will be a few days before they can travel to Illinois to watch over Jose. At first Sam did not like spending time with Jose, but he is growing very fond of the boy. Sam was an only child and never cared for children younger than himself. He seemed awkward at first around Jose. But now, the boy and Sam have become very close. Jose is a delight, skipping happily through life. He is teaching Sam to lighten up. That is good.

Sam would make an excellent father, although I don't think he realizes
it.

Back on her farm in Toleni, Leni has also been doing research on
the Arjogun serum to help us cure Fred, but we have been unsuccessful so
far. We wish to know if our doctors and scientists on Orisha can help. I
am attaching detailed documents that show human physiology. If you
can help, please send us the information as soon as possible. Sam is
growing frantic trying to watch Jose, visit both Cheryl and Fred in the
hospital and do his own work at the paper all at the same time. Sam is
back as Bureau Chief now because the economy is starting to slump,
and the paper is making cuts. He was told he could still work on the
Armando Cruz story, but only after the regular Bureau duties are taken
care of.

Leni and I have been secretly watching over the boy for Sam,
allowing Sam to work.

Right now, our one hope lies in an Arjogun spy we caught while
we were in Serbia on a mission. He helped Fred escape from an Arjogun
ship. I do not trust him, but Andy seems to think he will help us. I think
Andy is being very naive. You cannot trust an Arjogun. We plan to use
the Arjogun to locate Armando Cruz.

Please send any medical help you can for the human Fred. Thank
you.

Sincerely,
Captain Schaumburg Harmony
Commander, Mission to Earth

Response to request for Arjogun drug antidote for humans
To: Captain Schaumburg Harmony
Dear Captain Schaumburg,

Our doctors can supply a cure for the human Fred, but you will
have to gather the ingredients yourself. We are attaching a list and
recipe for cooking the formula.

We note that you have learned much about human culture, and
your reports from Earth are much more detailed than anything we have
gotten from the B.B.B. since Vil took over.

Since your discovery that Vil was actually an Arjogun spy surgically

THE TEDDY BEAR CONSPIRACIES

altered to look like an Orishan, we have been able to answer many questions we have had with regard to the B.B.B. We must not let Vil know we know that he is really an Arjogun. We also know that he knows that you know. Further, Vil knows that you are also the Paw. But he will never let you know he knows. And as long as you know he knows, you have the upper hand.

We understand that Vil is reporting to a human. We believe Vil's human supervisor, who is known as the Lemming, is very close to Samuel Arctophile. Do what you can to protect your human charges. Their destinies are interwoven with yours and your Hug.

As for the strange poles coming to life, we have never heard of such a thing either. We will advise if we learn more.

Orishan Command out.

January 31, 2002, St. Luke's Hospital, Montreal

After the Orishans concocted a batch of the antidote for Fred and Commander Black (who stayed at a secret Protector hospital), they administered it to Fred secretly. The doctors at the Montreal hospital could not explain Fred's miraculous recovery, instantly snapping out of his coma.

Cheryl recovered from her injuries received in the car accident as well. She suffered severe head trauma from hitting the windshield and a few broken bones in her accident.

Sam visited Cheryl in the hospital. Schaumburg and Louis came with him.

"How are you feeling today, Cheryl?" Sam asked her. She remained drowsy from her medication.

"My head is bandaged as well as my arm," Cheryl responded. "I have one leg in traction. How do you think I feel? I feel lousy. My brother said you are taking great care of Jose. Thank you for that . . . How is Fred doing?"

"He's finally snapping out of it," Sam said, winking at Schaumburg and Louis.

"Why are you winking at your teddy bears?" Cheryl asked, now growing more alert.

"Never mind. You just get better. You want to watch television or something?"

But Cheryl was back into a deep slumber.

"C'mon, Schaumburg, Louis," Sam said. "Let's see if Fred is ready to be discharged."

In Fred's room, Fred busied himself packing up his belongings, wearing street clothing once again.

"So, you tired of the room service in this hotel?" Sam asked.

"Sam!" Fred hugged his lifelong friend. Then Fred noticed Schaumburg and Louis.

"Where did you get the teddy bears?" Fred asked, realizing Schaumburg and Louis were Orishans.

"Actually, they just showed up at my apartment one day," Sam said. "Why?"

"May I?" Fred asked, gesturing for Sam to give Schaumburg to Fred.

Fred took Schaumburg and pressed his right paw, causing the Orishan to come out of his state of suspended hibernation.

"So it was you who saved my friend Fred from the Arjogun ship," Sam said to Schaumburg.

"Actually, it was an Arjogun spying for us. We had to create a special potion to counteract the Arjogun drug," Schaumburg said. "We administered the same remedy to Commander Black. I had to contact my home planet for an antidote. Fred and Commander Black are as good as new now."

"Sam, let's go find that sword now," Fred said. "The Orishans need it. It is the key to stopping the Arjogun."

"Hold on a minute, Fred," Sam said, now talking in hushed tones as a nurse passed by the door.

"I'm not leaving the area until Cheryl recovers. Besides, that map seems to show the sword is buried in a time capsule at the base of the Washington Monument. We can't just go digging it up."

"I thought *you* wanted to rescue Armando Cruz?" Schaumburg said. "*We* Orishans can go get the Sword of George Washington."

Fred and Sam looked at each other.

"These creatures are really very resourceful," Sam said. "And I did promise Cheryl I would find Armando."

Outside Fred's room, Cheryl's brother, Paul, was about to come in to greet Sam and Fred. But he paused to listen outside instead.

"Do you love her Sam?"

"I thought I did," Sam said. "And I am growing very fond of Jose. Now that we have evidence Armando is alive, and Cheryl has her brother here to watch Jose, I am beginning to realize that it can never be. Besides, she's a conspiracy nut," Sam said.

With that, Paul entered the room. Schaumburg immediately froze into suspended hibernation. Louis was still stiff.

"So my sister is not good enough for you, eh Anglo?" Paul asked.

"She's married anyway!" Fred protested.

"And if she were single, you would not have her because of the color of her skin?" Paul asked.

"No, it's not like that," Sam protested.

"It doesn't matter anyway," Paul said, now disgusted. "Why would my sister want to date such a scrawny Anglo like you? And one who carries around teddy bears!"

With that Paul stormed out.

"I don't get it," Fred said. "Isn't she married? Won't we find her husband now?"

"Paul and the rest of her family never believed Cheryl's husband was alive," Sam said. "They still don't."

"But he is alive," Fred said. "The Orishans showed me photos of the slave camp off the coast of Africa."

Sam awakened Schaumburg and Louis.

"Schaumburg, Louis, what do you Orishans know about Armando and this slave camp off the coast of Africa?"

"We believe it's on Madagascar," Louis said.

Schaumburg opened his trench coat and pulled out some photos, one showing Orishan slaves working alongside human slaves in the deep underground plant.

Another photo showed a man who looked like he could be Armando.

Lavender Grace, a beary growly Orishan, dreams of running an apothecary shop if she ever escapes from the Arjogun slave camp.

"Give me those," Sam said, grabbing the pictures from Schaumburg. He rushed out of Fred's room. Fred grabbed his suitcase, scooped up Schaumburg and Louis and chased after Sam.

Sam arrived at Cheryl's room, finding Paul talking to Cheryl.

"He's bad news," Paul said. "Prejudiced just like the rest of the Anglos."

Cheryl was crying.

"Cheryl, I have a photograph of Armando," Sam said. "He's alive!"

"Get out you creep," Paul said, standing between Sam and Cheryl's bed.

Sam looked at Cheryl, who now looked very sad.

"Don't you want to see the picture?" Sam asked.

"Just leave," she said to him, with a look of hatred he had never seen in her before.

Sam was thunderstruck. Fred caught up with Sam.

"It's over, Fred," Sam said, lowering his head in shame. "I've lost her." He took the photo that showed a man who looked like Armando and left it on a table near Cheryl's room door.

"Let's go home, Fred," Sam said and they stepped into an elevator.

After Sam and Fred left, Paul left Cheryl's room for a moment and noticed the photo on the table. Picking it up, he saw the man in the photo.

He crumbled it up and threw it into a nearby wastebasket then continued down the hall.

A nurse observing his actions went to the trashcan and recovered the crumpled photo.

Spies In Every Corner

The nurse flattened out the photo and brought it under a light on the nurse's station to examine it.

She picked up the phone.

"They know Armando Cruz is alive," she said. "No, the wife has not seen proof yet. But the journalist knows . . . No, they seem to have had a falling out. I don't think the journalist will be helping Mrs. Cruz anymore." She hung up the phone.

Suddenly from behind, a paw performed the Vulcan neck pinch on her. She slumped to the floor unconscious.

"Louis, every time you do that, you freak me out," Sam said.

"Quick, use the H.A.R.V.E.Y. unit to get the telephone number she just called," Lou suggested. Schaumburg complied and the phone automatically dialed the number. He handed it to Sam. The phone rang on the other end.

"Hello, Izzie Feinberg speaking."

Sam dropped the phone in shock. "Let's get outta here," Sam said softly.

As Sam, Fred, Schaumburg and Louis prepared to leave, Louis picked up the crumpled photo of Armando and snuck it into Cheryl's room, slipping it by Cheryl's head. She faced the opposite direction, fast asleep.

Afterward, Cheryl turned around moving her head onto the picture, which woke her up.

"What's this?" she asked, still drowsy.

Then her eyes focused on the photograph.

She immediately sat up, alert now. "It is true! Armando *is* alive," she said out loud.

At that moment, Paul came into the room. He saw her looking at the crumpled photograph.

"Cherylita, please," Paul said. "Your husband is dead."

Cheryl looked at the picture again.

"No, Paul," she said. "He is alive! I knew it! This photo looks like it was taken at some sort of work camp! We must find him."

"You just rest," Paul said.

Just at that precise moment, thousands of miles away, two Arjogunians interrogated Armando.

He sat tied to a chair under a hot lamp. A plain table set between the human and his alien interrogators. Armando wore tattered clothing and he looked weak, overworked.

The room where the questioning took place reeked with humidity, human sweat and other foul smells.

The Arjogunians wore special suits that kept them cool and protected from the tropical climate in the room. The suits had a paw crossed out on the chest plate.

"Human, in case you think you have a lovely wife and child waiting for you at home, you can give up on that hope," one of the Arjogun, Commander Snopple, said. "Give me the photograph, Polaris."

Polaris complied, handing Snopple a photo of Sam, Jose and Cheryl. The picture had been taken at the Chicago Field Museum.

"Look at the expression on your son's face," the Arjogun said, shoving the photo in Armando's face.

"He looks longingly at the man with your wife. You have a replacement, no? And look how the man and your wife are laughing in the photo."

The Arjogun slapped the photo face up on a table in front of Armando.

"Listen to me, human," the alien continued. "You have nothing left. We have robbed you of your existence. The world thinks you died in a plane crash three years ago. We have worked you in our camp here, preparing our weather station."

"This is no weather station and you know it, Snopple," Armando said to his interrogator.

"Silence human," Snopple said.

Polaris slapped Armando hard. "Show your respect for the general," Polaris commanded.

"You can beat me, make me your slave, but you can never take my family from me, as long as I live," Armando spat.

"Seems to me, human, your family has already been taken from you," Snopple said.

The aliens left Armando alone in the room.

Outside Armando's interrogation room, the two aliens had a conference.

"Do you think he was successful in making contact with the Knights in Blue Satin?" Snopple asked.

"I don't think so, but I know he has spoken to a Protector," Polaris replied. "Sir, you may have a difficult time breaking this human. He seems to care a lot for his wife and child."

"Do you think our agents faked that photograph of Cheryl Cruz?" Snopple asked indignantly. "She is really hanging around with another human male. We believe she has forgotten her husband. We must convince Armando she has. Have our agents in Illinois get us as much evidence as we can. We must convince Mr. Cruz his efforts against us are futile so we can learn who these Protector double agents are. We have spies working against us among our own and among the human government as well."

"Yes, sir!" Polaris said, snapping a salute that looked more like a hail to a god than a military salute.

Snopple looked into a window providing him a view of Armando. The former FBI agent peered at the photo. Then he broke down in sobs.

"I think this human will break after all," Snopple said, wringing his alien hands.

Snopple went back into the interrogation room.

"Human, I have decided to give you a . . . how do you say . . . break," Snopple said. "I will allow you to go back and join your work crew. We will question you no further today."

Snopple summoned a guard to haul away Armando.

The guard placed handcuffs on Armando and then untied him from the chair.

"Wait, Mr. Cruz," Snopple said. "You forgot your wife's picture."

Snopple handed the photo to Armando, who looked miserable. The guard led Armando away.

Later, in a filthy dining commons, Armando sat by himself picking at his food and staring at the photograph. Then he grew angry and began to rip the photo into pieces.

"No!" screamed a female from off in the distance. An Orishan slave, named Lavender Grace, rushed up to Armando.

"Let me see that picture Armando," she said.

Anyone watching these two knew they had a close relationship.

"Lavender, we are more than 1,000 feet below the earth's surface, and part of our job here is to dig a giant hole with special high-tech Arjogunian cutting tools," Armando said. "It's backbreaking work, and the temperatures down here grow hotter and hotter, the deeper we dig."

"Yes," Lavender replied, still looking toward the photo Armando held. She seemed distracted.

"We humans and you Orishan slaves had no protective air-conditioned suits like the Arjogun," Armando continued. "The Arjogun would die in that heat if they were exposed to it for too long. But they are too numerous, and much larger than you Orishans. The few humans here are not enough to overpower the armed Arjogun guards and officers running the camp."

"What's your point?" Lavender asked.

Her fur shimmered in the dim light, colored white with purple tips. The grime of working in the slave camp could not dull the luster from her fur. She wore a tattered silver pressure suit, without the helmet. The suit provided no protection for her against the searing heat and humidity at the camp.

"How can you still stay positive through all this?" Armando asked.

Lavender growled.

Armando hesitated, now pretending to tear the photo.

"Let me see it, Armando," Lavender commanded.

Armando grinned and gave her the photograph.

"Why, your wife is beautiful," Lavender said. "And look how happy she is. She must like this other human very much. And look at the expression on Jose's face. He is looking at the male human as if he adores him."

"Exactly," Armando said. "Snopple gave me this picture. He said my wife thinks I am dead and has found someone to replace me."

Lavender said nothing and continued to peer at the photograph.

"Suppose you and I don't get out of this horrible place," she said. "Wouldn't it make your heart glad to know your wife has found a new mate and your son is happy with a surrogate father?"

Armando sighed. He gently took the photograph back and peered at it more closely.

"Say, Lavender, that looks like an Orishan in the background," Armando said.

"Let me see," she said, snatching the picture back quickly.

"My God, that looks like Schaumburg, my brother-in-law," Lavender said. "I recognize him from family photo albums back on my home planet of Orisha."

"Schaumburg?" Armando said, wondering why an Orishan would be named after a city in Illinois.

"He and my sister, Millennium, were on a deep space mission to Earth more than 50 years ago and were lost," Lavender said. "I was born after Millennium left our planet. I never met her. I thought she and Schaumburg perished when their craft crashed on Earth . . . Hmm . . . That is strange . . . When was this photo taken?"

Armando took the photo back. "My wife seems about the same age as she would appear today. I suspect it was taken within the last few months."

"My brother-in-law Schaumburg looks not a day older than when he left our home world," Lavender said. "He should look a little older. Our species has a life-span of about 200 years, but he would not look as young as this—more than 50 years after he landed on Earth."

"Perhaps this is not your brother-in-law," Armando said.

"Something strange is going on here," Lavender said. "I will attempt to contact the Knights in Blue Satin to learn more. Meanwhile, you let Snopple keep thinking that this other man upsets you."

"He does upset me," Armando said. "He is stealing my wife and boy from me."

"No, Armando," Lavender said, gently. "He is taking care of your wife and boy for you. Let Snopple think you are insanely jealous. He will try to use it to break you. But we will learn more about him and perhaps about Schaumburg as well."

"Okay, Lavender," Armando said, gently tapping the furry creature on the head. "For you, I will do anything. I don't think I could have survived this long without you . . . And truly, my wife does look very happy with this man. I hope she is."

"I'm not suggesting we just sit back here and allow the nasty Arjogun to walk all over us, however," Lavender continued, growling again.

"What do you mean?" Armando asked.

Lavender said nothing.

"Are you thinking what I'm thinking?" Armando asked.

"If you mean trying to escape, that's exactly what I'm thinking."

"What do you have in mind?"

"We have to get to a bed up on the upper levels. We can use it to escape to Pawtropolis."

"A bed?" Armando said, thinking his Orishan friend had gone crazy from her forced incarceration. "How will a bed help us to get out of this God-forsaken place?"

"Beds on Earth all contain a portal to Pawtropolis and back to other beds," Lavender said. "But we will have to get past armed guards to get to the upper levels. The next time they take you to interrogate you, perhaps I can sneak in with you. How far up do they take you?"

"Just a couple of levels," Armando said. "But I think I could overpower Polaris and Snopple if they are distracted. Can you provide the distraction?"

"You bet I can," Lavender said.

"So, Lavender, what are you going to do when we get out of this hellish place?"

"I'm going to open up an apothecary shop," she said. "I was on my way to Earth to settle in Pawtropolis and open up my shop when I got nabbed by the Arjogun. The shop has been my dream ever since I was a cub."

CHAPTER 15

CAPTURED!

Sam busied himself at his office computer writing the stories for that day's paper. Two weeks elapsed since Cheryl spurned him and he learned that his managing editor could be somehow connected to the plot to help the evil aliens.

Schaumburg stood guard at Sam's desk as usual, dressed in trench coat and fedora.

Several men suddenly burst into the Versailles Bureau Office.

"Samuel Arctophile?" one of the men said. They all wore black suits, dark glasses.

"Yes, can I help you?"

"Grab the bear too," another man responded. Before Sam knew what happened, five men jumped on him, first taping his mouth shut, then handcuffing him and then putting a hood over his head.

They stuffed Schaumburg into a sack, but he remained stiff so as to not reveal his Orishan origins.

The men took Sam and Schaumburg into a waiting van and sped away.

Inside the van, Sam managed to feel his way around to wake Schaumburg from his suspended hibernation.

Schaumburg quickly assessed the situation and telepathically contacted Leni.

"Some strange men have abducted Sam and I," he reported to her. Alert Andy, Louis and Chocolate. These men may be working for Project Unicorn and have discovered Sam's involvement with us."

"We're on it, Schaumy. Hang tight. Can you activate the homing beacon on the H.A.R.V.E.Y. unit?"

"Right," Schaumburg said to her in his thoughts. Furtively, he reached down to the H.A.R.V.E.Y. unit and turned on the homing beacon. However, the unit began to malfunction again, shooting off sparks.

"Ouch!" Schaumburg yelled, revealing his presence to their captors.

"It's an Orishan!" one of the men said, quickly knocking Schaumburg out with a blow to the back of his head.

The H.A.R.V.E.Y. unit's beacon ceased to send a signal to Leni. Back at the Paw Cave, she told Mardi Gras the last known location.

"Schaumburg said they were in a van," Leni said. "He was in hibernation before entering, so he did not know a color or have a license plate. He said there were five men, dressed in black suits.

"That's got to be Project Unicorn men," Louis said. "I'll bet they identified Sam after that nurse called the Lemming."

"We've got to rescue them. Mardi Gras, eat some chocolate and fly out there to try and locate the van. Schaumburg is unconscious. I'll keep in touch through telepathy as usual and keep on eye on you with my crystal ball."

"Right, Leni," Mardi said as he gulped down some chocolate and packed more into his utility belt.

"Leni, I'll take up the F-117A with Chocolate," Louis suggested.

"There is no stealth mode on the ship," Leni said. "Schaumburg has H.A.R.V.E.Y. with him."

"I can out-fly any current aircraft the humans can throw at me," Louis said. "Mardi Gras may need some help."

"I agree," Mardi Gras said. "I'd be grateful for the help."

Leni reluctantly agreed.

Mardi Gras flew off and Louis and Chocolate soon followed close behind with the stealth fighter. Fortunately, the vehicle's natural stealth characteristics blocked it from radar. But it could still be seen by the naked eye.

"I see several vans in the vicinity of Sam's office," Mardi reported. "Using my X-ray vision, I should be able to locate the one carrying Sam and Schaumburg.

"When you find the right van, don't stop it," Leni instructed. "I want to know where those men in black are taking them."

"Roger," Mardi Gras said.

"Louis, keep an eye on Mardi Gras," Leni instructed on a separate radio channel to the F-117A. Keep him in sight at all times. He has never acted solo before. And after removing that Arjogun mind implant, Andy seems to be more quiet than usual. I am concerned about him."

"Leni, don't worry about Andy," Chocolate said. "I think he's just feeling guilty because of the things he did under the Frown's control. Mardi Gras is fine."

Louis looked at Chocolate suspiciously.

"We've been talking," Chocolate told Louis off the radio. "I am the mental health counselor for this Hug, am I not?"

"We'll keep an eye on him," Louis shot back over the radio. "Louis out."

"I've found them," Mardi Gras reported to Leni as he soared on his own power about 1,000 feet in the sky. "They're headed east on Interstate 80."

"Good, track them from a discreet distance," Leni said.

"Louis," Leni called over the radio. "Be beary careful. Both Mardi Gras and you are in danger if you are spotted."

"Got it," Louis called back. "Tell Mardi Gras to keep eating chocolate. It's been almost 20 minutes."

*   *   *

After about 1.5 hours, the van pulled off Interstate 55 near downtown Chicago. Mardi Gras descended to ground level and flew close behind the van.

Louis continued to fly high overhead.

"Leni, ask Mardi Gras to pull back," Louis called over the radio. "He'll be spotted."

Just as Louis finished the sentence, one of the men in black began to shoot at Mardi Gras.

"We've been made," Louis said. "Tell Mardi Gras to pull up quickly."

The bullets fired upon Mardi Gras bounced off his super hide, but they caused him to lose control of his flight. Mardi Gras fell to the ground, creating a gaping hole in a nearby sidewalk.

"Great!" Louis said.

"Stop it, Louis," Chocolate scolded him. "Just go down and pick him up. Leni can track the van with her crystal ball."

"Okay, I'll try to find a place to land."

But the van stopped and picked up Mardi Gras. He pretended to be unconscious and allowed the men to put him in the van.

"It's okay, Louis," Leni called over the radio to the F-117A. "He told me he was going to let them capture him. He plans to slip chocolate to Schaumburg too. But we still want to know where they are taking Sam and Schaumburg . . . Wait a minute."

"What's wrong, Leni?" Louis asked.

"I can't see the van in my crystal ball anymore. It's as if they can fog my magic."

"Great!" Louis said. "Tell Andy to keep on his toes."

"Don't call him Andy," Chocolate scolded Louis. "Our radio transmission may be picked up."

At that moment, a warning light began to buzz on Lou's control panel.

Louis checked his heads up display learning that an F-16 jet followed them in hot pursuit.

"Leni, we gotta book," Louis said.

He activated the hyper drive and zoomed instantly back to Toleni.

A fraction of a second later, Louis and Chocolate were back in the Paw Cave.

Louis activated the Paw Computer.

"Maybe I can remote activate the H.A.R.V.E.Y. unit's beacon," Louis said.

"If you can do that, why didn't you say so in the first place?" Leni asked.

"He just wanted to take out his toy airplane," Chocolate said.

"Stop it, ladies," Louis said. "It's a good thing I was backing up Mardi Gras."

"He seemed to be handling things ok without your help," Chocolate said.

Louis said nothing.

"I've just received a report from Mardi Gras," Leni said. "He's slipped chocolate to Schaumburg, and the confection woke him up. I instructed him to use knockout gas on the guards in the back of the van without alerting the driver or the man in the front passenger seat. Schaumy just reported that Mardi Gras successfully subdued the three guards in the back and they have untied Sam. Schaumburg informed Sam of our plan and he remains hooded so the driver and front guard will not suspect."

"Maybe we can finally nail these Project Unicorn guys," Louis said as he tried to activate the H.A.R.V.E.Y. unit's beacon with the Paw Computer.

"What happened?" Leni suddenly said. "I can't hear Schaumy or Mardi Gras' thoughts anymore. Louis, Chocolate, I've lost them. Can you activate the H.A.R.V.E.Y. unit's beacon?"

At that moment, the computer screen suddenly changed and the Frown appeared to all of them.

"You can kiss your friends good-bye," the Frown said. "I finally have them and your magic or technology will do you no good! Soon, that meddling journalist Sam, the Paw and Mardi Gras will all be martyrs for the Orishan cause! Ha,ha,ha,ha!"

Then the computer screen went blank.

Knights Come Under Government Suspicion

Top Secret Communication
Report on Police State Developing In United States
From The Knights in Blue Satin
To All Secret Operatives
February 12, 2002
Emergency Action Message

Terrorist legislation targets our organization:
    Since the terrorist attacks on America and the passage of the so-called Patriot Act, Attorney General John Ashcroft and his staff are drafting "The Domestic Security Enhancement Act of 2003," a sequel to the USA Patriot Act.
    If Orishans believed the USA Patriot Act was contrary to the principles

of freedom espoused by the Mystical Order of the Golden Paw, wait until you read about Ashcroft's newest legislative endeavor.

The legislation would reduce judicial oversight of surveillance, authorize secret arrests, create new death penalties and allow the government to revoke the citizenship of any American who is a member of or who gives assistance to a group identified as a terrorist organization by Ashcroft.

We have just learned that the Knights in Blue Satin have been designated by the United States government as a terrorist organization.

Two of our own have been arrested:

Furthermore, we have just learned of the secret arrest and possible execution of Scoop Schaumburg, Mardi Gras, and a human to whom Scoop Schaumburg has been assigned, a journalist named Samuel Arctophile.

All our resources are to be used to locate and rescue these three individuals. We have reason to believe that the Arjogun spy, Frank E. Vil, a.k.a. the Frown, is behind this abduction as well as his human, the Lemming. We have ascertained the identity of the Lemming. He is none other than Izzie Feinberg, managing editor of The Daily Press, the newspaper where Samuel Arctophile works.

Mr. Arctophile was instrumental in helping Scoop Schaumburg and his Hug obtain the F-117A last year, and is invaluable to our cause. He is also connected to the humans Armando and Cheryl Cruz, who are affiliated with the human organization known as the Protectors. Cheryl Cruz is about to be discharged from the hospital in Montreal after recovering from some automobile accident injuries.

Connection to the Arjogun slave camp in Madagascar:

We have learned that the accident involving her husband may have been staged. Commander Black, our liaison between the Protectors and the Knights in Blue Satin, has confirmed the location of FBI agent Armando Cruz. He is being held captive in the Arjogun slave camp along with a few human and Orishan slaves.

If our operatives are successful in rescuing Scoop Schaumburg, Mardi Gras and Mr. Arctophile from the Project Unicorn agents, we will proceed with our operation to rescue the slaves held in Madagascar.

The Sword of George Washington:

Also, we will send a unit to recover the Sword of George Washington, which we now believe to be buried in a time capsule at the base of the Washington Monument.

We have recently learned that the sword's purpose is linked directly with a defensive weapon designed by the great Bartholomew, and built into the Better Bear Bureau Arch in St. Louis.

We are still trying to determine how the sword will work. Any data on this that agents come upon would be helpful to our cause.

Thank you agents for your cooperation in this matter

Sincerely,
Perry Purple
President
Knights in Blue Satin
Pawtropolis, Illinois

February 12, 2002. Montreal, Illinois, 8:30 a.m., third floor office of *The Daily Press*

Fred Steinfeld approached Amy Sampson's desk.

"Amy, I didn't want to tell you this, but I'm afraid I need your top-notch investigative skills as a reporter," Fred said. "Sam was arrested last month by some secret police."

"What?"

"Yes, and we have no idea where he is or what they are doing to him," Fred said.

"We've got to find him!" Amy said.

"I thought you didn't like him anymore," Fred said.

"Of course I still like him," Amy said. "What can we do?"

"I have contacted a military black operations friend, a Commander Black," Fred said. "He believes he knows where Sam is being kept. But it's been a long time since you were in the military. The Gulf War ended years ago. I didn't know if your special forces training might help us. Unless, of course, you don't care about Sam anymore."

Amy arose from her desk. "You never forget that sort of training.

You knew I would help, Fred. We three have known each other too long for this. Now, where was Sam last known to be?"

"We have traced him to a hotel apartment in Chicago," Fred said.

"Take me there."

"What?" Fred asked, stunned.

"Take me there, now! My training here at the paper taught me a thing or two about investigating crime."

She packed up some plastic gloves and some plastic bags to gather evidence.

*   *   *

Fred and Amy took off for Chicago in Amy's 1972 Brown Chevrolet Impala. The beast, full of rust, ran like a well-oiled machine. As Amy progressed along Interstate 55 north toward Chicago, Fred noticed a sedan following them, containing two men in black suits. Fred caught a glimpse of a gun.

"We're being followed," Fred said. "It's those NSA goons. I recognize their great fashion taste."

Amy exited Interstate 55 in Joliet, and the sedan followed them off the highway.

"The key to winning a high-speed chase is not to make mistakes," Amy said.

"Did your military training teach you that?"

"Of course," Amy said.

"Don't let them get close enough to our car to force us to spin out," Fred said.

"Fred, don't worry," she said. "This old hunk of junk can't go very fast anyway. But in the city streets, I think I can evade them."

Despite her attempts to evade, the sedan pulled up alongside them and the driver pulled out his gun.

Amy stepped on the brakes and spun around to make a turn into a side street.

"Take that alley," Fred called out.

This confused their pursuers, but they continued on and eventually caught sight of Amy's Impala again.

Amy used the traffic to put several car lengths between them, weaving in and out of spaces between the cars. She drove up onto the curb and almost hit a parked car.

Fred covered his face, not wanting to see the crash, but she managed to swerve the car around the parked vehicle safely.

After she had created a great distance between her and the sedan, she sped across the lanes and pulled off onto another side street.

The sedan still pursued them. She entered the business district again and found a parking garage next to the Desplaines River.

"Why are you going in there?" Fred asked. "We'll be stuck if they follow us."

The sedan followed them into the garage.

"Trust me," she said to Fred. "This old Impala still has a trick or two. Crack open your window."

"Why?"

"Because if you don't and if the car is in water, the water pressure will make it impossible to open the window and escape."

"Water pressure?" Fred said, confused as he started to roll down the window.

Suddenly, at the 12th level of the parking garage, the top level, Fred noticed the sedan was very close behind them.

Amy sped straight toward the wall that faced the river 12 stories below.

The sedan almost overtook them.

Both vehicles zoomed at close to 50 miles an hour, headed directly for the wall.

Amy turned sharply to the left, screeching the tires just before hitting the wall. The Impala tipped onto its right wheels, but safely banked before hitting the wall.

The sedan driver did not do so well. He slammed on his brakes, but still hit the wall and went sailing over it into the river.

"Hope they cracked open their windows," Fred said, smiling at Amy. Neither wanted to wait around to find out.

Amy and Fred made it safely to the hotel apartment where Commander Black told Fred that Sam had been held captive. Black had secured an apartment key so they went directly to the apartment, number 3G. The room looked spotless.

"It's already been cleaned," Fred said.

Amy and Fred exited the apartment. They noticed a cleaning woman's tray parked outside in the hall.

"Did you just clean apartment 3G?" Fred asked.

"Yes," the woman said. She chewed a big wad of gum.

Fred pulled out his FBI identification and quickly flashed it like he was a special agent. His status as a research assistant qualified him to limited fieldwork, but only with express written permission. Technically, he was impersonating an FBI agent.

"I'm agent Steinfeld," Fred said. "Show me the refuse from 3G."

"It's all mixed together in the garbage sack," she said. "Help yourself."

The cleaning woman looked at Amy.

"Are you an FBI agent too?" she asked skeptically. Amy wore a pair of slacks and peasant blouse.

"She's assisting me in the investigation," Fred answered.

That satisfied the woman. "It's a good thing you guys came when you did," the cleaning woman said. "I found some bloodstains on the room towels from 3G. And there were some bloodstains on the carpet too. I was going to call the police anyway."

This alarmed both Amy and Fred.

"May we take the towels?" Fred asked.

"Yeah," she said, rummaging through the laundry. "Here's the ones from 3G. See, you can clearly see the blood on the towels."

Amy and Fred grew more concerned. But once inside Amy's Impala, Fred started to question the situation.

"If there was really blood on those towels from some sort of beating, they wouldn't have left it on the towels," Fred said. "Drive me to the FBI lab on 94th St. I have a buddy that will analyze this blood sample. I want to know if it's Sam's or not."

At the lab, Fred gave the towel to a friend, Dennis, who immediately examined it.

A few minutes later, he invited Fred and Amy into the lab.

He showed Fred the blood under the microscope.

"It's blood all right," Dennis said. "But it's not your friend's blood."

"How do you know?" Amy wanted to know.

"Because it's not even human blood."

This alarmed Fred, who thought it might be the Orishan's blood.

"It's from a pig," Dennis explained. This relieved Fred.

"A pig?" Cheryl said.

"Yes, and there's more," Dennis said. "There are traces of wood filings, traces of a leather sole, and some clay soil. I analyzed the soil and found some flora that can be found in Harvey, Illinois, near a former hog butcher warehouse."

"The Old Slaughter House," Fred said. "I know that place. I did some research on a case there once."

"One of the NSA agents must have cleaned off his shoes in the hotel apartment," Amy reasoned.

"Glad I could help you, Fred," Dennis said.

Amy and Sam rushed to the new location.

Fred opened the warehouse door with a key he obtained from the manager after flashing his FBI identification badge.

"I've never impersonated an FBI agent before," Fred said. "I've done it twice today. I'm gonna be in so much trouble for this."

"Pipe down, Fred. We have to determine what evidence the NSA goons may have left behind," Amy said.

"Are you kidding," Fred said. "These guys are professionals. There will be nothing here."

"We found this address, didn't we?" Amy said, putting on plastic gloves and handing Fred a pair as well as some empty plastic bags.

"Think like a criminal," she continued. "What happened in this room? Look for obvious evidence. Anything that can link these NSA goons to Sam while Sam was here."

Fred saw a portion of the carpet that appeared to have been recently cleaned because it was lighter than the rest.

She pulled out some plastic bags and put some samples of the carpet into them.

Amy noticed a cigarette butt in the trashcan. She bagged it.

"There's some hair on this brush in the bathroom sink," Fred called out.

"Bag it," she said.

She also found what looked like rope fibers in the trashcan. She bagged that as well. Then she saw what looked like glowing pieces of dirt or dust.

She bagged the glowing dirt as well.

"I hope this stuff isn't radioactive," she said to herself.

After scouring the warehouse, they decided to talk to the manager, Danny Wotowski. Wotowski, a surly, overweight man with few hairs left on his head, wore a sleeveless T-shirt. A cigarette stub hung from his mouth.

"You government boys have already been over this with me," Wotowski said.

"Just humor us," Fred said, trying to be official. "Where did they take their prisoner?"

"Boy, I'll tell you those guys in black sure bagged a loser," Wotowski said. "He was carrying two teddy bears with him, one dressed in a trench coat and the other in a super hero outfit. A grown man with teddy bears."

"When did they leave with the prisoner?" Amy asked.

"Last week."

"Did they say where they were headed?"

"No, but I overheard one of them say they were going to take him to the college, whatever that meant. That's government lingo for a prison, right?"

"Uh, yeah, right," Fred said. "Thank you for your cooperation, Mr. Wotowski."

Outside heading for the car, Fred showed concern.

"College is government lingo, but not for a prison," Fred said. "It's the NSA's version of a concentration camp."

"Where is it?"

"No clue," Fred said. "I know a few who can tell us."

*   *   *

Meanwhile, Snopple and Polaris prepared to take Armando away again for an interrogation session. Lavender, with Armando's help, managed to unlock her arm and leg chains. She slithered in the shadows and followed Snopple, Polaris and Armando onto the lift. Armando remained in chains.

Two floors up, Snopple and Polaris pushed Armando into the interrogation room. Lavender slipped in just before Polaris closed the door and hid under the interrogation desk as Polaris secured Armando to the chair.

While Snopple began his interrogation, Lavender worked the chains on Armando's hands and feet, freeing him.

Then she popped up, growling, and jumped onto Polaris. In that moment, Armando stood from his chair and put his hands around Snopple's neck.

"Snopple, you will take us both upstairs or I snap your neck right now!" Armando said, clenching his teeth. Polaris still struggled on the floor to get Lavender off his face.

"Lavender, you can let up on Polaris now," Armando said, still strangling Snopple. Lavender took her sharp claws off Polaris' face and stood erect. She pulled Polaris' and Snopple's Arjogun guns from their holsters, giving one to Armando.

"Now, take us upstairs," Armando demanded.

"Where?" Snopple wanted to know. He was rubbing his neck where Armando was applying pressure a moment earlier.

"We just need to get to the sleeping quarters," Lavender said.

Snopple pressed a button on his uniform located directly under his "no paw" symbol. This alerted Arjogun security.

As soon as Lavender and Armando led Polaris and Snopple out to the hallway, a group of Arjogun soldiers confronted them at gunpoint.

The Moving Prison

In the car on the way back from Chicago, Fred made a call from his cell phone.

"We have some physical evidence from the warehouse," Fred said. He was speaking to Leni in the Paw Cave.

"We'll analyze it," she said. "What else did you learn?"

"The warehouse manager overheard them talking about sending the prisoner to the 'college,'" Fred said. "I think they mean a special new prison constructed in a bunker by the NSA at some unknown location."

"Right," Leni said. "We'll see what we can find out."

"What do you want me to do in the meantime?" Fred asked.

"Meet me at Sam's apartment in Streator with the evidence."

Fred disconnected the cell phone.

"Whom were you talking to?" Amy wanted to know.

"My people," Fred said. "They have access to equipment that can analyze what we collected at the warehouse."

*   *   *

Amy went back to her duties at *The Daily Press*.

Fred took the physical evidence with him to Sam's apartment in Streator. Leni greeted him there. She brought him to Sam's bedroom.

"Fred, we have never allowed a human into Pawtropolis before," Leni said. "I will allow you into the Paw Cave, but I am going to have to establish some ground rules."

"Leni," Fred said. "Your husband and his friends saved my bacon more than once. I trust you."

"First, I will have to ask that you tell no one about what you see, even Sam."

"Check."

"Second, this is going to be a top secret operation. We don't know who we can trust among our own people at this point. After learning that the head of the B.B.B. is an Arjogun agent surgically altered to look like one of us, we cannot trust anyone."

"Check."

"You will likely see and hear things—technological devices and such, that you have never seen before. Expect the unexpected."

Fred agreed.

"Okay, Fred," she continued. "I am going to put a hood on you and transport you via the Teddy Bear Zone to the Paw Cave. The transport is instantaneous and harmless. I promise it will go quickly."

"I'm ready," Fred said.

She placed a black hood over Fred's head.

"Now crawl under the bed," she ordered. She put her paw in his hand and gently pulled him down.

Fred went down on his hands and knees, and then down on his stomach. He crawled under Sam's bed and Leni followed.

For a brief moment, he felt a swirling sensation and saw sparkling lights from beneath the hood on his head. He had a sensation of floating for a split second.

Then he was flat on his stomach on a cold smooth floor, different from Sam's wooden bedroom floor.

Leni pulled off Fred's hood.

Fred looked around. He saw a rocky surface on the walls, and a huge computer screen in the center of the room.

He also saw the Paw Mobile, and the F-117A. He knew about Sam's trip to Serbia with the Orishans to "procure" it.

Louis and Chocolate were already at work on the computer.

Chocolate took the bagged evidence.

"Thank you," she said. "I'm Chocolate. I will be examining the evidence."

She took the material in the bags over to a special scanner and what appeared to be a microscope.

"I'm particularly interested in those glowing bits of dirt," she said.

"I'm checking on that 'college' reference," Louis said as he banged on the keyboard to the huge computer. The keys looked like paw prints and had strange writing on each key. A ring surrounded the screen, which seemed huge by even human standards, with more strange writing upon it, and four paws made of shiny metal.

Fred had no idea what he was seeing.

Suddenly, writing in a strange language began appearing on the huge screen. It was a message from a double agent recruited by the Knights in Blue Satin.

"Here," Louis said. "We found a reference to the Homeland Security Agency's definition of college. It is a moving prison. It is located on an Arjogun cruiser and flies over Canadian air space."

"Where are you getting all this?" Fred said, trying to make out the strange writing on the screen.

"Oh, sorry," Louis said. He pressed a button on the strange keyboard, and suddenly the letters changed to English.

"This is from Gobador, an Arjogun who is working for us as a double-agent now," Louis said.

"We've met," Fred said.

"The Knights have been able to tap into the Homeland Security Agency's data base," Louis added.

"That's the second time you said 'Homeland Security Agency,'" Fred said. "I never heard of that. I thought this arrest of Sam and Schaumburg was an NSA operation."

"Americans haven't been told about the Homeland Security Agency yet," Lou said. "We only just learned of it a few days ago ourselves. The Lemming, who we now know to be Sam's boss at his newspaper, Izzie Feinberg, is one of the top officials in the top-secret agency. They answer to nobody except the General in charge of Project Unicorn. And they have been implanting mind control devices in human beings for longer than you have been alive. They do the medical operations onboard the Arjogunian ship known as the college."

Leni observed Fred's shocked expression.

"As we embark on a rescue operation to save Sam, Schaumburg and Andy, Commander Black and the Protectors are assembling a team of humans and Orishans to storm the camp at Madagascar as soon as we locate it."

"Cheryl will be happy when her husband is finally rescued," Fred said.

At that moment, Chocolate screamed out in tones of horror. "Oh, No!"

"What is it," Leni asked.

"These glowing pieces of dirt," she said.

"Yes?"

"It's from a stone which is from Orisha," Chocolate said.

"Yes?" Leni said.

"I fear this is being used to hurt Schaumburg and Andy."

"How can stone hurt them?" Fred said. "Aren't they super?"

"Only when they eat chocolate, and only then for 20 minutes," Leni said. "What is it, Chocolate? What have you found?"

"Hold on," Chocolate said.

"Louis, put this data into the Paw Computer and see what it tells us," Chocolate requested.

Louis took the data and punched in the information. Then he hit a query key and large amounts of data started streaming across the huge screen.

"What is it?" Leni wanted to know.

"Leni, we know that the reason Andy and Schaumburg have super powers is because they are brothers and share the same DNA," Chocolate said.

"Yes," Leni said.

"Well, when Schaumy and Andy eat chocolate, their bodies create a chemical reaction which is influenced by their power rings."

"Yes, go on," Leni said. "We know all this."

"The power ring is made of a refined ore on Orisha," Chocolate said. "The Elders of the Mystical Order of the Golden Paw forge the rings from volcanic lava. But unrefined Orishan volcanic ore can have the opposite effects on Andy and Schaumburg. It would make them weak instead of strong. It could actually kill them. The data base calls the unrefined ore Orishanite."

Leni put her paw to her mouth in horror. Louis also seemed shocked. Fred just seemed beary confused.

"Can we create an antidote to Orishanite?" Leni asked.

"We can try," Chocolate said. "It might take days, months, or even several years of research. I'll have to use trial and error."

"Make it a priority," Leni said.

"Got it," Chocolate said.

"Meanwhile, we've got to find out where that prison ship is and rescue them!" Lou said. "Before it's too late."

Lou tapped out a message to Gobador.

In response, a message came back. It was in English so Fred could read it.

"Samuel Arctophile is about to be implanted with an Arjogun mind-control device on board this ship. We are located near Ontario at present. I'll send you our exact coordinates in a moment. Move swiftly. The operation is about to begin."

H.A.R.V.E.Y. To The Rescue

At that precise moment aboard the Arjogun flying saucer soaring high above Ontario, Sam slept tied to an operating table.

Andy and Schaumburg sat in another room, looking very weak and sickly. Someone had placed a large Orishanite rock near them, causing their weakened condition. The rock set just far enough away not to kill them. They were tied at paws and feet as well.

An Arjogun doctor came in to perform an operation on Sam. He cut into Sam's neck with a laser knife that caused no blood to spill. The Arjogun swiftly and skillfully implanted a small electronic device in Sam's neck.

Izzie Feinberg entered the operating room with a medical mask covering his face.

"Doctor, was it successful?" Feinberg asked.

"Yes, Lemming," the doctor said. "He will answer to you when you say the prearranged code words to him. As soon as he hears those words, he will fall into a trance and perform any operations you command of him."

"What are his code words?"

"Is there nothing sacred," the doctor responded.

"That's appropriate for someone doing the bidding of the Lemming," Feinberg said. "Excellent. I will call upon Sam when needed. Have you wiped out his memory of this experience?"

"Yes sir, but he and the Orishans will suspect something because of the gap of a few weeks in their memory."

"Tell the Frown we finally have a solution to our super Orishans," the Lemming said. "They won't bother us anymore. And now with

Sam under my control, he won't be fishing around for information regarding Armando Cruz any more either . . . In the meantime, I have a special assignment for Mr. Arctophile. He will uncover the scoop of the century for *The Daily Press!*"

At that moment, the loudspeaker in the operating room crackled to life.

"Lemming, we are tracking an F-117A on an intercept course," a voice said.

"That's likely the Orishans' ship," the Lemming said. "Don't take any action. We'll allow them to rescue their friends now. Remove the Orishanite from our two Orishan captives."

"Aye, sir," the voice said.

The Lemming guessed correctly. Louis, Chocolate and Leni were on board the F-117A planning a daring rescue. They could not cloak the ship since H.A.R.V.E.Y. was with Schaumburg at the moment.

Louis moved his ship directly under the Arjogun saucer, opened the canopy, and then used a magnetic grappling hook to latch onto the saucer's lower hull.

As soon as Lou was about to climb up the metal cable attached to the saucer, Leni handed him a camera.

She looked at Lou who knew exactly what the camera was for. He pocketed it and climbed up the cable. Gobador was on board and opened a hatch to allow the Orishan onboard.

Gobador pointed Lou to the compartment where Sam, Schaumburg and Andy were being held.

"This is too easy," Louis said to Gobador.

"Do not waste time," Gobador said.

"Where's the Lemming?" Lou asked.

"In the control center at top," Gobador said.

"Great. I'll rescue our friends, then we'll be leaving you," Louis replied.

"Hurry," Gobador hissed.

Lou quickly entered the compartment where Sam, Schaumburg and Andy had been stashed, tied up. They all slept. He covered the Orishanite with lead and awoke them. He gave Andy and Schaumburg chocolate to revive their super powers as the Paw and Mardi Gras.

The Paw and Mardi Gras helped Sam climb down the rope back into the F-117A. The super Orishans flew back home on their own power.

"Where's Lou?" Sam asked as he entered the F-117A cockpit.

"He'll be here soon," Leni said. "He has a secret assignment on board that Arjogun vessel."

The next day, Chocolate had Sam on a table in the Paw Cave's operating room. She examined Sam's neck with an Orishan medical tool.

"Just as I thought," she said. "The Lemming has implanted one of those mind control devices on you."

"What?" Sam said, now horrified.

"It's all right," Chocolate said, calming Sam down. "We'll soon render it harmless."

She took the H.A.R.V.E.Y. unit and placed it over the scar where the Arjogun made the incision to implant the device.

A small electric spark sizzled Sam's neck for a split second.

"Ouch!" Sam said. "That stung! Can you remove the device now?"

"No!" she said. "Remember what Armando's report said about the government people that tried to remove the Arjogun mind-control device from human abductees? Removing it might kill you," Chocolate said. "I used the H.A.R.V.E.Y. unit to safely zap it into a hunk of fried scrap."

Leni, Louis, Fred and Schaumburg came in to see how Sam was doing.

"You look like you're back to normal, Sam," Fred said. "I'm curious to know what the Lemming and the Frown have in store for us."

"The device basically forces the victim to be subject to hypnotic commands," Leni said. "It is very primitive technology. Our H.A.R.V.E.Y. unit is able to disable it easily and safely."

"Boy," Sam said. "No wonder the Frown, or should I say Vil, wanted you guys to get rid of that H.A.R.V.E.Y. unit. It sure comes in handy. I just wish I could get this thing out of my neck."

"It's probably better it stays in," Schaumburg said. "If people suspect you, they may X-ray you to make sure you are still under their control with that implant. They have no idea we can neutralize it safely."

"How will I know when the Lemming wants to order me around to do some evil deed?"

"Funny you should ask," Louis said. "We have an inside man with the Arjogun now, thanks to Andy and Perry Purple. Remember that Arjogun who stowed aboard the F-117A in Serbia? His name is Gobador and he is now a double agent for the Knights in Blue Satin. He learned the word codes that will trigger your mind-control."

"What are they?"

"Is there nothing sacred." Lou said.

"I know what you mean," Sam said, not realizing Lou was using the code words. "I can't believe these goons would stoop to mind-control devices. Nothing is sacred to those Arjogun."

"No, 'Is there nothing sacred' are the code words that trigger your hypnosis," Lou said.

"Oh!" Sam said. "Looks like H.A.R.V.E.Y.'s zapping worked, otherwise I would be doing whatever you asked me to do right now, Lou."

"I want you to get me a bag of potato chips," Lou ordered, waving his hands in mock control.

"Your wish is my command," Sam replied. They all laughed.

At that moment, Andy ran into the room, excited.

"Paw, come quick," he said. "It's our team in Madagascar. They've been ambushed."

All of them ran out of the room except Sam. Sam walked, still woozy.

In the computer room, they watched a satellite camera showing infrared pictures of two factions facing off in a gun battle on Madagascar.

"Turn on the radio transmissions," Schaumburg ordered. Andy flipped a switch.

"We're pulling out," Commander Black said over the radio. Gunfire and mortars exploding could be heard in the background. Arjogun soldiers gunned down the "Protector" agents.

"I've lost three men already," Black continued. "This is a disaster. We'll have to regroup and formulate a new plan. They must have gotten word of our attempt to invade the camp here."

"Now what?" Schaumburg said.

"Those guys were trying to rescue Armando?" Sam said.

"Yeah," Fred replied. "They've been planning this for weeks."

The Paw phone suddenly rang.

"Paw, here," Schaumburg said.

"This is Perry Purple," the voice on the other end said.

"Yes, Perry," the Paw said.

"Our unit in Madagascar was ambushed," Perry said. "This will set us back months."

"We haven't lost yet," the Paw said. "Remember, we still have the map to locate the Sword of George Washington."

"I can't understand how the Protectors were discovered," Perry said. "I fear we have a mole here in Pawtropolis . . . In any event, I understand Schaumburg and Mardi Gras escaped from the HSA and brought back Samuel Arctophile safely as well. Were you able to neutralize the implant safely?"

"He's good as new," the Paw said. "We'll start working on finding that sword now. Paw out."

"Who was that?" Sam asked.

"That was our contact with the Knights in Blue Satin," Schaumburg said. "He was asking about your implant. We have a little surprise for the Lemming now with you back to normal. Let me go over our plan."

"Schaumy, we've managed to make the alterations to the Teddy Bear Zone portal under our bed here in Toleni," Leni said, almost blushing at the mention of their "bed."

"Can it teleport anywhere now, not just under other beds?" Schaumburg asked.

"Well, almost," Leni said. "With the help of Dreamwalker, we can now teleport under a car or airplane, not just beds."

"Well, that's something," Schaumburg said. "We can use that."

CHAPTER 16

THE DOUBLE CROSS

June 6, 2002, Versailles, Illinois. Sam's office

Months flew by without any strange events. Sam continued to work at the Versailles Bureau unmolested. Cheryl, now home from the hospital, continued to work at the museum. The FBI fired Fred so he found employment in Kankakee at a newspaper called *The National Investigator*, one of those tabloid rags people pick up at the supermarket as they check out.

Sam and Cheryl had little contact. She was glad he was back and safe, but she kept her distance.

"I'm sort of glad she's not keeping in touch," Sam said. "Now that we know her husband is alive, I have to back off. The less I see of her, the less it hurts."

"You should not stop your contact with her, Sam," Schaumburg said. "She and you have linked destinies. You should call her."

"Stop it Schaumburg," Sam said, now angry.

The advantage of working alone in the Versailles office is that as long as he filed his stories on time every day, nobody from the main office in Montreal bothered him much.

Sam had just filed his stories, signed off the clock, and busied himself by reading an article from Fred's weekly national scandal sheet.

"Listen to this, Schaumburg," Sam said as he unfolded the tabloid newspaper.

Canadian UFO sightings increase
sharply in first half of 2002

BY FRED STEINFELD
THE NATIONAL INVESTIGATOR

ONTARIO, CANADA—Round silver discs over Ontario and cylinders near Winnipeg and British Columbia have caught the public's imagination as UFO sightings increased dramatically this year, reports the Canadian press.

This has been a banner year for the sightings of unidentified flying objects over the country north of the United States.

"So far this year, we had the largest number of single sightings reported," said Charles Sanders, Mutual UFO Network (MUFON) spokesman for Canada.

"I wonder why there is so much UFO activity all of a sudden?" Sam asked.

"Maybe the Arjogun are evacuating the planet," Schaumburg wondered.

"Because the Arjogun don't want to be around when they set off their doomsday device?" Sam wanted to know.

But before Schaumburg could reply, his office phone rang.

"Versailles Bureau, Samuel Arctophile speaking," Sam said.

"Is . . . There . . . Nothing . . . Sacred . . ." the voice on the other end said.

"Yes master," Sam said, winking at Schaumburg. He pushed the record button on his special recorder to record the conversation. But the caller disguised his voice on the other end electronically. Sam knew it must be his boss, Izzie Feinberg. Sam also put the voice on speakerphone so Schaumburg could hear.

"What are your orders, master?"

"You are to plant a bomb at the residence of Cheryl Cruz," Feinberg said. "Be sure she and her son are home at the time. The boy is home from school by 3 p.m. The bomb material is being sent to you via courier this morning. After blowing her up, turn yourself into the authorities."

"Yes master." Sam hung up.

He was a little spooked by the coldness of the phone call.

"Feinberg will kill three proverbial birds with one stone," Schaumburg said. "He will be rid of Cheryl and her son and when you are caught, of you as well."

"Why isn't he asking me to destroy you guys?"

"I think the Frown is planning something along those lines," Schaumburg said. "Okay. Let's implement our plan. You know what to do?"

"Yes, Schaumburg. I only hope this works. At least it gives me an excuse to see Cheryl so I can warn her."

*   *   *

Sam knocked on Cheryl's office door at the museum. He was carrying Schaumburg with him, dressed in trench coat and fedora.

"Come in," she said.

Sam opened the door. Cheryl sat, back to him, reviewing books, letters and artwork related to George Washington.

She turned around. The minute she saw him, her expression turned cold.

"Oh, it's you," she said.

"Sorry to bother you Cheryl," Sam said. "But this is very important."

"As important as rescuing my Armando?"

"Just as," Sam said. He plopped down a tape recorder and played back the message from Feinberg telling him to blow her and Jose up.

Her large brown eyes seemed to grow larger with horror.

"What's going on?" she asked.

"When I was kidnapped, they planted a mind-control device in me," Sam said.

"But how?"

"Some people I know figured out a way to neutralize the implant,"

Sam said. "But nobody knows it. They think I'm going to blow you up. So we have to make them think that to flush them out."

"Who's 'them'?" she asked.

"The people who work for Project Unicorn," Sam said. "The same people who kidnapped me and your husband."

"Why should I help you?" she said coldly. "I'm just a conspiracy theory nut."

"Cheryl, I'm very sorry for those words I said in the hospital."

Cheryl looked deep into Sam's eyes. It made Sam very uncomfortable.

"All right, Sam," Cheryl said. "I'll help you. What's your plan?"

"Well, first, we have to get you out of here," Sam said. "Then we'll get Jose as well."

"How is that going to flush out the bad guys?" Cheryl asked.

"You'll see," Sam said cryptically. "Drive your car to my apartment. Fred is there waiting. I'll follow soon with Jose."

"Sam, don't do too much damage with that bomb," Cheryl said half joking. "That's my house, you know."

Sam did not reply.

Later, at Sam's apartment, Fred and Cheryl were sitting at Sam's kitchen table. Cheryl brought along a George Washington book to read while waiting for all this to blow over.

"What are you reading?" Fred asked.

"This is a biography of George Washington," Cheryl said. "It was written in 1800, right after Washington's death. It was dropped off at the museum as a donation. It's quite interesting."

Sam arrived with the boy. Jose jumped out of the car and tore up the stairs to Sam's apartment in Streator. He remembered it fondly from the days when Sam and Cheryl were seeing a lot more of each other socially.

He especially liked all the "teddy bears" that were there.

Jose began looking through the book his mother was reading. Suddenly, a yellowed piece of parchment fell out.

"What's this?" he asked himself.

He unfolded the yellowed paper which revealed a pen and ink drawing. It looked like a picture of two swords. It showed their dimensions, both nine-inches long. The drawing was labeled simply "The keys." It also said "Gifts from Bartholomew to George Washington."

"Hey, look what I found," Jose said.

He brought the sketch to his mother.

"Not now, Jose darling," Cheryl said, distracted by the bomb business.

"But mom, look at how small George Washington's sword is," Jose said.

"What?" Sam said, now curious. He grabbed the sketch from Jose and studied it closely.

"Cheryl, look at this," Sam said. He showed her the pen and ink drawing. It was signed by Gilbert Stuart, but unlike the oil on canvas, this was dated 1798, not 1796, the date of the famous painting.

Cheryl, remembering the letters from Bartholomew he and she had discovered with Fred, grew very curious about the drawing.

"Look, Cheryl, I have to go blow you guys up now, so I gotta go," Sam said. "Why don't you check into this tiny sword thing? I know some people that would be interested in that."

"Blow up?" Jose said.

"Never mind, Jose," Cheryl said. "It's a game. Sam won't be really blowing us up."

Sam scooped up Schaumburg and drove back to Versailles. On the way, he spoke with the Orishan about the drawing Jose had discovered.

"Those are the swords," Schaumburg said. "The Swords of George Washington given to him by Bartholomew. We have to locate them, Sam. It is imperative we find them before the Frown does."

"We'll look into it as soon as this bomb business is finished," Sam said. "Do Commander Black and Louis have the photos and everything they need?"

"Everything is set into motion," Schaumburg said. "And we can even prove that Feinberg made that phone call to you this morning. We have the phone records showing the time of the call and from where the call was placed. Feinberg used his own phone at work. Not too bright, that one."

Sam's eyes showed concerned now.

"I never knew my managing editor to be stupid or make a foolish mistake like that. Is this plan gonna work, Schaumburg?" Sam asked.

"Like a well-oiled machine," Schaumburg said.

Back in Versailles, Sam picked up the explosives. He used gloves to open the package and gave the box to Schaumburg. Schaumburg passed the box on to Andy who took it back to the Paw Cave with him.

Louis, Leni and Commander Black waited at the Paw Cave.

Cheryl and Jose stayed safe with Fred at Sam's apartment in Streator.

Sam picked up his phone and called Commander Black's cell phone.

"Okay, Commander," Sam said. "We are going to pretend to go to the Versailles police station with this bomb material. Get ready to apprehend the Lemming."

"We're on our way to Montreal right now."

Black and Louis took the invisible plane, now cloaked with a properly working H.A.R.V.E.Y. unit, to Montreal, arriving a second later at the newspaper office.

Commander Black took Louis to Feinberg's office door. Other Protector agents met him at the office door.

Commander Black's phone rang.

"It's time," Black said.

At that precise moment, the bomb parts lay on the Versailles Police Chief's desk. A C-4 plastic explosive was to be used, detonated by remote control by Sam. Sam and Schaumburg sat waiting at the police chief's desk to hear word of Feinberg's arrest.

Black's men burst into Feinberg's office.

"You are under arrest, Mr. Feinberg," Black said. "I'm Special Agent Black with the secret service." Black flashed his badge.

"What's the charge?" Feinberg asked.

"Attempted murder and attempted criminal damage to property for starters," Black said.

"That's preposterous," Feinberg said. "What murder? That girl was killed by Arctophile."

"I did not say anything about a girl, now did I?" Black said. Then Black played back the tape of the command to blow up Cheryl and Jose.

"What does that prove?" Feinberg asked. "That's not my voice on the tape."

Black plopped down phone records showing the call from his office to Arctophile at the precise moment the tape indicates the call was made to the Versailles Bureau.

"Circumstantial evidence," Feinberg said. Louis walked up.

"What's that, an animatronic teddy bear?" he asked referring to Louis.

Louis plopped down photos of Feinberg with the Arjogun doctors on board the Arjogun ship. One photo showed Sam still under as the operation was being finished. Gobador took that one for the Orishans. Louis took the rest after he rescued Sam, Schaumburg and Andy.

"So, you have some photos of me with some alien grays," Feinberg said. "What does that prove?"

"We can show Sam's still got the implant in his neck," Black said. "You might have killed that woman and boy, had we not intervened."

"You've been watching Arctophile, haven't you?" Feinberg said. "Ha! You fools! There's a post-hypnotic suggestion. Now that he has set off the bomb, Arctophile will turn himself in as the Cruz woman's murderer. You can't save him or tie it to me!"

"The bomb never went off, Feinberg," Black said. Black cuffed Feinberg and dragged him out of the office with other agents. Louis (in Black's arms) was back in a state of suspended hibernation, so he appeared to be a teddy bear to onlookers in the newsroom.

"This is all a misunderstanding," Feinberg said to his staffers. "I'll be back soon. Just keep working."

"You aren't going to be back for a long, long time if I have anything to do about it," Black said.

"You have no idea who you are dealing with," Feinberg said. "You Orishan lover! You and those teddy bear aliens are the ruin of mankind. They ruined my father. Now they will ruin us all! You're backing the wrong horse, Black. Let me go before it's too late."

At the entrance to *The Daily Press* building, as Black led Feinberg outside in cuffs, a group of Arjogun agents ambushed Black and snatched Feinberg away. All the Protector agents, caught off guard, were knocked out with a special Arjogun sleeping gas. The alien grays also snatched the incriminating evidence such as the photos and phone records.

After the Arjogun agents left the scene, Black woke up groaning. Then he woke Louis from his suspended hibernation.

"The plan to flush Feinberg has failed," Black said to Louis.

The Two Missing Swords

Cheryl Cruz's private journal, June 25, 2002

Dear Diary,

Today I learned the possible location of one of two missing swords once belonging to George Washington.

Scholars have long known of the location of five of the seven swords belonging to our nation's first president.

Small swords normally had thin blades and were designed for thrusting. They became an accepted accompaniment to an 18th-century gentleman's wardrobe. For this reason, small swords were readily available, and many military officers carried them into battle during the Revolutionary War.

Washington is known to have owned seven swords in 1799, the year he died.

To each of his five nephews, he bequeathed a sword with the requirement that they not be unsheathed for shedding blood, unless they were being used for self-defense or in defense of "their Country and its rights."

Washington did not approve of resolving quarrels with swords in duels.

Three of those five swords are currently on display in the collection of the Mount Vernon Historical Society and are exhibited in a museum on the grounds of Mount Vernon.

Two others are in private collections.

But the final two swords are lost to the pages of history.

It has come to my attention recently that at least one, if not two of these remaining swords are not swords at all, but tiny daggers, replicas of real short swords, measuring about nine inches long and made of elegant silver-mounted filigree hilts.

I believe I have located at least one of the two tiny replicas, since I have found writings dating back to the post-Revolutionary era when Washington reportedly laid a time capsule in the cornerstone of the plaza where the Washington Monument would be constructed years later.

However, the location of the final, and seventh sword, which I believe to be of the same nine-inch variety, remains a mystery.

Earlier this month, my son and I discovered a drawing by the great artist Gilbert Stuart. The drawing is done on parchment in pen and ink, is signed by Stuart. It refers to the two nine-inch swords as "keys" from Bartholomew. I have found a few arcane references to this Bartholomew, including letters to him from Washington himself. We have also discovered letters from Bartholomew to Washington and, I am almost ashamed to admit, secret writing created on letters between the lines using onion juice and lemon juice.

We discovered the writing by heating the paper. This was an ancient method of secret writing used at the time of Washington.

The only clues we have to this missing seventh sword are some references in letters.

In one letter to Bartholomew, he makes an obvious reference to this tiny sword. It is the earliest reference I can find:

Jan. 2, 1754
Dearest Bartholomew,
   It has been two years since you gave me your sword.

This would indicate the sword was given to Washington in the year 1752. He had not yet begun his rise in the military ranks when he was given Bartholomew's sword.

Washington makes a few strange references to Bartholomew's size. In one letter, he says Bartholomew is 18 inches tall. This could be some kind of code or something. However, I have also discovered other references to Bartholomew's size.

Could Bartholomew be the smallest midget on record?

Is that why his sword is only nine inches long?

And where is this tiny blade?

In an effort to answer these questions, I delved into many references to Washington in other historic documents and found some cross-references to Bartholomew.

Based on my research, I have become convinced that Bartholomew may have been an alien being who visited Earth more than two centuries ago, and helped guide our nation's leaders to found America.

Furthermore, I have discovered that this fabled missing seventh Sword of George Washington, if it is not buried at the base of the Washington Monument, must be secreted away someplace else. The seventh sword may have properties that are unearthly.

It could explain why Washington was able to ride into the fray of battles over and over and return without a scratch, while his horse was shot out from under him at least three times.

It could also explain why his coat was once found after a battle riddled with holes, while again Washington remained unscathed. Was this nine-inch sword magical, like the legendary Excalibur of King Arthur lore?

I will need to travel to the Smithsonian Institute to complete my research. I have also applied for a grant from the Mount Vernon Historical Society. They say they are very interested in my research. If I get the grant, I will be able to make the trip to Washington, D.C. It will be good to take Jose there, since he has never been to our nation's capital.

A local journalist who has several secret sources on George Washington and this mysterious Bartholomew has assisted me to a minor degree. He has not told me, but from his conversations, I am more convinced than ever that Bartholomew was an extraterrestrial. That would mean that if the sword given to Washington by Bartholomew has "magical properties," it is more likely that it contains some type of alien technology that seems like magic to humans.

Of course, these are all theories. I am meeting with the journalist tonight to obtain some more documents he promised. He has been helpful to me in the past, and I trust him. He is also becoming quite close to Jose, which is good since Jose's father has been gone for so many years.

I hope we can rescue Armando soon. I miss him so. It was this journalist, Samuel Arctophile, who finally confirmed that Armando is still alive. Certain elements in the government tried to rescue him, but the rescue attempt failed.

Meanwhile, other elements in the government, the ones Armando tried to warn the public about and the ones who imprisoned him, have made attempts on my life and on Jose's life as well.

These are very scary times. The man who most recently tried to engineer my death, Izzie Feinberg, was not punished for his crime. He is now missing.

Feinberg's plot to kill Jose and I, then frame Sam Arctophile for it has failed, thanks to the help of Arctophile. However, when Feinberg was being arrested, he was rescued by a mysterious group of gunmen. The evidence against him was stolen.

Mr. Arctophile said it is all connected to my missing husband and to this fabled Sword of George Washington. Therefore, my current task is to find this sword. I believe it will, ultimately, help me find Armando as well.

Cheryl Cruz
Versailles, Illinois

*   *   *

That same day, in the lowermost floor of the slave camp at Madagascar, Lavender and Armando planned their second attempt at escape during a short meal break.

"This time, we need to enlist the assistance of all humans and Orisha trapped here," Armando said. "If you can get us out of here with that portal, we just need to figure out a way to get up to the floors with the Arjogun sleeping quarters."

"I will discuss it with the Orishans here," Lavender said. "You speak to the humans."

"Whomever wishes to stay, should be allowed to opt out," Armando said. "They may just shoot us this time since this will be our second attempt at escape."

"Agreed," Lavender said. She hugged Armando.

That night, news circulated about an escape attempt. This time, they would overpower the guards just after the shift change when the new Arjogun would be preoccupied.

"But we will need some sort of weapon," Lavender said.

"Leave that to me," Armando said. "I stashed the laser cutters away in my sleeping bag. The Arjogun force us to sleep on this rock floor with just a sleeping bag for padding. The extreme heat precludes the need for blankets. But the temperatures also make it hard to sleep."

"I know," Lavender said. "Why are you telling me this?"

"Bear with me," Armando continued. "The heat combined with lack of sleep makes us slaves very weak, indeed . . . But with these laser cutters, we can even the odds. These will cut through anything, including Arjogun flesh," Armando said.

"I hope it doesn't come to that," Lavender said. "But I do hope we can get out of this horrible place."

"I have been stashing a laser cutter away every few days," Armando said. "As you know, the Arjogun throw them away when the batteries are dead. I have figured out a way to fool the cutter's computer mechanism into thinking the battery is dead long before it really is. Then I retrieve them from the refuse. In a few weeks, we should have enough of an armory to make our escape attempt."

"Brilliant!" Lavender said. "But don't go too fast and be sure your stash is unseen by the Arjogun! Here, let me keep some of them in my sleeping bag as well."

Connecting The Dots

Versailles George Washington Museum, June 27, 2002, 7 p.m.

Cheryl Cruz reviewed the letters from George Washington and the secret writing she uncovered which Washington had written in invisible ink.

A knock came at her door.

"I'll get it," Jose yelled. He was in the apartment, playing a video game.

Jose opened the door to Sam. He carried Schaumburg with him.

"Mom, it's Mr. Arctophile," Jose said, scurrying back to his game.

Sam went in unescorted to the back room where Cheryl busied herself with research.

"Sam, look," she said, pointing to the sketch of Washington's two small swords. "I think I've figured out something important. There were two small swords, not just one."

"What?" Sam asked, now excited.

She explained what she had discovered so far, and said she needed to go on an expedition for the second sword.

"We can't just dig up the time capsule under the Washington Monument," Cheryl said.

"I know some people who can," Sam said, grinning.

"You and your furry little green men?" Cheryl said.

"What?" Sam asked, taken aback.

"Yes, I know about the little furry aliens that look like teddy bears," Cheryl replied. "You and Fred have practically been blurting it out loud for months. I know those aren't teddy bears you keep with you all the time."

Sam handed Schaumburg to Cheryl.

"Press his left paw," Sam instructed.

She complied. Schaumburg suddenly came to life. His amber eyes lit up.

"What gives?" Schaumburg said.

"She knows, Schaumy," Sam said. "We might as well tell her everything."

Schaumburg gave her a quick summary, outlining the battle between the Orishans and the Arjogun, explaining that Earth is the location of the battleground.

"You must also know we are the good guys and it is the grays that are holding Armando captive," Schaumburg said.

"Yes. I had a long talk with your Commander Black the other day," Cheryl said. "He is very anxious to get back to Madagascar to rescue Armando and some Orishans trapped there as slaves. But he

said the place is like a fortress. He told me to concentrate on the sword
of George Washington. He said if we obtain that, the sword would
somehow give us a way to rescue Armando as well, and stop the evil
plot by these Arjogun."

"We still have a few months before their doomsday device is
supposed to be online," Sam agreed. "If these swords can stop it, I'm
all for finding them. But how can there be two of them?"

Cheryl showed Sam and Schaumburg weeks of painstaking research,
reading the secret writing and verifying the information with other
historical documentation she has at the museum and from other sources.

"I'm ready to find that second sword now," Cheryl said. "Are you
with me?"

"I'm not an archeologist," Sam said. "I am a journalist."

"Sam, we need to find out about that second sword," Schaumburg
said.

"This is the story of the century," Cheryl said. "Besides, there's a
local angle. I live here in Versailles. If I make this discovery, it's a local
story."

"I thought we were supposed to keep our distance," Sam said.

"I'm not asking you to date me, you moron," Cheryl said. "I just
need help, that's all. You can take this Orishan along as chaperone."

"I'll clear it with the temporary managing editor at *The Daily Press*.
It's an old buddy of mine. He'll let me go."

"Great, then it's settled," Cheryl said. "I'll take Jose with me. He's
not in school until the end of August. We should find the sword by
then."

"I hope so," Sam said, thinking this could very well take a long
time. They were headed for Virginia first, to find an old journal
mentioned in the secret writing. Cheryl also believed Schaumburg could
help her learn more about Bartholomew, who she now reasoned to be
an Orishan.

*   *   *

Schaumburg and Louis, the pirate captain, joined Sam, Cheryl
and Jose on their quest for the sword of George Washington. Louis
acted as the Hug's historical expert, and he had extensive knowledge of

Bartholomew. The Knights in Blue Satin charged Schaumburg with the task of finding the sword. Since Cheryl now knew they were aliens, they could speak freely to her, but only when Jose slept or played in another room.

Jose still thought Sam was just bringing along teddy bears for him to play with, which sometimes caused problems when Sam needed both Orishans with him on their journey.

They first stopped at a museum in Mt. Vernon to try and locate Bartholomew's secret diary. They met an elderly lady at the museum, Mrs. Harriet Abernathy.

"Welcome," she said to Sam and Cheryl, eyeing the two teddy bears Sam carried. "You can leave the toys outside, young man."

"These teddy bears stay with us, Mrs. Abernathy," Sam insisted.

"Very well, young man. This way to the archived book section. But as I told you on the phone, Mrs. Cruz, we do not have any secret journal by a man named Bartholomew here."

"Yes, yes," Cheryl said. "Please, let us see what you do have."

She left Cheryl and Sam alone, with the Orishans. Jose stayed busy outside in the main museum getting a private tour with one of the young female museum volunteers.

Cheryl began combing through the old books.

Sam awoke Louis and Schaumburg.

"Look for a leather journal with the words 'Weather Control' on the cover," Cheryl instructed Sam and the Orishans.

Sam lifted Schaumburg up to the top shelf so he could examine the dusty tomes there.

Sam placed Louis on a shelf on the opposite wall containing more ancient book stacks.

Unbound papers and drawings also filled the shelves, some being land survey renderings by Washington.

"Here's something," Sam called out. "It's a rolled painting with Washington and two tiny swords."

In his excitement, Schaumburg jumped down from the top shelf to look at the painting. Cheryl and Louis also went to Sam who rolled the ancient canvas out flat on a table.

The painting showed Washington holding two small swords in his palm.

"Look here," Louis said. "It clearly shows there are two of them. Plus there is a reference to a letter from Bartholomew."

The writing on the painting seemed cryptic. It said:

There are two swords. One for destruction. One for salvation. Both are keys to the beam, which will strike at the weather weapon.

"Strike at the weather weapon?" Schaumburg said. "This must be a reference to the Arjogun's beam of destruction."

"What makes you say that?" Louis asked.

"Because Bartholomew had seen it destroy another planet, remember?" Schaumburg replied.

"Uh, guys, you want to clue us poor ignorant humans into what you two are talking about?" Sam asked.

"Sorry, Sam," Schaumburg said. He sat down on the tabletop and began to weave a tale of death and destruction on another planet, far from Earth:

Every school cub on our home planet knows this tale. The story of Bartholomew and how he tried to save a planet from destruction by the Arjogun, but failed.

It is one of the reasons Bartholomew traveled to the Earth so long ago. He wanted to prevent the same thing from happening here.

It was in Earth year 1715, on the planet Modokai. Modokai contained inhabitants not unlike your Earth horses. Except they all have horns on their heads, and are all colored white or pink.

At this point in Schaumburg's yarn, both Cheryl and Sam looked at each other saying the word "unicorns," out loud in unison. Schaumburg said nothing in acknowledgement. He continued his tale.

The Arjogun visited the Modokai. The Modokai used very low tech, depending on magic for most of their creature comforts. The Arjogun wanted to settle on the planet, and the Modokai had no objections. At that time, Orisha assigned Bartholomew to be ambassador to Modokai.

Things stayed peaceful for about 10 years. Bartholomew tried to warn the Modokai about the untrustworthiness of the Arjogun. But the Modokai believed in the goodness of all creatures.

So they did not object when the Arjogun began building what they said was a weather control device. They bored a hole deep into the planet's crust, and created a special device that they said would control the planet's weather.

Bartholomew stumbled onto the Arjogunians' plans, and learned that the machine was actually a doomsday device. He learned that the Arjogun feared the Modokai and wanted to eradicate the species from the universe.

Bartholomew tried to warn the Modokai once again, this time bringing his evidence with him that showed the plans for the Arjogun device and its real purpose.

Most Modokai would not listen to Bartholomew. A few listened. He was able to transport those few safely off the planet before it was too late. One named Dreamwalker led the surviving Modokai. Some of his kind were already on the planet Earth, but remained hidden from humans by using magic that allowed them to vibrate at a different frequency from humans. That kept them safe from both humans and Arjogun when the Arjogun began to invade the Earth.

But back in the mid-1700s, no Arjogun came to this planet. The refugee Modokai joined other Modokai here and some have befriended those Orishans who are members of the Mystical Order of the Golden Paw.

But most Modokai perished when the Arjogun blew up their planet. The destruction of Modokai horrified Bartholomew, and he vowed never to allow the Arjogun to do that to another planet again.

"We believe that the Arjogun are building the same device here on Earth, and that Bartholomew left the sword here to prevent the Arjogun's destructive beam from destroying this planet," Schaumburg said. "But we don't know much more. And we had no idea there were two swords until you, Cheryl, discovered that from Bartholomew's old letters to Washington."

"That must be what Commander Black was talking about," Cheryl said. "He told me that if we find the sword, we could find the answers that will save Armando and the planet!"

Schaumburg peered closely at the painting. "Hello!" Schaumburg said. "What's this? A page number?"

Cheryl snatched the painting and peered closely at it.

"This says page 32," she said.

"And look, this painting has been torn from a journal," she said, examining one edge.

"Quick," Cheryl said. "Everyone back up to that shelf where Schaumburg was with the larger books. Find all the handwritten journals. All we need to do is find the one that is missing page 32."

But after an extensive search, they could find neither one missing a page, nor one hand-written.

"Something's wrong," Sam said. "This doesn't make sense."

"If all that survived of this journal is this drawing, it makes perfect sense," Cheryl said, a little depressed.

"What about secret writing?" Louis said.

"Of course!" Cheryl said. "Sam, you got a match or lighter?"

But Sam did not, nor did the Orishans.

"We have to get this painting out of here," Sam said.

"Hide it on one of the Orishans," she said.

Sam carefully rolled up the painting and handed it to Schaumburg who placed it inside his trench coat. It was so long, however, that it stuck up out of the top of his coat.

"Sam, carry him close to you like a baby, the way you always do," Cheryl said. "With his back to Mrs. Abernathy, she won't see the canvas sticking up."

Louis and Schaumburg reverted into a state of suspended hibernation, and the four of them headed for the main museum to pick up Jose.

"Did you find what you were looking for?" Mrs. Abernathy asked.

"Not today," Cheryl said and rushed Sam and Jose outside.

In Cheryl's car, Sam pulled out the painting.

"This is stealing, you know," Sam said. "And a national treasure, yet! We'll go to prison for this!"

"Hush!" Cheryl said. "It's in the name of science."

Back at their hotel room, Cheryl gingerly treated the canvas with heat, using a small, lit lamp bulb as a heat source. It worked quickly, as secret writing showed up on the drawing:

Find the tome marked weather control. It contains a map to the location of the two swords. Both swords are needed to stop the Arjogun destructive beam.

"There are two swords—one for destruction, one for salvation. Both are keys to the beam which will strike at the weather weapon." Cheryl Cruz found these words along with this painting by Gilbert Stewart showing George Washington holding two nine-inch swords on a canvas page torn from Bartholomew's journal. The page is marked "32."

CHAPTER 17

THE ARCTONIANS

At the Paw Computer, Mardi Gras received an electronic transmission from Perry Purple:

> *"We have reason to believe there are living descendants of the grizzly bears of old on Earth that stood erect and had the power of speech as we do. A human expedition deep into the North Atlantic Ocean discovered an island where a Big Foot sighting had been reported. The Big Foot later turned out to be a tribe of bears that have a culture and speak Orishan. We only just learned of it. But they are even larger than grizzly bears found in the wilds of America. They stand about 10 or 12 feet tall! We need the Paw and Mardi Gras to check it out for us. Please advise if you can contact them.*
>
> *—Perry Purple"*

Mardi Gras responded:

> *"The Paw is on assignment elsewhere looking for the Sword of George Washington. I will investigate these Arctonians for the Knights in Blue Satin.*
>
> *—Mardi Gras"*

"Leni, what do you think?" Andy inquired.

"They could be linked to our common ancestors," Leni said.

"I'm going with you," Chocolate said. "We can establish a link through genetics. I wish to sample their DNA."

"I'll notify Schaumburg about your mission. Use the Teddy Bear Zone to transport to a ship bound for the North Atlantic."

"Roger," Mardi Gras said, excited he was being trusted with his own mission.

After Leni left, Mardi Gras began filling his utility belt with needed items. Chocolate filled a medical bag with necessary equipment.

"I hope I don't screw up like the last time," Mardi Gras said to Chocolate.

"What?" she asked, surprised. "You didn't screw up. How could you have known those goons would shoot at you? We could not tell you to pull out quickly enough. That's why you got spotted. It's not your fault. We are a team here. We are all responsible. Understand?"

Mardi Gras was silent for a few minutes.

"Okay, Chocolate," he said. "I think I understand. And I am glad Leni is trusting me with this new assignment. Do you think these beings are part of the original grizzly bears who are said to be part of the original Knights in Blue Satin? The ones who were allies with humans ages ago?"

"Perhaps," Chocolate said, snapping shut her medical bag. "We Orisha are much smaller in stature to the bears of Earth. But dwarfism has its advantages."

"How?" Mardi Gras asked.

"We require less food, reproduce faster than larger species, and can hide easier from predators."

"I never thought of that," Mardi Gras said. "But doesn't being large have advantages too?"

"If you are bigger, you can reach food on treetops easier," Chocolate said. "Here on Earth, I learned that some larger mammals died out though, because their climate changed, and there were no longer tall trees to feed on . . . So, are you ready?"

"Yes," Mardi Gras said. "And I have H.A.R.V.E.Y. for invisibility."

In a few moments, Mardi Gras and Chocolate crawled from underneath a bed in a luxury cruise ship stateroom bound for the northern coast of Canada.

The Orishans quickly left the room. They had to hold paws (and hold H.A.R.V.E.Y.'s paws) to stay invisible.

Then they "acquired" a small boat and launched it from the side of the luxury liner.

"We have to head deep into this ocean," Chocolate said. "When we arrive on the island, we will have to trek toward the coordinates on foot."

For a few days, the two Orishans traveled by boat. They ate the fish that sometimes hopped onboard the small craft. They plowed through thick fog for days—using Orishan navigational equipment to find their destination. Their boat beached on an island before they knew they had struck land.

Once they disembarked from the boat and became visible once more, they found themselves inside the jungle of the uncharted island hidden by a deep fog.

"The humidity is so thick you can cut it like butter," Chocolate reported by radio back to Leni.

"I'm tracking you via American spy satellite," Leni said. "I'll be watching constantly."

"Have you heard back from Schaumburg?"

"Yes," Leni said. "They are chasing down clues to the second sword. Apparently, we need both of them to stop the Arjogun doomsday device . . . By the way, Louis says Andy should keep his paws off Chocolate."

"Tell Louis to stop being such a dope," Chocolate laughed back on the radio, knowing Louis was only joking too.

"Which way do we go from here, Leni?" Mardi Gras asked.

"Head due north," Leni said. "You have about 20 miles of thick jungle to traverse."

"We're on our way," he replied. "Mardi Gras, out." The fog slowly thinned.

"Do you think these creatures are friendly?" Mardi Gras asked.

At that instant, a human interrupted them.

"Can I help you two?" he said in English with an accent. He stood about five feet, had dark brown skin, and wore safari gear. He was not surprised to see two aliens that looked like teddy bears.

"Are you two babies lost?"

Mardi Gras and Chocolate looked at each other confused. Then Mardi Gras realized that he might think they were bear cubs.

"We are Arctonian cubs," Mardi Gras said. "We are lost. Can you bring us home?"

"Of course, little ones," the man said. "My name is Mkembe Olmo. I live near your city deep in the jungle. I was on my way back home now. I will guide you. Why are you so far from home?"

"We were playing hide and seek," Chocolate said, playing along with the ruse that they were children of the Arctonians.

"Ah ha!" Mkembe said. "Then you did not see the Mboro on your journey?"

"Mboro?" Chocolate asked.

"A ferocious carnivore that preys on Arctonians and humans alike," Mkembe said.

Mkembe pulled out his rifle. "I believe the word is 'lion' in English. I will protect you little ones if we are attacked," he said. "Do not worry."

Mardi Gras and Chocolate looked at each other with grave concern now.

Mkembe slashed away at the vegetation as he slowly cleared a path for all three of them to trek back to the Arctonian city.

Mardi Gras decided to ask some questions. "Why do you live so far away from the city?" he asked.

"My people are the tribe of Alcor," Mkembe said. "It is said that at one time, all humans and Arctonians were peaceful allies."

"Yes, I have heard that," Mardi Gras said.

"How many members of your tribe are there?" Mardi Gras asked.

"Why you know, little one," Mkembe said. "I alone am the last survivor of my tribe. A horrible disease wiped out my people not too many years ago. The grizzly bears seemed to be immune at first and tried to find a cure."

"You were not sick?" Chocolate asked.

"For some reason, I survived," Mkembe said. "The Arctonian doctors do not know why."

"Are the Arctonians going to die as well?" Andy wanted to know.

"We do not know," Mkembe said. "The doctors are working constantly to find a cure. Many Arctonians have already died. They even considered contacting other humans, breaking their highest law.

But the High Council of Paw City finally voted against it. The city had been built when there were many more inhabitants, deep within the jungle on this island constantly hidden by fog. The Arctonians usually put any stray humans who shipwrecked on the island to sleep with sleep darts and then carried them far away from the city. After repairing the human's boats, they set them adrift on the ocean again. Except for my people, no humans were allowed to enter the forbidden city of Paw."

Mkembe seemed very sad as he talked. He did not want to die, nor did he wish to see his friends, the Arctonians, die.

"Maybe I can help," Chocolate said. "I have medical training."

Mkembe laughed, thinking Chocolate only a child.

Suddenly, a loud roar filled the forest. An instant later, several large grizzly bears appeared. They pointed steel blowguns and crossbows at Mkembe and the two Orishans.

"Who are you bringing to us?" one bear asked, speaking what sounded to Mardi Gras and Chocolate very much like the language of Orisha.

"We are from the planet Orisha," Chocolate said in Orishan. "I have brought medical equipment and I wish to try and cure your disease."

The grizzly bears lowered their weapons. They all stood on their hind legs like humans and wore clothing. Their outfits appeared to be tunics made from sheepskins and wool.

The Arctonians spoke in hushed tones with each other for a few moments.

"You say you are from Orisha?" the chief bear asked. "Prove it."

"What sort of proof do you want?" Mardi Gras asked.

"We wish to see magic," another bear said. "It is said the Orishans can perform magic."

"I wish Leni were here," Mardi Gras said.

"Eat some chocolate and show them your stuff," Chocolate instructed Mardi Gras.

He immediately consumed a chocolate bar. Then Mardi Gras started soaring around the jungle like a bird. He landed near the head Arctonian, and took his steel blowgun out of his hand. He bent the steel blowgun in half, easily.

The Arctonians were impressed.

Suddenly, a small letter fell out of one of Mardi Gras' utility belt pockets. It was a note from Perry Purple written on Knights in Blue Satin stationery with the symbol of the crowned-snake in a circle and three crowned-rings within the snake circle.

"That is the sacred symbol of the knights," the lead Arctonian said. "You have been sent by Bartolo." All of the Arctonians instantly bowed down in worship of Mardi Gras and Chocolate. Mkembe bowed down as well. They recognized the ancient symbol of the Knights in Blue Satin.

"Bartolo?" Chocolate said. "Does he mean Bartholomew?"

"Wasn't Bartholomew rumored to have found the legendary city of Paw where an ancient race of grizzly bears lived?" Andy asked. "The same race that is rumored to be descended from the first bears who spoke and wore clothing here on Earth?"

"You have achieved much over time," the chief Arctonian said. "I am called Zumo. I am chief of Paw City. You will be my guests for as long as I am healthy. Alas, my days are numbered due to this dreaded disease."

For a long moment all the large grizzly bears looked beary sad.

Then Zumo smiled broadly and slapped Mardi Gras hard on the back in a friendly gesture. It knocked Mardi Gras down, even though he was still super-powered.

"You will regale us with your tales of Orisha," Zumo said. "We welcome your help in attempting a cure at our illness. If you cannot cure us, at least we will die knowing we finally made contact with our friends from Orisha once again. Mkembe, thank you for bringing us these treasures."

Zumo pulled up Mardi Gras and Chocolate, hugging them both warmly.

He carried them both all the way into Paw City, another hour's walk through the thick jungle. The Arctonians' large stature enabled them to easily traverse the jungle brush, stomping a path for Mkembe to follow without hacking away at the vegetation.

Inside Paw City, Chocolate and Mardi Gras were amazed to see the symbol of the Knights adorning all sorts of things such as artwork and clothing.

The architecture of the buildings seemed somewhat primitive. The Arctonians used stone in their building construction. The coolness inside the dwellings stunned Chocolate and Mardi Gras. The Arctonians had developed a method to circulate the air inside the dwellings and expel hot air through the roof using a special natural ventilation system. The more Mardi Gras and Chocolate learned about the Arctonians, the more they realized they were much more sophisticated than they seemed on the surface.

All welcomed the Orishans as long-lost friends.

Weeks passed. Chocolate determined the disease seemed similar to a plague that wiped out millions of Orishans hundreds of years in the past. She tested Mkembe's blood to see why he remained free of disease.

"Mkembe's blood holds the key," Chocolate told Andy. "We Orishans have lost the science to cure the old plague. The disease kills slowly, causing the Arctonian physiology to eventually dehydrate. They die of thirst, while drinking as much as they can. Leni has helped by contacting the Knights in Blue Satin as well as the Orishan High Command to try and obtain the ancient cure."

After two months of electronic communications between worlds, a reference to the cure was found on the home planet of Orisha. Chocolate finally found the element in Mkembe's blood that helped him survive the disease. Her attempts to synthesize a cure failed at first.

Meanwhile, more Arctonians were succumbing to the disease. There were 23 who had died since Chocolate and Mardi Gras arrived in Paw City.

Leni sent the data for a cure to Chocolate. However, she could not concoct such a cure in the jungle. She needed ingredients that could only be found in remote parts of Earth, such as plants and herbs grown in desert and arctic climates.

"Mardi Gras, I have a mission for you," Chocolate said. "I need you to use your super powers to fly around the world in search of these ingredients. Without them, we cannot create the serum to cure these Arctonians."

So Mardi Gras embarked on a hunt for various herbs and spices and other items needed that would combine for a cure to the Arctonian disease. He had to go to such places as the South Pacific, Brazil, North America, Canada, Africa and Utah (in search of a rare snake egg). He traveled for several days flying round the world. He carefully gathered the ingredients as per Chocolate's explicit instructions.

Zumo seemed to become more ill with each passing hour.

He called Chocolate to his bedside.

"I am dying little one," Zumo said.

"Mardi Gras will be back soon," Chocolate said. "Don't despair."

"I have a present for you," Zumo said. He was weak, and in pain. He drank a glass of water, and that helped for a moment. He got up to pull out a wooden box. Inside was a leather-bound journal. On the cover were the words "Weather Control" in plain English.

Chocolate did not at first grasp what it was she was holding in her paws as she leafed through the pages. Then she realized it was a journal written by Bartholomew. It contained detailed plans of the Arjogun doomsday device, how the device destroyed Dreamwalker's planet, and how the swords could be used to stop the beam. It also contained plans for a device built into the Better Bear Bureau Headquarters in St. Louis. It seems Bartholomew designed the Arch explicitly as a special structure that would counteract the destructive beam from the Arjogun's device. Bartholomew had agents construct the arch in the distant future to his specifications.

Chocolate knew she had to get this journal back to Schaumburg and the Knights in Blue Satin. But first, she had to cure her new friends, the Arctonians.

Zumo hung on for another day. Mardi Gras returned, and Chocolate swiftly prepared the remedy.

Zumo tested the brew first. In a few days, the preparation completely cured him. Chocolate made enough of the remedy to cure the entire tribe, about 300 Arctonian males, females and children.

Mardi Gras and Chocolate became heroes in Paw City from that moment. All hailed them wherever Arctonians spotted them.

Going on the Offensive

After learning about the journal Chocolate discovered in Paw City, she quickly contacted Leni who in turn contacted Schaumburg.

Schaumburg and Louis traveled with Cheryl, Sam and Jose to a remote mansion in Rhode Island that belonged to a very rich man named VanderBear. He built it for his wife in 1810. After the structure was completed, she divorced him.

But the mansion remained open to the public for tours. The building contained works of art adorning the walls as they do in European estates, as well as statues. The terra cotta walls reminded Cheryl and Sam of photos they had seen of palaces in France, Italy and Greece.

Something unexpected greeted the group when they entered the lobby to the house. They had security cameras, a metal detector and an X-ray machine for all guests entering the mansion. This posed a problem for Cheryl, Sam, Jose and the "teddy bears."

Sam pulled them out of the building and talked it over with Cheryl. The "bears" were still stiff so they looked like toys.

"Listen, we can't enter there and allow them to X-ray the 'teddy bears,'" Sam said.

"Will it hurt the teddy bears?" Jose wanted to know.

"Why, yes," Sam said. "That's it. It is harmful to teddy bears."

"I can help," Jose said.

"How?" Cheryl asked, now very curious about her little boy.

"I can throw a tantrum so they won't X-ray the teddy bears," Jose said.

Sam and Cheryl smiled at each other, knowing this might prevent the Orishans from being X-rayed, and subsequently discovered by security as more than just toys.

At the entrance, Jose started screaming.

"No! Don't X-ray my teddy bears!" he shouted. "You'll hurt them!" Then he started to cry and wail.

This distracted the guards, enabling Cheryl to enter with Louis and Schaumburg. Sam and Jose left after a few choice words with the guards. He took Jose back to the hotel room.

While taking a private tour of the building, Schaumburg, Louis and Cheryl studied the library left by VanderBear.

"Legends say he had some artifacts belonging to George Washington," Cheryl said.

While looking through the library, Schaumburg heard a call on his radio from Leni.

"Chocolate has found a journal written by Bartholomew!" Leni said excitedly. "It contains all the secrets we are looking for! It shows how the swords work, and has a map which will help us locate the second sword!"

Leni's news stunned Louis and Schaumburg.

"Send me some scans of the pages," Schaumburg said. They received the transmission via Orishan electronic radio pictures. A screen on Schaumburg's radio showed the pages.

The news shocked Cheryl as well.

"We have to get this book," Schaumburg said.

"This proves there was a second sword," Cheryl said. "I knew it!"

"Yes, and both are needed to stop the Arjogun doomsday device," Schaumburg said. "But the Arjogun don't know about that second sword."

"What are you thinking?" Louis asked, already knowing what Schaumburg planned.

"We have been on the defensive ever since we landed on this planet," Schaumburg said. "It's time we went on the offensive."

"What do you mean?" Cheryl wanted to know.

"I think it's time to play let's-fool-the-bad-guys," Louis said, smacking his hook against his paw. "This is going to be fun!"

"Let's go!" Schaumburg said.

"Go where?" Cheryl wanted to know.

"Home," Schaumburg said.

"But we still have to find the second sword!" Cheryl complained.

"We will," Schaumburg said. "It's about time for Jose to start back at school anyway. And what I have in mind will take some time. Mrs. Cruz, we will need your help."

"Anything I can do, I am willing," Cheryl said, a little confused as she rushed after Schaumburg who was walking beary fast to her car.

*   *   *

September 22, 2002. Back in Versailles at the George Washington Museum, Sam, Cheryl, Schaumburg, Louis and Leni sat around a light box in Cheryl's office. Schaumburg wore what appeared to be a human United States Air Force uniform. Louis had switched from pirate to U.S. Naval Commander duds, a gift from Chocolate.

They examined the map that showed the location of the second sword.

"What's your plan, Schaumy?" Leni asked. Mardi Gras and Chocolate listened in on the meeting via Orishan radio signal.

"It's quite simple," Schaumburg said. "We know how to stop the Arjogun device. The Arjogun have no clue they need both swords. All they know is what intelligence they have been able to steal by tapping into the Knight's computer system, or by using a spy in the Knights in Blue Satin. Whatever they are doing, we have to outfox them."

"We are going to give them forged documents?" Louis guessed.

"Precisely," Schaumburg said. "They keep stealing our intelligence, so we will give them false data. We will be able to stop their device and save the Earth!"

"How are you going to forge documents?" Sam wanted to know.

"Mrs. Cruz, a skilled calligrapher and archeologist, can create false copies of the journal pages."

"What is it you are going to have me falsify?" Cheryl inquired.

"First and foremost, we must not let anyone else know about the second sword or its importance. Everybody now knows about the first sword buried in the time capsule under the Washington monument. We will 'allow' the other side to 'procure' that sword, thinking we will need it to cancel their beam."

"I don't understand," Sam said. "How can you stop the beam if the bad guys have one of the two swords we will need?"

"You have to understand the Arjogun mind," Schaumburg said. "They are nothing if not logical. They will think we want that sword, above all else, to stop the beam."

"I still don't get it," Sam said.

"It's partly because you need to understand Frank Vil and his megalomaniac mind," Louis said. "We have known him for years. He will insist on trapping us at the Arch in St. Louis *with the Sword of*

George Washington. That will give us a chance to stop the beam by using both swords."

"So the bad guys will actually provide us with a means to stop their own death beam?" Cheryl asked.

"Yes!" Schaumburg replied. "It's beautiful! It's pure genius!"

"That's enough, Schaumburg," Leni said. "Your plan to fool the Lemming into getting himself arrested backfired, remember?"

"There are some risks here too," Schaumburg admitted. "Okay, here's the plan. We need two teams. Louis, you and Chocolate will help Cheryl forge the documents. We need them to appear like there is but one sword which will stop the Arjogun weapon."

"Check," Louis said. Cheryl nodded her assent as well.

"Mardi Gras and I will help Sam use this map to locate the second sword. We have to travel about in secret. We will need to use the stealth fighter with H.A.R.V.E.Y.'s cloaking device."

"Check," Leni said. "What about me?"

"We need you to stay at the Paw Cave and monitor both teams. Do NOT use the computer. I think the Arjogun have hacked into it. From now on, all transmissions will be by closed circuit Orishan radio. The Arjogun cannot track those signals."

"Schaumy, you are becoming so forceful," Leni said, putting her paw on Schaumburg's shoulder.

"It's the Bear Force military uniform," Schaumburg said.

"Mardi Gras, Chocolate, did you get all that?" Schaumburg asked. They remained in Paw City deep in the jungle on the hidden island.

"We read you loud and clear, Schaumy," Chocolate said. "I like your plan. I just hope we can find the second sword. Everything depends on it now."

The Lemming Attempts Subterfuge

Captain Schaumburg flew the F-117A on H.A.R.V.E.Y.-powered stealth mode to Paw City so he and Sam could pick up Chocolate and Mardi Gras.

Chocolate and Zumo exchanged a long hug awaiting the arrival of the aircraft.

Mardi Gras stood by.

"You want a hug too, Andy?" Zumo asked.

All three hugged.

"I don't know how we can ever repay you," Zumo said.

"We were glad to do it," Chocolate said. A tear streamed down her furry face.

"I just wish we could have saved you guys sooner."

At that moment the stealth fighter's engines roared and Schaumburg disengaged the H.A.R.V.E.Y. unit's cloak as the jet touched down on a rough dirt runway.

Schaumburg popped open the jet's canopy. Schaumburg and Sam climbed down from the plane. Chocolate and Andy (Mardi Gras) both ran up to hug Schaumburg. Sam was a little frightened by Zumo.

Zumo reached to hug Sam, who ducked in fear but reacted too late. The bear hugged Sam tightly, but not too tight. Sam, awkwardly, said thank you to the bear.

"You're welcome," Zumo said in perfect English. "It is good to see another human."

"I promise you, Zumo, you can trust Sam here," Chocolate said. "He won't tell anyone else about you or your city."

"No, of course not," Sam quickly said. "Uh, shall we go now?"

Sam began climbing back up the stairs to board the plane.

Chocolate handed the leather bound journal to Schaumburg. Andy ascended the stairs to the plane. Schaumburg and Chocolate climbed aboard as well. Before closing the canopy, Chocolate waved goodbye one last time to Zumo.

"I will always be in your debt, little ones," Zumo said as he waved good-bye. Tears streamed down the large bear's cheek now.

"C'mon, Chocolate," Sam said, still nervous around the large bear. "It's time to go. We have to get this journal to Cheryl and her team."

Meanwhile, the Lemming and the Frown made secret plans in the Frown's castle, Pawtropolis.

"You cannot go back to *The Daily Press*, boss," the Frown said. "We have lost our inside man there now and cannot keep as close an eye on that journalist and his Orishan friends."

"Perhaps I can trail him less covertly now," the Lemming said.

"What do you mean?" the Frown asked.

"There is no need to hide the fact that we are watching him now," the Lemming said. "I have known Samuel Arctophile for many years. I know how he operates, how he thinks. I may not be able to control his mind, but maybe I don't need to."

"I still don't understand," the Frown said.

"Oh, you Arjogun!" the Lemming said. "You are all about logic and conquest. Why do you want to give us your weather technology, anyway?"

"To help you control your enemies, of course," the Frown said, lying. The Lemming still had no idea the Arjogun were actually building a doomsday device.

"You are correct, boss," the Frown continued. "We should not be helping one faction on Earth to rule over other factions. It is not logical. Especially given your warlike, cruel tendencies. One day you may turn on the Arjogun."

"Exactly," the Lemming said. "So why are you helping the Americans with Project Unicorn?"

"There is a human saying that will explain the motivations of the Arjogun," the Frown said. "Keep your friends close, but keep your enemies closer."

"That sounds about right, coming from a paranoid race of conquerors," the Lemming said. "I will confront our journalist friend and explain to him how important our work with the Arjogun is. He will come around when he realizes he has backed the wrong horse."

"This is no horse race, boss," the Frown said. "This is survival."

*　　*　　*

After the flight back to Versailles and still under cloak, Sam asked Schaumburg about the motivations of the Arjogun.

"Why do the Arjogun build weapons that will destroy whole worlds?" Sam asked. "Isn't that counter to their cold logic?"

"The Arjogun are not like Mr. Spock on 'Star Trek'," Schaumburg said. "They have emotions and fear is one of their ruling emotions."

"So the Arjogun fear the human race?"

"They fear your potential," Schaumburg said.

"I'm not following," Sam said.

"The Arjogun think mankind has grown too powerful," Chocolate said. "When you created the atomic bomb in 1945, your race set off an intergalactic chain of events that is culminating with the Arjogun's doomsday device. They think your species will learn to fly across space and use your weapons of destruction to conquer them. The doomsday device is a pre-emptive strike."

"But what about the planet with the unicorns?" Sam asked. "They were not building atomic bombs."

"They have very powerful magic," Schaumburg said. "They are even more powerful than the Wizards like my wife Leni. If they were not loving beings, they could snuff out an entire planet with a thought."

The thought sent shivers down Sam's spine.

Schaumburg taxied the F-117A in a parking lot behind *The Daily Press* office in Versailles. Still cloaked, Sam descended with the journal of Bartholomew and handed it to Cheryl.

"This is going to take some time to reproduce this, you know," Cheryl said.

"Move as swiftly as you can," Sam said. "The clock is ticking. The Arjogun are in Madagascar building that weapon as we speak."

"Louis showed me some Orishan technology that will speed things up," Cheryl said. "They are light-years ahead of us in reproducing products. We have been able to reproduce the parchment used in Bartholomew's journal. But their technology cannot reproduce handwritten writing and drawings that look real. That will be up to me."

Chocolate descended from the F-117A and wobbled up to Cheryl.

"I'll help you too, Cheryl," Chocolate said. "Louis and I make a great team."

Cheryl picked up Chocolate and gave her a warm hug.

Sam hugged Cheryl too. As they moved away from each other, Cheryl stared deep into Sam's eyes.

"We have to do this to save the planet, and to save Armando," Cheryl said. "If it weren't for him, I would never have known about this alien invasion and could not have helped you or the Orishans. This was all meant to be, Sam."

She kissed Sam on the forehead and departed.

Sam watched her walk away, longingly.

"C'mon, hot shot," Schaumburg said. "We gotta go."

Sam climbed the ladder into the invisible plane and they sped off—destination: San Francisco, California in search of the second sword.

*   *   *

The F-117A stayed parked in a hotel parking lot, cloaked, off to the side near a dumpster. Sam reasoned nobody would try to park in its place that way. Schaumburg had explained that while cloaked, the ship was slightly out of phase with the vibrations of human technology and people, so nobody could disturb the ship anyway. The concept was difficult for Sam to grasp.

Sam picked up the two aliens, Schaumburg and Andy, who were now stiff and appearing like teddy bears.

At the hotel desk, he registered under an assumed name fearing the Homeland Security Agency might be tracking his movements.

However, the Lemming, otherwise known as Izzie Feinberg, waited for him in the lobby.

Sam spotted Feinberg and darted up to his room. Feinberg chased after Sam.

"Stop, Sam," Izzie shouted. "I'm not going to hurt you. I just want to talk."

Sam opened the door to his room and slammed it shut to keep Feinberg out.

"Let me in, son," Feinberg said.

"Why?" Sam asked. He put down the Orishans and awoke them from their state of suspended hibernation. "So you can implant another mind-control device in my neck?"

"I know what you are looking for, son," Izzie said in calm tones. "You should not try to stop the Arjogun. They are helping Americans create the ultimate weapon. No longer will America have to fear terrorists like Osama Bin Laden. We will finally be in complete control."

"So America is to be the land of the free as long as you agree? Is that it?" Sam asked.

Schaumburg whispered something to Sam. Sam opened the door.

"Ah, I see you have awakened your Orishan friends," Izzie said. "What I have to say to you is for you only. Can you and I go down to the hotel restaurant and talk? You can leave these things here in your room. Look at that one, wearing an Air Force uniform as if it were a human. Disgusting!"

"We'll be okay in the room, Sam," Schaumburg said. "I'll have Leni monitor things for us."

Sam took the room key and locked Schaumburg and Andy in the room. They turned on the television and relaxed on the two twin beds. Andy jumped up and down on one bed, having a great time.

In the hotel restaurant, Sam and Izzie began to chat as if no bad blood had been forming between them since the attempted mind-control-assassinate-Mrs. Cruz incident.

"Listen to me, Son," Izzie said, putting his hand on Sam's shoulder. Sam brushed Izzie's hand off in contempt.

"These Arjogun are our friends," Izzie said. "It is the Orishans who are the enemy. Don't you see? They look like innocent teddy bears. You can't trust them. They are trying to manipulate all of us into thinking they are cute, fuzzy, cuddly bundles of love. In fact, they are monsters."

"Are you truly that insane?" Sam asked. "These Arjogun are ruthless killers. The Orishans are gentle. What is wrong with you?"

"No! The teddy bears are the evil ones!" Izzie screamed. Veins began to pop out in Izzie's neck as his face turned beet red with anger. The other people in the restaurant began staring at Izzie and Sam.

"Leni, I could use a little help about now," Sam said, talking to himself, it appeared.

"You fool," Izzie said. "You are looking for that nine-inch sword! I know about that. We already know it's buried in a time capsule under the Washington Monument. Even if you get it, it's just a trinket. It won't be able to stop Arjogun technology! The weather control machine must go online May 5! It is imperative!"

At that moment, the Paw appeared at Sam's side, super-powered.

The next moment, the Frown appeared, carrying a chuck of Orishanite. The Paw sank fast to the floor, weak as a kitten.

The Frown and Izzie backed away, slowly. The other people in the restaurant had no idea what they witnessed.

As soon as the Frown and Izzie left the restaurant, the Paw got up, a little groggy, but all right.

Knowing he was in San Francisco, Sam attempted to make this look theatrical.

"Show's over folks," Sam said. "We were just rehearsing for a new television show about teddy bears that look like aliens. These animatronic teddy bears are pretty realistic, aren't they?"

CHAPTER 18

THE HUNT FOR THE SECOND SWORD

Dear Orishan Command,
Earth Date November 20, 2002.

Samuel Arctophile, Andy and I are traveling via F-117A jet in stealth mode to Alaska in search of a clue to the location of the second Sword of George Washington. I am sending this transmission via scrambled Orishan electronic Internet so the enemy cannot intercept it.

Sam is using the trip as a means to do feature stories about George Washington. He is taking some of the research we have been doing, combined with the photos he will take on our trip for the stories.

We have reason to believe there could be spies in the Knights in Blue Satin or elsewhere in Pawtroplis so I have devised a plan to keep this information secret even from the Knights. But the plan depends on our locating the second sword. I will report on our progress when we know more.

Captain Schaumburg Harmony, reporting from Earth on secret Orishan Command scrambled network.

As soon as Schaumburg, Andy and Sam landed secretly on a frozen runway at the Nome airport, they left the plane and headed for a nearby hotel. They already knew that Vanderbear possessed the second sword at the turn of the 19th century. Vanderbear purchased it from the Washington Estate and was a friend of the legendary Bartholomew, who outlived George Washington.

"I just hope that map of Bartholomew and the information we

obtained from the Vanderbear Estate is worth the price we paid," Andy said.

"A little honey gold can go a long way toward finding lost treasure," Schaumburg said. Andy and Schaumburg no longer wore their superhero identities. Schaumburg changed back into his Bear Force uniform. Andy donned his reporter duds. They reasoned their toned-down outfits would not raise as much suspicion when Sam hauled them around as "teddy bears."

Sam called his contact in Alaska, a former reporter for *The Daily Press* in Montreal, Illinois, Anton Goodwin.

"Anton, Samuel Arctophile here," Sam said. "I'm working on that story about George Washington artifacts. Can you get us into that private residence I spoke to you about?"

"Sure thing, Sam," Anton said. "I've already made the arrangements. What is it you are looking for?"

"Can't say yet," Sam said. "We have a sort of treasure map and we're trying to locate an artifact. The information we have indicates an acquaintance of Washington built this home here in Alaska and may have hidden something of Washington's in the house."

After Sam hung up, Schaumburg explained his theory to Andy and Sam.

"I think this Vanderbear is actually Bartholomew," Schaumburg said.

"Why do you say that?" Sam asked.

"Bartholomew traveled extensively around this planet after Washington died, according to his journal," Schaumburg said. "He may have traveled under an assumed name."

"Why would an Orishan need to change his name?" Andy wondered.

"Because he was disguised as a human," Schaumburg said. "Bartholomew was a skilled wizard. He could have used a spell to alter his appearance to humans."

"That doesn't explain why he would need to change his name," Andy said.

"It does if he was trying to cover his tracks," Schaumburg said.

"That still doesn't make sense," Andy countered.

"Okay, chum, you got me," Schaumburg said. "Bartholomew was no ordinary Orishan."

"How so?" Sam wanted to know.

"You may have noticed he did not follow the teachings of the Mystical Order of the Golden Paw," Schaumburg said. "He was a maverick. After the Arjogun destroyed the planet of innocent unicorns, he broke with Orishan Command and branched off on his own. Not too many Orishans know about his dark past."

"So that's why he manipulated George Washington," Sam said. "I thought it was strange for an Orishan to interfere with human history like that, and especially to encourage Washington to start the war with the British. I wonder if I can somehow work this new research into my feature story on Washington. Maybe I can quote Cheryl talking about Washington instigating the French and Indian War."

"Sam, please be careful about what you print," Schaumburg said. "We cannot allow the general population of humans to know of our existence. It could mean the death of many agents on your planet."

"I understand, Schaumburg," Sam said. "You know I wouldn't do anything to hurt you or your kind. I'm in this for the long haul. I'll do whatever it takes to protect your secrets. After all, you're protecting my entire planet, right?"

Schaumburg said nothing in response. But he thought to himself, "I hope I can protect your planet."

The next day, accompanied by Anton, Sam carried the two stiff Orishans with him to the mansion in Nome.

"This castle is said to be built by a mysterious stranger at the start of the 19th century," Anton said. "The name of the stranger remains a mystery to this day. Do you think he is connected to George Washington?"

"According to a source we have, this home was built by a man who had purchased a very valuable part of the Washington Estate, then hid it here," Sam said. "We'll see if my source is correct."

At the mansion, Anton introduced Sam to the groundskeeper, Frank Largetooth. Frank, a native of Alaska, stood about six-feet, five-inches tall.

Frank looked at the Orishans with obvious disapproval.

"You may look around to your hearts delight, take pictures, or whatever," Frank said. "Only, don't disturb anything. If you need help, just ring the servant's bell in whatever room you are in. And don't get in the way of the servants."

"You're on your own," Anton said to Sam. "I'll be back to pick you up after lunch."

Once alone in the house, Sam went to a room marked on his map as the library. He awoke Schaumburg and Andy.

"Okay, what does the map show about this room?" Sam asked.

"There should be a secret entrance to an antechamber somewhere," Schaumburg said. "Look around for a false door, something hidden under a picture, anything."

Sam, Schaumburg and Andy started examining various objects in the library to try and locate a device that would open the door to a secret room.

Sam pulled open the head on a bust of Beethoven. He pushed a button inside, but that just activated a movie screen. Sam quickly pushed the button again and the movie screen automatically retracted.

"That worked on the old Batman television show," Sam said. "I thought I'd give it a try."

Andy started trying to pull out certain books to see if that would activate a secret door, with no success.

Schaumburg looked at the map again, to see if it revealed any clues. Then he began to look at the books on the shelves. He found one on George Washington.

He pulled that one off the shelf. Instantly, the room's fireplace moved inward, revealing a passage to a secret room.

"In here," Schaumburg said.

The three quickly entered the secret room, which contained all manner of trinkets from the planet Orisha.

Sam noticed a crystal ball pedestal on a shelf.

He picked it up and as soon as he did, a light shone on him.

The light seemed to be a concentrated beam.

Suddenly, an image of Bartholomew appeared in holographic form before them. It started speaking in Orishan. Sam could not understand the words.

"If you are Orishan, and are looking for the second Sword of George Washington, then you have done well so far," Bartholomew said.

"What's he saying?" Sam wanted to know.

"Shhhh!" Schaumburg said.

"Take this glass pedestal, and travel to the second location, Moscow,

Russia. It is there in the Cathedral of St. Basil that I have hidden another part of my Bearacus. The Bearacus can detect silver, the material the sword is made from. Once in Moscow, you will learn where the final piece of the Bearacus is. Without the Bearacus, you will not be able to locate the second Sword. Remember, you need both swords to stop the Arjogun's doomsday weapon. Good luck, fellow Orishans."

Andy and Schaumburg looked at Sam's hands that held the pedestal.

"We're gonna need that, Sam," Schaumburg said.

"Yeah, and now we have to fly to Moscow," Andy added..

"Moscow?" Sam said. "What for?"

"To get another part of a device Bartholomew created for us to find the sword," Schaumburg replied.

"This seems like a lot of trouble," Sam said.

"Bartholomew wanted to make sure that the beings who found the two Swords of George Washington used them to stop the Arjogun," Schaumburg said. "This scavenger hunt he is sending us on is a sort of test. He knows it's Orishans on the trail, but since he is long dead, this is the only way he can be sure we are the good guys."

"Because only Orishans can understand his clues and the language?" Sam asked.

"That is in part true, yes," Schaumburg said. "But even more important, that beam which was shining on you was a sensor. It detected the goodness of the being who picked up the pedestal. It also senses our presence and knew there were Orishans in this room."

"Well, then let's go to Moscow," Sam said.

Memo

To: Orishan Command
From: Captain Schaumburg Harmony
Re: Access to St. Basil's Cathedral, Moscow, Russia
Earth Date: Nov. 30, 2002

Dear Commander,

We are apparently on the right trail, as we discovered several Orishan devices hidden in the mansion in Alaska. This was indeed the home of Bartholomew after the death of George Washington.

Bartholomew built a Bearacus, which as you know, will help us locate the second Sword of George Washington. But Bartholomew hid the parts of the Bearacus in different places around this planet. He is giving us clues as we go. My human, Samuel Arctophile, cannot gain entrance to Moscow or the Cathedral with a journalist's credentials, so we need some extra help. Do we have any operatives in Russia who can help us? Please advise ASAP.

Thanking you in advance.

Sincerely,
Captain Schaumburg Harmony

*　　*　　*

"I have a reply from Orishan Command," Schaumburg told Sam. They were still in their hotel room in Nome, Alaska. "They say we are to contact an Orishan in Russia who goes only by the name of Jack. If this Jack is who I think it is, we could have some trouble."

"Why do you say that?" Andy wanted to know.

"I have had dealings with Jack in the past!" Schaumburg said. "He and Leni dated years before she and I did. He still holds a torch for her."

"Can you contact this Jack?" Sam asked.

"I'll have Leni make the arrangements," Schaumburg said. "She can access the Moscow Hug of Orishans. She might get further than I would."

Andy and Sam looked at each other, both thinking Schaumburg seemed just a little bit jealous of this Jack.

*　　*　　*

"We have enough laser cutters to make our escape attempt," Armando whispered to Lavender during a meal break. "I'll give the signal tonight during our sleep period."

Lavender said nothing in reply. She was scared, but was willing to take the risk to escape from the slave camp. And she was beary tired of working endlessly to dig a tunnel for the Arjogun weather machine.

That night, Armando gave Lavender the signal, and they passed around the laser cutters.

Quickly and silently, they overtook the Arjogun guards, managing to knock all of them out before an alarm was sounded.

"Okay, now we have to take a lift up to one of the top floors where the sleeping quarters are," Armando said. "Lavender, you and the Orishans lead the way since you know how to use the portal."

They all plowed into a lift, eight Orishans and five humans. A few humans and Orishans stayed behind, not wishing to risk their lives in the escape attempt. But they helped the others by watching the guards and making sure nobody sounded an alarm. The lift took 22 minutes to reach a top floor, 1,000 feet above the slave camp. Finally, the lift opened. The Orishans and humans stayed against the wall until Armando signaled the hall contained no stray Arjogun.

"This place seems deserted for a weather control station," Armando whispered to Lavender. "I'll bet this really is more than just for weather control as I suspected."

"Hush," Lavender cautioned.

Armando opened the door to the sleeping quarters of several Arjogun soldiers.

Armando motioned for the Orishans to enter the quarters from the hallway.

Just as they entered, the light came on suddenly.

Snopple stood in the corner of the room holding an Arjogun weapon on them all. Polaris stood on another end with a force of armed guards.

"This is a trap!" Armando called out.

"Save your breath, human," Snopple said. "We won't kill you, though we should."

Lavender and Armando glanced at each other, surprised.

"We need you slaves alive to finish our weather control device," Snopple continued. "Then, soon you will all be dead anyway!"

Rebuilding A Bearacus

"You were right, Schaumburg," Leni said over the Orishan radio to her husband. "Jack is still carrying a torch for me. He agreed to help you get into St. Basil's Cathedral. But there is one catch."

"I was afraid of this," Schaumburg said. "What's the catch?"

"He wants you, Andy and Sam to help their Hug with their mission first."

"What does he need us to do?" Schaumburg asked.

"He said he'd give you the details when you arrive in Moscow. Land the stealth fighter on the Moscow Air Field. He said he would be waiting at these coordinates."

*   *   *

The flight to Moscow from Alaska was a short hop for the souped-up F-117A with an Orishan hyperdrive. But Schaumburg showed concern about Jack's request.

When disembarking from the stealth fighter, Jack pulled Schaumburg off the ladder and gave Schaumburg a big bear hug. Jack seemed large-bellied for an Orishan. He dressed more casually than Schaumburg's Hug. He wore a sport shirt and slacks, tennis shoes over dark-brown fur.

"My old friend," Jack said. "How are you? How is your lovely wife! It's been ages! How is Louis? I understand your little sister Chocolate has joined your Hug as well? Didn't you crash on Earth back in 1947?"

"Jack, we don't have time," Schaumburg said, somewhat disturbed.

"This is Andy Adorable," Schaumburg said.

Jack gave Andy a big bear hug as well.

"And this is my human, Samuel Arctophile."

Sam bent down to shake Jack's paw. Jack, a strong Orishan, pulled Sam down to hug him, but they both fell over onto the Moscow Airport tarmac.

All laughed.

"He doesn't seem so bad, Schaumburg," Andy said.

"Quiet, Andy," Schaumburg said.

"Come, I have a car waiting," Jack said.

To Sam's relief, Jack meant a human-sized car, not one the Orishans used to travel in. Those vehicles would be too small for humans.

A surly looking Russian drove the car.

"This is Petruschka," Jack said. "My human helping our Hug in Moscow."

"What is your mission here?" Schaumburg asked.

"We have to destroy an Arjogun station just outside of Moscow," Jack said. "That should be beary easy for you since you have an American stealth fighter, especially since it is really invisible, eh?"

Jack slapped Schaumburg very hard on the back forcing Schaumburg to fall off his seat.

"Hah!" Jack said. "You always were a weak Orishan, weren't you?"

Schaumburg started to get angry.

Andy put his paw out to help Schaumburg back onto his seat.

"Let's just concentrate on our mission, Schaumburg," Andy said.

"Right, Andy," Schaumburg said, dusting himself off.

"Jack, we can certainly use the stealth fighter, but it does not have any weapons on board."

"Doesn't matter," Jack said. "The Arjogun don't know that. If you fly the jet to the Arjogun base and materialize it right in front of them, you'll scare the willies out of those Arjogun! That will give our Hug enough of an element of surprise to set some charges and blow up their base!"

"This is how you plan to carry out your mission here on Earth?" Schaumburg said, shocked. "You'll kill dozens of Arjogun soldiers. You know we are never to use overt force against them or any other beings."

"You were always soft on those Arjogun, weren't you Schaumburg?" Jack said, slapping Schaumburg on the back again, forcing him off the chair again. "Isn't that why you still don't have your License To Hug?"

Andy flashed Schaumburg a puzzled look.

"Remember the mission, remember the mission," Schaumburg kept repeating to himself as he pulled himself back onto the seat.

"Perhaps there is a way to sabotage the Arjogun base without blowing it up," Sam suggested.

"What do you have in mind, human?" Jack asked.

"How about using the stealth fighter as you suggest to create an element of surprise, only without the H.A.R.V.E.Y. unit's invisible cloak. Then have Schaumburg and Andy call on their super-powered identities to destroy the base while they are cloaked."

"Super-powered identities?" Jack asked.

"We'll discuss it once we arrive at your house," Schaumburg said.

That night, after making detailed plans, Jack prepared his Hug to fly the stealth fighter to the base, without a cloak.

Schaumburg and Andy assumed their identities as the Paw and Mardi Gras inside the fighter. They hopped out and flew to the base, invisible by touching paws to H.A.R.V.E.Y.

The base included several barracks, and some concrete structures well lit from within. The Paw and Mardi Gras gently touched down in the middle of the compound, still invisible. They took in the surroundings, searching for armed Arjogun guards.

The Arjogun sounded an alarm when they spotted the stealth fighter in the night sky and started shining search beams.

"Smash their anti-aircraft guns so they can't shoot down the stealth fighter," the Paw whispered to his sidekick.

The Paw and Mardi Gras destroyed the anti-aircraft and other defensive guns on the base by smashing them. Hard steel suddenly curled before the eyes of the watching Arjogun. The Paw knocked one Arjogun soldier from his seat on an anti-aircraft gun, and he fell 5 feet to the hard earth. He pulled himself erect and started to flee in panic.

Another Arjogun soldier fired at the crumpled anti-aircraft weapon, blowing it up. However, the shrapnel did not harm the super-powered Orishans. Mardi Gras and the Paw flew down to grab that soldier's gun and pointed it at the Arjogun. Another Arjogun shot blindly at the air, hitting an ammunitions dump. The ammunition started sparking, then shot bullets, grenades and rockets in all directions, whistling and banging. The Arjogun fled for their lives. The Paw and Mardi Gras let go their grip on H.A.R.V.E.Y. The paw placed the unit on his arm. The two heroes quickly smothered the ammunition dump so it no longer posed a threat to anyone.

At that time, Jack's men landed the F-117A and planted the bombs. The Paw and Mardi Gras boarded the plane along with Jack's Hug of bears and put the H.A.R.V.E.Y. unit back in place to cloak the plane.

As the F-117A flew off the base, the charges planted on the Arjogun base began to explode. In a matter of moments, the charges destroyed the base in a monstrous ball of flames and smoke.

Jack slapped Schaumburg on the back again, beary hard.

"You did it!" Jack said. "I never knew such a pipsqueak could be so strong. Does that chocolate work on all Orishans?"

"No, fortunately," Schaumburg said. "And you can't tell any other Orishans about our powers, okay? Now, help us to get into St. Basil's Cathedral."

"Very well," Jack said. "I will make the arrangements tomorrow. By the way, Schaumburg, don't let anyone ever tell you that you do not deserve a License to Hug. You are an excellent soldier. I intend to put in a good word for you at Orishan Command."

*　　*　　*

Inside St. Basil's Cathedral the next night, Sam, Schaumburg and Andy secretly used their map to locate Bartholomew's hiding place.

"It should be underneath a priest's vestment closet," Schaumburg said in hushed tones.

Byzantine portraits of Christ lined the walls of the ancient cathedral.

"This is it!" Andy said.

Andy pulled out what looked like a portion of a crystal ball, another part of the Bearacus, shaped like a half-moon that fit onto the glass pedestal.

Instead of a hologram, the Orishans discovered a painting by Bartholomew. It depicted a chateau in Marseilles, France. On the painting they read the words "Look under the bedroom floor rugs for the third part of the Bearacus." The words were written in Orishan, of course.

"It looks like France is our next stop," Andy said.

The three sword-hunters embarked on a trip to France to find the chateau in Marseilles. This time, Sam made contact with Fred. Fred met the invisible F-117A at a remote field near the city of Marseilles. He escorted them to the Chateau. The Chateau rested on a lush green hillside in Southern France.

"Do I get an exclusive story, Sam?" Fred asked.

"Not this time," Sam said. "This time we have to keep our discovery a secret. I am beginning to understand how tough it is for our government to keep secrets now. And as a journalist, it is normally my job to reveal the secrets. Now I am operating on the opposite side of the fence, keeping secrets from journalists like you. It is very strange, isn't it?"

Inside the Chateau, Schaumburg led all of them into the bedroom. He examined the floorboards of the ancient home. He noticed some loose boards and pulled them up.

"There's a secret passage leading beneath the house," Schaumburg said.

They clicked on their flashlights and followed Schaumburg down into the dark passage. They soon found themselves inside a dark cave deep within a mountain. Orishan symbols and paintings, done by Bartholomew, adorned the walls. Schaumburg moved to one drawing of Washington with his nine-inch swords. Schaumburg touched the paintings of the swords and a blue flame started to burn around the swords.

Schaumburg backed away. The flames continued to burn until at last, a small hole was left, charred and black. Inside the hole they found the third part to the Bearacus.

Andy put the third part inside the glass "sphere" assembly on the Bearacus. At that moment, the Bearacus began to whir and whistle.

Another hologram appeared, this time the image of Bartholomew seemed much older.

"I hope by now you have discovered my journal among the Arctonians," Bartholomew said in Orishan. *"If you have, you also know that I have designed a way to stop the Arjogunians from harming the Earthlings. You have now completed the Bearacus. You will need it to locate the second Sword of George Washington. Now you must travel to the tomb of Chocolatl in the rainforests of Central America. There you will find George Washington's sword. Good luck, my friends."*

After the hologram finished speaking, it dissolved and an image of the tomb showed before them.

"We have to go to the tomb of Chocolatl in the rainforests of Central America, Sam," Schaumburg translated for the human.

"I know that tomb," Sam said. "I read an article about it in a *Geographic National Magazine*. It's in Guatemala!"

*   *   *

Back in the Montreal newsroom of *The Daily Press*, Amy Sampson combed through that day's mail. A manila envelope addressed to Samuel Arctophile stood out among the letters. Normally, she would have merely sent the mail unopened to the Versailles Bureau for Sam to open. But something told her to open this envelope. It came from an address in Nome, Alaska, which struck Amy as odd.

"Perhaps this is part of Sam's features he is turning in about Washington," Amy thought to herself.

Frank Largetooth wrote the letter. The letter shocked her.

> *Dear Mr. Arctophile,*
>
> *You were very professional on your visit to the mansion recently. I was impressed, although I thought it was strange for a grown man to be carrying around teddy bears. Then I looked at the surveillance cameras that were filming you while you were in the mansion. We photographed you and the two "teddy bears."*
>
> *I just wanted you to know that the real owner of this mansion, Bartholomew, was not a human being. He was, like your "teddy bears" from the planet Orisha. Since I surmised this was what you actually carried, I allowed you into our sacred mansion. Our people befriended Bartholomew more than 150 years ago when he came to our land. We know about his mission and why you have come. Please let me know if there is anything we can do to help. I have access to some military hardware and some other people who will fight to protect the Earth from the enemies of both Mankind and the Orisha.*
>
> *Sincerely,*
> *Frank Largetooth*

"Wow!" Amy exclaimed to herself out loud. "Just what have you gotten yourself mixed up with, Sam?"

Amy immediately called up the Internet on her computer and found the website for the mansion Largetooth cared for.

She furtively looked around the newsroom to make sure nobody was watching her. She slipped out a small device that resembled a credit card from her purse, except this card had a wire attached to it. The card had a U.S. Army special forces logo on it. She connected the "card" to her computer.

She started banging on her computer.

"C'mon, baby, show me your security videos," she said under her breath.

Suddenly, a message came across the screen. It said simply, "Type in your access code."

"Access code?" she said, surprised.

She tried a number of encryptions to hack past the site's security files.

After several unsuccessful attempts, she said to herself, "Let's try thinking outside the box on this one."

She typed in "Teddy Bear."

The response was "Invalid access code."

Then she tried "Schaumburg."

Still nothing.

She tried again for several minutes, trying to guess what the code would be.

Frustrated, she looked at Frank's letter again.

"Bartholomew," she said. "I'll bet that's it."

She typed in Bartholomew and the site's security video camera library showed on her screen.

"Yes!" she said. Another reporter looked over to her but just assumed Amy was doing research for a story.

Amy watched the film. The videos contained images of Sam, Schaumburg and Andy, watching a holographic image of Bartholomew. She gasped as she watched the video of Sam climbing into what appeared to be an invisible aircraft, following by the two "teddy bears" climbing an invisible ladder.

"Obviously, those aren't just teddy bears Sam has been carrying around with him," she said.

Amy immediately picked up the phone.

"Information, get me a listing for a Frank Largetooth in Nome, Alaska," she said. "Yes, I have the street address."

The Connection to King Arthur

January 20, 2003, Somewhere deep in the tropical rainforests of Guatemala

Sam, Schaumburg, and Andy disembarked from the F-117A, which remained cloaked.

"A Guatemalan native, Juan, should meet us here," Schaumburg said. "Juan is one of a few humans on Earth that know of the Orishans' existence. He is helping us in our covert fight against the Arjogun."

Juan approached Sam and the Orishans.

"I don't think there is any treasure in those old ruins, Senior Schaumburg," Juan said. "Those particular ruins have been picked clean by scavengers. When some archeologists from *Geographic National* did a dig there a few years ago, they found a tomb. Other than bones, no treasures were there."

"I have a map that might help us locate some very valuable treasure," Sam said.

"I know you said you cannot tell me what it is you are looking for, but perhaps I could help if you told me what it is," Juan said.

"It's not that we don't trust you," Sam said. "We are just trying to keep as few people as possible in the loop about this. Please trust us on this one."

Juan directed Sam and the Orishans to his jeep located nearby, and they all hopped in, loading up the jeep with their gear. Juan's jeep trudging off in the direction of Chocolatl.

Andy took out a strange device that looked like a glass sphere. It contained the symbol of the Knights in Blue Satin. Juan recognized the symbol immediately.

"Ah," Juan said. "So you are working with the Knights. You are looking for the Sword of George Washington, no?"

Sam and the Orishans all looked at each other.

"How did you know that?" Schaumburg asked.

"The chatter among the Protectors, the humans working with the Orishans, is that the sword will stop the Arjogun's weapon. But I thought it was buried in the Washington Monument?"

"It is," Schaumburg said.

Andy continued to move dials on the device.

"What is that?"

"It's some sort of computer," Andy replied. "We found part of it in Alaska, part in Russia, and part in a cave in France," Andy said. "The map led us to it and it directed us to come here to Guatemala. According to Bartholomew's Journal, he invented this device. It is unlike anything on Orisha or Earth."

"How does it work?" Juan asked as he sharply turned the jeep's wheel to the left to avoid a large tree trunk that had fallen in the middle of the dirt road. They were winding through the rainforest and sometimes the flora fell on the road.

"It is currently homing in on the silver," Andy said.

"Shhhhh!" Schaumburg said.

"It's okay, Schaumburg," Andy said. "He already knows what we are looking for."

For the rest of the bumpy ride, nobody said anything else.

At the Mayan ruins near a village called Nueva Cadiz, Juan let his passengers out.

"Here's the ruins you are looking for," Juan said. "But I still say there is nothing to find in there."

Schaumburg took out the map. It pointed to a false door inside the pyramid tomb.

"There!" Schaumburg said pointing to a corner of the ruins. "We have to bust through that door."

"I cannot allow you to do that," Juan said. "This is protected by the Guatemalan College of Antiquities. I was able to obtain a permit to explore here, but not to destroy anything."

"Andy, use your utility belt," Schaumburg commanded. Andy, who wore his Mardi Gras costume underneath his regular clothing, knew exactly what Schaumburg wanted him to do. They had already agreed they would have to put the guide to sleep so he could not see them in case they located the sword in the ruins as promised by the map and Bartholomew's journal.

Andy took out a special glass bulb and threw it, causing it to smash on the ground in front of Juan. Gas seeped out, which put Juan to sleep. The gas dissipated before it could reach the Orishans or Sam. Sam, Andy and Schaumburg dragged Juan's slumbering form into the jeep.

They entered the tomb, flashlights beaming. The light showed them paintings of Mayan guards keeping the "door" shut.

"Here!" Schaumburg said. "That's the false door. Quick, Andy. Use your laughing powder to take down the door. Be careful not to hurt anything else in the tomb."

The Orishan laughing power caused the Mayans painted on the door to start laughing. They began to laugh so violently, that rocks and dust fell to the dirt floor. Then Sam, Schaumburg and Andy saw what lay behind the false wall—an inner chamber filled with Orishan technology, blinking and whizzing with electronics.

Against the opposite wall of this inner chamber they spied a painting in blue of the snake in a circle, crowned. Inside the circle were three rings, also crowned. This was the symbol of the Knights in Blue Satin.

Andy read the inscriptions written in Orishan.

"Greetings, fellow Orishans. If you seek the Sword, remove it from its bed just like King Arthur."

Schaumburg and Andy looked at each other puzzled. Sam wondered what the inscription meant as well. They could see neither sword nor any base for one.

"Andy, what is the Bearacus telling you?" Schaumburg said.

"It says there is some silver here," Andy responded.

"Remove it from its bed? Does Bartholomew mean base?" Schaumburg said.

"That sounds like the King Arthur legend," Sam said.

"What's the King Arthur legend?" Schaumburg said.

"It tells of a king who as a boy had to pull a sword from a stone. Many strong knights tried to pull out the sword, but only Arthur could pull it out because he was destined to become King of England."

"Isn't this King Arthur connected to legends about the constellation Ursa Major?" Schaumburg asked.

"I don't know," Sam said.

Schaumburg pulled out his Orishan radio.

"Leni, what can you tell me about the King Arthur legend and his connection to the constellation Ursa Major? Cross reference him in the Paw Computer."

"I'm already on it," Leni said, searching through her ancient tomes.

"Okay, here it is," Leni said after a few minutes of research. "In Celtic lore, the constellation is said to be a great wagon pulled by King Arthur. Legend has it that Arthur is named after the bear. He is sleeping in a cave and will return some day to save his people."

"Thanks Leni," Schaumburg said and shut off his radio.

"Arthur is sleeping in a cave and will return to save his people," Schaumburg said to himself out loud. "Remove it from its bed just like King Arthur. Perhaps, the sword is imbedded in the rock walls."

"Imbedded, like sleeping in a bed," Sam said. "Of course."

Andy put the Bearacus up against the walls. First, Andy put the device on the walls to the right and left of the opposite wall with the Knights in Blue Satin painting—no sword. Then Andy used it on the wall with the painting. As soon as Andy placed the Bearacus up against the painting, the Bearacus began beeping loudly.

"This is it," Andy said. "The sword must be imbedded in this wall."

Andy slid the device up and down and across the wall until it beeped even louder. Then it pulsed with a blue light.

"Here," Andy said. "This is where the sword must be."

Schaumburg took out a laser knife and began cutting out a piece of the rock wall. After carefully removing the piece of wall he cut out, the nine-inch silver sword pinged down to the dirt floor beneath him.

Sam, Andy and Schaumburg jumped for joy, howling with delight.

Suddenly, their joviality was stopped short by a voice.

"Hand over the sword," they heard.

They twirled around to see Juan pointing a gun at them.

"I thought you were our friend," Schaumburg said.

"I am a friend of whomever pays me the most," Juan said. "This artifact you have found will pay me handsomely."

At that moment, a blinding light and smoke filled the room, distracting Juan.

Then a buzz filled the ancient tomb. Leni suddenly faced them all.

"Hand over the gun, Juan," Leni said.

Juan lunged at Leni, and she raised her paw, yelling, "Nap time." Juan slumped to the floor in a peaceful slumber. Everybody stared at Leni in disbelief.

"This paw is loaded," she joked.

"But how?" Andy asked.

"I used the modified Teddy Bear Zone portal to transport under the jeep," Leni said.

Sam grabbed some rope from Juan's jeep and tied Juan.

"Thanks for saving our hides," Schaumburg said to Leni. "Now, let's get back to Versailles and help Mrs. Cruz and the others with those false documents."

CHAPTER 19

DEFENSE AGAINST DOOMSDAY

February 24, 2003, Versailles, Illinois, George Washington Museum

Cheryl busied herself creating a phony version of Bartholomew's journal.

Meanwhile, in another room, Louis and Chocolate conducted a high tech "slide show" showing photos and giving information to Sam, Schaumburg, Andy and Leni. A special Orishan projector caused holographic images.

"We have been studying Bartholomew's journal while you folks have been away on the hunt for the second sword," Louis said. "You are about to see what Bartholomew created to defend against the doomsday device."

The projection on the wall showed a picture of the Arjogun weapon that bored deep into the core of the planet to be destroyed.

"The Arjogun weapon uses the super heat of a planet's molten core to power their ingenious doomsday device," Louis continued.

"In other words, the power source for the weapon is the planet's own molten core?" Sam asked.

"Precisely," Louis replied. "The weapon triggers a series of spasms in the planet's core which erupts in the planet's crust in the form of earthquakes and volcanoes. Finally, the stress causes a polar shift."

The photo of the planet on the screen first erupted in volcanic explosions, and then shifted suddenly and violently to the left. The entire mantle, or crust, shifted position, causing the oceans to be displaced.

"This causes massive destruction as the land masses move across the surface of the planet," Louis said.

"But that's not the end," Chocolate added. "After the polar shift, the molten core continues to heat up, eventually overloading the planet's system and blowing it to pieces."

The slide changed to a planet exploding.

Chocolate moved to the next "slide," a drawing by Bartholomew of the Arch that had yet to be built in St. Louis.

"This is the Gateway to the West, the arch in St. Louis," Louis said. "It was designed by Bartholomew 100 years before it was actually constructed. The humans built the arch in the 1960s. Bartholomew's plans were handed down to Eero Saarinen, the man credited with designing the arch in 1947, the same year we crashed on Earth. Saarinen was secretly working with the Orishans. The Orishans built their secret headquarters at the top of the arch without human knowledge, without realizing that as they followed Bartholomew's plans precisely, they were actually creating a device he designed that will defend the Earth against the Arjogun's doomsday weapon."

"I always wondered why the arch looked like a structure from another planet," Sam said.

The slide changed, showing the arch creating a vortex inside the concrete walls that stretched to hundreds of feet into the air. Then the vortex changed into a concentrated beam that shot into the Earth's surface.

"The real reason for the arch's weird design is to form this multi-dimensional vortex," Louis said. "This vortex can be concentrated into a single powerful beam which when aimed at the Earth's core, can neutralize the Arjogun's doomsday device on the opposite side of the planet."

Chocolate changed the "slide."

"This next drawing shows the location of Bartholomew's control panel inside the secret Orishan HQ at the top of the arch," Louis continued. "As you can see, there are two slots in the panel."

Chocolate adjusted a control on the "slide" projector, which changed the slide to an animated photograph of two silver swords.

"Here are the two 'keys' to activate Bartholomew's defense mechanism. By the way, Bartholomew called it his 'Fire Eater.' These two nine-inch silver swords were designed to fit exactly into these slots on the Fire Eater's control panel. It's the silver in the swords that completes the electronic circuit, combined with their unique shape. Without this manual of Bartholomew's, we would never have been able to figure out how to concentrate this beam that stops the Arjogun doomsday weapon. You see, one sword starts the vortex."

The photograph "slide" changed to show one sword placed inside one slot and the vortex outside in the arch it created.

"The second sword," Louis continued, "starts the concentrated beam which stops the weapon. You can't stop it with just one sword. Bartholomew knew that. That's why he kept the existence of both swords top secret. It wasn't until Cheryl Cruz read those letters and discovered the secret writing that we even knew of the existence of both swords."

"Cheryl is rewriting the journal to show just one sword is needed," Chocolate said.

Chocolate hit some more buttons and images of the phony journal appeared on the projector.

"Mrs. Cruz is forging the documents very close to the original, using paper which actually is from the 1830s," Chocolate said.

"Uh, Chocolate?" Cheryl said.

"Yes, Mrs. Cruz?" Chocolate asked.

"Those papers are not from the 1830s," Cheryl replied.

"Then how did you get them to look so old?" Chocolate asked.

"I made color photocopies of them, and then stuck them in the oven to age them," Cheryl explained.

"Clever humans," Chocolate said. "As you can see, in her version, there is only one sword needed to both activate the vortex, then create the concentrated beam."

On the slides, a succession of phony journal pages are shown, similar to the originals, but altered to make it appear Bartholomew designed just one sword for the Fire Eater.

"This is great work," Schaumburg said. "You both have done a lot of research on this device. And Mrs. Cruz's fake journal pages look beary close to Bartholomew's originals. The Arjogun will not know the difference."

"The beauty of this is that if they really do steal the phony journal, only we will know how the defense mechanism really works," Andy said.

"Have you instructed the Knights in Blue Satin to discontinue their attempt to have the time capsule dug up under the Washington Monument?" Sam asked.

"Yes, but Perry was a little reluctant to follow my advice since I could not reveal to him my entire plan. However, he trusts me," Schaumburg said.

"What about destroying this weapon that the Arjogun are building?" Sam asked. "Won't Bartholomew's device only neutralize the weapon?"

"Good question," Louis said. "In fact, Bartholomew's concentrated beam not only stops the Arjogun weapon from destroying the planet, but it causes an overload in the weapon itself, causing it to implode. Basically, this causes the Arjogun device to self-destruct."

"We left that out of the phony journal, too," Chocolate added. "The Arjogun won't know the swords will actually trigger the Fire Eater that will in effect 'eat' the Arjogun's massive planet killer."

"But what about those Arjogun, Orishans and humans building the weapon in Madagascar deep underground?" Leni asked.

"I thought of that too," Schaumburg said. "We'll need a team to fly a human Army Ch-47 Chinook rescue helicopter, large enough to carry all the Arjogun, humans and Orishans to safety after the Arjogun weapon starts to self-destruct."

"Just what are you planning, Schaumburg?" Leni asked. "How are you going to get the Frown to start the vortex at the arch with that first sword?"

Schaumburg ordered that the lights be turned back on in the room.

"Okay, folks," Schaumburg said. "Here's my plan. The Frown wants to kill me and Andy as the Paw and Mardi Gras. We know the Lemming has ordered our deaths."

"We're with you so far, Schaumy," Leni said. "So how do you get the Frown to do your bidding and bring you to St. Louis with his sword?"

"As long as I have known Vil, he has been beary competitive," Schaumburg said. "After he steals the phony journal and then manages to obtain the sword buried in Washington, D.C., he will think he has won and relax."

"Okay," Leni said. "Go on."

"We have to let the Knights in Blue Satin know about our attempt to rescue the humans and Orishans in Madagascar," Schaumburg continued. "That way the spy in the Knights will tip off the Lemming and the Frown of our plan."

"Holy sneakiness!" Andy said. "I think I see what your plan is. The bad guys will think we are all headed to Madagascar to rescue those enslaved there."

"The entire planet depends on me succeeding, Leni," Schaumburg said. Leni looked into Schaumburg's amber eyes. She could see fierce determination in them, as if Schaumburg was willing himself to succeed.

"Let me give you some insurance then," Leni suggested.

"What have you got in mind?"

"I will contact my order of Wizards," Leni said. "I think I can give you some extra help at the right moment."

"What happens if after we hand over the phony journal and first sword to the bad guys, and they don't follow through and challenge Schaumburg as he suggests?" Sam asked.

"First things first," Schaumburg said. "We have to complete the fake journal and figure out a way to allow the bad guys to get it."

"Leave that to me," Chocolate said. "I've got an idea."

Amy Investigates

Amy arranged for a one-on-one phone interview with Frank Largetooth.

"Just who exactly are these Orisha you spoke about in your letter?" Amy asked.

"If you are a friend of Mr. Arctophile, you must know that they are aliens that appear to be teddy bears," Largetooth replied. "Bartholomew, who was an Orishan, devised a plan to stop evil aliens from hurting Mother Earth."

"Wait a minute," Amy said. "Evil aliens? You think these Orishans are evil?"

"No, no, no!" Frank said. "The Orishans are very good beings. But wait! If you are *truly* a friend of Mr. Arctophile, you would know that, wouldn't you?"

Amy searched quickly in her mind for an answer. "I was just testing you," Amy said. "You are talking about the alien grays, aren't you?" Amy guessed.

"Yes, the Orishans are battling the Arjogun," Frank responded. "As you know, the Arjogun are sometimes called alien grays."

"Just how are these evil alien grays going to hurt Mother Earth?" Amy asked.

"Are you sure you are Mr. Arctophile's friend?" Frank asked, now very suspicious of Amy.

"I work with Sam," she confessed. "I saw your note to him. I was trying to figure out what kind of a mess Sam is in."

"I can tell you are a true friend," Frank said. "I can hear trust and love in your voice. I will tell you what you want to know."

"What are the evil aliens planning to do to Earth?"

"They have a weapon which will destroy our planet. Bartholomew invented a defense against it. That's what Sam is helping the Orishans do."

"I don't understand," Amy said. "What is Sam helping the Orishans do?"

"Sam is helping them find the keys to activate the Fire Eater, the defense Bartholomew invented more than 150 years ago to stop the Arjogun from destroying our planet!"

Amy thanked Frank and hung up the phone.

"I may be able to get more out of Fred than Sam at this point," she said to herself.

* * *

Amy knocked on Fred's Kankakee apartment door late one evening.

Fred peered through the peephole and was pleased to see his longtime friend, Amy.

After opening the door, Amy surprised Fred by pushing herself in and violently shutting the door behind her.

"What's wrong, Amy?" Fred said.

"Shut up!" Amy shouted back. "How could you and Sam deceive me like that? For as long as we have been friends? How could you? Especially Sam!"

"But, Amy, I . . ."

"I said 'shut up'!" Amy shouted back. She pushed him backward by poking him in the shoulder until he sat down backwards on a kitchen table chair.

"Now, tell me what you know about these aliens who call themselves Orishans!" she demanded, throwing the photos of Sam, Schaumburg and Andy on his kitchen table.

"Oh, so you know about the Orishans?" Fred said, nervously.

"Tell me!" she screamed.

Fred knew he was in trouble.

"Okay, but don't yell any more," Fred said.

"I won't yell," Amy said, trying to calm down. "Tell me everything."

Fred filled Amy in on everything he knew, including the missing pieces to the puzzle about Sam's abduction and the strange behavior of Izzie Feinberg.

"So, what is the Orishans' plan to stop the Arjogun doomsday weapon?" Amy asked.

"Well, it's a two-pronged assault," Fred said. "Schaumburg, Sam's Orishan friend, will use the keys to set off Bartholomew's device."

"The keys are these Swords of George Washington?" Amy asked.

"Yes, and the Arjogun know about the Fire Eater," Fred said. "But they don't know exactly how it works or that they need two keys. Sam and the Orishans forged a copy of Bartholomew's journal and will allow the Arjogun to get a hold of it. This will convince them that the Fire Eater works with just one sword, not two."

"What's the second 'prong' in this mastermind military assault?" Amy wanted to know.

"Sam and I along with some other humans known as the Protectors will launch a secret attack on the camp in Madagascar where the doomsday device is being built."

"Why are they attacking the doomsday device camp?" Amy asked. "I thought you said the Fire Eater will cause the device to self-destruct?"

"Yes, it will," Fred said. "But there are human and Orishan slaves at the camp who will be killed unless they are rescued."

Fred could see a light dawning on Amy's face.

"These Orishans are great tacticians at defense," Amy said, speaking from her experience as a soldier. "They seem to lack experience on offense."

Fred looked at her with a puzzled expression. "What do you suggest?"

"I've got a lot of ideas," Amy said. "I'd like to talk to this Schaumburg and Commander Black. Actually I already know the Commander."

"What?" Fred said, now very surprised.

"I carried out a number of assignments for him during the Gulf War," she said. "He was a very good soldier. I trust him. But you and Sam shouldn't be involved with such dangerous missions. What kind of training is he giving you?"

"We are training heavily with the other Protectors on our mission to Madagascar, learning simple combat and self-defense techniques. Our old Judo lessons have been coming in handy."

"Okay," Amy said. "I can't let you and Sam go on this mission so naked. I'm going to help. And I have some others who are willing to join us. Get me into a strategic planning meeting with you and the Orishans."

"Amy, I'm sorry I could not tell you everything," Fred said.

"You lied to me, Fred, and so did Sam! How could you?"

"Would you have believed us if we came to you and said, 'Hey, Amy, we need your help fighting evil aliens who are going to destroy the Earth,'? You would have told us we belonged in a mental institution."

"And I would have thought you *were* crazy until I saw how crazy Izzie became. Mind control? This is all so fantastic! Is Sam okay?"

"As you said, the Orishans are very good at defense," Fred said. "They devised a way to neutralize the mind-control where our best human scientists failed. Sam is fine, thanks to your help as well."

"You came to me knowing I could help you find Sam," Amy said. "You wanted to tell me about all this back then, didn't you?"

Fred said nothing.

"Sam and I have been in danger for several years," Fred said. "You have no idea how close we all came to being killed, more than once. We could really use your help, especially now."

"You know I will," Amy said, putting her hand gently on Fred's face. "You guys only had to ask for my help."

The Frown steals Bartholomew's journal

April 24, 2003, Pawtropolis Capital building steps

Chocolate Harmony spoke live to Pawtropolis television reporter Fatima Furbulous about her recent discovery, the journal of Bartholomew.

A large remote television monitor displayed the broadcast for a huge crowd of Orishans watching off to one side of the Pawtropolis Capital building.

"Please tell us, Ms. Harmony, what kind of secrets did the Great Bartholomew write down in his journal?"

"Well, for one thing, he explained how the Arjogun are going to destroy this planet," Chocolate said. "He gives alarming details about the Arjogun's doomsday device and how to prevent the destruction of the Earth."

Chocolate opened the forged journal created by Cheryl Cruz and the camera zoomed up on a drawing of the Arjogun doomsday device in the journal.

"Here's how the Arjogun weapon will be used to destroy this planet," Chocolate said. A collective gasp of horror sounded through the crowd watching on the monitor.

"Here's the device that Bartholomew created to neutralize the weapon," Chocolate continued. "You see, this nine-inch silver sword is actually a key to operate the Fire Eater, Bartholomew's invention which will stop the Arjogun's weapon."

"Amazing, Ms. Harmony," Fatima said. "Do you and your Hug intend to operate the Fire Eater to save the Earth?"

"That's the plan, Ms. Furbulous. We still have to obtain permission to dig up the time capsule buried under the Washington Monument. Schaumburg, the head of my Hug, is coordinating those efforts with the humans as we speak."

Fatima Furbulous turned to the camera.

"There you have it, fellow Orishans," she said. "It looks like Scoop Schaumburg and his Hug may earn their License To Hug after all if they pull this one off. There's nothing like saving an entire planet from destruction to help boost your standing with Orishan Command. Fatima Furbulous, reporting live from . . ."

Just as Fatima prepared to sign off the air, the Frown rushed up in his evil Frownmobile, an ugly convertible vehicle painted in his horrible colors of navy blue and black with a huge frowning face painted on the hood.

The Frown leapt out of the vehicle, snatched the journal from Chocolate's paws, and hopped back into his car, speeding off.

"Ha,ha,ha,ha,ha,ha,ha,ha,ha!" he laughed as he zoomed away to his castle. "Come get me if you can, Paw! Ha,ha,ha,ha,ha,ha,ha,ha!"

"Did you get that?" Fatima asked the Orishan operating the camera. The camera Orishan nodded, indicating the camera broadcast all of it live to Pawtropolis citizens.

"What does this mean?" Fatima said. "Will you fail in your mission now?"

Chocolate said nothing, pushing Fatima's microphone away.

Fatima turned to the camera again as Chocolate stomped off camera.

"You saw that here live, folks," Fatima said. "We just witnessed the theft of the journal of Bartholomew containing a way to stop the Arjogun's doomsday device. Will the Paw get it back from the Frown on time? Where is the Paw? We haven't seen him here in Pawtropolis for months. Come to think of it, we haven't seen any stories by Scoop Schaumburg in *The Daily Times* for a while, either. What's your brother been up to? Chocolate? Where did she go?" The camera operator panned, showing no sign of Chocolate.

"This reporter wonders what the Paw has done for Pawtropolis citizens lately? Why wasn't he here to stop the Frown? Why would he foolishly allow such a valuable piece of history to fall into evil hands? Will the Frown prevent Schaumburg's Hug from earning their Licenses To Hug after all? Will the Arjogun destroy this planet with their doomsday weapon? I, for one, have no faith in either the Paw or Chocolate's brother, Schaumburg Harmony. He's failed to carry out his missions before, which is why he has not earned his License To Hug. We'll bring you a live update when we know more about the Paw's efforts to reclaim the famous journal of Bartholomew . . . If the Paw can get it back . . ."

Back at *The Daily Times*, Andy, Schaumburg and Perry watched the television. Perry's face betrayed his horror.

"Write this up, Andy," Perry ordered. "And you, Schaumburg, contact the Paw as soon as possible. We have to get that journal back. This could spell doom for all of us. Why is Fatima turning on the Paw like that, anyway?"

"I'm on it Perry," Schaumburg said, pulling on his trench coat and fedora, and leaving for the bearavator. "I'll see you at home, Andy. And Perry, don't worry about Fatima Furbulous. She's just a television journalist. They're more concerned about getting pictures that look dramatic on television than on reporting the news."

"Agreed," Perry said. Then he looked at Andy. "Start writing!" Perry barked to Andy.

"Right, boss," Andy called back as he began banging out a story about the live events as they had unfolded on television.

Meanwhile, at the Paw Cave later that evening, Leni contacted the Mystical Order of the Golden Paw via crystal ball.

"Master, please help us," Leni said. "We need to protect Schaumburg from the Frown. I need a spell that can help him carry out his mission."

"Leni, this is Nerwonduh on the planet Bengali," came back an answer. She could see the wizard in her crystal ball.

"Yes, Nerwonduh," Leni said. "Do you know about Schaumburg's plan?"

"I do, and we also know of the two swords. Cast a spell of Excalibur on Schaumburg's sword. It will make a difference in his battle with the Frown as they struggle at the arch."

"A spell on the sword?" Leni asked. "But that spell is for protection in sword fights."

"Exactly," Nerwonduh said. "Trust me, Millennium. This spell will protect your husband."

"Yes, sir," Leni said, still not convinced.

Leni picked up the gleaming silver sword that Schaumburg, Andy and Sam found in Guatemala a few weeks earlier.

It sparkled in the soft light of the Paw Cave. Dreamwalker pranced up to her. Leni instinctively patted Dreamwalker's forehead. At that instant, Leni saw a flash, a premonition, when she touched the unicorn's forehead. She saw an image of Schaumburg in a sword fight with the Frown. She also saw Andy, Louis and Chocolate there with Schaumburg. That put her mind at ease.

"Is this what will happen or what could happen?" Leni asked the unicorn. The unicorn remained silent. Then the unicorn used his horn to point at the sword.

"You want me to cast the spell, don't you boy?" she said to the unicorn. The magical creature nodded his head in agreement.

Leni closed her eyes and waved her magic wand over the sword. She waited until the stroke of midnight exactly. She lit some frankincense to give the room a magical aura and help her concentrate. She lit two candles on either side of a simple table where her crystal ball stood on its pedestal. She placed the sword on the table, point away from her, between the candles. She closed her blue eyes tightly and concentrated. Three times she repeated the following blessing:

"TO THE GREAT BEAR SPIRIT IN HEAVEN, i HUMBLY ASK THAT YOU BLESS THIS MAGICAL SWORD AND ITS WIELDER, SCHAUMBURG, AND PRESERVE THEM FROM ALL EVIL, SO THAT THEY MAY SERVE THEE

BY BANISHING THE EVIL AND PROTECTING THE GOOD. SO LET IT BE WRITTEN. SO LET IT BE DONE."

Then she took the sword and held it before her for a moment, point upward.

As soon as Leni finished the spell, the sword started glowing with a bright white light.

For an instant, the sword floated above Leni, then drifted back down to her paws. She could feel its power surging through to her paws.

Then she took a special black leather scabbard she crafted which contained magical symbols, including the Golden Paw, and gently placed the sword in the scabbard. She put the sword and scabbard into a blue box lined with special velvet and closed the box.

"I hope this works, Schaumy," she said to herself, softly.

At the Frown's castle, the Frown pored over the journal that had been altered by Cheryl Cruz.

"This is fantastic," the Frown said to himself. "This Orishan Bartholomew figured out a way to stop our Planet Destroyer. We can't let the Orishans have this kind of information. It could spell disaster for Arjogunia!"

He immediately called upon his human, the Lemming, for help, using a special computer telephone. Instantly, the image of Izzie Feinberg showed on the Frown's monitor.

"Boss, we've got to devise a plan to stop the Paw! If he carries out his plan, our device will never be activated! Your military will never have its weather control device."

"Your attempts to kill the Paw have failed in the past," the Lemming said. "We have to come up with a better plan. Perhaps you can trap him with the Splotch."

"The Splotch!" the Frown said. "But that horrible monster will kill every being on this planet if it goes unchecked."

"We have no alternative," the Lemming said. "As you said, we have to stop the Paw. Set it up. Trap the Paw! The Lemming, out."

PART 3

THE SECRET WAR

CHAPTER 20

BACK TO THE FUTURE

Late April, 2003, in Samuel Arctophile's Versailles Bureau office

The Paw, Mardi Gras, Leni and Jose discussed the past four year's events with little Jose.

"Boy, you Orishan teddy bears really are heroes," Jose said. "Schaumburg, are you gonna have to fight the Frown at the Arch and use those swords to save our planet?"

"I am, my boy," Schaumburg said. "And Sam here is going to help in rescuing your father while I'm in St. Louis. Have you made the arrangements for the U.S. Army Ch-47 helicopter with the Protectors yet?"

"Yes, and we leave for Africa in a few days," Sam replied.

Jose suddenly started to worry.

"What if you fail, Schaumburg?" the boy asked.

Schaumburg waddled up to Jose and gave him a big hug. Then he pulled out the second Sword of George Washington. "Leni cast a magic spell on this sword. I've got my H.A.R.V.E.Y. unit. I'll be all right. I promise. I will not fail."

Jose saw that same determination in Schaumburg's eyes that Leni had seen a few weeks earlier.

Suddenly, the phone in Sam's office rang.

"Sam, this is Louis in the Paw Cave. Tell Schaumburg to turn on his Orishan Radio and listen to this transmission."

"Right, Louis," Sam said.

Schaumburg turned on the Orishan portable radio and turned up the volume so all could hear.

"This is a challenge to you Paw," came the familiar voice of the Frown.

"Meet me at the Arch in St. Louis and try and stop me from turning your precious Sword of George Washington into a lump of silver! Ha,ha,ha,ha,ha,ha,ha,ha,ha,ha!"

"He's taken the bait just like we thought he would," Leni said.

Preparations For Final Battle

Samuel Arctophile received a call the next day at his office in Versailles.

"Sam, this is Amy," the caller said.

"Hi ya, Amy," Sam said. "What can I do for you?"

"Since Izzie has been gone, the upper management has been kicking around names for managing editor to replace him."

"Yeah, so?"

"You are being mentioned prominently," Amy said. "The General Manager asked me about you—wanted to know what I thought of you taking over."

"What'd you tell him?"

"I gave you a glowing review of course," Amy said. "So you better give me a big fat raise when you get the job!"

Both laughed.

"They want you to come into Montreal as soon as you can for an interview."

"Why didn't the GM call me?"

"To be quite honest, I think he's a little afraid of you, Sam."

"Afraid of me?"

Sam thought this quite humorous since the GM was a large man, 6 foot, 5 inches, who could easily pound Sam into submission if he wanted to.

"Not physically, you dope," Amy continued. "He's afraid of your character."

"Say what?"

"He's worried you might slay some of the paper's sacred cows with your crusades as editor."

Sam understood now. All papers had sacred cows, organizations or companies that stayed off limits when it came to reporting corruption or any bad news about them. For example, a railroad company owned a newspaper that he once worked for. So consequently, stories about derailed and wrecked trains were not news in that publication. Sam promptly quit when he learned about that. In Versailles, he has been able to go after just about any story he wanted since the main office and sacred cows seemed to all be in Montreal. But working out of the main office would be different.

And all this was coming at a time when he prepared for a trip to Madagascar to help rescue people and Orishans from the Arjogun. The timing could not have been worse.

"Okay, Amy," Sam said. "I'll drive in ASAP. I have to file one story and I'll leave then. I'll be there in about an hour."

After the interview with the GM, Sam took Amy out for a quick lunch.

"Listen, Amy," Sam said in hushed tones. "I want this job, especially since it looks like Izzie has gone looney tunes. But I've got to finish up an assignment first."

"What are you gonna do?"

"I told the GM I would let him know my decision next week, after May 5."

"What's so special about May 5?" Amy wanted to know.

Sam hunched down low in the booth where they sat.

"I have to go on a sort of military mission," Sam said.

"Oh, that," Amy said. "I already know about that. It's about time you told me."

"What?" Sam asked loudly.

Amy plopped down the photographs of Schaumburg, Sam and Andy in Nome, Alaska.

"I interviewed Mr. Largetooth," Amy said. "Then I cornered Fred. I know everything and I want to help. Get me to a meeting with the Orisha and these Protectors ASAP."

"Amy, you and I have known each other since high school," Sam said. "But I have never known a moment in our friendship when I have felt more grateful to you. Please help us. Your military background will be invaluable. Come to my apartment tonight, 7 p.m."

*   *   *

At Sam's apartment later that night, Amy knocked on his door. Fred greeted Amy with a warm hug. Fred wore army camouflage with a blue satin beret. The beret contained symbol of a crowned snake in a circle with its tail to its mouth with three crowned rings inside the circle.

When Amy walked into Sam's apartment, she saw a room full of walking, talking teddy bears, as well as Sam and Cheryl. She recognized Commander Black but others there she did not know. Most wore the same outfit as Fred with the blue satin berets.

"Surprise," Sam said, and gave her a big hug. Schaumburg walked up to Amy.

"I don't believe we have been formally introduced," Schaumburg said. "I am Captain Schaumburg Harmony, a member of the Bear Force from a planet called Orisha. These other Orishans with me are part of my Hug, or squad."

Schaumburg quickly filled Amy in on the mission and the logistics of having to rescue people in Madagascar before the camp self-destructs.

"Your plan for rescuing the people in Madagascar is sound, but I don't like the business of you going alone to St. Louis," Amy said.

This stunned Schaumburg.

"You have to have backup, Schaumburg," she said. "You can't take on this Vil character alone. He's likely to have backup defending his six."

"Six what?" Schaumburg asked.

Amy laughed. "That's Army slang for defending your back," Amy explained. "Schaumburg, how are you getting to St. Louis?"

"I was going to travel via the Teddy Bear Zone."

"I suggest you take your F-117A, and therefore, will need other Orishans to help you fly it."

"I volunteer to go with you Schaumburg," Andy said.

"I agree with Amy," Leni said. "You do need backup."

"I can't risk your lives as well, Andy," Schaumburg said.

"All our lives are at risk," Andy said. "Please, let me do this."

"Schaumburg, one of the lessons of command is sometimes giving orders that could put your men in danger," Amy said, gently placing her hand on Schaumburg's shoulder.

"Why is it necessary for us to use the F-117A to fly down to St. Louis?" Schaumburg asked.

"Backup," Amy said. "If something goes wrong in Madagascar, you and others can fly to Africa instantly with the F-117A Orishan hyperdrive, right?"

"Good thinking," Schaumburg said. "But we can't fit too many beings in that tiny cockpit."

"That's an excellent suggestion, Amy" Black said. "But Schaumburg is right. That ship cannot carry too many safely. I suggest that an entire Hug of Orishans lead a secret assault on Vil and the Arch in St. Louis. Leni can stay behind in the Paw Cave to monitor via crystal ball. But Andy, Louis, and Chocolate should be with Schaumburg. Vil may have some Orishanite there, you know."

Schaumburg thought it over for a few minutes.

"Understood," Schaumburg said. Amy smiled an ear-to-ear grin at Schaumburg.

"Okay, so it's settled," Sam said. "Andy, Louis and Chocolate will go with the assault team led by Schaumburg to St. Louis to confront the Frown and activate the Fire Eater. The rest of us will travel to Africa and take the chopper to Madagascar to mount our rescue effort as soon as the Fire Eater is activated."

"We won't meet much resistance this time in Madagascar," Black said. "We have been monitoring Arjogun ships leaving the planet at an alarming rate. I suspect there will be few left in Madagascar to guard the doomsday device."

"Just the same, we may hit some resistance," Amy said.

"Granted," Black said. "And we have determined that the slaves are being kept at the lowest levels, down in the final construction phase. We will have to climb far underground to reach them. The choppers

can't fly down there. That could take time and we won't have much
once the self-destruct begins."

"I know where we can 'borrow' another Chinook Ch-47 chopper
and some muscle as well," Amy said. "Bartholomew made a lot of
friends when he was on this planet, apparently. May God protect us all.
Sam, Fred, we have some training to do. Sam, Fred and I will meet
Commander Black and the rest of your team in Africa at the prearranged
spot at 0600 hours on May 4."

Leni handed the sword to Schaumburg.

"I cast the Excalibur spell on it," Leni said as tears streamed down
her furry white cheek. "Please come back to me."

"I will," Schaumburg said. They hugged each other tightly.

*   *   *

At the slave camp on Madagascar 1,000 feet below the surface,
Armando and Lavender enjoyed a short break together. Both were
grimy with sweat, grease and soil.

Lavender spoke in hushed tones.

"I learned about my brother-in-law," Lavender said. "He and his
Hug are on a dangerous mission to stop the Arjogun."

"That's great," Armando said, a sparkle lighting his brown eyes.

"There's more," she said. "This monstrosity we are building. It is
not to control weather, as we were told. It is a special weapon called a
doomsday device. I have heard of it. It will destroy your entire planet.
That is what Schaumburg's Hug is going to stop."

"That's good news, right?" Armando asked.

"Sort of," she said. "The problem is, as soon as the doomsday
device is deactivated, it will self-destruct."

"With us down here at the bottom of hell," Armando said. "Figures.
It was nice knowing you, Lavender."

"It's not over yet, human!" Lavender scolded Armando. "Don't
you give up hope on me. Part of Schaumburg's Hug is executing an
airlift rescue. They have a team of humans and Orishans ready to
pounce on this facility as soon as the device is neutralized."

"You mean like those crack commandos defeated by the Arjogun last year in their attempt to break us out?"

"If they fail this time, we all die anyway," Lavender said, now looking a little scared.

Armando hugged her.

An Arjogun cracked a whip near Lavender and Armando.

"Get back to work you two," the Arjogun screamed at them. "Break is over!"

"I'd like to wring that gray alien's neck," Armando said under his breath to Lavender.

"I wouldn't," she whispered to him. "His name is Gobador. He is spying for the Orishans. He's one of us."

That stunned Armando. He quickly got back to work digging the ground with a laser shovel.

*   *   *

Leni sat alone in her house at Toleni, fretting over the coming mission. She spoke to her pet dragon, Scorch. Her two baby owls, Hoot and Nanny sat quietly perched nearby.

"I am glad Schaumburg agreed to take the rest of the Hug with him to the Arch, Scorch," she said to him. "But something is still bothering me. I'm going to contact Jack in Moscow."

Scorch nodded his head approvingly and gave Leni a verbal raspberry.

"Jack, this is Leni," she said into her Orishan radio. "I need your help again."

"Leni, have you finally decided to leave that drip Schaumburg and come crawling back to me?" Jack said.

"In your dreams," Leni replied. "Jack, seriously, I want you to provide backup to my Hug on our mission. Are you guys available?"

"Yep!" Jack said. "We were just making preparations to journey back to Orisha. Our ship's ready to fly. What can I do for you, doll?"

Leni outlined the details of how Schaumburg planned to activate the Fire Eater.

"That's suicide!" Jack said. "There will likely be Arjogun soldiers all over that Arch now that they know it can be used against them! Sorry, honey. This Orishan is heading for home!"

"But Jack . . ."

"Sorry, doll! See you on Orisha!"

A Crystal Butterfly

Schaumburg and Louis practiced their sword fighting in the Paw Cave while Andy and Chocolate worked in the lab on a formula to counteract Orishanite.

"I don't think we'll be able to find a cure in time," Chocolate said. "We have just a few days before that weapon goes online."

"Then Schaumburg and I will just have to go to the Arch without using our super powers," Andy said.

"There will likely be a hoard of Arjogun soldiers there," Chocolate said. "We have to have some sort of advantage."

Andy thought for a moment, fondling the Bearacus that he had used to locate the second sword in Guatemala.

"You know, I've been thinking," Andy said.

"Yes?" Chocolate asked.

"Why would Bartholomew go to all the trouble to hide this device in three different parts of the planet just so we could locate the second sword?"

"It is kind of goofy," Chocolate said. "But then, Bartholomew was said to be a bit eccentric. Just look at those B.A.R.T. Bearavators he invented."

"No, this has to be more than just a device to find the sword," Andy said.

Suddenly, Andy accidentally cocked the globe-like Bearacus into a different position. It clicked opened, revealing a small pen-like object inside.

Andy took out the "pen," made of a crystal-like structure.

"This looks like some kind of stylus," Andy said.

"Let me see that," Chocolate said, taking the "pen" and putting it under her microscope.

"This is not a stylus," Chocolate said. "It is a living organism."

"What?" Andy said.

"Schaumburg, Louis, come quick," Chocolate yelled. "Take a look under this microscope."

Louis and Schaumburg looked at the "pen." It seemed to be a living "worm" when seen under the microscope.

"What is this?" Schaumburg asked.

"It came from the Bearacus," Andy said. "I found it by accident."

"Contact Cheryl," Schaumburg said. "See if the real journal of Bartholomew has anything about this strange being."

*   *   *

Amy busied herself instructing Sam and Fred on some quick combat moves. They walked through Starved Rock Park, near Utica, toward a canyon to practice mountain climbing. After receiving the secret plans to the Arjogun base at Madagascar from Gobador, the Protectors learned that the only way down undetected by the Arjogun would be to descend a rough-hewn shaft, 1,000 feet straight underground. The rescue squad needed to reach the bottom of the shaft to reach the slaves. The Protectors reasoned they could take the Arjogun lifts back up to the surface.

"Everything depends on split-second timing, and we had very little margin for error built into the plan," Amy said. "A few days of mountain climbing should get this rescue squad into shape. I contacted Frank Largetooth in Alaska who is sending a team to Illinois to train with Commander's Black's squad."

"A few Orishans from another Hug are fitting the helicopters with Orishan hyperdrives so we can instantly transport out of harm's way once the Orishans, captured Arjogun and humans are safely aboard," Fred said.

"Why did you ask Largetooth to help us, Amy?" Sam wanted to know as they started to climb down the mountainside.

"The way I was taught to fight battles, you never want to be undermanned or outgunned," Amy said. "Gobador predicted there would be a skeleton crew of just 12 armed Arjogun remaining when we arrive in Madagascar. But the camp has many built-in defense weapons. I want to have double the amount of personnel on our side."

"But why two helicopters?"

"Again, just in case," Amy replied.

By this time, all three were slowly descending the rock face with mountain climbing equipment.

"You know, Amy, I've never seen your military side before," Sam said as he arrived at a flat outcropping. Fred continued down. Amy stopped on the landing with Sam as well.

She looked down at Fred and waved. Fred was unaware the two had stopped and continued to concentrate on climbing down. Amy trapped Sam against the side of the mountain.

"I am always prepared, just like a Boy Scout," Amy said. Then she leaned in to kiss Sam softly.

"You're no Boy Scout," Sam said after they kissed. "Why did we stop dating anyway?"

"Good question, tiger," Amy said, kissing him again. "I think it happened when I scared you away with talk of marriage and children."

Fred began to tug on their ropes.

"We better keep on climbing or Fred will get suspicious," Sam said.

"Fred knows how I feel about you," Amy said, brushing her bangs out of her blue eyes. She peered into Sam's eyes and kissed him again.

"How *do* you feel about me?" Sam asked.

"Like this," she said and kissed him again.

"But you know, company policy does not allow supervisors to date employees," Sam said, now a little nervous. "If I take that managing editor's position at the paper, we can't date."

Amy started tickling Sam while still holding his arms still.

"Hey, what gives?" Sam protested.

"You listen to me Samuel Arctophile," Amy said, forcing Sam to squirm and giggle. "You will not refuse to accept that promotion just because you want to date me!"

"Who said I wanted to date you?" Sam said, now joking with her. Amy tickled him more forcefully, causing him to laugh and squirm more. They were still about 20 feet from the ground. Fred was already down below.

"We'll fall!" Sam protested, then laughed some more. "Okay, I'm sorry. Uncle. I like you, okay?"

"And if we do decide to pursue this relationship, the company doesn't have to know about it for now, right?"

"Are you thinking of quitting the paper?" Sam said as Amy stopped tickling Sam.

Amy kissed Sam long and sensuously.

"Just don't let our feelings for each other get in the way of your career, ok?" Amy said.

"Anything you say, 'boss,'" Sam said mockingly. Amy started tickling him again. Sam, now free of her grasp, began to descend the mountainside very quickly to escape the "torture."

*   *   *

"I think I know what that wormlike creature is, Schaumburg," Cheryl told the Orishan over special Orishan radio. "I found some passages in his journal about it. It is not a worm. It's sort of a chrysalis. The Bearacus acts as a cocoon."

"You mean this is going to change into a butterfly made of crystal?" Schaumburg asked.

"It's from one of the planets Bartholomew visited in the past," Cheryl said. "It has powers which repel the Arjogun."

"Could you elaborate?" Schaumburg asked, now very interested.

"I'll get back to you on that," Cheryl said and ended her transmission.

"Andy, can you get this thing back into the Bearacus?"

"I think so," Andy said. "Why?" Andy practiced clashing swords with Louis just then in the Paw Cave. Andy held a broadsword known as a Claymore. Louis wielded a cutlass fit for a pirate, even though he now donned a naval commander's uniform.

"Because it's like a cocoon for the being inside," Schaumburg replied. "And I think we want it to change into a butterfly for us."

"A butterfly?" Andy said, as Louis scored a "hit" with his sword on Andy's chest.

"Don't drop your guard, Andy," Louis said. "You know the Arjogun love to fence with Orishans when in close combat. We'll have to be better than them. Everything depends on it."

Andy put down his Claymore sword, about 10 inches in length, ignored Louis, and walked over to Schaumburg. He picked up the "worm" and placed it back into the Bearacus. The globe shut once again and started to glow blue.

"I think you may have been right about this Bearacus," Schaumburg said to Andy. "It's not just a device to find the second sword. I think it will also help us stop all those Arjogun at the Arch.

"I hope you're right, Schaumburg," Leni said. She had just walked into the cave. "You are going to need a lot of help on this mission."

At that moment, the Bearacus burst open, and a sparkling blue crystal butterfly flew out of the globe. It gave off a melodic sound.

"Schaumburg, Cheryl's calling on the radio," Louis said as they all watched the crystal butterfly flutter about the cave.

"It's a being that will stun the Arjogun with its song," Cheryl said. "But its range is only about 20 feet. In a closed room, you could stun an Army of Arjogun with that thing!"

At that instant, the Paw Computer sparked awake and a grisly visage of the Frown greeted the Orishans.

"Well, Schaumburg, I've been waiting for days! When are you coming?" the Frown taunted him. "Come and get your precious Sword of George Washington and save this puny planet for these humans, if you dare!"

"This is obviously a trap, Schaumburg," Louis said.

"We leave at 5:30 a.m.," Schaumburg said, grimly.

Schaumburg (left) and Louis prepare the F-117A for their trip to
St. Louis to confront the Frown and engage the Fire Eater.

CHAPTER 21

WITH A LITTLE HELP FROM SOME FRIENDS

"Circle the Arch slowly," Schaumburg ordered Louis who piloted the F-117A toward St. Louis. The craft was invisible thanks to the attached H.A.R.V.E.Y. unit.

"Commander Black, this is Schaumburg," he called over secret Orishan radio. "Commence Operation Cleanup. We are approaching the target now. Give us exactly 30 minutes to engage Fire Eater."

"Roger," Commander Black called back.

"There!" Andy called out watching on the Heads Up Display showing infrared visual of the Arch below. "I saw an Arjogun guard!"

"There will be dozens of them, I'm sure," Schaumburg said. "Chocolate, do you have our secret weapon ready?"

"The butterfly is right here," Chocolate answered, showing Schaumburg the crystal blue butterfly fluttering around inside a special cage they built for it. The Orishans heard its melodic tune.

"As soon as we touch down, use it to subdue those Arjogun guards at the door to the arch."

"Aye, Captain," Chocolate said.

"Leni, are you monitoring?" Schaumburg called out, seemingly talking to himself.

"I see everything, Schaumy," Leni answered him back through telepathy. "There are five guards at the door and two inside. Will the butterfly's song carry through the door?"

"We'll find out soon enough."

"Schaumburg, they have chunks of Orishanite on them as well," Leni said. "You and Andy cannot use your powers, as we suspected."

"Understood," Schaumburg said. "Andy, Leni said she sees chunks of Orishanite on the guards besides their weapons. No super powers, understood?"

"Aye, Captain," Andy said.

At that very moment, inside the Better Bear Bureau Headquarters, the Frown monitored outside as well. But the F-117A remained cloaked with the H.A.R.V.E.Y. unit.

"Where is he?" the Frown asked himself. Several Arjogun soldiers patrolled the B.B.B. headquarters.

"It's been days. Why hasn't that stupid do-gooder attacked me yet?" the Frown complained to nobody in particular. "Killing him has been so very difficult these past few years. Schaumburg is bound to attack soon. We go online with the weapon in less than six hours."

Leni looked at her crystal ball and observed the Frown.

"Schaumburg, he's waiting for you," Leni said. "Be careful. As the humans say, 'Godspeed' to all of you."

"Set her down, Louis," Schaumburg ordered. "Let's do it."

Chocolate emerged from the invisible ship and deployed her butterfly "weapon" immediately. All the Arjogun guards outside the arch doorway on the ground level dropped to the ground unconscious.

The rest of the Orishans descended from the invisible ladder and approached the door.

"The guards on the other side are unharmed, but are also unaware of the attack so far," Leni told Schaumburg.

Schaumburg motioned for Chocolate and Louis to stand on one side of the door as he and Andy stood on the other.

Schaumburg took out some of his laughing powder and busted down the door. Chocolate immediately deployed the butterfly again, whose song stunned all attacking Arjogun. But the noise of the broken door alerted the Frown upstairs at BBB HQ.

"They're here!" the Frown screamed. "Put all our forces from here to ground level. Stop them from getting up here!"

Several Arjogun soldiers ran down to the pods that normally carried tourists from the observation level at the top of the arch and back down to ground level. The pods took about 20 minutes to climb downstairs, however, giving Schaumburg and his squad time to ascend the arch themselves in a different pod. By the time Schaumburg and his group arrived upstairs, all the Arjogun save three and the Frown made it downstairs.

Once they arrived at the top, Louis used his cutlass sword to skewer the control panel for the pods, so they could not be used any longer without repairs.

The Frown twirled around to greet Schaumburg and company.

Chocolate tried to deploy the butterfly, but an Arjogun stabbed it with his sword and flung it out of Chocolate's paws. The cage smashed, allowing the butterfly to flutter away. The Frown pulled out his Sword of George Washington. It gleamed in the office neon light. Schaumburg faced the Frown. Schaumburg pulled out *his* Sword of George Washington.

"So, you have your own Sword of George Washington," the Frown sneered. "It will do you no good, Schaumburg! I told you when you left Orisha you were on a fool's errand."

The two Swords of George Washington clashed in battle.

Schaumburg knew that by moving in closer to the Frown's blows with his sword, he could cut off the power of the Frown's force.

Schaumburg could feel power surging from his sword, thanks to Leni's magic. He countered with his sword as the Frown tried to stab the Orishan.

"You fence well, Schaumburg," the Frown said. "You've been practicing."

"It's over, Vil," Schaumburg said. "We've already won!"

The Frown struck a blow to Schaumburg's head, which Schaumburg quickly deflected. Schaumburg pushed Vil farther and farther back against the wall of the Better Bear Bureau office.

Louis had already subdued his Arjogun attacker. Chocolate did not do so well.

"Are you okay, honey?" Louis asked her.

"I could use some help, Louis," she said as she deflected blows from her own Arjogun attacker.

Louis took up his opponent's sword and used both to attack the Arjogun who had Chocolate on the run.

Andy defeated his own attacker with a swift blow to the Arjogun's head from the hilt of his Claymore broadsword.

Andy and Louis helped Chocolate overpower the Arjogun attacking Chocolate.

Meanwhile, Schaumburg and the Frown continued to clash in deadly combat.

Schaumburg watched for the Frown to make a mistake. Schaumburg deflected an attack from the Frown to the side, throwing the Frown off balance. Schaumburg knocked the sword out of the Frown's paws. It clanked to the floor in front of Schaumburg, who stepped on it.

The Frown kicked Schaumburg in the chin forcing the Orishan to fall backwards on his fanny as the Frown snatched up his sword once again.

Schaumburg stood up.

"You never did learn to fight dirty, did you Schaumburg?" the Frown asked.

"I never needed too," Schaumburg said as he lunged forward, moving his sword in swift steady blows from left to right, pushing the Frown farther and farther back.

The Frown raised his sword above his head for a final huge blow. That left the Frown open for Schaumburg to punch the Frown in the stomach with his paw, knocking the wind out of him.

At that moment, Andy and Louis fell on the Frown and pinned him to the ground.

"Grab the sword," Louis called to Andy who kneeled near the Frown's sword.

Andy threw the sword to Schaumburg.

Schaumburg took up both swords. He placed one into the Fire Eater control panel.

"Nooooooo!" the Frown screamed. "If you activate that device, it triggers the weapon automatically," the Frown said. "We'll all die!"

"What?" Schaumburg said, now concerned.

"We knew you would try this, so we rigged a trigger here that sets off the weapon in Madagascar," the Frown screamed. "You lose anyway! Ha,ha,ha,ha,ha,ha,ha,ha!"

The vortex began to materialize in between the concrete walls that form the arch. It caused a sucking wind that drew in everything around—trash, newspapers, and a passing bird.

"Leni, did you hear what the Frown just said?"

"Yes, Schaumburg," Leni replied.

Meanwhile, the timetable preset before the attack was at the 30-minute mark. The two rescue helicopters had launched for an instantaneous trip to the Arjogun camp in Madagascar.

"We can't call back the Protectors," Leni told Schaumburg. "They've already left."

"Rats!" Schaumburg said. "If I put in the second sword, it activates the neutralizer beam, and the self-destruct begins. But it also begins the weapon's systems. What will happen?"

"They're going to turn it on in a few hours anyway and destroy the planet," Chocolate said.

"But Chocolate, we did not expect to be neutralizing an activated weapon," Louis replied. "Our people are going to be down there at the bottom of that pit when the weapon begins to heat the planet's core."

"It's likely they're already starting to climb down the hole toward the bottom in Madagascar as we speak, Louis," Andy said.

"You see, Schaumburg," the Frown said. "This has all been for naught! I have won and you will finally be dead!"

"So will you, you birdbrain!" Louis yelled at the Frown. Andy and Louis still held him down.

At that moment, a door from the fire escape staircases burst open. Jack emerged, hopelessly out of breath from climbing several stories upstairs.

"What are you doing here, Jack?" Schaumburg asked.

"I'm here at the request of your lovely wife," Jack said, catching his breath. "She thought you might need some help. All the Arjogun downstairs have been neutralized, by the way."

"Did you overhear anything?" Louis asked Jack.

"They said the trigger for the weapon was connected to a wire which is activated by the green button on the Frown's computer. If we unplug the computer, it cuts the circuit."

"Wait!" the Frown screamed and Louis and Andy tied him up with rope.

"Stupid Arjogun technology!" Jack said under his breath. Jack approached the computer, stabbing it with his sword. Sparks flew wildly all around the office.

The computer monitor went dead.

"That should take care of that," Jack said. "Now put in the second sword, boy!"

Schaumburg took the second sword and placed it into the second slot.

"Ha,ha,ha,ha,ha!" the Frown cackled. "I knew you would do that! The Arjogun anticipated your every foolish move. You fools have triggered your own deaths! The Earth will be destroyed now! The weapon has been activated! Ha,ha,ha,ha!"

Schaumburg, Louis, Andy, Chocolate and Jack all looked at each other, now concerned.

"Is he right?" Andy asked.

"Let's hope not," Schaumburg said. "We leave for Madagascar now! Let's move!"

"But you can't leave me here to die!" the Frown complained as the Orishans left the room, zooming down to ground level.

The vortex outside swiftly turned a red-orange in color and concentrated into a single beam of power. The beam shot straight through the center of the Earth aimed directly toward the weapon buried 1,000 feet under the surface in Madagascar.

The self-destruct sequence began. Unfortunately, at the same moment, the weapon began to activate just as the Frown predicted.

At the same time, Commander Black and his group reached the bottom of the shaft, where they spied more than 20 human and Orishan slaves (and Gobador) chained to a cylinder.

"They're strapped to the bottom of the doomsday device with metal chains," Amy said.

At that instant, the beam struck the bottom of the device, causing a brilliant ball of light to cascade up the cylinder walls of the weapon.

The Protectors immediately ran to free the slaves.

The concentrated beam burst from the vortex created within the arch shooting straight into the surface of the Earth.

Fancy Flying

"I hope this thing is self-destructing and not activating," Commander Black said.

Sam and Fred looked at each other worried.

"It looks like it's heating up," Sam said. Sam and Fred tried to use some heavy tools lying around to break the chains.

Amy noticed a set of keys hanging on a nearby wall.

The weapon began to rumble inside.

She used the keys to unlock the slaves.

"Use your heads, boys," she said to Sam and Fred, grinning from ear to ear.

"There's a lift this way," Armando called out to the Protectors. He pulled up Lavender and held her close to him like she was a baby and ran for the lifts. They had to run across a huge room to reach the lifts, more than the length of a football field.

Unfortunately, the lifts opened before anyone arrived and Arjogun guards spilled out, firing light-beam weapons at them.

Two of the Protectors fell with fatal wounds. An Arjogun weapon hit Commander Black in the leg.

"Get back," Amy screamed at everyone, pulling Fred down behind a barrel for protection.

A gun battle erupted inside the cavern as the doomsday weapon continued to heat up on its prearranged path to destroying the Earth. At the same time, the beam of light from the Arch continued to bathe the weapon in hot orange colors and caused it to vibrate.

"It's gonna blow!" said Frank Largetooth. "We gotta get outta here!"

"We're pinned down," Commander Black said as he clutched his wounds. More Arjogun soldiers arrived in the lift, firing a barrage of weapons at them.

Back in St. Louis, Leni told Schaumburg to hightail it to Madagascar along with Jack and his crew.

"They're pinned at the bottom of the caverns below Madagascar and the weapon is about to blow up," Leni screamed. "Get over there on the double!"

Orishans onboard Jack's Orishan saucer picked up all the Orishans in the Gateway Arch, dropping off Schaumburg's Hug at the F-117A. Then Jack's saucer instantly zoomed to the Madagascar site followed swiftly by the F-117A. Because of the size of the shaft, the Orishan vessel, like the Ch-47 Chinook helicopters that waited safely above ground, could not descend the shaft. But the F-117A could. Schaumburg and Louis soared down the shaft, leaving Chocolate and Andy behind aboard one of the choppers.

"Captain, we don't have any weapons on board, you know," Louis said to Schaumburg.

"I intend to use the ship as both a weapon and a shield," Schaumburg said. "We'll fly between the Protectors and the Arjogun first. Turn on the outside loudspeaker."

"Roger," Louis replied. Louis said as he pulled back hard on the stick and dived deep into the shaft. Louis noticed crimson dripping down the side of Schaumburg's Bear Force outfit near his shoulder.

"Schaumy, you're bleeding," Louis shouted in alarm.

"Vil nicked my shoulder in the sword fight," Schaumburg said. "I'll live."

As the F-117A arrived at the bottom, it flew between the rescuers and the Arjogun soldiers, effectively stopping the gunfire from both sides.

"Attention, Arjogun!" Schaumburg said over the loud speaker as his ship streaked past all of them then banked against the wall. Then the plane turned back toward them.

"This place is about to blow!" Schaumburg continued. "Either leave with all your prisoners and the others up the lifts now, or you will die down here!"

The Arjogun started shooting their laser weapons at the F-117A.

However, Louis flew the jet so low and slow that it forced the Arjogun to move away from the heat exhaust given off by the jet's engines. This opened a clear path to the lift doors.

The doomsday weapon continued to throb and rumble and the beam from St. Louis continued to do its work. Also, it continued to arm itself to destroy the planet at the same time.

"Let's go for the lifts," Armando called out and all the prisoners and rescuers packed inside them and traveled back to the surface.

Some of the Arjogun dropped their weapons and followed the slaves and rescuers up in another lift.

One Arjogun got off a lucky shot and struck a dorsal fin on the F-117A.

As soon as the lift doors closed, Louis punched the controls and soared straight back up the shaft. He noticed the controls were sluggish and almost hit the side of the shaft on the way up.

Schaumburg became alarmed, realizing Louis could lose control of the ship.

In the lifts, the prisoners, rescuers and Arjogun soared at super-fast speed to the ground level, however they had a long way to go.

"I'm not sure we're going to make it folks," Commander Black said. Lavender, whom Armando held close to him, growled at Black.

"We'll make it," she growled at him. "Have a little faith."

"Don't mind her," Armando said to Black. "She's a little growly for an Orishan." Black's leg started to bleed onto the elevator floor.

An explosion rocked the bottom floor of the camp as the beam caused the doomsday weapon to begin to self-destruct. However, the device continued to arm.

A great ball of fire and shrapnel began wildly flying up the shaft after Schaumburg's plane. The black jet emerged safely as flames followed the F-117A up the hole.

"Schaumy, I'm losing it," Louis said.

"Don't tell me you're going to crash one of my ships again," Schaumburg joked as he assisted Louis.

Suddenly, the broken dorsal fin flew off, breaking off part of the wing on its way.

"We're going down, Schaumburg!" Louis yelled.

The lifts finally arrived on the surface and all the slaves and rescuers raced to the helicopters. Two human Protectors dragged Black to the choppers. Waiting Orisha helped them board. Some of the Orisha hopped onboard Jack's saucer too. Jack could squeeze about four more onboard.

Sam stopped to look up. He noticed that the F-117A was flaming and nose-diving to the ground.

The stealth fighter hit the ground in a deafening explosion of flame, dust, and shrapnel.

"Schaumburg!" he screamed and he stopped his race to the waiting Chinook helicopter.

The force of the choppers' whirling blades caused a strong enough backwash to knock a full-grown man off his feet, so the Orishans had even more trouble reaching the choppers.

Some humans picked up Orishans and trudged against the strong winds to safety.

Chocolate, aboard one of the choppers, grew alarmed as well, thinking Louis and her brother went down on the F-117A. Her mouth hung open as tears formed in her dark brown eyes.

"I've lost Schaumy and Louis," Chocolate said softly to herself. "Are we all doomed? Will that Arjogun device destroy the Earth after all?

"C'mon, tiger!" Amy yelled at Sam. "I'm not leaving you here to die!" She grabbed his shirt and started to drag him to the chopper.

Sam started to run as fast as he could against the strong winds to a chopper. Tears streamed from his eyes. Amy followed. The force of the Ch-47 Chinook blade's props seemed like a 60-mile-per-hour windstorm.

"They'll be okay," Andy said to Chocolate as they watched the F-117A burn. "They have to be." Tears began forming in Andy's eyes as well. He hugged Chocolate as she sobbed softly.

Another explosion shot flames and debris from the shaft onto the surface, pelting those outside with dust and dirt. Nobody knew if that meant self-destruct for the weapon or if it continued to arm itself.

At that moment, Sam noticed a streak of red and blue carrying Louis toward the chopper for which he and Amy headed. Now, a tear of joy started to stream down Sam's cheek.

Schaumburg had gulped some chocolate, busted a hole in the plane's canopy, and then grabbed Louis. He flew them out of the stealth fighter as it dove straight down.

More explosions continued to rock Madagascar as the weapon that was intended to destroy the Earth continued to explode in searing heat and noise.

As soon as the last Arjogun guard safely crawled on board the choppers, the choppers slowly lifted. A few more Orishans scrambled on board Jack's ship, which shot straight up and disappeared. One final huge explosion erupted in the camp, spewing a flame so high, it almost licked the bottom of one of the choppers that had already lifted more than 20 feet above the ground.

The dark, morning sky turned as light as day as the doomsday weapon created a ball of white-hot flame.

Finally, molten lava began spewing from the hole where once stood the Arjogun camp. All onboard the choppers knew the Fire Eater prevailed, destroying the weapon before it could destroy the planet. The lava covered all evidence there had ever been a camp at that location. Later, any native of Madagascar, known as the Malagasy, who happened upon the site would see nothing but a black thousand-foot-deep hole in the ground.

But just now, a firestorm raged out of the hole. Schaumburg leaned against the helicopter bulkhead soothing his wound. He got up to look out a window at the carnage erupting below. "It worked," he said softly to himself. Chocolate noticed her brother.

The wash from the Chinook's props were blowing the firestorm away from the choppers. He remembered the ancient Orishan prophesy about the Knights in Blue Satin, reciting it out loud:

The Knights in Blue Satin will ride out on winged horses, one black, two with wind-wings, creating a windstorm to save Earth from the Arjogun's fire.

Chocolate started tending her brother's wounded shoulder.

"The choppers are the horses with wind-wings," she said. "The black winged horse was the F-117A and the blue satin is on the berets the Protectors wear."

"I wonder how the ancient Orishan prophets knew," Schaumburg said to himself just as the choppers hit hyperdrive and zoomed away from Madagascar at light-speed.

*   *   *

Back in the Arch, the Frown watched in horror as the Fire Eater machine itself began to self-destruct—erupting in sparks and flame. He remained tied at hands and feet.

"Fire!" he screamed. "Somebody call 9-1-1!"

Unexpectedly, a form from the dark grabbed a fire extinguisher and put out the flame.

Then the small being with light reflecting on her glasses threw the Frown into a Bearavator, closed the door and smashed the controls. The B.A.R.T. lift tossed the Frown to and fro, endlessly. She had used the altered Teddy Bear Zone portal so that she could materialize under a desk at the B.B.B. headquarters.

"Get me out of here!" the Frown screamed. "Untie me!" But nobody even knew he was there. Nobody except Leni, that is. "You need a major time-out!" she said to herself. She giggled as she swiftly rode through the Teddy Bear Zone back to the Paw Cave.

*   *   *

The choppers and Jack's saucer all landed safely near the Paw Cave. Leni and the unicorns ran out to greet them.

Chocolate and Louis began to apply first aid to some of the slaves.

Lavender ran up to Leni. Although covered in grime, Lavender's furry smile shone brightly in the moonlight.

"Hi ya, big sister," she said to Leni.

"Huh?" Leni said. "What do you mean?"

Cheryl waited with Jose and they embraced Armando with hugs and kisses.

"I knew you'd come for me," Armando said. "Thank you."

Cheryl kissed Armando long and hard.

"You can thank Sam and his Orishan friends," Cheryl finally said, then kissed him again.

Sam walked up to Armando and shook his hand.

"Armando, the initial research you did helped us all to save the planet," Sam said. "You're a hero!"

"No, my friend," Armando said. "I just blew the whistle on this plan. You folks, human and Orishan, are the heroes!" He warmly shook Sam's hand. "And thank you for looking after my family."

Cheryl kissed and hugged her husband again; tears of joy streaming down her cheeks. Then Armando threw Jose up into the air and caught him.

"Hey, Mijo," Armando said to his son. "How'd you get so big?" Then he hugged his son warmly.

Amy waltzed up to Sam.

"Hey, how about some of that, tiger?" she said to Sam. They hugged and kissed.

Schaumburg sat resting at the base of the ladder to Jack's saucer. The exhausted Orishan still bled at the shoulder. Schaumburg seemed oblivious to all the rejoicing. Dreamwalker slowly pranced up to Schaumburg, touching Schaumburg's wounded shoulder with his horn, healing it instantly. Schaumburg patted Dreamwalker's forehead affectionately.

"This is my little sister, Lavender," Leni suddenly said to her husband, who jumped.

Schaumburg peered at Lavender.

"Leni, is all your family that dirty?" he asked with obvious affection in his voice.

"You're not exactly squeaky clean yourself, Schaumburg, with all that blood on your superhero uniform!" Lavender screamed back.

"Whoa!" Schaumburg said. "She's a feisty one!"

"Leni is going to help me start an apothecary shop in Pawtropolis," Lavender said. "We're going to call it 'The Growly Orishan.'"

Schaumburg and Lavender laughed, then hugged.

Then Leni slowly approached Schaumburg. She looked deep into Schaumburg's eyes.

"You did it, husband," she said. "I'm proud of you." She hugged him warmly.

Scorch the Dragon cooks up a batch of hot dogs and other goodies for the gang as they relax after the Arjogun's weapon is destroyed in Madagascar. At home on the early afternoon of May 6, 2003, in Toleni are (foreground) Scorch and

EPILOGUE

Former Managing Editor Arrested For Vagrancy

BY FRED STEINFELD
THE NATIONAL INVESTIGATOR

SAN FRANCISCO, CALIF. (May 6, 2003)—San Francisco Police reported today they arrested Israel "Izzie" Feinberg, former managing editor of The Daily Press, *published in Montreal, Illinois.*

Feinberg, 60, has been wanted by police for attempted murder and conspiracy to commit murder involving one of his reporters, Samuel Arctophile and the curator of the George Washington Museum in Versailles, Illinois. Arctophile is the Versailles Bureau Chief for the Montreal daily newspaper.

A spokesman for the San Francisco Police Department said they managed to arrest Feinberg on a fluke.

"He was prancing around the Filmore District, spewing sermons about how teddy bears were going to kill human beings," the spokesman said. "He was very erratic, and an officer on the beat took him downtown for questioning. We first thought he was a homeless man until we discovered his true identity."

Police are holding him at the county jail until a hearing to set bond. He may be extradited to Illinois to stand trial for the counts of attempted murder and conspiracy to commit murder, both Class A felony charges.

Feinberg could not be reached for comment.

May 6, 2003, 3 p.m. at a special Orishan ceremony, Bartholomew Hall, Pawtropolis, Illinois.

Schaumburg stood at the end of a line with his wife Leni beside him to his right. Next in line stood Louis, Chocolate and Andy. Lavender Grace stayed very close to Andy's right. She liked him. Next to Lavender stood the sole Arjogun present in the building, Godador. Pawtropolis television broadcast the ceremony being held in a great hall live to Pawtropolis, Paw City, the planet Orisha and other parts of the universe.

The heroes all faced an audience of several hundred Orisha and humans.

Nerwonduh, the Master Wizard, had his back to the audience. He held up several rolls of parchment. Then he slowly gave one roll to each Orishan standing before him and to Gobador, the Arjogun who spied for the Knights in Blue Satin.

Nerwonduh turned to face the audience.

"On behalf of the Mystical Order of the Golden Paw, the Orishan Command, the Protectors of Earth, and the Knights in Blue Satin, I hereby present a special gift to Captain Schaumburg Harmony and his Hug. We have been watching Schaumburg for a beary long time."

Nerwonduh turned to face Schaumburg.

"Tell us, Schaumburg, what have you learned from this mission?" the Wizard asked.

"I have learned that the bottom line when Orishans are out in the field is to accomplish the mission," Schaumburg said. "Sometimes that means taking risks, which includes putting yourself and your crew in harm's way. But you do what must be done with minimum risk to all concerned."

"Very good Schaumburg," Nerwonduh said. "You have summarized the challenge of command very well."

Nerwonduh turned back to face the audience.

"We knew Schaumburg had the gift of command, but Schaumburg needed to learn to balance his desire to not harm others with his need to complete the mission. We think Schaumburg far exceeded requirements this time by saving an entire planet. Therefore, it is with extreme pleasure that I award his Hug their long-deserved Licenses To Hug."

Tears welled up in Schaumburg's eyes. The audience erupted in applause and began to stand, continuing to clap loud and long.

Sam sat in the front row, standing up to clap. He began to weep openly, proud of his Orishan friend. Amy stood from her seat next to Sam, admiring both Schaumburg and Sam for what both had accomplished. Tears also formed in her eyes. Armando, Cheryl and Jose stood up too. Jose sat on Armando's shoulders clapping and whistling proudly for his "teddy bear" friends. Fred, Commander Black, Frank Largetooth and the Orishans Jack and Perry also stood up to applaud.

Then Nerwonduh spoke the audience again, motioning them to stop their applause.

"Next, we have a special presentation for Millennium Harmony," the tiger said. "Would you please step forward, Leni?"

Leni, surprised, stepped to the front of the stage next to Nerwonduh. An Orishan in a black Wizard's robe came out with a wand lying on a blue pillow.

Nerwonduh picked up the wand.

"This is the wand of a Wizard," Nerwonduh said. "They are conferred upon any Wizard who has completed his or her training, and who has demonstrated they have the power to wield their magic for the good of all beings. It is made of copper and contains two crystal globes at each end. The one on the bottom, which is opaque, is for the questions which life throws our way. The clear globe at the top is for the Wizard to see clearly the answers."

He placed the wand in Leni's paws.

Then he hugged her and the hall erupted in applause once again. Schaumy's chest puffed out with pride as more tears streamed down his furry face.

"Thank you Nerwonduh," Leni said. "And now, I have a presentation to make as well. Nerwonduh and I spoke, and we have decided to confer a new award here on Earth to humans and Orishans who have proven themselves worthy to be called a friend to the Mystical Order of the Golden Paw."

At that instant, some Orishans brought out a long platform with a staircase leading to it. The platform stood in front of the Orishans and Gobador on the stage. She motioned for the Orishans and Gobador on stage to move back.

Then another Wizard brought forth an ornately decorated chest and handed it to Leni.

She opened the chest and first pulled out a rolled parchment.

"Will the following humans and Orishans please step onto the stage behind this platform," she said. "Commander Albert Black."

As soon as Leni said Black's name, Fred leaned across Amy to Sam and said, "So that's what his first name is."

Amy shushed Fred.

The audience erupted in applause again.

"Fred Steinfeld," Leni said.

The applause increased in volume.

Fred stood up to take the stage.

"Frank Largetooth," Leni said. More applause filled the hall.

The large Eskimo walked up to the stage.

"Jose, Armando and Cheryl Cruz," Leni said. "Amy Sampson and Samuel Arctophile." All people in the audience now stood up to give the humans a standing ovation.

"And now, the following Orishans should come up to the stage too," Leni said.

"Captain Jack Davis and Perry Purple."

The two Orishans wobbled up to the stage.

Leni pulled out golden paw pins from the chest, first pinning them on Jack and Perry.

"I am bestowing upon you each the Golden Paw, a pin symbolizing your efforts to assist the Mystical Order of the Golden Paw," Leni said.

As she pinned Jack, he smiled at her.

"Thanks, toots," Jack said. Leni winked at him. "Don't get any ideas Jack," she whispered.

Leni walked onto the long table, the humans now standing behind it.

She pinned a golden paw on each human. The humans had to bend down to Leni even though she stood on the platform.

Sam hugged Leni after she pinned his golden paw on him.

"We could never have done it without you," Leni whispered to him as she kissed Sam on the forehead.

The audience continued to fill the hall with loud applause, hoots and hollers.

"We ask that the humans receiving the golden paw pin wear them always, so that any Orishans who see it will know that you could provide them sanctuary if necessary," Leni said.

Suddenly, Fatima Furbulous burst through the crowd from the back of the room, brandishing an Arjogun weapon.

"It won't do you any good, Leni and Schaumburg," she yelled. The audience panicked and began to scramble for the doors.

Fatima shot the laser at the ceiling, yelling, "Everybody halt!" The panic stopped.

Fatima began to slowly march toward the honored heroes. "These aren't heroes," she said. "They are buffoons. They barely managed to stop the Arjogun from destroying this planet. Well, I'm going to finish the job that the Frown started."

Fatima aimed the weapon right at Schaumburg's heart.

Andy and Schaumburg looked at each other with a special signal.

They each gobbled a piece of chocolate, switched at super-speed to the Paw and Mardi Gras and soared to tackle Fatima.

They easily disarmed her.

The Paw tied her paws with some rope in his utility belt.

"Why, Miss Furbulous? You must have been the spy we suspected in the Knights," Schaumburg said.

Suddenly, the Paw's H.A.R.V.E.Y. unit began beeping. "This is an Arjogun surgically altered to look like an Orishan," the unit said, sparking.

"Holy alien gray!" Mardi Gras said. "That explains it."

Orishan police officers led Fatima away in chains. Fatima's actions cut short the festivities. Mardi Gras and the Paw quickly changed back into their civilian clothing away from onlookers behind the stage. The two emerged on stage. Schaumburg looked sad. The audience began to file out of the hall.

Leni walked up to Schaumburg.

"What's wrong, hero?" Leni asked.

"She tried to kill me," Schaumburg said.

Nerwonduh put his paw on Schaumburg's shoulder. "Don't be sad, son," Nerwonduh said. "You cannot change the hate that is in another being's heart. All you can do is love them."

"You mean love beings like Frank Vil?" Andy asked as he walked up to them.

"Vil?" Leni said shocked. "I left him in the Bearavator yesterday at the Arch. He must still be tumbling around up there."

Then she started to giggle. All of Schaumburg's Hug surrounded Leni and Schaumburg and started to laugh. "We better go get him," Leni said. All agreed.

Sam, Fred, Cheryl, Armando, Jose and Amy circled Schaumburg's Hug on stage. They all laughed out loud and hugged.

"So, Schaumburg?" Sam asked. "Congratulations on your License To Hug . . . Schaumburg, you and your people have taught me so much. Mostly, you taught me to love freely and unconditionally, like a child. And now, I'm not so afraid of the prospect of being a father."

"Thank you for that, Schaumburg," Amy said, popping up and grasping Sam's arm affectionately.

"And you taught me to stay on task—never to lose sight of the final goal," Schaumburg said to Sam. "Don't fret about getting married and having children someday, Sam. You'll make a great father."

Amy blushed.

"Congratulations are in order for you too, Mr. Managing Editor," Schaumburg said.

"You going to go back to your job at *The Daily Times* here in Pawtroplis?" Sam asked.

"Sam, I have some bad news for you," Schaumburg responded.

"Bad news?"

"The Orishan Command has recalled me to Orisha," Schaumburg said. "Something about a new assignment. I don't know how long I'll be gone."

Gobador sought out Schaumburg and bent down to hug the Orishan.

"I understand now why you saved me on Serena," Gobador said. "Thanks."

"No, thank you," Schaumburg said. "We could not have pulled

this off without you. I understand too. I should have trusted you the way Andy did."

"Trust must be earned," Gobador said.

Suddenly, Jack walked up.

"Your ride's here, Schaumburg!" Jack said, slapping Schaumburg on the back. "C'mon! We gotta get to Orisha pronto! Something big is on the horizon!"

"You mean you're leaving for good?" Sam asked, visibly upset.

Schaumburg walked up to Sam, his arms outstretched for a hug. They hugged each other warmly.

"I'm gonna miss you, Sam," Schaumburg said. "I'll visit if I can."

Sam closed his eyes and held back a sob.

"I'm going to miss you too, Schaumburg."

Jack poked Schaumburg on the shoulder.

"C'mon, Scoop," Jack said. "Orisha Command is expecting us."

"'Bye, Sam" Schaumburg said.

Leni tapped Sam on the side as Schaumburg walked off with Jack.

"He'll be back," Leni said.

"How do you know?" Sam asked.

"Because I'm here," Leni replied. "He's just getting briefed on our new assignment."

"Will you have to go off planet?" Sam asked.

"Don't know," Leni said.

Amy and Sam watched Schaumburg walk out of the auditorium and head for Jack's saucer.

"Hey, Tiger," Amy said. "Why the long face?"

"I'm really going to miss him, Amy," Sam said. He hugged her tightly for a long time.

*   *   *

The next day, in the Versailles Bureau, Sam slowly packed up his personal belongings so he could move into the managing editor's office in Montreal. Sam picked up a photo of Sam and Schaumburg sitting on his desk. He started to pack away the photo, then stopped to stare it.

"I'm really going to miss you, Schaumburg," he said, a tear forming in his right eye. Absentmindedly, he put his hand on the golden paw pin on his shirt lapel.

Without warning, Schaumburg pushed the glass door to Sam's office open. "Sam, Sam," Schaumburg said. He wore a black vest, white shirt, his fedora, and he had a silver revolver blaster in a holster on his left hip. On his right hip was the Sword of George Washington in its black leather scabbard. Both the holster and scabbard bore Golden Paw symbols. On his chest was a golden badge, similar to those worn by police officers on Earth. This one said, "Better Bear Bureau, Chief Schaumburg."

"I need your help," Schaumburg said, very excited. "This is terrible."

"Schaumburg!" Sam screamed and he rushed to greet the alien, hugging him.

At that instant, the door to Sam's office burst open and Dr. Daniels stormed in.

He shoved some official documents in Sam's face. Schaumburg froze and Sam put the Orishan on the counter next to Daniels.

"This is a court order for you to return to my institution for further examination," Daniels said. "I have convinced a judge you are deranged and a menace to yourself and others."

Sam looked at Daniels, exasperated. Meanwhile, Schaumburg awoke from suspended Hibernation and placed his paw on Daniels shoulder from behind.

Daniels slumped unconscious to the floor.

"Lou taught me the Vulcan neck pinch," Schaumburg said. Sam hugged Schaumburg again, happy to see him.

"Not now, Sam," Schaumburg said, pushing Sam away. "You don't understand. Orishan Command has learned about a potential disaster of intergalactic proportions. We need your help."

. . . . Only the beginning.

Captain Schaumburg Harmony, Orishan Space Command, has earned his License To Hug.

THE SECRET OF
THE UNIVERSE

In light of the events outlined in this work, the people of Orisha decided to provide humans with the secret of the Universe. The following is from the Book of the Orisha upon which the Mystical Order of the Golden Paw is based:

THE SECRET OF THE UNIVERSE CAN BE BOILED DOWN INTO ONE SIMPLE SENTENCE:
IN THE END, WHAT REALLY MATTERS IS HOW YOU HAVE TREATED YOUR FELLOW BEINGS. THAT IS THE ESSENCE OF ALL WISDOM AND ALL YOU REALLY NEED TO KNOW TO HAVE ALL YOU DESIRE AND TO PARTAKE OF LIFE'S BOUNTIFUL TREASURES. WE HOPE THIS PEARL OF WISDOM HELPS YOU IN YOUR JOURNEY THROUGH LIFE.

LOVE,
SCHAUMY

ABOUT THE TEDDY BEAR 'AUTHOR,' SCHAUMBURG:

So, many people may be asking themselves, "Is this Schaumburg the real author or is Myke Feinman?"

In a previous story, *In Search of the First Teddy Bear*, Schaumburg travels 100 years back in time. All Myke will say about that story is Schaumburg really did travel back in time 100 years to discover which company really manufactured the first teddy bear, and Schaumburg really did tell Myke that he came from the planet Orisha which orbits a star in the Ursa Major constellation, a.k.a. The Great Bear.

Now, in case you think that's a load of bull, for *The Teddy Bear Conspiracies*, consider that Myke contacted the astronomers at the University of California at Berkeley while doing research for this book. He learned that there is a Jupiter-like and Saturn-like planet orbiting the star in Ursa Major and could very likely be an Earth-like planet.

He learned this *AFTER* Schaumburg told him he came from Orisha which orbit's a star in the Ursa Major constellation.

We should also tell you that Schaumburg has proof of his time-travel back to the year 1902 where he met Theodore Roosevelt, Clifford Berryman, Rose and Morris Michtom and Richard Steiff. All four are key players in the creation of what we on Earth refer to as teddy bears. His proof is a bent hat. The hat did not have a bend when Schaumburg left for the past. Upon his return to the present, the hat was bent because Schaumburg was hit over the head in the past. Myke cannot explain otherwise how the hat got bent.

Myke said he stuffed Schaumburg on November 24, 1999, for his 43rd birthday.

Schaumburg claims he has been around much longer than that.

Of course, Schaumburg also said he believes Myke is an alien, so go figure (actually, a lot of Myke's friends think Myke is from another planet, too).

Schaumburg, meanwhile, has many careers. He has been a reporter, an astronaut, an pilot in the Bear Force, a Rough Rider (circa Spanish-American War with Teddy Roosevelt), a police officer, a monster-hunter, a private detective, a cowboy, a Wizard, an archeologist, a magician, a swashbuckler, a superhero, and is currently the Better Bear Bureau Chief.

He obtained a trench coat and fedora in late 2002, by ordering one from the Vermont Teddy Bear Company.

He wears his fedora as BBB Chief.

He also carries various weapons, such as his H.A.R.V.E.Y. unit, which resembles a three-inch white bunny rabbit but is in reality a sophisticated computer device that can render large objects and beings invisible, and a pistol in a holster. The pistol looks very much like a Glock or Smith and Wesson compact automatic revolver, only smaller, of course.

But the revolver will only put enemies to sleep, and they wake up with a much better attitude, Schaumburg says.

So, is Schaumburg really just a toy, a mere teddy bear with stuffing inside instead of internal organs?

Well, we all know Schaumburg at least has a heart. And he likes hugs, too.

ABOUT THE HUMAN

AUTHOR:

Myke Feinman is editor of *The Paper*, a weekly newspaper. He's worked at *The Daily Times* of Ottawa, *The Times-Press* of Streator, and the *Herscher Press*. He is also author/illustrator for two graphic novels and wrote a children's book, *In Search of the First Teddy Bear* with photos by his son, Anthony.

The Teddy Bear Conspiracies is his first novel. Of course, Schaumburg says it is a true story, with a few name changes.

Before Myke considered becoming a reporter, he made up stories to entertain his friends in school. For example, in the first and second grade, sources at Ink and Feathers Comics have learned that Myke told his schoolmates that he saw flying saucers land in his back yard, and claimed there were marks in the grass to show where the landing gear touched down. Aliens left the ship and made contact with Myke, he claimed. Some believed his wild tales. Were they really true?

Feinman, 47, has worked as a professional journalist since he was between his sophomore and junior years in high school.

He graduated from Andrew Hill High School, San Jose, California, in 1974.

He obtained his Bachelor of Arts degree in journalism from San Jose State University in 1978. He worked his way through college as a busboy/waiter at Farrell's Ice Cream Parlor Restaurant at the Eastridge Mall in East San Jose.

Upon graduation from college, he entered management at Farrell's where he stayed until the start of 1980. Leaving the restaurant business for a job as a bill collector for an insurance company, American

Hardware Mutual Insurance Company of Menlo Park, California, he stayed there until he moved to Illinois.

Myke transferred to Illinois as an insurance sales representative in 1984, moving his wife Cathy and six-year-old son Anthony with him.

Myke grew bored with insurance sales and quickly began working for newspapers in Illinois, where he started working as a correspondent for *The Daily Journal* in Kankakee. By 1985, he worked full time in the field of journalism.

He published his first novel-length comic book, *The Mask Conspiracy*, in 1991. He and his wife established the Ink and Feathers art scholarship at Herscher High School that year, giving away $250 a year to HHS graduating seniors.

In 1993, with a fellow journalist and cartoonist, Jim Ridings, he published the *Ink and Feathers Comic Publishers Guide*.

During the time of his first two publications, he worked as editor of two weekly newspapers, *The Herscher Press* and the *Reddick-Essex Courier*. He and his family resided in Herscher, Illinois, where they eventually purchased a home.

He obtained a position as City Editor for a daily newspaper, *The Times-Press* in Streator, and moved to Streator in the fall of 1996.

At this point, Anthony stayed behind in Herscher to finish at Kankakee Community College.

In 1998, he published a sequel to his first graphic novel, *The Crystal Skull Files*. The second graphic novel was the basis for a second scholarship, the Freedom Journalism Scholarship that donates $250 a year to journalism students graduating from Streator High School. The art scholarship also continues at Herscher. Ironically, this book contained one character, Alvie Odell, who carried a teddy bear around with him everywhere. Sound familiar?

Shortly after finishing his second graphic novel, he was offered an opportunity to transfer from *The Times-Press* and take the Marseilles Bureau Chief position for *The Daily Times* of Ottawa.

It was at *The Daily Times* that Myke's relationship with teddy bears began. He and his wife Cathy went to a Build-A-Bear workshop in Schaumburg on November 24, 1999, each building their first teddy bears. Schaumburg is Myke's bear and Millennium, or Leni, is Cathy's bear.

Myke began corresponding with the Build-A-Bear people because he wanted an outfit for his bear that included a trench coat and fedora (to this day, Build-A-Bear does not offer such an outfit).

He began communicating with two people at the World Bearquarters in St. Louis, Danielle Swanner and Maxine Clark, the Chief Executive Bear.

Meanwhile, Myke became lonely working at the Bureau in Marseilles and began to bring Schaumburg to work with him. This was about spring of 2001.

That summer, he went to St. Louis to meet Clark, Swanner and many others at the World Bearquarters in St. Louis. At that time, he decided to write his novel, basing it on the premise of a reporter who brings his teddy bear to work with him every day.

Myke began doing research for the novel, in part keeping track of all the reactions people had to Myke and Cathy carrying around teddy bears to restaurants, to the supermarket, all over the place. People's reactions were varied. Some people thought Myke had lost his marbles. Others already knew Myke was not playing with a full deck, so the bear thing did not bother them.

After September 11, 2001, Myke began writing a weekly electronic newsletter using Schaumburg as the real "author."

Myke's research on the history of teddy bears resulted in his learning that in 1902, two companies claimed to make the first teddy bear, Ideal Toy and Novelty Company of New York and Steiff of Germany. Both claimed to be the first, but neither could prove it.

So, Myke's teddy bear Schaumburg decided to travel back in time to the year 1902 to learn once and for all which company created the first teddy bear.

In August 2002, he published online Schaumburg's journey that became the book later that year, *In Search of the First Teddy Bear*, now in its second printing.

Meanwhile, Myke continued work on his novel.

He stayed at *The Daily Times* until early 2003 where he took the job as editor of *The Paper*, a free-circulation weekly newspaper published in Dwight, his current position.

Myke and Cathy continue to reside in Streator and now have many teddy bears in their "hug."

ABOUT THE
PHOTOGRAPHER:

Anthony Feinman, 26, currently works for Heartland Bank & Trust in Bloomington, Illinois. His photos have appeared in the *Herscher Press*, *The Times-Press* of Streator, *The Paper* of Dwight and *The Heartbeat*. He is also the author/illustrator for a comic book, *Escape in a Dirigible*, based on Myke Feinman's comic book hero, Terry Freedom. His photography and pagination skills can also be seen in Myke Feinman's one-shot magazine, *In Search of the First Teddy Bear*. It was the first publication to showcase Anthony's graphic design abilities.

The Teddy Bear Conspiracies is the second book displaying his photography.

Anthony was born in San Jose, California. In between his fifth and sixth year on this planet, he was stuffed into snow pants and a coat then whisked off to Illinois with his parents. He soon grew to like the snow and flatland.

He graduated from Herscher High and continued his education at Kankakee Community College. The institution kicked him out after he received his A.A. in Liberal Arts. In 1999, he transferred to Illinois State University to pursue a major in Theater Arts. By the end of 2000, Anthony then transferred to Heartland Community College to study the basics of Computer Graphics, Graphic Design, and Web Design. He is currently still learning. At this point, Anthony is still unsure of what he would like to be when he grows up.

In between his spurts of education, Anthony has had a wide variety of jobs. He has been a construction worker, a bookseller, a banker, a factory worker, and stuffer and pre-press artist for a local newspaper.

Anthony's love of the arts is unparalleled due to his parents' fondness for the arts. On top of being a freelance photographer, Anthony is also an artist, cartoonist, actor, and a freelance graphic design artist and web designer. Anthony also likes to dance around in his underwear in his apartment. He is best known for doing this in the middle of tornado warnings.

In 2001, he was given the Best Dancer Award at Monmouth College. Anthony is best known for doing numerous performances of *Horton Hears a Who* and *How the Grinch Stole Christmas* by Dr. Suess at local Barnes & Noble stores. He can act out the entire stories from memory. He has also done performances of these two stories at Limestone Grade School and St Joseph's in Kankakee County. In addition, Anthony has spoken on cartooning to summer school classes in Geneva, IL.

Anthony designed a new Website for Ink & Feathers Comics (www.if comics.com). He is also writing and illustrating the last in the comic book trilogy about Terry Freedom, his Dad's character. Anthony will be working on more projects as time allows in the coming years.

ACKNOWLEDGEMENTS

Many people helped make this project possible. First and foremost, I would like to thank Anthony Feinman, my son and fellow enthusiast in the realm of comic books, movies, science fiction and fantasy novels. Without his marvelous photos (which are each a work of art that Anthony spent countless hours to create) *The Teddy Bear Conspiracies* would not have been possible. His eye for composition is matched only by his vivid imagination. He also helped edit the manuscript, making sure I added some scenes to explain certain events in the story for the reader, and eliminated some inconsistencies in the manuscript. My wife Cathy also helped with the artwork, editorial concepts, and editing. Cathy inspired the female leads in the story. As she read through the manuscript, she helped me keep the "teddy bears" in character, an invaluable asset to me as I wrote the story. She created some of the names, like "The Paw," and gave us the idea for the design of an Orishan spacecraft. Jody Bourne, Jim Ridings and June Enger also edited this work, three very talented journalists I have had the pleasure to work with on past publications. Other people helping include Stanton Friedman, the Roswell UFO researcher and author, who provided us with news clippings from around the nation after the crash at Roswell; and the astronomers in California who found a Jupiter-like and Saturn-like planet orbiting the North Star in the constellation Ursa Major (the Great Bear). The astronomers told us it is highly likely there is an Earth-like planet orbiting the star as well. Thank you to Geoff Marcy, professor of astronomy at U.C. Berkeley. Schaumburg always said his planet was in that constellation. I don't know why I ever doubted him. Also, Anthony Feinman created the photograph of the Paw flying over a city skyline, but the background photo is a portion of a panoramic aerial view of Chicago by Mark Segal, a Chicago photographer. Mark generously allowed us to use his background photo in this publication. Thank you. Thank you also to Rebecca L. Grambo, author of "Bear, a Celebration of Power and Beauty" for allowing us to use her quote that appears at the beginning of this book. Thank you to Sheila Brockman who provided research material on George Washington and the photo of the Gilbert Stewart painting of George Washington (to which Anthony added two tiny swords). Besides the people helping with the research and editing, readers should note that the majority of the "teddy bears" photographed for this book and their outfits/accessories are from Build-A-Bear Workshop. Build-A-Bear Workshop provides customers with an interactive retail experience where customers stuff new friends with love, then choose outfits for them. My wife and I fell in love with the bears after our first visit to such a Build-A-Bear in Schaumburg, Illinois on November 24, 1999. However, not everything in the photos is from Build-A-Bear. Exceptions include Scorch the dragon, a Ty product, and the Frown (a bear we purchased at a Michael's craft store in Kankakee). Cathy Feinman handcrafted Scorch's cooking hat and apron with love. She also crocheted Schaumburg's beret that he wears with his Army outfit. Scoop Schaumburg's fedora and trench coat are from the Vermont Teddy Bear Company. The Arjogun, Gobador, is based on an interactive talking Alien Pal we purchased at a Spencer's with a few computer "enhancements" by Anthony. I want to also acknowledge the inspiration for the Orishan H.A.R.V.E.Y. unit, named for Elwood P. Dowd's invisible friend.

Myke Feinman
Streator, IL
Fall 2003

For more information about Schaumburg, visit him on the web at: www.ifcomics.com or to subscribe to his free online weekly newsletter, write to: *mefeinman@webtv.net*.

No teddy bears were injured in the production of this publication.